DATE DUE

MAR 0 2 2005	
MAR 1 4 2005	
APR 0 6 2005	
APR 2 1 2005	
MAY 0 9 2005	
JUN 1 1 2005	
JUL 3 0 2005	
NOV 0 5 2007	
AUG 2 1 2009	

The Library Store   #47-0107

IRISH CREAM

IRISH CREAM

A Nuala Anne McGrail Novel

ANDREW M. GREELEY

A TOM DOHERTY ASSOCIATES BOOK

NEW YORK

IRISH CREAM

This book is printed on acid-free paper.

A Forge Book
Published by Tom Doherty Associates, LLC
175 Fifth Avenue
New York, NY 10010

www.tor.com

Forge® is a registered trademark of Tom Doherty Associates, LLC.

Library of Congress Cataloging-in-Publication Data

Greeley, Andrew M., 1928–
    Irish cream : a Nuala Anne McGrail novel / Andrew M. Greeley.—1st ed.
        p. cm.
    "A Tom Doherty Associates book."
    ISBN 0-765-30335-3 (acid-free paper)
    EAN 978-0765-30335-6
    1. McGrail, Nuala Anne (Fictitious character)–Fiction.   2. Women
detectives—Illinois—Chicago—Fiction.   3. Donegal (Ireland : County)—Fiction.
4. Hit-and-run drivers—Fiction.   5. Clergy—Diaries—Fiction.   6. Irish
Americans—Fiction.   7. Married people—Fiction.   8. Chicago (Ill.)—Fiction.
9. Psychics—Fiction.   I. Title.

PS3557.R358I73 2005
813'.54—dc22
                                                                    2004056322

First Edition: February 2005

Printed in the United States of America

0   9   8   7   6   5   4   3   2   1

For Tamra and others like her.

And in fond memory of Brian Shannon, who, unlike some of the people in this story, understood what Notre Dame means. His departure has left a big hole in the lives of many of us. He watched every game of the women's basketball team when it won the national championship and laughed when I told him that they might think about hiring Muffin McGraw as coach of the football team.

IRISH
CREAM

— 1 —

"BEFORE YOU hire me, Mr. Coyne, I must tell you one thing about myself. I am a convicted felon. I killed a man."

A moment before Day O'Sullivan had seemed a bright, alert young man, eager for the job we had offered him. Suddenly he became a condemned criminal, awaiting a sentence. His angelic face twisted in a grimace of guilt and a haze of pain slipped over his pale blue eyes.

Harm had been done to him, me wife had said.

"Tell us about it, Day."

"Involuntary manslaughter," he said softly. "I'm afraid I don't know much about it. Five years ago. I got drunk one night at the club, took my father's car, and in the dark. I rolled over one of his oldest friends, Mr. Keefe. It was terrible. I usually don't drink and now, of course, I don't drink at all. I have no memory of what happened. My father worked out a plea bargain with the state's attorney. He said he thought a time in jail would be good for me but he didn't want any more disgrace to the family than I had already caused. So I'm on probation for five years, only six more months left. My father tells me that I won't be able to stay out of trouble that long, but it's been more than four years already."

Nuala had put on our mystery-solving face. This meant that there was a puzzle which we had to solve. There were never any options. I forced myself to look away from the outline of her breasts beneath her light blue knit top.

"We won't hold it against you, Day," I said, knowing that's what Nuala wanted me to say—and what I wanted to say too. Damian O'Sullivan, or Day as everyone called him, was our dog boy. Nuala had hired him, subject to my approval, one day in early April at the dog park. I was afraid that she had added just one more responsibility to her responsibility-laden life.

"He's coming over to meet you tonight, Dermot," she had assured me. "I know you'll like the poor kid."

She does the hiring and the firing in our family. My consent to her decisions is always presumed. Normally she doesn't even bother to explain them to me. To bring him over so I could perhaps veto the hiring was unheard of.

Damian Thomas O'Sullivan certainly seemed harmless, an innocent, who was loved by dogs and children. Indeed, I had hardly opened the door to let him in the house and he had scarcely the time to say, "I'm Day O'Sullivan, Mr. Coyne," before the two snow-white Irish wolfhounds were all over him, yelping with joy.

They are barred from our parlor because they tend to scare the living daylights out of guests who have not met them. Under proper circumstances, Nuala dispenses from that regulation. This time they hadn't waited.

They hugged Day, kissed him, wrestled with him, and threatened to knock him to the floor.

"Girls!" Nuala warned sternly.

Reluctantly Fiona and Maeve sat on the floor, hemming Day in so that he couldn't move.

"You are not even supposed to be in here."

They lifted their very large bodies off the floor and, tails drooping, withdrew to the rear of the house. They were immediately replaced by four children, our three and Katiesue Murphy, all of whom hugged him.

Thin, just a little above medium height, clean-shaven, with closely cut blond hair, kind if somewhat aimless pale blue eyes, a sweet smile, and a seraphic face, Damian Thomas O'Sullivan seemed like a harmless Peter Pan, a perpetual youth who had thought about growing up and had decided against it. He wore faded jeans and an old millennium tee shirt under a thin beige windbreaker.

"All right, kids, back to the playroom. You too, Nelliecoyne."

"Ma!"

"You heard me!"

"Bye, Day." Socra Marie waved at him.

We have three children: Mary Margaret, usually called, but not by her teachers, "Nelliecoyne"; Micheal Dermod, ma-Hall DEAR-mud, aka "the Mick"; and Socra Marie, aged, respectively, six, four, and two.

Socra is an old Irish-language name of undetermined meaning. It is pronounced *Sorra* and if you don't get that first syllable right in our house, you are corrected.

Day was not so much Peter Pan, I decided, but the pied piper of Lincoln Park West.

"I didn't mean to create a scene like that," he apologized, a faint flush on his face.

"We have an exuberant family," I admitted. "Those dogs are perhaps the calmest of the lot."

"As I told Mrs. Coyne, they are wonderful characters, so affectionate, so intelligent, and so well trained."

"Mrs. Coyne is me mother-in-law. I'm Nuala Anne."

"You'll find, Day," I said, putting on my paterfamilias face, "that you and I are the only totally sane persons in the ménage. You're welcome as long as you can put up with us."

Me wife smiled approvingly. For a man, and one often more dense even than most men, I had managed to say the right thing. She produced a pitcher of iced tea and poured us all a glass.

"Damian O'Sullivan?" I had said dubiously before he had arrived at our door on Southport Avenue. "To take care of the dogs?"

"They're dear sweet things," she had replied, "but they take up a lot of space, make a lot of mess, and consume a lot of time."

TELL HER THAT SHE SHOULD HAVE KNOWN THAT.

"'Tis true," I had agreed.

"And when we go to Grand Beach for a weekend, we can hardly bring them along, can we now? And, sure, won't the poor things be lonely here all by themselves?"

"They will."

"And won't Damian take them for runs and over to the dog park and clean up the basement and the backyard and even plant flowers there, the poor dear lad?"

"Will their ladyships accept him?"

"Och, don't they adore him altogether like?"

"Is he a dog man by profession?"

"A handyman. Doesn't he do odd jobs and himself living in a little attic above a store over on Fullerton?"

"How old is he?"

"Well . . . isn't he a lot younger than you and maybe a little younger than meself?"

"Da," Nelliecoyne had put her two cents into the discussion, "he's grand altogether. He has such a beautiful golden halo."

"Halo?" I said with a sinking feeling in my stomach.

"You know, Da," she said, impatient with my slowness, "just like the saints over in church."

"Just like the saints?"

Me wife pointedly avoided my questioning look.

"Not just like them, is it now, Nellie?"

"No, Ma, it's all hazy and misty like around real people."

"Do I have a color, Nelliecoyne?" I asked cautiously, fearful that the door of the fun house might slam shut at any moment.

"Ma, isn't it a pretty blue like his eyes and doesn't it have a lot of little lights in it?"

"'Tis, dear," she said, still avoiding my pretty blue eyes.

SEE WHAT YOU'VE GOT YOURSELF INTO NOW!

"And your ma's color?"

"Da, you *know* what it is!"

"Sometimes I can't see it too clearly."

"Isn't it just like the sun shining on our silver tea set?"

"Of course, just that . . . Does it change when she looks at me?"

"You *know*"—she stamped her little foot—"that it becomes kind of rose."

Halos for sexual attraction! Wasn't that cute!

"Your little sister?" I asked, figuring I ought to know about these off-the-wall phenomena that were happening in my perfectly sane home on Southport Avenue, City of Chicago, County of Cook, State of Illinois, United States of America, Earth, Solar System, Cosmos.

With her brightest smile, Nelliecoyne said, "Oh, Da, such a pretty red, just like the robes Cardinal Sean wears sometimes."

"Everyone has halos, Nellie?"

"Some people you hardly notice," she admitted. "Anyway, Da, we call them auras, don't we, Ma?"

"Yes, dear."

Nelliecoyne drifted off to the playroom where Socra Marie was playing with our neighbor down the street. Katiesue Murphy is a couple of months older and with as strong a will as our daughter's. Her father is the little bishop's nephew and teaches anthropology at Loyola University and her mother is Cindasue McLeod, a lieutenant commander in the Coast Guard, though I suspect she's really a gumshoe for the Treasury Department. Katiesue, who almost always wears some kind of Coast Guard uniform, and Socra Marie seem to get along just fine, though I become uneasy when my little girl says, "Shunuff!" with a perfect Appalachian accent.

"You never told me about the auras," I began, when Nelliecoyne was out of the room.

"You never asked."

Her head was averted.

"You can tell when I'm thinking obscene thoughts about you?"

"I don't need the aura to know that."

"I can't see your aura when it turns silver rose."

"I'm sure you could if you tried hard."

Her face had turned rose.

Idiot, a voice inside me, not this time the Adversary, observed, you can pretend to see it.

I'd never fool her.

"Sometimes," she said in her professorial tone, "I hardly notice someone's aura, just a few little colored dots. Then sometimes it's like a brief burst of light. Other times it's dazzling, almost blinding."

"Oh," I said in a tiny voice.

"Yours is always dazzling," she said, "well, almost always. I knew what kind of a man you were the moment you came into O'Neill's on that foggy night and I saw that wonderful blue glow all around you. Wasn't I hoping that none of the other women in the place saw it?"

This was, I suspected, mostly blarney. You could never be sure, however, about Nuala Anne. Truth and blarney interacted in strange ways in her mystical soul. Some things were simply true, others were true "in a manner of speaking," and yet others were True in some transcendental fashion even if they were at odds with the known facts.

"Were you now?" I replied with a question since we were talking Irish talk.

"Wasn't I now? Something terrible. And didn't I say to myself then and there, 'Nuala Anne McGrail, you're just going to have to sleep with that man.' And didn't I now?"

"A long time later, after we were married."

"Sure, didn't I know that if I seduced you that night, I'd shock you something terrible, and you Yanks being so shy?"

Fiction by now had caught up with fact and passed it. Among her many personae, one of the core masks, a proto Nuala Anne, was the shy, mystical Irish-speaking virgin, a role she still played with considerable appeal on some occasions, especially when I was attempting to undress her.

"So you want us to hire this Damian O'Sullivan because he has a golden aura?"

"Dermot Michael Coyne, I most certainly do not! I want to hire him because we need someone to help with the dogs. All the aura tells me is that there is no harm in him. Harm has been done to him, but there's no harm in him."

Ah, that added another dimension. In fact, we were hiring Damian O'Sullivan because he needed our help and was going to get that help whether he knew it or not, indeed whether he liked the prospect of our help or not.

THAT'S WHAT YOU GET, BOYO, FOR MARRYING A WITCH.

So after I had listened to Damian's confession, I said to him, "If you don't mind putting up with us, you're welcome to the job."

My wife smiled at me. I had recited my lines well.

"Thank you, sir. I don't drink anymore, and I get around on my bike and the bus and the L. I'll try not to embarrass you."

That night after we made love, Nuala whispered in my ear, "That poor boy never killed anyone."

Which meant we were supposed to find out who did.

Thus did he join our family. His care of the hounds had relieved some of the burden on my wife, though now Damian himself was a burden. Who had done harm to him and why?

He cleaned the yard and the basement and planted flowers in the garden, which the dogs were warned to avoid. Astonishingly they did. He came and went quietly and never upset the order of our family life, such as it was. He chatted shyly with Ethne, our Galway-born nanny who was a graduate student at DePaul. She seemed to find him mildly interesting.

"He's a nice boy," she informed us. "Everyone in the neighborhood likes him. There's some extreme heavy thing with his family. They undercut him all the time."

"Do they now?" Nuala murmured.

I went over to the dog park once to watch the hounds frolic with him. They are big dogs, very big dogs compared with the others in the park. When they arrive it's like a whole new game begins. Fiona and Maeve chase the others and then they chase back. No one tries to mess with the hounds, not even the occasional Rottweiler that might wander in. They're friendly, good-natured pooches. They also have big teeth, very, very big.

They respond instantly to Day's call, though when I've been responsible for playing with them, they tend to ignore me. But my aura is only pretty blue, not bright gold.

He attached the expanding leashes to their collars, a process they did not like but of which they were forbearing when Day was doing it. Then as they prepared to return to our prefire home on Southport, four little kids accompanied by two dubious mothers approached the hounds—from a safe distance.

"Big doggies," said a little girl, braver than the rest.

"Are they dangerous?" one of the mothers asked dubiously.

"Not at all, ma'am," Day said with a dazzling smile. "They love little kids . . . Fiona, shake hands with the little girl."

Fifi, as my wife calls her, promptly extended a paw in greeting. Hesitantly the kid extended her right hand.

"Mom, she's so sweet!"

"Maeve, roll over for the little boy!"

With evident delight, the biggest wolfhound bitch in all the world (or so Nuala Anne insisted she was) rolled over and waved her paws in the air.

"She wants you to scratch her stomach."

He did just that. Maymay made a purring noise. Then the other kids joined the fun. They hugged and petted the dogs and even permitted the dogs to kiss them. Day presided over the game with evident glee.

"I suppose they're not very good watchdogs," one of the moms said, a Lincoln Park Limousine Liberal, I thought, who had to be politically correct on all occasions: you had to have a reason to let such monsters into your house.

"Best in the world," Day said proudly. "They can smell the difference between good and evil, can't you?"

He rubbed their big heads.

"Shall we go home!"

At the word "home" the dogs climbed to their feet and prepared to run.

"Say good-bye to the nice kids."

The hounds barked. The kids waved good-bye. Day and his entourage were off and running. Great little show.

I was looking forward to meeting his father, John Patrick O'Sullivan. I was quite certain that herself would enact a scene for him. No, it would be more than a scene. It would be a performance.

$$— 2 —$$

OUR TWO wolfhounds howled in protest as if the Danes were landing on Fullerton Avenue and storming down the street. Fiona hurtled down the stairs at full tilt, followed by my poor wife, who stumbled at the bottom and might have broken a leg if Maeve were not there to grab.

"The little brat is having fun again!" Nelliecoyne complained.

Socra Marie, our two-year-old, had come into the world more than two months early and weighed less than a pound. Somehow she managed to survive, by sheer willpower, the neonatologist had said. Those three months were hard on the whole family, especially my poor wife who was convinced, despite everything that the doctors told us, that it was her fault that our daughter had been born prematurely.

Now that she was two, our onetime eight-hundred-gram, twenty-five-week little girl thought that just about everything in her life was fun—like, dolly clutched firmly in one arm, sneaking out the front door of our prefire house on Southport Avenue, climbing down the stairs to the street, and setting off on a walk across to St. Josaphat school, which her brother and sister attended.

I put aside the Irish manuscript from the nineteenth century I was reading. Slow-moving oaf that I am, I barely made it to the top of the steps before Nuala Anne, her face twisted in a mixture of anger and relief, rushed up the stairs with the tyke bundled in her arms. The two wolfhounds, baying in dismay, followed like they were members of a funeral procession.

It was a lovely Saturday in April, with green lace appearing at last on the stark trees and lawns green overnight, as though the mayor had sent out paint crews. Just like the day we brought the little terror back from the hospital.

"Didn't your daughter try to kill herself?" Nuala accused me, as though it were all my responsibility.

"Me go for a walk, Da," the child informed me cheerfully.

"And she's going for a long time-out."

"Ma!"

Unsurprised by the scene, our two other children stood behind me.

"She dropped her glasses," our six-year-old Nelliecoyne observed. "I'll get them."

Nuala Anne said something in Irish which I think meant that Nelliecoyne should not go out on the street.

"Ma!" the perfect little daughter exclaimed.

Four-year-old Mick sighed loudly, protesting the disruption to his Lego project.

Socra Marie had reached the age of two, at which time, the doctors had told us, her developmental process would have caught up with that of other children her age. Her only apparent problem was weak eyesight. We were afraid she'd reject the glasses—which made her tiny face look even more elfin. She loved them, however, and would shout when she woke up in the morning, "Ma! Glasses!"

"I think her eyes will improve as she gets older and she won't need the glasses anymore," the doctor had said soothingly.

"She won't go blind, will she now?" Nuala Anne had demanded anxiously.

Though she knew better, my wife still feared in the depths of her superstitious Irish soul that she was somehow responsible for the premature birth of our third child.

"Certainly not," the doctor had replied soothingly. "There may be some later developmental problems, but I don't think so. She's fine, a very healthy and lively little girl."

The woman understood that she was treating Marie's ma as well as the little girl.

"Marie fine." The child who had climbed into the doctor's arms twisted about and grinned at us.

Nuala was uneasy.

"Isn't all this energy a little suspicious, Doctor?"

The pediatrician, a blonde maybe my age, smiled.

"There aren't many two-year-olds who are as curious and as energetic as our little friend here, but she's certainly within the normal limits."

"Me normal!"

I was sure she didn't know quite what normal was. She'd figured it was good.

"Neonates like Socra Marie," the doctor continued, "expend a lot of energy just staying alive. She doesn't need so much anymore, but she enjoys it, just like she enjoys bonding with you."

She handed the two-year-old back to her ma.

"Me normal," she said, cuddling in her ma's arms.

Then she would want to cuddle in my arms and with her big sister should Nelliecoyne be around and then with her big brother, who would put up with her, though with a considerable show of impatience.

The wolfhounds would be next.

"She has," the pediatrician said, perhaps unnecessarily, "strong affiliative needs."

Not reassured, Nuala Anne murmured, "Somehow she doesn't seem normal."

The doctor, Polish if one were to judge by her name, did not want to touch that bit of Irish superstition.

"She's a remarkable little girl, Nuala. God has blessed you with a wonderful child.

My wife muttered something in Irish.

One of our children was apparently normal—the Mick, who like his father was big, blond, laid-back, and maybe just a little lazy—though my wife became furious whenever that description was suggested of either of us. Mary Margaret, as her teachers at St. Josaphat properly called her, was, according to her mother, even more fey than Nuala herself had been at that age.

"Dear sweet little Mary Margaret," as the teachers called her, was the social leader of her class. "She always knows when someone is hurting. She's so kind."

"Little manipulator," her mother had murmured, wary of compliments of her children and even more wary of the lack of compliments.

Fey perhaps our graceful little first grader was, but unlike her mother she was even-tempered, sunny, and predictable. Nelliecoyne had inherited the fey part of my wife. Socra Marie, her madcap, manic part.

"She's not fey, at all, at all," Nuala explained to me. "Lucky little brat!"

Back in the family room Socra Marie was banished to the chair in the corner, her face clouded by an injured pout—an innocent unjustly persecuted.

"Time-out for a half hour!" Nuala ordered.

"Ma!" She clasped her dolly to her chest.

"Not a word from you, Ms. Coyne! And don't you dare leave that chair!"

The children became Coynes only when they engaged in bad behavior.

"Ma," Nelliecoyne asked as she worked on her coloring book, "what's a heifer?"

Nuala turned quickly. Her rules said that she had to give as much attention to our two older children as she gave to the little terrorist, lest they be "destroyed for life altogether!"

There were no signs that this was happening. Nelliecoyne and

Mick were at times exasperated by their little sister and more often amused. Neither seemed particularly cheated out of maternal love. But what did I know?

My wife had not changed much physically since I had first encountered her in O'Neill's pub on College Green in Dublin, the Danish town of the Dark Pool. Despite her jeans and her Chicago Bears sweatshirt (which matched the garb of our little terrorist), she was still an Irish goddess, not that I had ever encountered any exemplars of that group of women—slender, lithe, dangerously sensuous, with a voice in which you hear the sound of distant bells over the bog land, long black hair, flashing blue eyes, and a pale, ever-changing face that adjusted to the role she was playing at any given time. As I watched her she was playing the role of the mother whose patience had been driven to its outer limits, a role that was all too familiar these days.

She had resolutely refused to permit three pregnancies to affect her figure. To look at her was still to desire her. However, the sudden appearance of three more personalities in our house—not counting the two wolfhounds—had taken its toll on her tranquility, never all that stable to begin with. She suffered from postpartum depression after the Mick and then had struggled with the task of keeping Socra Marie alive, as though God could not be fully trusted to do His part—an idea I had never dared to raise. She had abandoned her singing career and threw herself into responding to the challenges of motherhood, the standards for which would have been too much even for the Madonna. She had plenty of help—Ethne, our babysitter, Danuta, our housekeeper, and even Nelliecoyne, who loved to play the role of little mother. Indeed, as far as I could see (and I kept my mouth shut) the last-named was the principal agent in the toilet training of the Tiny Terrorist. I was available on demand, though my wife had little confidence in my abilities as a "minder."

However, Nuala reasoned that she was still responsible not only for the children, but also for her associate caregivers and, on rare occasion, me. Also, arguably as the little bishop says, the two snow-white wolfhounds before me.

Only an insensitive brute would try to force himself on such a stressed-out woman. Her graceful breasts, however, still tormented me when I permitted myself to notice them.

"A heifer, dear, is kind of a teenage girl cow."

"What color should she be?"

"Any color you want."

"Are there purple heifers, Ma?"

"I don't think God has made any that color yet, but if you do a good job on her, God might think it's an interesting idea."

She was good with the kids, I had to admit. Yet the lines appearing around her eyes were lines of worry.

"I'm a focking, frazzled mess," she had admitted to me tearfully one night. "A nine-fingered gobshite of a mess."

"Beautiful though."

"I'm old before me time, I won't live to be thirty."

"Woman, you will."

"A lot you know."

So you marry a beautiful woman, the Adversary whispered, and you figure you're going to make love to her daily for the rest of your life and then these three little hellions invade your house and take her away from you.

The Adversary is a voice which lives in one of the dusty subbasements of my soul and periodically bothers me with its complaints. I am not responsible for any of his ideas.

In another year or two they'll all be in school. I'll have her to myself then.

She'll still worry about them and will be running back and forth to school all the time. You'll have to wait till they're in college, and by then you'll need Viagra.

It wasn't that we didn't make love. We did and we enjoyed it, more or less. But it was an interlude of brief escape from the chaos of our nursery school.

The good days are over, boyo. It serves you right for marrying a neurotic twit.

She is not!

Up to a point, I feared, maybe she was. Or maybe it was just part of the life cycle if you were married to a sensitive woman. Sensitive Irishwoman.

The phone rang. Before Nuala could turn to answer it and before I could lumber out of my comfortable chair, Socra Marie bounded out of her chair and grabbed it.

She babbled into it, imitating as best she could her mother's impatient tone. Then she shouted "Go away!" and hung up.

"Me answer phone," she said with a proud smile, clearly expecting applause.

I lifted her up and returned her to the time-out chair.

She began to sob.

"Da make me cry!"

"An hour on that chair," Nuala ordered implacably. "Don't ever, ever do that again, Socra Marie Coyne."

" 'Twas her father's genes again," I said aloud.

My wife actually giggled. She did that occasionally, even when we were not in bed.

"Certainly not her mother's. We didn't even have a phone in Carraroe when I was a child."

"You learned how to use it quickly enough."

"Isn't it a grand means for finding civilized talk when you're surrounded by little monsters all the day long?"

"Monster, Ma," Nelliecoyne corrected her.

The phone rang again. This time I got to it before the Tiny Terrorist, though the demonic expression on her face hinted that she was about to break out of the penalty box.

"Dermot," I said.

"This is John Patrick O'Sullivan," a resonant baritone voice informed me, "Damian's father. I just tried to get through to you."

His tone was pleasant and friendly enough. My demon (who is distinct from the Adversary) took over.

"I'm sorry about the confusion. We're teaching our two-year-old how to answer the phone. She's making a lot of progress."

Nuala Anne, who had slumped to the floor in total exhaustion, looked up and grinned. Still the imp, still indeed the shite-kicker.

"I'm happy to hear that," John Patrick O'Sullivan replied easily. "Never can begin too young."

"Absolutely not."

"I wonder if I might stop by and see you tomorrow after Mass . . ."

There was a hint of suspicion in his voice. We were probably the kind of young Catholics who didn't go to Mass.

"My wife sings at the eleven o'clock Mass at Old St. Patrick's. Anytime after two-thirty would be fine."

"Good. I'll be looking forward to meeting you . . . and that long-distance operator in training."

It was a funny comment, but I didn't like it.

"Damian's father?"

"Yeah."

How did she know? Don't ask me. She just knows.

"I don't like him."

One doesn't argue.

"Whatever Damian's problems might be, he's part of them."

"He wants to see us tomorrow."

"I'll be ready for him."

Thus spoke the implacable Irish goddess. Normally they come in threes. My Nuala Anne, however, could kick enough shite for three of them.

Sure enough, in a few minutes, our younger daughter, still clutching Dolly, was sound asleep.

"The poor little thing." Nuala Anne sighed. "The point is that all of that was just too much for her."

The words sounded different when she spoke them because the Irish language has no "TH." So what I heard was, "Da poor little ding, da pint is dat all of dat was just too much for her."

I am so adjusted to that language tic that I sometimes drop my "h" after "t," for which Nelliecoyne corrects me.

"You're a Yank, Da. You can't talk that way."

My wife picked up the "ding" and, humming da Connemara lullaby, carried her upstairs.

"Don't worry, Da," Nelliecoyne reassured me, "eventually she'll grow up. I did."

"You were never a Tiny Terrorist," I replied.

"I know the doctors say that she needs a lot of sleep because she expends so much energy," Nuala complained when she rejoined us. "It still doesn't seem natural."

"She's a very healthy little girl, Nuala," I said, echoing the doctors.

"That's what *they* say, but what do they know?"

I didn't try to answer that question.

"Mothers always worry too much, Ma." Nellie held up her purple heifer. "Weren't you after telling me that yourself?"

Nuala giggled again and rolled her eyes.

"Well, I know one thing: don't I already dislike that gobshite John Patrick O'Sullivan and meself not even knowing him yet."

"Don't say gobshite, Ma. It'll shock the Mick."

I decided at that moment that I would make fierce love with my wife that night.

Nuala always knows when I begin to think this. Don't ask me how she knows. She *knows*.

She glanced at me, then glanced away quickly.

YOU DON'T HAVE IT IN YOU.

You just wait and see.

— 3 —

OUR LIFE on Southport Avenue is regulated by an elaborate scheme of rules. The only way my wife could sustain the weight of her responsibilities to three children, two dogs, two "helpers" (three now that Day was on board) and, oh yes, one husband, was to impose order on chaos by making rules. To a considerable extent, however, her passion for order was violated by the fact that for every rule there were exceptions, either ones that she had legislated on the spur of the moment or systematic. Thus the rule said that when the door to the master bedroom was closed, the room became an inner sanctum into which neither child nor dog was permitted to enter.

Fair enough.

But what if there were an emergency that we did not pick up on our four monitors, one in the Mick's room and three in the girls' room, two for Socra Marie? The systematic exception was therefore legislated that the door would be ever so slightly ajar so that a large canine snoot or a small human face might cautiously peek in. That this exception negated the whole purpose of parental privacy was not a position I was ready to debate.

The other side of the coin was that Ma became very angry when someone took foolish advantage of the exception. So we were only occasionally bothered on our nuptial bed. The possibility of this happening, however, was an impediment to abandoned passion.

So the night before John Patrick O'Sullivan was to visit, Fiona pushed her large muzzle into our Holy Place, very tentatively, and looked around.

"Your police dog friend is here," I murmured.

"Hmm? . . . Oh, Fifi, it's all right." She sighed. "Weren't your man and I just playing around?"

The good Fiona did not understand the words, but she knew the tone of voice. Discreetly she withdrew and presumably returned to the "girls' room," which was her chosen overnight station. Better her inquiry than the Tiny Terrorist.

" 'Tis your fault," Nuala Anne insisted, "and yourself making all that noise."

"I thought it was my wife who did the screaming."

"Only because you made me," she whispered contentedly, as she snuggled closer to me. "You're a desperate man altogether."

"Desperate" is a hard word to translate from Irish English to American English. It may be a fourth level in the comparison of the adjective "grand" as in "grand," "super," "brilliant," and finally "desperate." It was on a higher level than "dead focking brill," the kind of expression Nuala Anne had given up out of respect for my American relatives and our children. In some places in Ireland "desperate" yielded position to "right focking whore," which was very high praise indeed. Nuala disdained that expression on the grounds that it was "chauvinist."

"The room is a terrible mess," she murmured as I caressed her gently.

"Is it now?"

"It smells like illicit sex."

"How would you know what illicit sex smells like?"

She giggled, as she often did during our postcoital cuddling.

"Ah, that would be telling, wouldn't it"

"It smells like perfectly legitimate marital sex."

"The sheets are soaking wet and crumpled up, our clothes are all over the floor, and it's a terrible, terrible mess—like a room in a disorderly house. I'll have to clean it up before Danuta comes in the morning." She sighed loudly. "Sure, isn't that the way of it?"

Heaven forefend that Danuta would suspect that we had made moderately violent love. Indeed, the marital bed was always neatly made before she arrived in the morning, even if it were Sunday morning and she would not show up.

Having stated her obligation, Nuala Anne did not move to get out of bed and begin to impose order on our disorderly room. Instead, she snuggled yet closer to me.

"Hold me tight, Dermot," she begged.

"If you insist on that, you might just get assaulted again."

"You wouldn't dare."

Which defiance was in fact an invitation.

"You think I'm too old to do it?"

"I think I have no secrets from you at all, at all."

I held her tightly in my arms so she couldn't move.

"I'm a terrible wife, Dermot Michael Coyne."

"Woman, in the last hour or so you provided excellent proof that's not true."

"I wear meself out worrying and fussing all day long and then at the end of the day I'm too tired for yourself."

"Maybe I shouldn't let you wear yourself out."

"'Tis not your fault that I'm an obsessive bitch." She was crying softly. "Och, Dermot love, I'm terrible sorry."

"You're not an obsessive bitch," I argued. "You're my Nuala Anne at a particularly hard time in your life cycle. It will get better."

I believed that, mostly.

"I should get up and straighten out the room."

"You'd just have to do it again later."

She giggled again. "Sure you wouldn't dare!"

I took a breast into my mouth and flicked my tongue against its nipple.

"Dermot Michael Coyne!" she gasped.

"Besides, tomorrow is Sunday and Danuta doesn't come."

" 'Tis true."

We were wakened very early in the morning by the Tiny Terrorist bellowing, "Glasses! Glasses!"

The little brat had learned to shout right at the monitor.

"Dermot, would you ever . . ."

"On my way."

Normally she would ask.

"Da! . . . Where's Ma!"

"She's all tired out," I said, arranging the glasses on her tiny, and quite adorable, nose.

"Aw, poor Ma!"

Nelliecoyne opened her eyes.

"She knows how to put them on herself, Da."

"I know, but she wants to be sure that we're still alive."

Nellie closed her eyes. Socra Marie turned her full attention to getting her dolly dressed for Mass.

"What time is it, Dermot Michael?" Nuala said, as I slipped back into bed.

"Five-thirty. We have three hours before we have to get up."

"We should feed the kids."

"Nelliecoyne can do it this morning."

"And I have to sing at Mass."

"Woman, you do."

"And my voice destroyed altogether."

"No, it's not."

"And that awful man is coming this afternoon."

"Maybe he's not awful."

"Och, Dermot, I know he is."

"Nuala Anne McGrail, go back to sleep."

"I don't know whether I'm safe in this bed."

"Probably you're not."

But she was. For the time being.

I have long since given up trying to account for Nuala's behavior. For the Eucharist at Old St. Pat's she dressed herself in a white sleeveless dress and found similar dresses for her daughters, even for "Dolly." Each of them wore a blue ribbon as trim. Blessed Mother blue. Her son wore a blue jacket and white slacks as indeed did the boy's father, because those were the clothes laid out for him on the neatly made marital bed. Fragrance spray had cleansed the room of all smell of sex, illicit or licit.

The four of them, Tiny Terrorist in her mother's arms, created quite a scene as they swept in to Old St. Patrick's Church. Heads turned as they walked up the steps and people whispered. Socra Marie waved at them. I followed along behind as security guard and spear-carrier.

We were in Easter season and the white was appropriate. Whether our romps the previous night suggested resurrection and rebirth, I did not know and I did not ask. Like the auras around us, the less I knew the better.

I was given charge of the threesome in the back of the church while she sang with the choir. Nelliecoyne knelt in solemn devotion, and sang the hymns and recited the prayers. Loudly. The Mick played with his trucks. The Tiny Terrorist roamed the pews. She smiled at strangers, climbed in and out of pews and ran around the back of the church and the vestibule, ducking in and out of places that might prove useful for hiding. I followed her out and discovered that she was already four steps up on her way to the choir loft (where the choir never performed). I carried her the rest of the way up.

"Pretty!" she announced at the view of the church from the loft.

Then, despite allegedly weak eyes, she spotted herself up with the choir in the front of the church.

"Ma!" she cried out. "Hi, Ma!"

Most of the people in the loft turned around and smiled at the pretty little imp. The priest who was preaching smiled too.

I brought her back down the stairs.

Nuala tried to blend with the choir, holding down her vocal power so as not to steal the show. Yet you couldn't miss the sweetness and clarity of her now-well-disciplined voice, especially when the melody of the song took possession of her.

A long time ago, when we were just married, I hired Madame down at the Fine Arts Building as Nuala Anne's coach. She had proved a quick and apt pupil, never to be an operatic soprano, but now a skillful singer of pop and standard songs—and Catholic hymns. At my insistence she quit her job at Arthur Andersen. When I remind her now that Arthur is in such deep trouble, that I saved her from all that, she waves her hand airily and announces that she was ready to quit anyway. She knows that she can't get away with it, but, like I say, Nuala Anne is a shite-kicker.

At Communion time I assigned Nelliecoyne to watch the Mick and carried the Tiny Terrorist up to the front of the church. She flirted outrageously with the priest (who thought she was adorable), then waved to her ma.

"Hi, Ma!"

Nuala waved back.

After Communion the congregation was to sing the English version of the old Latin hymn, after my wife had sung it in the original and much richer Latin form.

O filii et filiae
Rex caelestis rex Gloriae
Morte surrexit hodie
Alleluia!

Et mane prima sabbati
Ad ostium monumenti
Accesserunt discipuli
Alleluia!

Et Maria Magdalene
Et Jacobii et Salome

Venerunt corpus ungere
Alleluia!

In albis sedens Angelus
Praedixit mulieribus
In Galilaea est Dominus
Alleluia!

Discipulis astantibus
In medio stet Christus
Dicens pax vobis omnibus
Alleluia!

In hoc festo sanctissimo
Sic laus et jubilatio
Benedicamus Domino
Alleluia!

Herself was not only a singer but an actress. The joy of the song took possession of her body and soul as she clapped her hands with the rhythm.

"Now let's sing it all in English," she urged, "just like we were there on the happiest day in human history."

Ye sons and daughters, let us sing!
The King of heaven our glorious King,
From death today rose triumphing. Alleluia!

That Easter Morn at break of day,
The faithful women went their way
To seek the tomb where Jesus lay. Alleluia!

An Angel clothed in white they see
Which sat and spoke unto the three
Your Lord has gone to Galilee. Alleluia!

That night the apostles met in fear
And Christ in their midst did appear
And said, My peace be with you here. Alleluia!

On this most holy day of days
To God your hearts and voices raise
In laud and jubilee and praise. Alleluia!

The congregation clapped, which probably it should not have done. Though maybe they were celebrating the song more than the singer. Socra Marie pounded her little hands together enthusiastically.

"Ma sing good, Da."

"She always does, dear."

"And she didn't practice hardly at all," Nelliecoyne marveled.

One manic sexual episode would not lead herself back to her singing. She always had been ambivalent about it. Somehow it was calling too much attention to herself. She really did not have to work very hard to earn her fame. So when she went into postpartum depression after the Mick was born, music was the first thing she abandoned. Now, with the responsibility of her family, she didn't have time for it. The first time around it was the psychosis speaking. Now she had an excuse to turn away from something that might interfere with her being a good mother.

Only a neurosis.

When she emerged from the church, the crowd cheered. Socra Marie shouted, "Ma! Ma! Ma!" and twisted to escape my arms. I put her on the ground and she ran to her mother, who scooped her up.

"Ma awesome! Totally awesome!"

Nuala, an accomplished performer, no matter what, waved her hand and smiled graciously at her admirers. I knew her well enough to know that she didn't like it.

"Awesome! Awesome! Awesome," our youngest chanted.

She didn't quite know what it meant, but she liked the sound of it.

"That word is your fault, Nelliecoyne."

The perfect six-year-old laughed.

"I might have taught her a worse one, Da."

My wife leaned over to kiss my cheek.

"Friggin' eejits," she told me. "They shouldn't clap for a singer in church!"

"Maybe they were cheering the song and not the singer."

"Give over, Dermot Michael, that doesn't mean a thing at all, at all."

"Awesome, awesome," the Tiny Terrorist insisted.

"Give over yourself. Maybe they were clapping for the Nuala behind Nuala."

I was referring to Nuala's version of Irish mysticism, in which there was always a reality, hiding behind the reality that appeared to our senses as in "the real mountain, the mountain behind the mountain." Not being much of a mystic meself, ah, myself, I had no idea what she meant.

She pulled away from me and frowned.

"You mean because God raised Jesus from the dead? And ourselves too someday?"

"Didn't someone say this was the happiest day in human history?"

"So when I sing again in church, that's a kind of resurrection? I meant no such thing at all, at all."

"What do I know?"

"Awesome! Awesome!"

"Hush, dear, your da already knows that he's awesome . . . And Dermot Michael Coyne," she whispered in my ear again, "you should not stare so lasciviously at me and meself singing in the holy choir."

"I was not staring lasciviously."

"You were so."

"Well, at least it was respectful lasciviousness."

We opened the door of the old Benz and arranged the brood in their car seats.

"And you think that I rose from the dead because of last night."

I really didn't think that either.

"Would I ever think anything like that?"

"You would, Dermot Michael Coyne. You know too much altogether."

"Awesome! Really awesome," Socra Marie murmured as she drifted off to sleep.

We stopped at a bistro on Wells Street for brunch, a practice of many of the Old St. Patrick's crowd. Nellie and Micheal dug into their French toast, I demolished a stack of pancakes with real maple syrup and whipped cream.

"Whipped cream, is it now?" Nuala remarked with a twinkle in her eye, as she toyed delicately with her bacon and scrambled eggs.

She often insisted that I devoured her with my eyes the way I lapped up whipped cream. I argued that it was her metaphor, not mine, but it was a good one.

"It was wonderful last night, Dermot Michael," she said eyes averted. "Thank you."

The Tiny Terrorist woke up and demanded to be put on the floor. She walked about the bistro, shaking hands with everyone like they were old friends. Of course they thought she was adorable.

"Thank YOU," I replied.

"You deserve a better wife," she said as she poured tea for me. We had given up coffee altogether.

"For the moment, I'll keep the one I got."

I heard someone tell Socra Marie that her mother was a fabulous singer. She rushed back.

"Ma fabulous!"

"Thank you, dear." She picked up the mite and kissed her. "Don't bother the nice people while they're eating their breakfast."

"Fabulous!" our daughter said proudly as she scampered around the room to bother more nice people.

"I guess I went over the waterfall," Nuala continued our mysterious discussion, her face now suffused in a becoming blush.

"I like that metaphor," I said, having no idea what she meant.

Before we could play the reprise of our romp, the Mick cried out, "Ma, she's heading for the kitchen."

Nuala sprang up, turned abruptly, and knocked over the teapot, which discharged most of its hot contents on my poor wife and her Easter dress.

"Ouch," she cried, and dashed for the kitchen.

"We have real trouble now," Nelliecoyne observed.

A moment later my wife emerged from the kitchen, much of her skirt dark with tea and her lips compressed in pain.

Fast-moving fellow that I am, I had managed to climb out of my chair.

"Take her," Nuala snapped at me. "I have to see if I can save this dress."

"I'll help, Ma." Nelliecoyne rose and followed her mother to the women's washroom, accompanied by the woman of the house, who was only a year or so older than my wife.

"Can I have some more French toast, Da?" the Mick asked.

His mother would have told him that he already had enough and his eyes were bigger than his stomach.

"Sure, Mick, enjoy it while you can."

"Ma mad," Marie said, as we sat down.

"I think so, dear."

"Me not spill tea."

"I know that, dear."

She cuddled in my arm, aware that she was in trouble but not quite sure why.

Sometime later, as I finished off the French toast that the Mick couldn't eat, Nuala emerged from the women's room, encased in a robe that the establishment had somehow produced. She carried the fragile white dress, soaking wet, on a hanger.

"I think we saved it," she said, still angry.

"And you're not badly burned?"

"Not at all, at all."

"We put ointment on it," Nelliecoyne confided.

"Ma love Marie?" the tiny one asked anxiously.

My wife melted. Altogether.

"Unconditionally."

She took our energetic little child into her arms and sang the Connemara lullaby. The patrons applauded. Nuala Anne beamed and waved again.

"Unconditionally," the Tiny Terrorist used her new word. Nelliecoyne rolled her green eyes.

I thought better of trying to resume the conversation that Socra Marie's excursion into the kitchen had interrupted.

My wife said hardly a word as we navigated up to Southport. She was thinking through what she thought I had said after Mass.

"Well, Dermot love," she informed me, as she carried the sleeping little terrorist up the stairs, "you're probably right again as usual. So I'll have to go back to practicing every day. Only fifteen minutes, mind."

"We'll all be there to listen."

One of the rules of our marital discourse was that I was rarely right at all, at all, and then only when I agreed with my wife at the beginning of the discussion. Yet on this Sunday after Easter hadn't I won an argument that I didn't know was going on.

I SUPPOSE YOU THINK THAT THIS MEANS YOU'LL SCREW HER MORE OFTEN. The Adversary was being inappropriately cynical.

I take the opportunities when they come.

Inside the house, Nuala put our youngest in her crib, arranged the playroom for the other two, and warned them that when Day's father came, they were to stay in the playroom. She opened the door for the hounds to frolic in the backyard. They immediately renewed their wrestling match, which neither ever won.

"I'm going upstairs to change," she informed me.

"For Mr. O'Sullivan."

"Would there be anyone else coming to visit us this afternoon?"

It would be not only a performance, it would be solemn high.

"Should I change?"

"Whatever would make you think that?"

It doesn't matter what supernumeraries wear.

I would bide my time before the solemn high performance by reading the first segment of the manuscript that Ned Fitzpatrick had left for us. My wife argued solemnly that a century ago Ned knew about us and left it for us because he wanted us to solve the mystery.

Sure, time isn't all that important is it now?

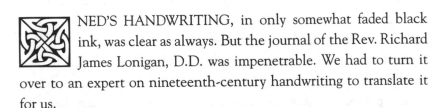

NED'S HANDWRITING, in only somewhat faded black ink, was clear as always. But the journal of the Rev. Richard James Lonigan, D.D. was impenetrable. We had to turn it over to an expert on nineteenth-century handwriting to translate it for us.

"This man is Irish?" the expert, a young mother about the age of herself, said to me skeptically. "He writes like he's a Spaniard."

We would learn later that Father Lonigan had studied at the University of Salamanca, which probably explained his writing style.

My brother, George the Priest, had come upon the manuscript down in the subbasement of his old rectory at Immaculate Conception parish on North Park.

"I can't make head or tail out of it, little bro. But there might be something in it that will hold the attention of that witch to whom you're married."

The word "witch" was a compliment. My brother didn't believe in psychic powers (unlike the little bishop, his sometime boss down at the Cathedral) but he did believe that Nuala was just a little scary and that despite the fact she always treated him with enormous respect. She invariably addressed him as "your riverence" while the cardinal was simply Cardinal Sean and the little bishop simply Bishop Blackie.

Ned's introduction to the ms was indeed inviting.

I'm not altogether sure why I am placing this manuscript in my archives. It depicts, fairly I believe, what life was like in Donegal at the outer edge of Ulster, in time after the Famine and before the Land League Wars. Father Lonigan was clearly an acute observer of this culture which is now dying out. I had accompanied my wife Nora on a return visit to her Irish home some twenty years after I had carried her off to America (along with her baby daughter Mary Elizabeth and her niece Josie) after her first husband Myles had been unjustly and cruelly executed in the Galway Gaol for a crime which everyone knew he had not committed. If I had not done so, the mother and child would surely have died of starvation.

We visited Galway again and prayed for Myles Joyce outside the great, ugly jail where he was murdered by the British Empire and where he was buried in quicklime. Both of us wept for that great and good man.

We stayed in the same room at the Railway Hotel in which we had consummated our marriage twenty years previously. It is a tribute to my wife to say that our love is stronger and more passionate now than it was then.

Our reception in Maamtrasna was strained, as she knew it would be. Some of the actual murderers were still alive. While most of the people in the townland shunned them, their presence was a reminder of who had done the killing and of the silence of the townland when the innocent were hung. Nora's presence reminded them of their failure. It would have been more in keeping with the melancholy mythology of the West of Ireland if she and Myles's infant daughter had starved to death. Instead she returned twenty years later a beautiful and prosperous "Yank."

"Won't they be glad to see us go?" She sighed. "Still we owed it to poor Myles to come back, didn't we, Ned?"

I could not have explained why we did, but I knew she was right.

"Let's see this Paris place," she said with a wan smile. "No one there will know me."

She has read this manuscript carefully. While she had never visited Donegal when she was growing up, she said that Father Lonigan's picture of the fringes of Donegal on the edge of the Atlantic in the decades after the Famine fit the beliefs of the time. "It was bad in Galway, worse in Mayo, but worst of all out there on the ocean. Don't they say that Colmcille might have gone to Donegal, but God stayed away."

Despite the silent resentment which greeted us at Maamtrasna, life was much better than it had been when Nora and Josie and Mary Elizabeth had rode away. It's the twentieth century now. Ireland won the Land League Wars. It cannot be long before home rule finally comes.

We showed the manuscript to Josie when we returned to Chicago. She read it carefully, then grinned her impish smile. "Isn't it clear who the killer was, Uncle Neddie? But now's not the time to name names, is it?"

With that verdict I leave this diary of Father Richard Lonigan, D.D. (Salamanca) to whatever posterity might discover it.

My wife believes that she is the same line as Josie and that some of her own fey traits are connected. She'll even tell me that she *knows* that Josie and Nora expect us to solve the mystery. I learned very early in our marriage not to try to argue with such a conviction. Then I put aside Ned's introduction and began to read the diary of Father Richard Lonigan.

March 8, Feast of St. Cathal of Taranto.

Another Irish exile. Fitting that I should begin my exile here on the brink of the Atlantic Ocean on such a feast day, though Sicily would be warmer than the outer edge of Ulster. The Cardinal has had his revenge for the strange ideas I brought to Maynooth from Spain. If I had simply given up those perfectly orthodox ideas, I would be sipping port in the Common Room at the College.

I would not do that. So here I am, my fingers so cold that I can scarce hold the quill with which I write. The ocean roars in the distance, the wind howls through my crumbling parish house, bringing with it the foul smell of the sea, and I shiver because my slovenly and slatternly housekeeper is conserving firewood. I shall pension her off and replace her with someone who is less committed to the ways of my saintly predecessor.

"Everyone adored the Canon, Your Reverence," says Mike Pat Branigan, the bald, corpulent, red-faced publican who has appointed himself to educate me about the townland. "Sure we'll not see his like again."

That is the none-too-gentle speech pattern of these sullen people. The new priest must understand that he should not attempt to change the ways to which his people have been accustomed.

I do not reply to Branigan's advice on this or any other matter. Rather I ignore him. He apparently takes my silence for agreement. I'm sure that when my piano arrives he will whisper in my ear that the people cannot understand a priest that plays the piano. I will ignore that advice too.

I will also rebuild the parish house and hire some good and presentable woman who has no objections to a house that is clean and warm and to food that is edible. I will also set out to extirpate from the parish the three chief vices of the Irish peasantry—wakes, holy wells, and "patterns" as they call the patronal feasts which are little more than an excuse for drunkenness and violence, both of which are an insult to St. Colm. I will pry the school away from Dr. Landry, the local Protestant parson, and install a young Catholic who speaks both Irish and English. I'm sure Branigan will disagree with all these ventures.

"Best not to disturb them, Your Reverence. Give them time now to get used to you."

They will indeed get used to me, sooner rather than later. Just as I have no choice but to be here, they have no choice but to suffer me as their parish priest for the rest of my natural life. If they don't like me, it is their problem, not mine.

April 24, Feast of St. Flann, Abbot of Iona.

Branigan tells me that the people find my sermons "very intelligent." By which he means they don't understand my theology. After Mass on Sunday, a mother with three children clinging to her skirts offered a somewhat more positive opinion. "Sure, Fr. Lonigan, didn't the old Canon preach a fine sermon too, but it took him three times as long to get to the point as it takes you."

A poor short sermon, our homiletics teacher told us, is much to be preferred to a poor long sermon.

Ah well.

"They're not used to having a doctor of theology preach to them," Branigan warns me.

I beat him to his next remark.

"Especially one who plays the piano a half hour every day."

A presentable woman, somewhere between thirty-five and fifty years old, came to the parish house two weeks ago, a child hiding behind her back. She was, I had reason to know, in desperate straits. She whispered meekly, yet bore herself with a certain grace that I might almost call elegant. She was a cut above the illiterate savages who constitute my parish, which was probably part of her problem.

Her husband had died after ten years of marriage, collapsed in the field one day and himself a big man and a hard worker, though he was sixty years old. He had left nothing to her, of course. His family had reclaimed the house in which she and Eileen (apparently the child was a daughter) had lived. There was no one in her home townland down in Mayo to whom she could return.

She had heard that I might be needing a housekeeper . . .

Branigan had warned me about her of course. Some of the women in the parish disliked her and others felt sorry for her. Because of this "difference of opinion" she would not be "fitting" for my housekeeper, especially since the people had liked Mrs. O'Malley so much. I ought to be very careful to hire someone who was like Mrs. O'Malley and herself working so hard for the late Canon.

The marriage patterns here in Ireland after the Famine are a disgrace. Her husband must have been at least fifty when he married her, a good twenty-five years older than she and finally brave enough to bring another woman into the family house where she was, technically, the one in charge. As soon as he was dead, the others got rid of her and her daughter.

Branigan's opposition disposed me towards the woman before I met her.

"Would that be Eileen hiding behind you?" I asked.

"It would, Fr. Lonigan . . . Eileen, say hello to the good priest."

The child peered around her mother and smiled. It was a winsome, heartbreaking smile on the face of a tiny angel.

"Jesus and Mary be with you, Father," Eileen murmured in Irish.

"And Jesus and Mary and Patrick be with you," I replied. "Would you want to be living in the little house behind the parish house and helping your mother?"

"I wouldn't mind it, Father. I'm a quiet little one."

Somehow, even then I found that hard to believe.

"It's not good for a child to be too quiet, Eileen O'Flynn."

"No, Father."

"Mrs. O'Flynn," I said to her mother, "I fear you will find me a harsh taskmaster. I expect a clean and neat house, food properly and punctually cooked, and peace and quiet."

"I'll do my best, Fr. Lonigan."

"See that you do."

I had not the slightest doubt that she would.

Several days later when I was indulging in my half hour of music in late afternoon, I noticed Eileen O'Flynn standing outside the window and listening with rapt attention. I almost warned her off.

I am invited tonight to dinner at the manor house of Milord Robert Skeffington. We shall battle over control of the school and I shall win.

April 26, Feast of Assan, Patron of Raheny in Dublin.
Whence I come, not that he has ever done anything to protect
me from the folly of my own mouth and the harshness of my
own soul.

On the way to the "Big House" I rode by the famed Holy Well of
St. Colm (not to be confused with the one at Glen Colmcille). It
is on a ledge a quarter mile from the sea, which was quiet yesterday
under a blue sky and a bright spring sun that bathed the shrine in
gold as it raced on towards America.

It is more elaborate than most such "wells"—a steady flow of
water from stone cairn, which fills a small pond and sinks back into
the earth. Spring fed, I thought, though this close to the Atlantic
it could be salt water.

I tasted the water in the pond with my fingertips—fresh, sweet,
and clean. This place surely had been a shrine as long as people
had dwelt in the vicinity. Its marvelous appearance, so close to the
sea, and its pleasant taste suggested that there was something
sacred, almost divine about it. The stones, which lined the inside
of the pond, could have been there for a thousand years.

Next to the pond was a stone cottage, the "drying house," since
it was necessary if one was to gain the full benefits to walk into the
water of the pond and climb out the other side. An English trav-
eler, having nothing better to do, had described it forty years ago.
He claimed that men and women disrobed on the patronal feast
and immersed themselves into the pond. I could scarce believe
that, though this part of the country is so savage that almost any
pagan custom could survive. I consoled myself with the thought
that the cold water would probably kill off concupiscence.

In the distance, the vast rock—St. Colm's mountain they call
it—looms over our townland like a grim and punitive spirit, not
unlike my friend the Cardinal. I'm sure its foreboding mass has
made it a target for superstitious fear since long before St. Colm
came out here, if he ever really did. Branigan tells me that my people never mention it to one another because that would be bad

luck, not that they've had anything but bad luck since Cromwell invaded Ireland. I find myself thinking of it as the Cardinal's mountain—massive, stubborn, and dumb.

I resolved that I would denounce all superstitions at my Mass on Sunday, not that it would do much good.

My parish stretches along the Atlantic coast in a half-moonlike curve with mountains behind us and hills at either end, the ones at the right leading to Colm's mountain on the coast. A massive headland rises above the shingle strand, which appears and reappears with the tide. Some men do swim in the ocean though the huge rocks along the strand make it difficult and dangerous. The village—church, cemetery, the new school, pub, store, RIC barracks, a few homes that are a bit better than the surrounding farmhouses—is in the middle of the saucer created by the mountains, the hills and the headland, a kind of prison from which the outside world is entered only by an old road that winds through the valleys beyond the manor house at the right-hand end of the crescent.

The land itself is poor, sustaining only corn, potatoes, a few peat bogs, some cattle, sheep, and goats. It might well be dairy country if the people, tenant farmers and the few day laborers left from the famine years, could purchase more than their tiny herds.

Streams cross the land, generally draining towards the clefts in the headland, but sometimes towards a river that flows by Colm's mount and drains an ominous lake set back in the hills, from which the local folks are afraid to draw fish though the occasional tourist fisherman draws a large catch. Somehow the lake is thought to be cursed, for reasons no one today can explain. There is no ocean fishing here because there is not even the semblance of a place that might be a tiny port.

Poor, wet, cold, rocky, and cursed.

Lord Skeffington's ancestors could not have been very important in whatever invading army he had fought. The land which had been taken away from the people and given to that ancestor was not very good land and the holding could not have been, even in the best of times, very lucrative. The "Big House" was not very big and was as worn and weary as the whole region. Bright flower gardens, however, lined the drive up to the house and ringed the house itself—an effort of the new Lady Skeffington if one could believe Branigan's tales.

"A lovely young woman," Mrs. O'Flynn had told me. "Very kind and gracious."

Mrs. O'Flynn could not find a harsh word for anyone, even her in-laws, who had actually waited on me in the parish house to demand that I discharge her because she did not "belong to the parish."

I had told them that they were very poor Christians and dismissed them with a wave of my hand.

Lord Skeffington had inherited the land and the title when his cousin had died—a hard, hard man, I had been told. He returned from India, found himself a proper wife in an impoverished noble family, and moved to Ireland, where he could hunt and fish to his heart's content. Typical English landlord.

Inside the house was cool away from the blazing fires and draft. However, Lady Mary Margaret had applied her woman's touch to brighten the place up and make it habitable if not palatial. She was a pretty young woman with bright brown eyes, curly hair, and a quick smile. If she was depressed by her new home in a land at least as savage as India, she did not show it.

"I'm told you're a pianist of some talent, Fr. Lonigan," she said. "Would you favor us with some music before supper? I'm afraid our house is not big enough to keep an orchestra."

I was both embarrassed and pleased, so I played Mozart, a divertimento followed by a minuet.

Lord Robert Skeffington watched with a smile of generous amusement. He probably knew nothing about music, but he sensed that this papist cleric was hitting all the right notes. He was a tall, handsome man, with black hair edged in silver and a military bearing matched by the cut of his clothes. I noticed that he treated his young wife with affection and, more to the point, genuine respect. The latter you don't see often in English gentry.

Dr. Landry, complete in gaiters and a ruffle at his neck, was in my judgment a typical Church of Ireland parson—overweight, pompous, and losing his hair. He was also, unless I mistook the signs, not very intelligent. His wife was a tiny nervous woman with graying hair and an expression of permanent disapproval. They were the kind of people who lived off the taxes imposed on Irish Catholics and did nothing because their congregation was so small that they had nothing to do. Loyal servants of the Queen, of course.

Yet the people of the townland were as polite and servile to them as they were to me.

The worst thing about my parishioners, I had begun to think, was the servility behind which lurked disapproval and resentment stored up through long years of incompetent clerical rule. They would be glad if I took the school away from Dr. Landry, but they would never admit it to me.

"Bravo, Fr. Lonigan," mine host applauded. "There are drawing rooms in England where Mozart has never been played so well."

"And some few which would even know it was Mozart!"

He chuckled generously. I must be careful or I would begin to like the man.

" 'Father' is appropriate is it not? Or should it be 'Doctor'?"

"Salamanca," I said and instantly regretted the boast. "Father, however, is just fine."

"An ancient and honorable university, is it not, Dr. Landry?"

"I'm sure I wouldn't know, milord."

"Do you like it here, Father?" Lady Mary Margaret asked me.

"I'm still feeling my way, milady. It's a challenging assignment. And yourself?"

"I love it! The scenery is so dramatic and the people so charming and when the wind blows I fancy that it comes all the way from New York and carries many loving messages from those who have left."

Her husband beamed with unabashed admiration. I realized that she was a better Christian than I was, though her exile to the end of Europe was as complete as mine. She shared it with an adored and adoring husband.

On the other hand, I thought as Mrs. Landry twittered and tweeted about how poorly educated the Irish were and how much good would come from proper education, I decided that I would rather be lonely than share my life with someone like her—and like all the other Church of Ireland wives I had known.

I said nothing about education. My opinions on the subject would wait till the ladies had withdrawn. Dr. Landry, however, bragged to Lord Skeffington about how much good the school was doing and how enthusiastically the previous lord had supported it. He was sure that there would be no trouble finding a new schoolmaster.

There would be a great deal of trouble if I had anything to say about it.

His Lordship complained to us about how difficult it was to understand the condition of his holdings. His agent, Tim Allen, was taciturn and not much of a help.

My parishioners feared Allen as a cruel man who stole from everyone, including the late Lord Skeffington. He also spent several nights a month at the house of a widow at the far end of the parish, a woman known only as Widow Cudahy.

"The old Canon would read her from the altar," Branigan had told me. "The people admired him for it, even though it didn't do any good."

I promptly resolved that I would not denounce her.

"So we're both trying to get the lay of the land, are we not, Father?"

"You, I am sure, milord, with a lot more tactical experience than I."

He chuckled again.

"Perhaps."

At dinner he asked about the Holy Well.

"Did you ride by it on the way over, Padre?" he asked me."

"I did."

"What did you think of it?"

He refilled my glass of claret. Even though it was first-rate, I drank only a sip. I noted that he limited himself to a single glass.

He was not the kind of English landlord who would drink himself into a stupor every night to escape the boredom and the deathlike smell of the sea.

"Very old, pre-Christian certainly. With a veneer of Christianity laid over it. I will denounce it as superstition, but I'm sure that will not stop devotion there, some of which is doubtless authentic."

"But hardly pleasing to God," Dr. Landry insisted pompously.

Mrs. Landry twittered away about the evil of Irish superstition.

"I know a bit about superstition, ma'am," Lord Skeffington interjected. "This one strikes me as rather harmless and charming in its own way. After all, water is one of God's primary gifts to us."

"Out here," I added, "it seems to be just about the only gift that is left."

"Quite so," Mary Margaret Skeffington agreed tersely.

Her husband's eyes twinkled. Obviously she could do or say no wrong, not even if she sounded like a Fenian.

After the women had withdrawn, port had been poured, and cigars offered (which I declined), Lord Robert turned to the business of the school.

"Since you two are the important members of my board, I hope we can reach a quick agreement about finding a new schoolmaster."

"I think not, milord," I spoke out immediately. "I will reserve to myself the right to nominate a schoolmaster for your consideration. The people in this townland are Catholics. They speak both Irish and English. It is only fair that they be taught by someone who is Catholic and who speaks both languages."

Dr. Landry sputtered.

"Your late cousin did not agree, milord. It would be a terrible mistake to depart from his custom. It would encourage the Fenians in this area of Ireland. The old Canon never objected. Donegal was too close to Belfast for there to be many Fenians."

"How many children are there in the school, Dr. Landry?"

No holds barred, no quarter given.

"Fifteen, I believe."

"No, sir," I replied. "Only ten, six of them Protestant, four from one Catholic family. Originally there were more than thirty. The Catholics withdrew their children gradually when they discovered that the school was in fact an agent for proselytizing activity. The old Canon did not have to urge them to do so. They may be superstitious savages, milord, or maybe that's all they can be under the circumstances. Yet they are Catholic and will remain so. I will oppose the school with all the power at my command, but my opposition will merely stiffen a few hesitant backbones. My people want education for their children, but not at the cost of attacks on their faith."

A grim mask seemed to spread over Lord Skeffington's face and his eyes hardened. He'd been a colonel, a regimental commander. I was seeing his look before battle.

"You make your point effectively, Father," he said softly.

"Milord," Landry continued to sputter, "you cannot permit the school to become a place where the children of my flock will be subject to attacks on her faith. You are, after all, sir, a servant of the Crown."

"And of the Queen Empress," Skeffington said lightly.

"There will be no attacks on anyone's faith," I said. "I will guarantee that any nominee of mine will respect every faith under heaven. Any complaints on this subject should be brought promptly to my attention and, if necessary, I will recommend to His Lordship that he dismiss the schoolmaster."

"I cannot accept a guarantee of that sort," Dr. Landry announced. "I will not accept the word of a papist cleric."

I almost responded. Then I realized that the best strategy would be for me to be quiet.

"Well, gentlemen, your positions are both clear. I will take the matter under advisement and inform you of my decision about a schoolmaster when it is convenient for me to do so."

It was a typical statement of an English lord. Or a colonel in the Indian Army.

Just the same I had won.

The conversation turned to the weather and the prospect for the spring crops. Then we "joined the ladies," to the obvious relief of

Lady Mary Margaret, who seemed to have been quite overcome by Mrs. Landry's twittering about the ignorance of the "mere Irish."

Shortly thereafter the Landrys took their leave.

"I'm delighted, milord," said Dr. Landry, "that you see things my way on the school."

I wondered if we'd been in the same room.

I was about to leave too, but Lord Skeffington put a strong hand on my shoulder.

"Stay a moment, Father Richard."

We walked back into the parlor of the house. The wind had picked up. Drafts danced around the room. The fire rose and fell in response to teasing wind.

"Mary Margaret, would you bring a drop of poteen for the good father and me?"

"Only a drop, Father. You're going to have to ride back in the storm that's brewing."

"Yes, ma'am," I agreed.

"It is said," His Lordship said with a sigh as he opened his cravat, "that the poteen from this part of Donegal is the best in all of Ireland."

"Really?"

"Mary Margaret is quite right. Only a sip. I wouldn't want the pope or the Cardinal blaming me for the death of a new parish priest here. You know that there are stills all over your parish?"

"I did not."

No reason anyone would tell me that.

"Poor devils stay alive on the income. Farms aren't worth much in many places hereabout. Too poor to own many head of cattle. They're very clever about hiding it. The customs men are after them constantly, but the local constables are in league with poteen men . . ." He puffed on his cigar. "Would you denounce my wife, Father Richard, if she should bathe in your Holy Well?"

"I don't denounce people, milord. I merely denounce superstitious practices. In any case your wife isn't Catholic, so I could hardly denounce her."

"She'd keep some of her clothes on, I think. Unlike the people my idiot countryman claims to have seen earlier in the century. She wants a child, as do I. We have not been successful so far and, as you might well imagine, it's not for lack of effort. She has heard that the well has powers of fertility . . ."

"Water is the source of life, milord," I said. "I'm sure that pond has been credited as a fertility cure since long before St. Patrick. There is some reason to be skeptical . . ."

He laughed.

"I know, I know. I'll warn you beforehand if we ride over there. I wouldn't want to embarrass you."

"Here's your draught, Father." Lady Skeffington appeared and presented me a tiny glass with a splash of clear liquid in the bottom. She gave her husband a somewhat larger ration.

"Bob needs it to get those two out of his system. Otherwise, he won't be able to sleep."

I didn't know whether she was serious or joking or offering a bit of a nuptial hint to her husband. He merely laughed.

"They're terrible people, all right, but then we all have them, don't we, Dick?"

So now I was "Dick." I didn't want to get too close to the Establishment.

"I could give you a long list of ours," I agreed, and raised my glass to toast them.

"*Slainte!*"

He responded, "Your very good health, Dick."

I indulged in a tiny sip of the poteen. My whole body caught fire. I put the glass down on the table next to me. Lord Skeffington downed his with a single toss.

"You don't have to drink any more, Father," Lady Mary Margaret assured me. "Bobby's stomach was ruined out in India. He doesn't even feel it as it goes down. It will catch up with him later."

"I drink it only once a week, Dick." He sighed. "It's too easy an escape from our problems. In a quarter hour I'll feel all's forever right with the world."

"Which it isn't," his wife added.

She enveloped him in a smile that made me think that a man whose wife smiled at him like that did not need poteen.

"Before that happens, Dick, let me ask you whether you have a schoolteacher in mind for our school."

"I do, milord. He's young and has been taught by the Jesuits in Dublin. He knows Latin, Greek, and Irish as well as English. And he writes poetry . . ."

"All you mere Irish do that . . ."

The poteen was already catching up with him.

"He's from Galway and is eager to return to the West of Ireland."

"He's coming out here?"

"In July."

"We'll talk to him then."

"Thank you, milord."

"It's the only fair thing," Lady Mary Margaret said in approval.

The English are great people for fairness, given the unfair situations they create.

They escorted me to the door, His Lordship's arm around his wife, though I doubt he needed her support yet.

They waved good-bye to me as I rode off into the wind and the stench of the sea. The moon had disappeared. It would rain before I returned to the parish house. The spring mood had already disappeared. Lightning scratched the western sky. More love messages from New York?

Mrs. O'Flynn would have a light on in her little hut so I could find the house. When she heard me put the horse in the stable, she would blow out the candle.

It had been a strange evening. Now two days later, I still don't know what to think of it. I wonder how much the poteen explains the passivity of my people.

I will add drink to the evil of superstition, which I will denounce from the altar on Sunday.

— 5 —

WHEN I came to the part of the manuscript in which Ned described him and Nora returning to the hotel room in which they had consummated their marriage, I closed the manuscript folder and, carrying it in my hand, ambled down to the master bedroom. I arrived just in time to discover my wife emerging from the bathroom, a towel wrapped around her body.

"Dermot Michael Coyne!" she protested. "Whatever are you doing here? You're violating my privacy! You're stealing my modesty."

"A man has a right to watch his wife dress and undress," I replied with mock innocence.

"So long as she doesn't object!"

"You usually don't object."

I choose my times for such amusement only when I'm pretty sure she won't object.

"You look at me like I'm one of your chocolate malted things that you gulp down for your pleasure!"

"With lots of whipped cream!"

"I'm just a thing for you to enjoy!"

She threw the towel at me.

"I'll leave if you want," I said.

The preliminary conversation was babble to cover the touch of sweet embarrassment, which mixed with her delight at my attention.

"Now that you're here"—she sighed, a woman offended beyond all toleration—"you might as well stay . . . You drink in every woman you look at, Mr. Coyne."

"I don't!"

"You do so! Weren't you ogling that bitch Clare Conley at the bistro and herself old enough to be my mother."

"She's not . . . Besides I only look at her with respect."

"That's the problem. You respect them all, so they really don't mind you undressing them with your eyes! You're a terrible man altogether . . . Here now, make yourself useful and hook me bra for me."

"I leave some of their clothes on," I protested.

Feigning clumsiness, I hooked her up. Then my arms crept around her and my fingers dug into the firm muscles of her belly.

"Didn't you have enough of me last night, Dermot Michael Coyne?" She slumped against me.

"Woman, I did not!"

I rested my lips against hers.

She sighed, her West of Ireland sigh of a woman whose patience has been too long affronted.

"Didn't I say that to meself the first night at O'Neill's pub? Didn't I say to meself that big lout is a cute one, but he'll never get enough of me? If he once gets his hands on me, will he ever leave me alone?"

"If all the things you said to yourself that night were laid end to end, wouldn't you have been saying them for a couple of months?"

I increased the pressure of my lips against hers. She sighed again.

"Would you ever please go sit on the couch and read Ned's manuscript and let me get dressed, so I can deal with Mr. Pigface when he comes?"

"A reasonable request."

She had never met the man. How did she know he was a pigface?

He would encounter my wife in beige—tight beige slacks, a form-fitting beige cashmere sweater, and a beige ribbon in her long hair.

"Dermot love?"

"Yes, Nuala Anne?"

"I'll begin to practice singing again this afternoon. I'll do it for fifteen minutes and cut my time in the exercise room from a half hour to fifteen minutes."

"Woman, you will not! It will be a half hour for each!"

I glanced up to look at her face in the mirror. It was clouded up as though thunder and lightning were about to appear.

"Och, sure, Dermot Michael, don't you have the right of it? Whatever would happen to me if you weren't around to take care of me?"

We prepared very carefully for the coming of Mr. Pigface, aka John Patrick O'Sullivan. Nuala arrayed a row of alcohol bottles on the mantel, as though we were the kind that serve cocktails every evening at precisely five-thirty. She filled a bucket with ice, though her Irish prejudice was that only friggin' Yanks ruined perfectly good booze with ice. She sternly warned Nelliecoyne that she and the other kids should stay in the playroom till Day's father left.

Then we sat in the parlor and waited, I patiently, herself impatiently.

I couldn't quite figure out why the setting or should I say scene for this encounter had to be contrived so carefully. I knew that if I asked, I would be informed that wasn't it obvious altogether.

"It was a good show," I murmured, referring to our interlude in the bedroom while she was dressing.

"What was a good show? . . . Och, Dermot, you're being vulgar!" She blushed in pleased embarrassment.

At precisely two o'clock I heard the noise of a car pulling up in front of our house.

"What's he driving, Dermot Michael?"

"A powder blue BMW 750."

"Custom paint job. Figures."

I don't know why it did, but I'm not the psychic in the family. Nor do I see auras.

I opened the door as soon as the bell rang, lest I be ordered to hurry up and answer it.

My first impression of John Patrick O'Sullivan was of his scent, a strong masculine aroma which suggested, that freshly powdered and burnished, he had just stepped out of the locker room after a successful round on the golf course. Let there be no doubt about it, he was a real man. If you didn't believe it, just sniff. People walking on the street, a floor down below us, could probably smell him too. (Like many homes in our neighborhood the entrance is on the second floor, harking back to the days when the city was a swamp.)

Nuala buys my scent.

"The important thing," she lectures me, "is that no one even notices, except perhaps whatever woman you're sleeping with."

"Jack O'Sullivan," he said, thrusting out a genial hand and a genial Irish smile.

"Dermot Coyne," I murmured diffidently as I successfully resisted his effort to crush my hand.

He then thrust his business card at me. It was pale green with a darker green border with hints of shamrock. It announced "O'Sullivan" in large green letters. Under that it informed the world that the business was "Specialty Electronics."

"Either he or someone who has worked for him is a brilliant engineer," Mike Casey the Cop had informed me. "He grew up in Englewood while the blacks were moving in. Father a cop. Family was poor. Didn't have the proverbial pot to piss in. Went to Mount Carmel, then on to the Golden Dome on a football scholarship. Not quite good enough for the pros. Bought this tiny company in the northern suburbs with money from his Notre Dame admirers. Built it up from nothing. They're so good at what they do and what they do is so important that the downturns in tech stocks have never hurt them. Bet you own some of his stock."

"Feds after him?"

"They take a good hard look at everyone like him. Haven't found a thing. He's either honest or very smart."

He certainly radiated bluff, open Celtic honesty in his navy blazer, light blue slacks with a jeweled stars and stripes in one lapel and a small, solid gold shamrock in the other. His French cuff links, gold on navy blue, carried a jersey number. He was a big guy, my height—six-four—and maybe twenty pounds heavier, most of it not fat. His slicked black hair, above an abbreviated forehead, was jet-black edged in silver, a dye job so professional you would hardly notice. However, nothing artificial could hide his red Irish face and pale blue eyes, which bored relentlessly into me despite his genial Irish smile.

"You went to the Dome, didn't you?"

I inclined my head slightly.

"Play football?"

"Not really."

That was true enough. I had quit the team at Fenwick and turned to wrestling because I detested the coach. I'd walked on at Notre Dame for a few days and decided that it was too much work.

"You would have made a great linebacker."

"That's what they told me."

"My position. I played it back in the sixties. Huarte and Snow."

"Number one till the last game," I said, showing off my knowledge of Dome arcana.

"We should have beat the Trojans that last game," he insisted.

In fact they should have. But they didn't.

When two big guys meet each other, they automatically size each other up, trying to figure who can take whom. Despite the fact that professional trainers had kept John Patrick O'Sullivan in good condition, I knew I could take him. I could have taken him when he was playing for the Dome. I was quicker and smarter and pretty good at wrestling. Also vain, a fault my wife contended that I shared with all males of the species.

"A lot of things have changed since those days," he said. "Not really a Catholic university anymore. Nor a Catholic football team."

It was my own fault I had flunked out at Notre Dame.

"Kind of a Catholic theme park," I said, a contradiction to what he'd said that was too subtle for him.

"Now they've got this new coach. I don't think it's going to work out. Maybe he can civilize some of the savages they recruit these days.

I liked to think that if this new coach, lifted from the Stanford Cardinals, had been coaching at the Dome when I was there I would have stayed and become all-American and maybe played a year or two with the pros. However, I would never have met Nuala Anne. She disagrees vehemently. "Didn't God mean me to find you?"

I introduced him to Nuala Anne.

"Jesus and Mary be with all who come to this house," she said in her thickest Galway accent. "Dermot Michael, would you see what Mr. O'Sullivan will have to drink?"

Nuala never asks that question of a visitor.

"Scotch and water on the rocks," he said automatically, "even though it's a little early in the day."

Incurably South Side Irish. Has bought enough good taste so that he thinks he's urbane and polished but doesn't know what the words mean.

"Won't I have a splasheen of Green Bush, Dermot love? Straight up."

Me wife does not ordinarily drink whiskey.

As I fixed the drinks I heard the rustle of canines behind me. As discreet as they try to be, the two hounds make a lot of noise because there is a lot of them. I had not heard herself summon them, so they must have responded to a telepathic signal, which happens occasionally. Maeve lifted herself to the couch on which Nuala was sitting, causing it to sink perceptibly. Fiona curled up on the floor at her feet and watched John Patrick O'Sullivan intently. Cleopatra with her pet leopards.

I poured her substantially more than a splasheen and a tiny drop for meself.

" 'Tis yourself that has the heavy hand." She sighed, taking the Waterford glass with a perfectly straight face, which warned me not to spoil her act.

"Those are big dogs, Mrs. McGrail," our guest said nervously as I gave him his scotch and water on the rocks, light on the water.

"Mrs. McGrail is me ma. I'm Mrs. Coyne or Ms. McGrail . . . Aren't they dear ones? Maeve here is the largest wolfhound bitch in the world. Fiona is a retired police dog. They're both as gentle as newborn kittens. They'd only chew your throat out if I told them to."

Maeve laid her huge snoot on my wife's lap and made her noise not unlike a purring kitten. We would have to remove every hair from the parlor before Danuta showed up on the morrow.

"What part of Ireland are you from, Mrs. McGrail? I get over there every year with a group of friends for a golf tour."

"Connemara," she said softly.

My wife does not normally answer the question that way. Rather she tells you the name of her hometown, assuming that anyone with intelligence knows where Carraroe is.

"Yeah, I know the place. There's a great golf course there, right above a town called Salt Head."

"Salt Hill. Me husband has a three-stroke handicap at Poolnarooma because he doesn't practice very much."

Not the total truth. I don't practice enough, but I haven't played there often enough to build up an official handicap. Three is about right, however.

"Me wife," I added, "won the women's championship there a couple of times."

Total truth.

Said wife smiled modestly. "Wasn't that ages ago?"

"We play a different course every day," O'Sullivan went on. "Ballybunion, Adare, Postmarnock . . . Great way to see Ireland, good friends, good food, good golf."

"Sure, doesn't it sound like a brilliant cultural experience?"

Her irony was lost on him.

We got down to business. John Patrick O'Sullivan spoke to me. Nuala answered him. I remained silent. I noted that hard eyes were a much better indication of his temperament than the lighthearted, happy Irish smile that seemed frozen on his face.

"This is a picture of my four oldest kids, Dermot. First-rate young men and women. All went to Notre Dame. Damian spoiled our perfect record. These kids are real Irish cream. Kathleen is a pediatric surgeon, Sean is a lawyer, so is Maura, Pat works with me at our company. I'm proud of them. Five grandchildren already, another in the oven. All married Irish spouses."

All four kids were clones of the old man, tall, athletic-looking, black Irish, who would have been handsome if not for their grim expressions. They could just as well have been an IRA cell. I passed the photo over to me, er, my wife.

She glanced at it and nodded imperceptibly. "Handsome."

"I'm very proud of them. Like I say, they're the cream of the crop."

"Damian isn't in the picture."

"He would have ruined the picture." He bowed his head and shook it. "Damian has the habit of ruining things."

"He seems like a very nice boy," Nuala said, scratching Maeve's huge head.

"Boy is the right word! The doctor says he might have a Peter Pan personality. Refuses to grow up. Damian is almost twenty-five. By the time I was that age, I had two kids and owned my own company. He takes care of puppies, draws pictures, and babysits. He refuses to assume adult responsibility."

"Psychiatrist?" Nuala asked innocently

"Of course not! No son of mine needs a shrink! . . . He refused to apply himself in school. Graduated from Faith, Hope grammar school only because we made a contribution. Flunked out of Loyola Academy. Was accepted at Notre Dame because of my clout and wouldn't go. Ruined our perfect record. Absolutely refuses to apply himself."

"Maybe he needs testing," Nuala Anne murmured.

"No kid of mine needs testing," John Patrick O'Sullivan said grimly, his fallacious smile fading for a moment. "He's just lazy."

The man's pain is real enough though he's patently an asshole.

I took his empty Waterford tumbler.

"Just a short one. I have to drive up to the club."

He continued to speak to me, though Nuala Anne played our role in the conversation.

"My daughter Maura, she's the youngest, thinks he's gay. I won't believe that a son of mine could be gay. He's just immature."

"Doesn't Ethne, our cute little babysitter, tell us that he gets along fine with the girls here in the neighborhood and themselves liking him?"

Nuala Anne never calls Ethne a "cute little babysitter" and does not refer to young women as "girls." But she was in the role now and playing it to the fullest.

"I tried to get him a seat at the Board of Trade . . ."

"I hear they're cheap these days," I said brightly.

"Expensive enough . . . He worked there for a couple of days and quit. Would rather draw his crazy little pictures . . . There's no money or respectability in that."

"I know a young man," Nuala said, "who flunked out of Notre Dame, didn't graduate from any college, and failed at the Exchange. He tries to write poetry. As you know there's no money in that. His family thinks he's lazy. Didn't he seduce a poor innocent little Irish lass?"

Witch. She didn't add that I made a couple of million on a Friday afternoon, admittedly by mistake, and promptly retired and had since written a couple of successful novels. Even published a few poems here and there. About her and her children. Won the occasional prize.

"That's Damian's problem. He's lazy . . . I have to warn you that he might be dangerous. He got drunk out at the club and drove our car over a good friend of mine. A little twit of a public defender wanted to go to trial. We would have looked real bad in the media . . . I had to hire a topflight lawyer and use all my clout to get him off with five years' probation."

"Bad enough family disgrace as it was . . ."

"I don't like the way he hangs around kids either. Doesn't look right. What kind of a twenty-five-year-old male hangs around kids, tell me that?"

"A priest, maybe?"

He missed her irony.

"They'd never take him in the seminary . . ." He put his empty glass on a coaster. "I had to warn one family here in Lincoln Park, which had hired him as a babysitter . . . Can you imagine that? A twenty-five-year-old man acting as a babysitter."

"They discharged him, did they now?"

"Sure they did. Couldn't take the chance. I didn't want a suit on our hands. Or another court case."

His red face had turned purple. Anger at his youngest son had become a demon that possessed his soul.

Damian the Leper.

"Sure, doesn't the poor lad have a lot of troubles?"

"We're the ones who have the troubles, Mrs. McGrail," he said, as his genial smile and voice returned. "He's going to destroy us . . . What's the matter with that dog?"

"Hush, Fiona. 'Tis all right. The poor man doesn't realize he was shouting at me."

Fiona suspended her low growl. Temporarily.

"I'm sorry if I shouted. The kid is driving me crazy. I beg you to get rid of him before he ruins your family too . . . How many kids do you have?"

Nuala didn't answer. It was up to me.

"Three," I said. "Two little girls and a little boy."

"For the love of God, get rid of Damian! He's dangerous to them."

"Not while our two friends here are around."

"He charms dogs too."

"We appreciate your warning, ah," Nuala glanced at the card, "Mr. O'Sullivan, and we understand your pain. Nonetheless, we think you are doing a terrible injustice to Damian and probably have done so for a long time. We'll not discharge him!"

Not a single question in the whole paragraph.

"You must!" he sobbed.

"Dermot Michael, will you show Mr. O'Sullivan to the door."

I did.

"You gotta think about the risks," he told me at the door. "The kid is a misfit. Totally unreliable!"

"We will think about what you've said," I replied in the interest of civility.

I watched him walk down the steps to the street, his shoulders slumped, his head bowed. Poor bastard.

As I closed the door, I realized that the two hounds were behind me wagging their tails dubiously. Then they took turns standing on their hind legs and licking my face.

"Irresistible, Dermot Michael," my wife observed, "aren't you now?"

"To dogs and little children!"

I sat next to her on the couch. Both pooches curled up on the floor.

"Just like poor Day."

"Except he didn't seduce a poor lass from Ireland."

She giggled.

"I admit that I went too far . . . Still, we got a lot out of him didn't we . . . You know my methods, Dermot. What did you observe about your man?"

"I caught the Sherlockismus, love. What I noticed most of all was that he seems to have produced five children, four of them pure Irish cream, without the necessity of a wife."

"You noticed that, did you now?"

"I did."

"Mr. O'Sullivan is a friggin' gobshite," Nelliecoyne informed us.

"Nelliecoyne!" we both exploded.

"It's all right to use the words," she argued. "We're all three Irish, and we know that we mean no harm by those words."

"The little children!" Nuala protested.

"I don't talk that way around them. Anyway, they'll learn it soon enough . . . Poor Day probably has a learning disability."

I don't know whether the Irish vulgarity or the American psychological cliché on the lips of our gorgeous little red-haired six-year-old was more of a surprise.

"How many times have I told you not to eavesdrop on adults when they're talking!"

"A lot, Ma."

"And you still do it!"

"Don't I have to find out what's happening in this house?"

She hugged Maeve, who had sidled up to her. Fiona, unwilling to pass up affection, nudged her for a hug. Nelliecoyne obliged.

"Go back to the little kids," Nuala said sternly. "I'll deal with you later."

"Yes, Ma."

"What about Socra Marie?"

"She was grumpy when she woke up. Bad dreams about who spilled the tea. Now she and I are working on her coloring book."

"Whatever are we going to do with that one, Dermot Michael Coyne? She's worse than her sister."

"I suspect that you will have a nice serious talk with her and explain why it isn't fair to adults to listen to what they say and that you'll explain to her everything she needs to know. That may work for a while."

She sighed loudly.

"They'll be the death of me altogether . . . By the way, I'm glad you liked the show."

"The one here with John Patrick Sullivan?"

"Of course not. That was just a way of finding out a lot about him . . . No, the one in the bedroom. You're very sweet, Dermot love. When you look at me in that adoring little-boy way, don't I tremble all over and want to collapse?"

"You mean you like being whipped cream?"

"When you make me whipped cream, isn't it dead friggin' brill?"

These days she rarely returned to the expressive Dublin street argot she had learned at Trinity College. She could use it about me, however, anytime she wanted.

"I'll keep that in mind."

"Now, about your man." She changed the subject quickly. "Not only doesn't he have a wife, he doesn't think much of women. The twit who thought she could get Day off in a trial was obviously a young woman. He was unimpressed with our quotes from Ethne. He's a locker room male, at ease only with men, especially on their golf trips to Ireland, from which women are banned . . . Don't you ever dare to think of doing that, Dermot Michael Coyne!"

"Wouldn't I be out of my mind if I did!"

"Did you notice anything else?"

"Well, he talked to me and you answered him, an interesting conversational style."

"And?"

"Let's see, oh yes, he's enthused about Ireland but doesn't seem to be aware that you are a well-known singer of Irish music, which means he really doesn't give a damn about Irish culture beyond that which he encountered at the Golden Dome four decades ago and on Irish golf courses more recently."

"And?"

"Day is an obsession with him. He's had this perfect life and perfect family, then one rotten apple comes along and spoils it all."

"Serious obsession . . . And the other kids?"

"They look grim and ruthless. Like a cell of IRA killers."

"You've got the right of it, Dermot Michael. He's afraid of women, even his daughters, though they're probably tough enough in their style to please him. Day is the only child who doesn't look like him. Probably the image of his wife. He's afraid Day's queer."

"His mother is likely a sweet little woman, who the others in the family ignore because Daddy does. Sweet and very strong, Dermot Michael. I'm not sure if the sweetness is real. We'll have to talk to her if we can . . ."

"Talk to her!"

"Sure, don't we have to find out what happened that night at the country club when someone killed someone?"

"Where do we start?"

"With that twit of a public defender. Where else?"

"Good on you, Nuala Anne."

I was Dr. Watson again, the spear-carrier. For a woman like my wife I would gladly carry spears forever.

"What's that story like?" She gestured at my dossier.

"Dark, very dark. I can't quite figure out why. There's lots of passionate people in it."

"Would you ever let me read it now? I need to go back to the nineteenth century. I'll read it while I'm on the treadmill."

"I'll go down and play with the kids."

We have three floors in our house—the ground floor with the laundry, the furnace, some storerooms, the playroom, and the dogs' room.

Beneath the ground floor was a dark gloomy basement. "For the ghosts," me wife said.

Some one of these days, we'd have to finish the basement and use it as game rooms and study rooms.

On the second floor, where the entrance is, there's the parlor, the dining room, the kitchen, the breakfast nook, and the music room where Nuala practices—when she practices at all. At all.

On the third floor we have four bedrooms and two offices, both of which can be converted into temporary bedrooms. We also have five bathrooms scattered around the house, which Nuala thinks are "excessive altogether." She also thought that the master bathroom was "excessive," but she didn't object to its various facilities.

We had added an exercise room in the attic, of which my wife and I made separate use. Nuala Anne in shorts and running bra, twisting and turning and running was too much of a distraction when I wanted serious exercise.

I walked down to the playroom, where the three kids were playing, Nelliecoyne with her coloring book, the Mick with his Legos, and the Tiny Terrorist with her dolls. Who could ask for children who were more quiet, more dutiful, more intent on their play?

"How's herself?" I asked Nellie.

"She had bad dreams that told her she had spilled the tea on Ma. I told her the dreams weren't true. Ma spilled it on herself."

"Ma love Socra Marie, unconditionally."

"Yes, she does," I agreed, lifting her up into the air and spinning her around. Many kids her age would have been frightened by such a spin. My younger daughter chortled gleefully.

"Where are the doggies?"

"Day took them for a run."

Better he than I, I thought.

"Day color doggies," Socra Marie informed me, when I restored her to terra firma. She held up a sheet of drawing paper. "Fabulous!"

This time the word was appropriate. In crayon he had captured the two snow-white giants on green grass panting after furious exercise, possibly wrestling with one another. They huddled together in mute affection, empresses of all they surveyed and ready to rebuff any dog that threatened their domains. He'd even caught the differences in their personalities; Maeve more laid-back, Fiona more vigilant as befits a retired police dog.

The composition, the color, the craftsmanship were superb. The kid had talent, some of it natural, some of it acquired by discipline and practice. Of that skill his father certainly would not be proud.

"It certainly is fabulous, Socra Marie. Can I put it over here to show Ma?"

"Ma spill tea," she insisted.

"Yes, she did," I agreed.

I would not report this exchange to her mother. Nuala would worry that she had created a major psychological problem for the child, which it might take years of therapy to resolve.

I began to turn over in my mind a poem about three kids in the playroom—black, red, and blond hair, of their intensity at their games and myself wondering how I came to have such three rapidly growing rugrats.

A chorus of barking dogs erupted in our backyard.

"They're back!" Socra Marie rushed into the dogs' room and hugged the canine Moby Dicks as they entered.

The foundation of our house had been laid before the Great Fire, which had missed it, though just barely. The ground level was near the ground until the city built up the streets in its never-ending battle with mud and eliminated the possibility of ground-floor entrance. However, the yard in back was some three feet lower than the street level. Hence there was a back door.

"Hi, Dermot," Damian said with a happy grin, not unlike his father's except his geniality had not yet turned bitter. "Quiet, girls, you know how herself doesn't like all that barking in the house."

Except when they're barking at her in something like hyperdulia in the good old Catholic days.

"My dad was here, wasn't he, Dermot. It looked like his car in front."

"He was."

"And?"

"Herself and the dogs scared him away."

"I've tried. I can't please him, no matter what I do. I keep trying . . ."

No one tells Nuala Anne McGrail whom she can hire."

"That should be obvious after a moment's conversation!" He grinned happily. "Dad always undercuts me because he wants me to grow up and become a man. He used to bribe my teachers to give me poor marks because he told them good marks would go to my head. He bribed the man at the secretary of state's office so I wouldn't get a driver's license. I got it on my own six months later."

"He didn't undercut you with us," I said firmly.

At that point, my good wife appeared in running shorts and sweatshirt, virtuously sweating after an enthusiastic workout. My fantasies became dirty at once.

"Don't mess with me, guys," she announced breathlessly. "Haven't I been practicing me martial arts? And after supper, you know what, Socra Marie, I'm going to practice singing again! Your da made me do it!"

He most certainly did not! But the cheers from the troops made it difficult to reject credit!

"Ma unconditionally!" exclaimed our youngest, hugging her mother's thigh.

"You can't come and listen till I improve!"

"Ma!" the three of them shouted, the Mick looking up from his Legos.

"You can too listen," I insisted.

"Well," Nuala Anne said with a sigh. "Like I tell you, Da is the boss, isn't he now?"

"Yes, Ma," they said dutifully, though they knew better.

"Da, show Ma Day's colors!"

"Yes, ma'am."

At the sound of Day's name the hounds yelped and danced around him, expecting that they would have another run.

"Girls!" Nuala ordered.

They sat down obediently but continued to pant.

I handed her Day's crayon sketch of the hounds.

Nuala glanced at the drawing. Then an expression of intense con-centration flashed across her face. This was very serious business.

"What do you think, Dermot Michael?"

I am almost never consulted on artistic matters.

"Reilly Gallery," I said, "maybe some sort of contract. They'll ex-hibit him and broker deals for him to paint people's dogs."

"You have the right of it as always, Dermot Michael."

She did not add the usual, "Wasn't I thinking of the same thing meself."

"Do you know the Reilly Gallery, Damian?" she asked.

He had suddenly been promoted to Damian. Wasn't he, after all, a fellow artist?

"Sure, I stop in there every once in a while to look at Superinten-dent Casey's paintings. Mrs. Casey makes herbal tea for me and serves oatmeal raisin cookies."

"Naturally," I said.

"You do a lot of paintings of dogs, do you now, Damian?"

"Dogs and people, kids especially."

The rest of us listened silently, knowing somehow that this was an important conversation. Even the doggies seem to understand that herself was up to serious business—the business of befriending a sup-pressed talent, one of my wife's favorite indoor sports. It was, she told me often, an obligation that her own surprising career imposed upon her.

"I don't suppose you have a lot of work like this around your apart-ment."

Day, or Damian as I must now call him, seemed baffled. What was this catechism all about?

"Tons of them, I'm afraid, Nuala. That's about all I do when I'm not studying art books or working."

Nuala sighed, her most expressive West of Ireland sigh, a woman's protest against the failure of reality to organize itself properly.

"And you learned how to do this stuff, mostly by looking at books?"

"Like I told Dermot, I didn't want to do the kind of stuff that the students down at the Art Institute want to do. There's nothing wrong with it. I just like to draw other stuff. I found a couple of books about painting dogs. That's why I hang around the dog park. I like dogs. They tell us a lot about ourselves if we'd only listen."

He sat on one of the many stools in the playroom, one across from my wife—two artists at work. The hounds curled up on the floor between them.

"Weren't we after breeding them to reflect our own traits? Isn't that true, Dermot Michael?"

" 'Tis," I said, but without the appropriate sigh.

Now I was being asked to confirm what she said. Something that happened rarely in my marriage. What the hell is going on?

"When I was a little girl," Nuala Anne began again, "I wanted to be an opera singer. I knew I wasn't quite good enough, so I decided to be an accountant and I came to this city to work for Andersen. And doesn't this sweet boy I met at O'Neill's pub in Dublin say to me, Nuala Anne, you can have a lot more fun singing popular and standards and folk songs than being an accountant? I thought he was crazy, but I did what he said, like I always do."

PURE BULLSHIT.

For once I agree.

"Uh-huh."

Damian O'Sullivan listened intently to this sweaty beautiful woman, dimly seeing a faerie big sister or maybe an angel who was pointing towards a glimmer of hope in his life.

I sat in the old easy chair, which was my designated seat in the playroom, where I could be convenient when herself needed me to confirm what she was saying. The Mick returned to his Legos, but he was listening. Nelliecoyne pretended to be working on her herd of purple heifers that might change the Deity's mind. Socra Marie crawled onto her ma's lap and confirmed the thrust of the conversation.

"Day color fabulous."

"I'm not saying they'll hang your work in the Art Institute or that you'll become as wealthy as your father, but I am saying you could have a lot of fun and earn a very good living."

"Painting dogs?"

"And kids and grown-ups too maybe, isn't that true, Dermot Michael?"

"'Tis," I said, managing to sigh this time.

"I never thought of that . . . It would be fun. What do I have to do?"

"What do you think, Dermot Michael?"

This was getting to be too much.

"I don't suppose you could pick out maybe ten of your best works and bring them over tomorrow morning. Nuala would bring them down to Mrs. Casey to get her opinion."

"Day draw Socra Marie?"

"I sure will! . . . My stuff at the Reilly Gallery . . . I can't believe it."

"No promises, Damian," I said. "But unless my wife's taste is wrong—and I've never known it to be—you've got it."

"Gosh!"

For just a moment, his eyes lit up. Then quickly they dimmed.

"My dad will ruin it. He always does."

"If he tries," Nuala said grimly, "he'll find that he's encountered a rather different set of adversaries, won't he, Dermot love?"

"He will indeed."

Learning martial arts, I hardly need remark, did not make Nuala Anne a fighter. It only helped.

Mike Casey was the head of Reliable Security, for which many of the city's best cops worked when off duty. Then there was the little bishop, who had more clout than anyone I ever met. If John Patrick O'Sullivan tried to interfere with Nuala's plan, he would find he'd run into a buzz saw.

It was patently (as the little bishop would say) her plan, despite her attempt to make it all seem like my idea.

WHAT THE HELL IS GOING ON?

Don't ask.

So Damian went home, his eyes wet with tears and glowing with hope, and we ate our Sunday supper—sandwiches with the crusts cut off, Irish style, a sure way I thought to spoil children. Naturally I kept that opinion to myself.

After supper we all trooped to the music room, where the materfa-milias began to renew her singing career. The kids clapped and cheered, even Socra Marie, whose head was nodding and her dolly held at half-mast.

However, while the bells still rang clearly over the peat bogs, Nuala Anne was rusty, very rusty. She could sing church hymns and lullabies without too much effort, but you quickly realized that her voice was ragged around the edges and her breathing was out of focus.

"Don't try to do it all at once, Nuala Anne," I warned her. "There's no rush, is there now?"

She glared at me, took a deep breath, and murmured, "Don't you have the right of it again, Dermot Michael . . . Would you ever call Madame for me and see if I might go down to the Fine Arts Building and get some help?"

"No."

"But, Dermot love, won't she be furious at me?" Close to tears.

"She'll go through her act, Nuala love, but you're her most success-ful pupil and you know how much she adores you."

"I can't do everything, Dermot Michael. It isn't fair of God to want me to do everything."

"Ma no cry," Socra Marie begged.

"I think if you bring herself down with you, Madame will melt."

"Isn't that a brilliant idea altogether!"

It was all of that, especially since my wife had thought of it from the beginning of the conversation.

"You have more minutes to sing, Ma," the implacable Nelliecoyne reminded her mother. "Sing a couple of lullabies to put herself to sleep."

The Tiny Terrorist was deep in the land of Nod at the end of the first. The Mick was yawning. It was easy to get them all into bed.

"I should practice at bedtime every night, shouldn't I, Dermot Michael?"

I didn't answer, not till I figured out what the game was.

Later, I lay in bed working on my poem while Nuala, in an unnec-essarily chaste gown and robe, sat at the foot of the bed, reading the first installment of Father Richard Lonigan's diary. She was wearing her reading glasses, which meant that it was very serious reading.

"Very dark indeed, Dermot Michael Coyne!" she said, with one of her better sighs as she put the manila folder aside. "Bad things are going to happen!"

We were both too worn from the previous night's exertions to consider lovemaking.

"They happened long ago, Nuala."

"We have to figure them out. But . . ."

"Otherwise, Ned Fitzpatrick wouldn't have left the diary for us."

" 'Tis true," she murmured sleepily. "And we have to figure out who framed poor Damian."

She hung up her robe and crawled into bed next to me.

"Good night, Dermot Michael, I love you."

For all her worries, she went to sleep as easily as had her younger daughter.

And left me to ponder as I tried to sleep the peculiar change in my wife. She had regressed to the greenhorn country girl from the Gaeltacht.

Which, unless I was very much mistaken, she had never really been.

— 6 —

"LOVELY RING," I said to the young public defender. "You got it on Easter, I bet."

She covered it up immediately, embarrassed that I had read the signs.

"Is it that obvious?" she said, her fair face flushing.

"Is he South Side Irish too?"

"Are there any other kind?"

"And he's a lawyer too?"

"Are there any other kind?"

"He works for the state's attorney?"

"No, thank God! He works in the mayor's office!"

Mary Jane Healy was a lovely young woman with long blond hair, deep blue eyes, though not as deep as my wife's eyes, and a willowy figure that must have been distracting to judges and juries. She had been skeptical of me when I first asked to see her.

"I cannot talk about my previous clients," she had insisted curtly.

Then I recognized her radiance for what it was.

THE OLD COYNE CHARM, the Adversary insisted.

We were talking in her small, windowless office at the Cook County Courthouse at 26th and California.

"I assume he understands who the boss is?"

"All Irishmen know that!" She laughed. "He's a good guy though. Very sensitive and kind."

"God bless you and grant you many happy years together."

"Thank you very much, Mr. Coyne," she said, flushing again.

"My dad's Mr. Coyne," I replied, borrowing one of Nuala's lines. "I'm Dermot."

Actually he was R. Coyne, but that was not relevant to the situation.

"Why do you want to know about Damian O'Sullivan?" she said, the tough litigator again, but not quite so tough.

"My wife and I are convinced he was framed."

"He may well have been. All I know is that the state's attorney had no case against him. There was no evidence. Sure, they found him drunk at the edge of the pool. But there is no evidence that he drove the car that banged into Rod Keefe. None. The police arrested him because his father and his brothers and sisters all said he had stolen the car and driven off with it. Except they didn't find keys on him or in the car or anywhere else. Maybe he did kill Keefe. Probably he did. But he was innocent till they could prove him guilty and there was no way they could do that. I was asking for a bench trial and would have moved for a dismissal on grounds of lack of evidence. I might have won."

"No evidence?"

"Not a bit . . . then this tight-assed little black Irish bitch comes to see me. She's Maura O'Sullivan, like I'm supposed to be impressed. Associate at Minor, Grey she tells me, DePaul graduate, Law Review. They want a plea bargain. I tell her I was Law Review at The University and all she says is that everyone knew that our graduates were no good as litigators. I say good enough to know that there's no persuasive evidence against your brother and that Judge Mikolitis will almost certainly grant a motion to dismiss. She waves that off. The family does not want a trial. Keefe was her father's closest friend. They hurt enough as it is. They want a plea. Negligent homicide. I say he could get ten years. She tells me that he deserves it—his sister, his fucking sister, excuse me, Mr. er Dermot, Jerry doesn't like me using that language and he's right—his sister wants to send him to jail. So I remind her that I'm Damian's lawyer and I will not seek a plea when I am convinced he's innocent. She says then they will have to hire their own lawyer. The O'Sullivans don't need a charity lawyer. Little bitch!"

"And Damian agrees to the change?"

"The poor kid doesn't know whether he's coming or going. They bring in a real heavy, senior partner in another firm who's a tax specialist. The state's attorney who is a real asshole offers them five years, which includes time off for good behavior. The gangs would make him a sex slave. He probably wouldn't survive. They buy it."

"The judge gives him probation anyway? How did that happen?"

"I meet him at a Bar Association golf outing. I'm in his foursome and am beating the shit out of him. So he asks me how come I'm out of the case and they're pleading. Not exactly a proper question, but he's the judge and smells something funny. So I tell him. He turns around and gives Damian five years of probation. The state's attorney is furious. So are the little bitch and her father, who are in court. They want him to do time. I'm in court because I want to see how it plays out. I thought the father was going to beat up the judge."

"That's incredible! Could Damian sue the lawyer for malpractice?"

"He sure could. I know some tort guys who would jump at it . . . Cindy Hurley is your sister, isn't she?"

"The way I hear it, I'm her brother, her little brother."

"Cool woman . . . What I say can't be used in court. But she could look into it and maybe come up with something that's respectable."

"Yeah . . . You know, Mary Jane, this smells."

"Real bad. So do a lot of things around this place. I bet you could find that there was some effort to get Mikolitis off the case. Put one of their guys in. That's not a hard one to pull off around here. They must have blown it . . . Hey, you're married to that totally gorgeous singer, aren't you?"

"I'm her husband," I admitted. She missed the irony.

"She's really great. What's she like?"

A brash question, but that's the way the South Side Irish are.

"I'm a very lucky guy, or so she tells me every day."

"I have all her discs."

"I'll ask her to autograph one for you. That doesn't violate any ethics, does it?"

"Not out here."

"Your guy is from St. Gabe's?"

"Sure," she said, grinning happily. Is there any other? . . . "So am I."

"I figured."

I should never have said that. Patronizing River Forest snob looking down on the barbarians from Canaryville. No harm was done. She took it as a compliment.

And I wouldn't have to tell Nuala Anne.

This would be a tough case. No one in the O'Sullivan family would talk to us. Well, maybe Damian's mother would, but how would we get to her. Perhaps someone else had wanted Rod Keefe dead and Damian was charged because his family wanted him charged. Maybe they were covering for one of their own or for someone else who was more valuable to them than Damian.

Vile people.

Someone might well have murdered Rod Keefe. His family had put the blame on poor Damian. I was no lawyer, but I knew enough law to know that such a person could be charged as an accessory to the crime. Maybe we could get at them through my big sister Cindy Hurley.

"Ever since you got mixed up with that gorgeous Irish witch," Cindy, a lovely matron in her early forties, said to me, "you been involved in some strange events."

"Witch" was not a hostile word in context. None of my siblings believed that Nuala Anne was fey, including George the Priest. His onetime boss, the little bishop, confidently assumed that of course she was. They all adored her and yet there was still, they'd whisper to one another, something a little odd about her. And they didn't know the half of it. However, they confidently asserted that she would make something out of me, though what was not something they were prepared to define. Moreover, the assertion that she would remake me, once spoken as a future event, now seemed to become an ongoing and constant project as in, "I think she's really making something out of Dermot. Have you noticed how good he is with kids."

They had forgotten that I'd always been good with kids.

"'Tis true," I admitted, imitating Nuala's sigh.

"Let me get this straight. O'Sullivan replaced the public defender who might have kept his son out of jail with a tax man who pleaded him for five years in prison."

"Right."

"Why the hell did he do that?"

We had neighbors like that in River Forest I reminded her. People for whom bloodlines (or more recently family DNA) were sacred responsibilities for which much would be sacrificed. We both knew of a family that had disowned a son who had flunked out of Notre Dame and thus disgraced three prior generations of Domers.

"Sure, Derm, but everyone knew they were crazy."

"Some Irish are like that, Cindy. They have to undo generations of losers to confirm that they are truly winners."

"We weren't like that, were we?"

"Nobody wanted to disown me or put me in jail because I was a loser."

"Then you came home with that woman and we had to admit you weren't a loser, at all at all, as she would say."

See what I mean?

"And Rick Mikolitis rejected the plea," Cindy changed the subject, "and gave him probation? That sounds like the kind of thing he might do all right. We'd have to get the record of the plea bargain agreement to see exactly what he said. I'd bet he just about accused this tax lawyer guy of incompetence."

"Could we sue?"

Cindy never asked who "we" might be. Obviously the Clan Coyne, all those dark-haired foreigners, *contra mundum*.

"Hell yes, little bro, and we could depose the whole O'Sullivan

family and embarrass them for years on end. Serve them right. I'm not
sure how that would help this kid who runs with dogs and paints. Nor
does it find us the real killer or killers."

"Nuala will figure that out."

She was silent for a couple of moments.

"I don't doubt that for a moment . . . The country club is up in one
of those North Shore suburbs isn't it?"

For the Coynes any region of the city north of Irving Park Road,
was like Great Britain beyond Hadrian's Wall.

"Yes. So we can't count on Mike Casey having as much clout with
the local police as he does in this city."

"I can talk to this Mary Jane person, who sounds kind of cool."

"She hinted that she would talk to you and herself not even knowing I was going to have lunch with you."

Good feminist-bonding material.

I ambled over to the *Sun-Times* Building to see what its archives
had to say about the death of Rodney James Keefe. The obit was brief,
all-American halfback at Notre Dame, served in Vietnam, awarded
Distinguished Service Cross, Silver Star, Purple Heart, joined with his
teammate John O'Sullivan to found O'Sullivan Electronics, responsible for products which made possible the Internet, survived by wife
Helen and three sons, Rodney Jr., Mark, and Mathew. Mass at ten-
thirty at SS Faith, Hope, and Charity.

He had not been all-American at the Dome; neither for that matter
had Jackie O'Sullivan, as it turned out both his friends and enemies
called him. I had phoned my father, who had all such information at
his fingertips. While the good doctor rarely said anything unpleasant
about anyone, he commented, "Not everyone who played football
at the Dome became an all-American. A lot of their memories become
blurred later in life. Rod played enough minutes to earn a letter, but he
was really a third-stringer. Jackie O'Sullivan was second-string MLB
during his senior year but started the last four games of the season because the first-stringer was hurt. He was famous for tackling the wrong
man and earning unnecessary roughness penalties."

"I'd say that's pretty selective memory, Dad."

"Not as bad as the memories of those who never made the team but will tell you that sure they played football at the Dome. Most people don't check."

"And you wouldn't call their bluff?"

"They don't usually fib to me."

"What about their wives?"

"Let me think for a moment . . . Jackie married a girl from St. Leo who went to St. Mary's, Madge Clifford, pretty little blond kid. Rod was on his trophy wife. Dumped Joanne Kennedy from St. Sabina or one of those South Side parishes maybe ten years ago. He was always kind of a jerk. Drank a lot. Brilliant though. Everyone says that he was the genius behind their company. Made millions for Jackie, who didn't really know the time of day."

"How did he die?"

Dad had hesitated, searching his memory.

"Some kind of auto accident as I remember, five, six years ago maybe."

He had asked about Nuala and the kids and chuckled at my stories about Socra Marie.

"Funny little kid. Just like your sister Cindy at that age."

Perhaps. However, I suspected that the Tiny Terrorist's energy came from the McGrail genes.

He didn't ask why I wanted to know about these Domer football heroes. He probably figured that I was my wife's Dr. Watson again.

There was nothing besides the obit in the papers about Rod Keefe's death. The violent death of a Notre Dame football player and successful industrialist should have earned more notice. I checked the sports sections. Not a word.

Jackie O'Sullivan, as I now thought of him, must have used a lot of clout to keep the stories out of the papers.

I found a headline that said, "Friend's son gets probation in death of Notre Dame all-American."

The piece was short. Judge Rick Mikolitis had sentenced Damian Thomas O'Sullivan to five years' probation after he had pleaded guilty to negligent homicide in the death of Rodney Keefe, a football

all-American at Notre Dame. O'Sullivan is the son of Mr. Keefe's business partner, John Patrick O'Sullivan.

That was all.

There were several obvious stories that had been missed. Why such a lenient sentence? Why no discussion of the judge's decision to go easy on Damian O'Sullivan? Why no comments from the victim's wives or sons? Why no references to how Keefe had died?

Smellier and smellier, to paraphrase Lewis Carroll.

I phoned home to report my successes to herself.

Danuta answered the phone.

"Missus take baby out, kids in school, girl come soon, boy play with dogs."

Herself had perhaps called Madame and brought along the Tiny Terrorist for protection. Knowing that little conniver, I was sure that she would turn on her charm and act as grown-up as her big sister.

I met Larry Ryan, a contemporary from Marquette, at Billy Goat's, a subterranean bar on lower Wacker Drive once notorious as a watering spot for journalistic drunks but now a tourist spot because of the taxidermy of the Billy Goat who had allegedly cursed the Chicago Cubs.

Larry, a sophisticated analyst of Chicago businesses, was waiting for me, as were a busload of tourists. He was sipping some kind of dark brew.

"Diet Coke," he said dyspeptically. "Deirdre said she'd throw me out of the house if I didn't stop drinking."

"High time," I said.

"I told her she should have done it five years ago." He shrugged. "She agreed."

"You look great."

A wispy little guy with faded brown hair and innocent freckled face was once more the weary angel he had been in college.

"I should. I've lost weight. I sleep at night. No hangovers."

"Should we be meeting here?"

"No problem! When I see the drunks here I realize that would be me in a couple of years if Dede hadn't lowered the boom . . . What'll you have to drink?"

"Same poison as you."

He laughed.

"You on the wagon too?"

"I never did drink much."

"Lucky you . . . Well, what can I do for you?"

"What can you tell me about O'Sullivan Electronics?"

He hesitated, as if not altogether certain how to begin.

"Well, he's a phony shanty Irishman who's made a lot of money, but I gotta give him credit, he runs a profitable company, well within the limits of the law, though you wouldn't want to work for him. He saw the electronics revolution coming, figured out what kind of miniature chips they'd need for pagers and phones and Palm Pilots and that sort of thing and mass-produced them. He undersold the potential competition and hired the kind of engineers who have kept him one step ahead of the game. A shrewd, tough son of a bitch. You wouldn't want to mess with him."

"Me personally?"

"He'd come after you if he thought you were a threat and he's not smart enough to learn how much clout you have."

"Me?"

We both laughed.

"He has no business problems?"

"Do you remember DEC?"

"Computer company that merged with Compaq?"

"Right, because it couldn't keep up with the flow of the game . . . Remember Compaq?"

"Yeah, it did a noisy merger with Hewlett-Packard because it couldn't keep up with the flow of the game."

"The computer game is the closest thing we have to real capitalist competition in this country. Compaq was number one a few years ago, then along came Dell and Gateway and creamed them. Top management gets arrogant, thinks it can't be touched and bingo, a year or two and they're looking for a white knight to save them."

"That's happening to O'Sullivan?"

"Word on the street is they're on the edge. It's a closely held family firm, though the widow of Rod Keefe, who was a partner in the firm for a long time, holds maybe thirty percent of the stock. They continue to be profitable, which is better than most such firms are able to do just now. Worry is about his kids."

"Kids?"

"Look, Derm, if a guy is running a company, he's gotta be very careful about putting his sons in top-level jobs. Maybe the kid is as good as you are, hell, maybe he's even better. But maybe he's not quite as good or quite as driven or maybe he's a lout but you can't see it. Get what I mean?"

"Not that I have a company or ever will, but you're saying I get a dispassionate outside evaluation of my son before I make him COO?"

"Right! Jackie O'Sullivan doesn't see it that way."

"How does he see it?"

"He thinks his kids are as tough and as smart and as obsessive about work as he is. The word is out that the two he's got up there aren't in the same league as he is, only he can't see it."

"Yeah?"

"Sean went right from Notre Dame into the company's senior management. Nice kid, they say, and as smart as the old man, but doesn't much like to work. Enjoys playing with the company plane. His father can't see anything wrong with him. Patrick, the second son, works hard, but he couldn't make it at a small-bore Loop law firm. Put the two of them together and maybe you have one minor-league Jackie O'Sullivan. Smart young engineers don't want to work for them. Deadly, see what I mean?"

No mention of Damian O'Sullivan, the invisible son. Damian the Leper.

"Aren't there a couple of daughters?"

"Jackie O'Sullivan let a daughter into the management of his firm? No way. Capitalism is for men."

"What do they do?"

"One's a doctor, pediatrician I think. The other's a lawyer at one of the big firms. Supposed to be an obnoxious bitch; even the other women lawyers can't stand her."

Larry could run down every important Chicago company in the same fashion. Moreover, he'd share his information with a friend and not ask why the friend wanted to know. Maybe he knew about Nuala Anne's mystery-solving adventures, but he wouldn't mention them.

"So you're saying the vultures are gathering?"

"I didn't say that, Derm, but you're right. The smart money is saying that Jackie has another year, two at the most, and he'll have to sell out. He won't go down without a fight. He's one of your South Side Irish types who think there's always a way to tilt the playing field, but that doesn't work when the big boys close in on you. He'll make a ton of money of course, but take all the competition out of his life, he'll fade pretty quickly. So will that pasted-on smile."

"What happened to Rod Keefe?"

"He ran into the front end of Jackie's car up at their fancy country club. They say that one of his kids was driving it. Nothing ever came of it. Rod was a genius and a fall-down drunk. He was giving Jackie a lot of trouble . . ." Larry shrugged. "I think it probably was an accident, but a convenient one for Jackie."

"His second wife inherit the stock?"

Larry's eyes turned shrewd. He knew I was up to something. However, he didn't much care. I was his friend and I was entitled, therefore, to any information he had.

"No way. His first wife is one tough lady. She got the stock in the divorce settlement."

I finished my Diet Coke, thanked him for the information, and told him to give my best to Dede. He smiled and said she was some woman. We agreed that we'd get together sometime soon. I'd tell this to Nuala Anne and that would make it certain that we would indeed get together. She argued that such a promise, however pro forma it might be when men made it, still had to be kept.

My final stop was at the Reilly Gallery. My wife and younger daughter had already been there with Damian O'Sullivan's drawings. As Annie Casey brewed the usual apple cinnamon tea for me and served up the oatmeal raisin cookies that were de rigueur for visitors she heaped praised on Socra Marie.

"Such a poised and pretty and well-behaved little girl. You're very lucky, Dermot, to have such a grown-up two-year-old."

I didn't know that they were going to stop at the Gallery on the way down to Madame's studio in the Fine Arts Building. However, I wasn't surprised by my daughter's behavior. I knew that the little terrorist could become a manipulator when the occasion provided the opportunity. Like her mother, she could shift roles quickly.

I said none of this, however, to Annie Casey. Rather I acknowledged that we were indeed fortunate.

"That young artist of yours is very gifted, Dermot. If he does his work in oils or watercolor and on good paper, it will definitely be commercial. We'll be happy to represent him. I kept two of his drawings. We'll frame and hang them. People want paintings of their dogs and their children. Incidentally your daughter's two wolfhounds are handsome creatures."

"Socra Marie's dogs?"

"Well, she kept saying, 'my doggies.'"

We both laughed.

"That's one you're going to hang?"

"Certainly!"

Mike Casey drifted in, wiping paint off his hands. He too praised my daughter, my wife, my young find, and my doggies. Then we adjourned to his workroom.

"I had to call in a marker from the Kenilworth police to get the details on Rod Keefe's death," he said, with a wink of his eye. "They're more snooty than their taxpayers, but since we hire some of their people for off-duty work at Reliable Security, they finally gave in."

Until he winked, he looked like Basil Rathbone in the very old Sherlock Holmes films. Then he looked like Holmes as a sometime Chicago Police Department superintendent.

"I assume that young artist herself has taken under her wing was the alleged perpetrator in this case." He looked at me, his blue eyes shrewd and penetrating."

"Naturally," I said.

"Well, we both know that she's one of the dark ones and is seldom wrong. He apparently admitted his guilt, but the evidence against him was weak."

I recounted my interview with the good Mary Jane. Mike nodded solemnly.

"There's no doubt that the O'Sullivan BMW ran down Rod Keefe. Ran him down, backed up over him, then ran him down again. They found him under the car. His blood alcohol content was .22. Apparently he had collapsed on the way to his own car and fell asleep in one of the aisles of the parking lot. Whoever drove the BMW backed out of his spot, turned, and encountered the sleeping victim. Whether he deliberately hit him or not is problematic. It was a moonless night. The parking lot is illuminated, but not all that well. Someone might have hit Rod Keefe without ever being aware of his presence. He might have backed up to see what he'd hit, seen Keefe, then run over him again."

"Or he might not have seen him in the dark and decided that he hadn't hit anything."

"Especially if he were drunk," Mike agreed, "which the alleged perp admits he was."

"Then what?"

"Maura O'Sullivan, one of Jackie's kids, came out of the club. Her Corvette was in the same aisle. She was surprised to see her father's car in the middle of the aisle. She approached it, observed the blood under the car, and ran back to the clubhouse screaming. She had the presence of mind to call the police while the rest of the family poured out of the clubhouse. When the police arrived, Jackie identified the victim. Sobbed hysterically according to the police, though he and the victim had a loud public argument at the club shortly before."

"About what?"

"About Rod's drinking, according to all the witnesses. The trustees of the club had been debating whether to withdraw Rod's membership because of complaints about his behavior."

"It must have been pretty bad for those rich Irish even to have noticed it."

"It was the Calcutta night, which happened every year on Labor Day weekend . . . You know what a Calcutta is I presume, Dermot?"

"I golf, Mike. I'm not a big-stakes gambler. I quit that when I left the Board of Trade."

"And herself?"

"She's Irish," I replied. "She's willing to bet on anything, even the gender of a baby before it's conceived. She won't take the winnings because she says she *knew* beforehand. I don't let her near a casino. The Outfit doesn't like people who win all the time."

"Well, Jackie O'Sullivan lost a big bundle that night and was presiding over a celebration to give the illusion he had won. Everyone says that neither he nor any of his family had left the clubhouse. Except Damian, whom nobody seems to have remembered because he was hardly worth noticing."

· "However, they did remember seeing that he was drunk?" I asked

"Sort of vaguely when they were asked. He was certainly drunk when the police found him at the edge of the swimming pool."

"The family told the investigators that they hadn't seen Damian for an hour or two. He had been sleeping quietly in a corner in the lobby of the clubhouse. They also said he had a long history of alcoholism and that he had been forbidden to touch the family car."

"Setting him up nicely?"

"One could interpret it that way. Ms. Keefe was screaming hysterically at the investigators to find Damian and kill him. They found him at the edge of the pool and arrested him."

"Pretty quick rush to judgment?"

"They had powerful people shouting at them for action, Dermot."

"The key was still in the ignition of the car?"

"You're getting good at this investigation stuff, Dermot."

"I read your text so that I could better help herself who, as you know, operates on a different plane of reality in this stuff."

"You're right in your implication. The key was not in the ignition. Nor did they ever find it. It wasn't on the person of Damian O'Sullivan or in the pool or anywhere on the grounds of the club, though there was an intensive search for it."

"But the fingerprints of the alleged perp were on the steering wheel of the car?"

"They were not, Dermot. There were so many different prints on the wheel that it was impossible to recover most of them."

We were both silent for a moment.

"It smells, Mike."

"It does, Dermot."

"My man might have done it, but they had no solid proof against him, other than his own confession, obtained spontaneously when the rest of his family was shouting at them?"

"I don't know that for sure, but I don't doubt it."

"Maura O'Sullivan might have recognized the key case and snatched it."

"Arguably"—Mike tilted his head forward in a nod—"as our friend the little bishop would say."

"Curious about the wife, wasn't it?"

"Very."

He smiled, acknowledging the Sherlockismus. There was no mention in the story of her. She was the little woman who still wasn't there . . .

The rain had stopped when I left the Gallery. I walked down Oak Street to Michigan, crossed under the urine-drenched underpass and walked to the deserted beach. Before long it would be covered with both the fair and fat, all too willingly sacrificing their skin to the sun.

What was I to make of the case of Damian Thomas O'Sullivan?

At most his family had shown unseemly if unanimous (excepting his mother) taste in blaming him for the death of his father's friend and colleague and in conspiring in his arrest, indictment, and conviction. Granted that they had formed a group think paradigm about him (much like the one my family had constructed about me, though in a very mild and not altogether unjustified mode), that was one thing. It was quite another to decide that because he lay in a drunken stupor some distance away from the dead body of Rod Keefe, he had in fact driven the family BMW over him three times. Yet they had done so instantly and apparently by unanimous consensus.

Damian is a leper, OK. Damian is a killer? That's a big leap.

Yet they had made it. And quickly.

Now if I started out with Nuala Anne's assumption that Damian was a total innocent (and naturally I had to start out there), they were covering either for a terrible accident or a murder. They despised the youngest member of the family, but it did not seem likely that they would use the death of Jackie O'Sullivan's partner to get rid of him unless there was some other motive. It must have been clear to Maura when she saw the bloody body that something must be done instantly. Most likely she grabbed the keys before she called the police. Was the motor still running? Had the killer abandoned both the car and the keys and fled?

If she had taken the keys, she must have recognized the key case. Hence she knew who the killer was—if she were not the killer herself. Was she married yet? Was it possible that she would go home without her husband? Perhaps they had a marital tiff and she was running home in the family car? Had she come to the others and blamed the killing on Damian. They all quickly bought into that explanation, perhaps to protect John Patrick O'Sullivan himself, maybe half-knowing that it might not be true but happy to have an explanation that would do less harm to the family than any other.

That might explain why she ran so quickly to Mary Jane Healy to get her out of the case.

All very ruthless, but they were probably a ruthless family, dominated and shaped by their father's pride in their genes or their blood or Notre Dame loyalty or whatever. They were, after all, Irish cream, were they not?

Where were the mysterious keys? Doubtless in the possession of the one who had driven the BMW. The police would never find them. The family would assure them that Damian had a set of keys. On the face of it, that seemed unlikely. John Patrick O'Sullivan would hardly trust his despised youngest child with the keys to his car. Damian could perhaps have borrowed them from someone, perhaps his invisible mother.

All of these speculations assumed that Nuala was right that Damian had been framed. The explanation the police bought was less baroque.

STOP THAT, OH YOU OF LITTLE FAITH.

OK.

How were we to break the case if no one in the family would talk to us?

On the way back to Southport Avenue, I picked up the next installment of the diary from the outer edge of Europe.

— *7* —

 July 12, Feast of St. Ultan of Cork, a disciple of St. Finbarr.

I celebrated the day by preventing Tim Allen from dispossessing a family.

Mrs. O'Flynn came to my study after breakfast while I was read-ing my breviary and thinking, irreverently, that David was not a Christian.

"Isn't Tim Allen evicting the Hanleys over by the sea and them-selves with five young children?"

"How much money do they owe?" I put aside my breviary.

"Ten pounds, Your Reverence. 'Tis a lot of money."

"I think I'll ride over and put a stop to it . . . Are they the ones in the tiny cottage at the highest part of the bluff?"

"And the winds tearing it apart every day?"

I took ten pounds out of my desk, collected my mare, and rode over towards the bluff.

The day was spectacular. A clean wind had swept away the fog, the ocean was brilliantly blue with big whitecaps breaking against the rocks. Not a cloud marked the clean sky. A perfect Irish-summer day.

A wonderful day to be thrown out of your home.

I arrived just as Tim Allen finished reading the notice of eviction.

Three constables, including Sergeant Kyle, stood awkwardly by. Two formally dressed bailiffs waited on either side of Allen.

He was a tall, lean man, dressed like he was an English lord in riding boots and tweed jacket and astride a huge white stallion. It was the first time I had seen him, since he did not come to church. He was, I guessed, in his early forties and had the look of a Kerry man about him—wild, handsome, and hateful.

"Bailiffs, take possession of that shack and destroy it. Constables, drive these people off His Lordship's land. If they do not take this rubbish with them, push it over the edge of the cliff."

I rode into the scene. The Hanleys were young, hardly thirty. The children were poorly dressed, but attractive. The parents had not lost the bloom of youth, despite the despair that froze their faces. Their pitiable possessions were piled near the edge of the cliff. Neighbors stood around watching. Some of the neighbor children were chasing one another as children always do, no matter what the setting.

I rode into the center of the group.

"Do not obey those orders," I barked. The demon was upon me. My temper, usually under tight rein, flamed like a bonfire.

"Don't interfere, Father," Allen snarled. "This is the law."

"English law," I replied. "How much do these poor Irish people owe?"

"Ten pounds . . . His Lordship has been patient . . ."

"His Lordship be damned! Here is ten pounds, traitor. Now take his money to His Lordship and take your police and bailiffs with you."

I threw the ten pounds at the feet of his horse. One of the bailiffs picked it up and handed it to Allen.

"The debt is paid, sir," he said anxiously.

"You have no right to interfere."

"Right or not, I just did. Now leave these poor people alone."

He turned his horse and rode off, the constables and the bailiffs riding behind him.

"Now, you people, stop gawking and help the Hanleys move back into their house."

I dismounted and picked up a battered chair and walked into the house. Finbarr Hanley, tears pouring down his cheeks, grabbed my hand."

"God bless you, Father. With a good harvest we'll be able to pay."

"Let me know if he ever tries this again."

I calmed down as I rode back to the parish house. I felt complacent for a few moments, then guilty about my outrageous behavior. Tales about my being a wild man would spread around the parish before sunset.

"Did you drive him off?" Mrs. O'Flynn asked when I returned and picked up my breviary.

I looked up at her.

"He's a terrible man."

"He is, Your Reverence. Poor man has lived a hard life."

Irishwomen are by nature contrarian.

"And himself keeping a slave woman up in the hills," I continued.

"That's not quite the way of it, Your Reverence, if it ever were . . . Sure, wouldn't she be dead or worse if it weren't for him. Her husband's family drove her out when he died."

"Just like yours?"

"In a manner of speaking."

"What's wrong with Allen?"

"The old lord treated him unkindly when his family died and no one in the parish would take him in. He's still angry at us all."

That was another side to the story.

A couple of hours later, His Lordship entered, gently brushing Mrs. O'Flynn aside, a broad grin on his face.

"That's all right, Mary Catherine, the priest has damned me to hell and I come to seek absolution."

So Mary Catherine was her name. I had never asked.

"His Lordship be damned! Ah, 'tis yourself, Father, that has the terrible temper! I never would have thought it."

He threw himself on my couch and laughed loudly.

"Can I buy an indulgence or something of the sort?"

I found my face turn hot.

"I was not speaking literally."

"Well, I'm glad to hear it. I would think that a curse from a Catholic priest, especially one with a degree from Salamanca, would have great effect!"

He laughed again.

"Here's your ten pounds back, by the way . . . I would love to have been there and witness the scene. Our regimental padre out in the Northwest territories was the same kind of man. Dressed me down repeatedly, God be good to him."

"He's dead?"

"Killed by a Pathan sniper . . . I've told Tim no more evictions without my explicit approval. Which means there won't be any. This is not a good holding, but ten pounds from poor people won't make any difference. I have my pensions and Mary Margaret has an excellent income. I tell her all the time that I married her for her money. She thinks that's very funny."

Milord was in an expansive mood.

So Mary Margaret was not impoverished nobility after all.

"It wouldn't hurt," I said, "if you rode over to the Hanley house and told them not to worry."

"That's exactly what Mary Margaret told me." He slapped his boot with his hand and stood up. "It's safe to do it now that I know your curse is not real."

Laughing still, he left the house.

"Don't cross him, Mary Catherine," he called to Mrs. O'Flynn. "Doesn't he have a terrible temper?"

I put aside the breviary and went to my piano. Eileen and her crowd of urchins appeared from nowhere, even though it was early in the day for them to come.

August 14, Vigil of the Assumption of Mary, Lady Day in Harvest.

Not a great harvest here, but good enough and better than many.

I went to my first wake last night. Granny Murtaugh, to whom I had administered the final rites last week, passed away in her sleep. She looked like she was eighty but in fact she was only sixty, worn-out by miscarriages and hard work. The family had not seemed greatly worried by her sickness. The doctor, a Protestant who drinks too much but all we have, had told them there was nothing he could do. Sure, we're terrible crowded in the cottage, her daughter Kate told me. Granny has lived too long.

Granny had brought that woman into the world, nursed her, bathed her, seen her through sickness, rejoiced at her marriage, adored her children and now the poor old woman meant nothing more than an extra bed.

That's what happens to poor and oppressed people, I tell myself. Blame the English. Blame Bob Skeffington and his ancestors. Yet I wonder if we Irish are to blame and maybe we priests. Maybe we talk too much about heaven and not enough about decent lives for people here on earth. Or maybe since the Famine our people are cruel because they have no choice. Too many died.

I do not know why I am wasting good ink in these ruminations.

In any event, the priest is expected to minister to the sick person, then slip quietly away lest he interfere with preparations for the wake. I have been told by priests out here in the West of Ireland that wakes are the only entertainment that the people have. If we succeed in crushing them, we will make their lives all the more miserable. And are they not a celebration of the life that is to come?

I don't know. However, perhaps because I thought that Granny was a gallant woman, I resolved to go to the wake and lead the Rosary.

It may not have been a wise decision. The insufferable Branigan warned me not to, but I told myself he feared that less of his drink would be consumed if I was present even for a half hour.

It was still light when I approached the cottage. I heard singing and dancing and the fiddles and the tin whistles from perhaps a half mile away and also the ungodly keening which is counterfeit sorrow. I encountered no lovers in the fields, but if that custom persisted—and I have been assured that it does—it would probably be practiced after dark.

Somehow they must have learned that I was coming, because by the time I reached the cottage, silence had come upon it, a resentful silence I thought. I resolved that I would not let their sullen faces intimidate me.

The cottage smelled like a public house, tobacco and drink. I may have been the only sober person inside.

"Granny survived the Famine as a little girl because she was young and strong. She served her family through her life with all the strength she had. Now her strength has finally failed her and she has left us behind, all of us the poorer for her absence. Those who knew her long ago must remember her as a strong, brave young woman. Those of you who are young must realize that she was like you are now. We all die, most of us grow old and die. We find courage from our faith that Granny is young again as so we too will be as God has promised us. Let us now pray for her and pray for ourselves."

At first their responses to the prayers were weak. They wanted to get back to their drink, their tobacco, their keening, and their party. But as I progressed through the mysteries their voices picked up. Perhaps their dogged Irish faith had reasserted itself. I don't know. The final decade was a shout that filled the countryside.

Kate sobbed through the Rosary. It was not artificial keening. When I left, she kissed my hand and thanked me for coming—the smell of whiskey strong on her breath. The crowd of mourners was decently quiet as I rode away. Doubtless they were happy to see me go.

The wake I conclude is a pagan custom to which some Christianity is attached. I could stop it as easily as I could scream down the ocean or move Colm's great ugly, evil rock.

They do not have requiem Masses in this part of Ireland, perhaps because the custom did not survive the penal times, perhaps because the people felt they did not have the money to pay for it. Yet the custom that the body was carried directly from the wake to the cemetery is strong. They do not want to give it up.

So I waited for them at the entrance to my leaky old church as the rain beat down. The burial was to be "in the morning," with no precise time given. "They won't come before noon," Mrs. O'Flynn predicted quite accurately.

They finally straggled up the road to the cemetery next to the church. My tiny acolyte and I braved the rain to walk to the graveside. The unctuous Branigan raised a leaky umbrella over my head. I realized that the whole funeral party—several score of people— were both soaked to the bone and drunk. I was shivering uncontrollably and my teeth were chattering. Nonetheless, I was determined that Granny Murtaugh would receive the full Latin ceremony for commending a Christian soul to her maker.

"Your Reverence needs a small drop against the cold," Branigan said.

I ignored him.

I would not desert Granny Murtaugh until the last shovel of earth was piled on her grave.

Eternal rest grant unto her O Lord and let perpetual light shine upon her.

Back at the parish house, Mrs. O'Flynn had a warm pot of tea and a small sip of poteen for me.

"Your Reverence needs a bit of warmth."

"What will they do now?"

"Won't they go to the public house and keep on drinking?"

"They're all drunk now."

"Doesn't a burial require a lot of drinking?"

I would like to have asked whether her husband's funeral was similar. At least I had the sense for once to keep my mouth closed.

I sipped the whiskey, drank the tea, and ate the warm meal that Mrs. O'Flynn had prepared for me. Then I left the house to walk into town to the pub. I wanted to witness the entire burial ritual. The rain had stopped and in the distance over the roaring ocean a bit of blue sky was beginning to appear. I will not try to describe the degradation of the scene. Half the mourners were unconscious, the rest were quarrelling with one another. Kate was in the corner, still sobbing, with a whiskey bottle in her hand.

"You shouldn't have come, Your Reverence," Branigan told me.

"Yes, I should have come. There will be no more of these binges after burials. Do you understand? I will condemn them from the altar and condemn you if there is another one."

"I need the money," he pleaded.

"You will not earn it off the grief of these poor people," I told him, turned on my heel, and walked back to the parish house, feeling that once more I had made a fool of myself.

St. Colm's massive rock seemed to stare at me with implacable scorn.

As I played late this afternoon Eileen O'Flynn brought some of her young friends along to stand outside and listen silently.

Not much good as a priest, but a great entertainer of children. A man could have a worse epitaph.

We have a new doctor, younger than his predecessor and, I think, more intelligent. And, thanks be to God, Catholic! However, he drinks too much, as did his predecessor. I wonder whether he can do much more than bind up a few wounds and perhaps repair the occasional broken limb.

Lord Skeffington has appointed young Liam Conroy as schoolmaster for three years. Liam arrived three days ago. He is an innocent, a true Israelite in whom there is no guile. A tall handsome Viking, with long blond hair and a gentle smile, he is young in a place where everyone is old, even those who are not yet twelve. Will his hope survive in a school where the children of the old are already old themselves?

How many years will it take to turn Eileen O'Flynn into Granny Murtaugh?

August 22, Octave of the Assumption, Feast of St. Andrew of Fiesoli, brother of St. Donatus, first bishop of Fiesoli.

Two more wandering Irish missionaries. Fiesoli, I thought, high above the Duomo of Florence, would have been a great improvement over anything they left behind, to say nothing of my own exile here.

I preached today against superstitions and paganism. The Irish people would never amount to anything until they left behind the paganism that they had permitted to slip back into their religion despite all the fine work that Patrick and Brigid and Colm had done in spreading the pure Christian faith. The English were right in their judgment that the Irish were poor, ignorant, superstitious savages. They were poor and ignorant because they believe in such things as holy wells and sacred mountains, which were a survival of pagan times. Good St. Colm is ashamed in heaven to know that his name was associated with superstitious practices and with the abuses of the patterns and the wakes, which were also survivals of paganism.

I would preach on these abuses until they stopped. Moreover I would absolutely forbid visits to the public houses after a burial. Unless the relatives of the deceased promised on their solemn honor that they would not permit such drunken orgies, I would refuse to bury the deceased in consecrated ground.

That created a stir in the congregation. Refusal of a Christian burial was a great punishment, not to the deceased, who would probably be on his way to God (whose love I had assumed would forgive the Irish many things because of the acute pain of their lives, one of my opinions that greatly upset the Cardinal), but to the family. It would be a disgrace that would linger for centuries and cause bad luck.

I was using one superstition to rout another, which was also a sacrilege.

They were sullen after Mass, the men touching their forelocks but with little sign of real respect, the women looking down, more humiliated, I thought, by their own degeneracy than the men were. Branigan simply shook his head in despair. A handful commended me, some of the women who would have approved of what the parish priest said, even if he had preached in Russian, and others like the new schoolteacher, the new doctor and his wife, and, of course, Mrs. O'Flynn.

The last said with her usual firmness, "It's time those things be said, Your Reverence."

September 15, Feast of St. Ciaran of Clonmacnoise, one of the greats in Irish history.

His monastery survived the Vikings, Irish kings, and the Normans, only to be destroyed in the sixteenth century by the Protestants under Cromwell.

Lady Skeffington bathed in the Holy Well today, two weeks before the feast.

Bob, part of Cromwell's inheritance here, did not warn me, which is just as well. I could hardly have ridden over to the well to warn her off. She was, after all, a Protestant and I had no jurisdiction over her soul, even if she and her husband were friends.

Nor had I any right to judge what was superstitious for an Englishwoman. Fortunately she came early in the morning. Mrs. O'Flynn reported to me that several of the women of the parish were there to protect her modesty. She didn't say whether she was among them. I didn't ask. I presumed that she was.

What would happen if she conceived after her visit to Colm's well? I would have to rejoice and also perhaps conclude that God has a sense of humor and is not subject to the jeremiads of a parish priest.

September 16, Feast of St. Nimian, an Irish convert who antedated St. Patrick and brought religion to the Scots, a poor venture at best.

A troop of redcoats rode through the parish yesterday. The rumor spread that they had come to help the customs men search for stills. Panic spread as many of my parishioners moved their stills by the dark of night, fearing that there might be an informer in our midst who would report to the redcoats the location of every still in the townland.

The people of the parish turned out to watch them, silent, sullen, threatening. The troopers looked neither to the right nor the left, but some of the younger ones seemed intimidated.

I was invited to dine with Lord and Lady Skeffington to meet the two callow subalterns who commanded the troop. They were barely twenty years old, fresh out of Sandhurst and sent not to the extremes of the British Empire but to a place which might be more dangerous than India. The Fenians were still around, if silent and brooding, as they awaited the time for another rising, one doubtless more ill planned and ill led than that bloody disaster. Nor did the local Ribbonmen like the idea of redcoats in our town- land. They wouldn't risk doing battle with the whole troop of twenty lance-carrying men. But they might pick off an occasional straggler or two. The men would simply disappear. There would be a frantic search for their bodies, which would lie at the bottom of the ocean. The constables would hunt for the killers. Everyone in the townland would know who was responsible, but no one would say a word, for fear the Ribbonmen would take vengeance on them- selves and their families.

They were pleasant enough lads, though arrogant as young men wearing red coats and carrying lances and carbines would be. At first they thought I was the local Church of Ireland parson. Who else would be on a first-name basis with the lord of the Big House?

Mary Margaret Skeffington, who at first would not look at me, gently corrected them. "I say, sir," the more callow of the two, a young man with unruly blond hair said to me, "can't you do any- thing about these 'patterns'? Isn't it rather a disgrace that a troop of the Queen's cavalry has to be called in to help the local author- ities maintain order? And what exactly is a 'pattern'?"

"You might think of it as a kind of village fair," I said pleasantly enough (I was after all, Bob's guest), "combined with ancient pagan practices on a festival day, which here at any rate honors one of Ireland's great saints, Colm. Horses and sheep and cattle are bought and sold, races are run, both human and equine, people bathe in a pool of springwater, which the locals claim was caused by the saint striking it with his crosier. It is icy-cold water which does more harm to the health than benefit. Poteen is bought and sold, though with utmost discretion—His Lordship may explain that to you. Then at the end of the day, someone whispers an unguarded word to someone else and a duel ensues between two factions which both the initial combatants represent. The tension has been growing all day long as everyone awaits the spark, some fearfully, others eagerly."

"I say!" exclaimed the other one, a tiny fellow whose cockney-like accent said that he had to be a promising soldier for Sandhurst to make him an officer and a gentleman. "Do they fight with swords and pistols?"

Milord Skeffington laughed, bitterly I thought.

"Ensign Cadbury, few men here on the outer edges of Europe possess such weapons, for which Her Majesty's government should be grateful. When they engage in revolution which they will every twenty years more or less until Westminster permits them to govern themselves, they use pikes. In these fights they use good stout clubs, shillelaghs they call them, since the intent is not to kill, which pikes tend to do."

"No one dies, then?"

"The odd person does occasionally, but through mischance and drunkenness. They intend only to wound and maim."

"How barbaric!"

Neither Milord nor I disputed the point.

"What will happen if a score or so of British lancers should line up?"

"They'll run as fast as they can," I answered. "It's not Balaklava, you know." I had failed again in the custody of my tongue. The reference to the ill-fated light brigade at the siege of Sevastopol was uncalled for.

"Nor are they a warrior people like the Zulus," Milord added, commemorating another glorious British defeat, one more recent.

It occurred to me that for a veteran who had been a regimental commander at a very young age, His Lordship was more than a little cynical about Her Majesty's Army.

"Your men," I told them, "will be in more danger from knives in the dark. You'll be perfectly safe during the daylight hours, which are very long this time of the year, but once darkness sets in, you might as well be in Zululand."

"Which reminds me, Bobby," Mary Skeffington interrupted our conversation, "you must insist that your guests spend the night here."

"No, ma'am!" they insisted bravely. "We couldn't possibly do that!"

"You can and you will, gentlemen. If I have to make that an order, I will. You will learn in time that bravery is only taking necessary chances. There is no moon tonight. Father Lonigan is correct. For British officers after dark, this is enemy country."

"For you too, sir?" the short man asked in horror.

"That could happen, though I think it won't. I'm held in sufficient regard here that if such a plot were afoot, I would hear about it beforehand."

A lord had been killed down in Mayo in recent memory. But he had been a cruel tyrant. Most of the local people respected Robert Skeffington, some loved him. Yet it could happen, especially if the Fenians decided to stage another rising.

Lady Mary Margaret rose from the table.

"I'll leave you gentlemen to your cigars and brandy."

I had noticed that the two young officers had devoured her with their eyes all evening. She was only a couple of years older than they were.

"I think we can do better than brandy, can we not Mary?"

"I'll send the butler in with it," she said primly.

It was the bottle of clear liquid. "Gentlemen, this is the drink that the men in the faction fight on the festival day will have consumed for most of the day. It's amazing how much courage it bestows on a man with a club in his hand . . . No, Father? I gather you don't need the creature to be courageous."

I rode home in the dark of the moon. It was not raining but there was a chill in the wind and a mist in the air. The ocean was growling sullenly, and the stench of salt was thick in the mist. I will never get used to that stench. I was aware that there were men lurking in the mists as I turned away from the sea. I paused and waited for them to come closer.

"Go home, you fools!" I shouted. "'Tis only the parish priest. You might want to kill him, but you'd be afraid to. You'll not catch the soldiers tonight. Do you want to bring all the might of the British Empire down on this poor townland? You will surely die if you do. So will many others. So will many innocent women and children. Go home now and be content with maiming one another in honor of good St. Colm."

I nudged my mare and galloped off.

I have already sent my groom with a note to Bob warning him that there were Ribbonmen about and that there was no telling what they would do.

Would they use the violence of the pattern to attack the constables and the redcoats? The Ribbonmen had done more foolish things. The fact that this looked like a good year for the crops, a chance for the tenant farmers to catch up on their debts, would not deter them.

I doubt it.

This afternoon I played Irish reels for Eileen O'Flynn and her friends. Very hesitantly at first, then with cautious enthusiasm they danced to my music. I had learned in Spain that God made us dancing creatures and approves of dances if they are proper. What proper is, like so many other things, depends on time and place. I felt also that good Colm might not mind either. The Cardinal would, but he's a long way away.

I also noticed that Eileen O'Flynn was a little older than I had originally thought. The decent food of the parish house had come at the right time in her life. I prayed to God that she would find a man who was not a brute like some of them or an insensitive lout like many of them, but rather a decent, upright, gentle man who would love her and treasure her.

I warned myself that I was thinking like a father and then dismissed that foolish fear.

September 18, Feast of St. Keemgel, one of the early Irish women saints. She probably thinks I'm a fool too.

I have a pretty clear memory of the patronal feast. There are some blanks, but the main events are etched in my memory. The church was filled for Mass. The people were dressed in their finest clothes. We sang some old Irish-language hymns and I surprised the congregation by my knowledge of their language. I preached on Colm and his generosity and dedication, especially when he had to go into exile on Iona, the most barren and desolate place in all the world and how his goodness turned it into a holy place, which it still is.

I wondered to myself if Iona was any more desolate than my own parish. That was self-pity, however, which I despise.

The fair was just outside the town, between the town and the Holy Well. I resolved that I would stay away from the well, at least for this year. It was the faction fight I intended to stop.

By the standards of England or Spain or even the Pale, our town fair, as I liked to think about it, was not very impressive. Yet for the edge of Europe it was a pleasant and lively day. Shy young couples watched anxiously as their parents negotiated the terms of their marriages. Shrewd horse breeders argued and insulted one another in high good humor. Women sold lace shawls and wool sweaters on which they had worked all winter and prayed for sales that might give them a few extra coins with which to manage their families' lives. Happy crowds surrounded storytellers from other places. Musicians with fiddles and drums and pipes and tin whistles entertained for a few pence and led the songs and the dances.

I was exhilarated by the vitality of my people when the sun shone and the sea was quiet and the crops were promising. This was the way life in Ireland ought to be all the time. Then we would not need pagan miracles or faction fights or revolutionary bands.

The Cardinal has accused me of undue optimism about the Irish people. Perhaps he was right, yet in the morning and early after-noon of the pattern I sensed the possibilities in our land.

As the day wore on, however, a certain manic mood crept over the celebration, like fog seeping in from the sea. Men's voices were louder, curses and insults more elaborate, warning about what might happen if someone didn't hold his tongue. More ominously, moth-ers chased their children home and followed them shortly after. Engaged couples slipped away, perhaps to visit the well and pray for marital happiness. The great rock, stark against the sky, seemed grimmer as the light of the sun moved west.

The faction fight was about to begin—the west end of the town-land against the east end. For immemorial reasons these two groups of men, friends and coworkers all their lives, often even related by marriage, would summon up from the depths of twisted memories age-old grievances and, minds dulled by the poteen, decide that now was the time to settle all the old scores.

"You should be going now, Father," the ubiquitous Branigan whis-pered in my ear. "You don't want to be here when the fighting starts."

"I do want to be here," I replied. "I intend to stop it."

"It won't stop," he insisted, "till the redcoats come and we may have a few surprises for them."

As I had feared, the Ribbonmen were planning to take on the English army. They might kill a few lancers, but a squadron or per-haps even a regiment would descend on our edge of the world and work vengeance. Would the English be aware of the danger?

Two small groups of men, four or five in each perhaps, emerged from a tent. They screamed at one another and waved threatening clubs. This was how it began. I strode towards them.

"Stop it, you fools," I am told I said. Then, it would seem a wild Celtic battle cry went up and scores of men poured out of the tents, ready to begin the battle. According to those who were watching in horror, I planted myself between the two converging mobs of drunken and angry men. I myself can remember only darkness. I think I wondered if this was what death was like. I did not have time even to think of an act of contrition.

Others assert that when I went down a hellish groan swept through both mobs.

"They've murdered the priest!" a woman cried out.

Murdering a priest in Ireland is counted to create the very worst of bad luck. Hence I was not surprised to learn that the men hesitated in a moment of blind horror, then scattered in all directions. Apparently I lay on the ground, blood streaming from my head.

Unlike Blucher at Waterloo, the redcoats arrived a few minutes too late, thank God. The pattern ground was deserted. The diminutive lieutenant recognized me and sent for the new doctor.

Later, much later or so it seemed, my head hurting as though a tree had fallen on it, I opened my eyes with great effort, then closed them again, dizzy because of the wavering shapes in what seemed to be my room. Apparently I was not quite dead yet. I forced my eyes open again. Milord Skeffington was watching me closely.

"Who am I, Dickie?"

"That's easy," I said, closing my eyes, "you are General the Lord Cornwallis." .

People laughed, relieved laughter I thought.

I opened my eyes again.

"Would you identify the other people in this room?"

"Don't you know who they are?"

"I want to see if you know who they are?"

"Of course I do!"

"Then tell me their names."

"Liam Conroy, schoolteacher; Jarlath McGrath, retired medical doctor; a man in an elaborate police uniform whom I do not know; Mrs. O'Flynn, housekeeper; Eileen O'Flynn, student; Her Ladyship the Honorable Mary Margaret Skeffington . . . I do not understand why the three women are weeping . . . Now I have a very bad headache and I'm going back to sleep."

They told me that I had to stay awake lest I slip back into the coma.

I don't really recall that absurd scene. I cannot believe that I spoke so absurdly. However, the others insist that I had acted like a comedian. If I did, I am ashamed of my levity.

The policeman, some sort of senior official from Belfast, informed me that by breaking up the faction fight I had disrupted the plans of the Ribbonmen and prevented a bloody battle with English troops. He seemed unhappy that I had frustrated the opportunity to kill a few score Irish Catholics.

"I saw a lot of brave folly in the Khyber," Bobby Skeffington said later. "Yours is the mark of a man who doesn't care whether he lived or died."

I think I replied that I really didn't care.

"There'll be no more faction fights," Mrs. O'Flynn had said confidently. She was right. In Ireland there's nothing like the fear of bad luck to curtail violence.

October 21, Feast of St. Mel.

"His Lordship the Bishop will be coming to visit us the day after tomorrow," I had said to Mrs. O'Flynn yesterday.

"What will he be wanting?" she had said in a tone of voice which implied that "no good will come from that."

"He'll be wanting dinner," I said. "About half one, I should imagine."

There was no point in telling her that this particular bishop was an insufferably fussy man and that he was coming to complain. I was not particularly afraid of him. If he removed me, he would have to find another priest to assume this benefice which would not be easy and he would have to explain to the Cardinal why he had done so. He would fear that the Cardinal might take it as a personal offense that he had removed one of his priests and thus presented the Cardinal with another problem. It was always difficult to predict His Eminence's reactions. He might be delighted to have his own judgment about me confirmed or he might be furious that this foolish little man had dared to dismiss me. Hence Milord Bishop would do nothing but be unpleasant.

The bishop arrived at one o'clock today in the midst of a particularly nasty Atlantic rainstorm.

"Well, Father Lonigan," he greeted me at the door, implying that it was my fault that he had to drive across half the county in such terrible weather.

My groom took his buggy around to the back and I conducted him into the parlor and offered him a glass of sherry or claret. He declined.

We sat in opposite chairs in front of the fireplace, in which a warm fire burned. It did not improve his disposition.

"I see you've improved the house," he began the charges against me.

"I'd say rather that I made it habitable," I replied, determined not to give an inch.

"It was good enough for the old Canon."

"It was cold and drafty. The roof would be leaking above your head if I had not made the changes."

"Hmnn . . . I suppose you paid for it out of parish funds."

"There are very little in the way of parish funds, milord. I take no money from them. As you know I have an income from my late parents."

"Hmnn . . . And you discharged the Canon's housekeeper."

"Rather I pensioned her off with the same salary she received from the Canon, which wasn't very much. She was slovenly and resisted my attempts to keep the house decently warm. She also destroyed perfectly good food with her cooking."

"Hmnn . . . I hear you got yourself in trouble protecting some redcoats."

"I'd rather say I ended a faction fight before the lancers arrived. I hope there will be no more such fights."

Mrs. O'Flynn invited us to the table.

The bishop raised an eyebrow.

"The woman is attractive, isn't she?"

"If you say so, milord."

He blushed as though I had caught him in an indecency.

Mrs. O'Flynn, like her daughter, had benefited from eating decent meals. Color had returned to her face. She was no longer scrawny. I noticed for the first time that she was indeed attractive. Very attractive.

"I suppose she lives here in the house?"

"Please, milord, I may be a fool, but I am not that big a fool. She and her daughter live in the small domicile behind the parish house. I improved that when I improved this place."

"Hmnn . . . People will talk, you know."

I despised myself for playing his silly little game.

"She was destitute, milord, driven out of her own home by her husband's family after he died—and without repaying her dowry. And she is, as I'm sure you've noted, an excellent cook."

"Hmnn . . . It might not be prudent, Father Lonigan."

"I judge it to be prudent, milord. I will not discharge her. If you wish do to so, you may, of course."

There was no chance of the old fool doing that.

"Have you been able to see to the school matter?"

He had heard all the vicious stories. He had not heard about my triumph with the school.

"Milord Skeffington has seen fit to appoint a young scholar who is Catholic and who has Irish as well as English."

"Hmnn . . . You must be careful not to offend Lord Skeffington, Father Lonigan. He is very highly regarded by Dublin Castle, you know."

"That matters not to me, Your Lordship. He is a cultivated and civilized gentleman."

"He has received their highest decoration, you know, the Victoria Cross."

"I did not in fact know that. Neither he nor his wife mentioned it to me."

"He is a Protestant."

I was to receive no credit for my friendship with the lord of the Big House. Rather it was to be an occasion for another warning.

"I believe all in his class are, milord."

Mrs. O'Flynn removed the remnants of her sumptuous beef stew and replaced them with apple crust and heavy cream.

"Hmnn . . . Now what's this about his wife bathing in the so-called Holy Well of St. Colm?"

He had heard that, had he now?

"I was told after the fact about that event, Your Lordship. I was not present at it. I accept that the reports are true."

"You did not try to prevent it?"

"How was I to prevent it when I did not know that it was to happen?"

"You certainly did not permit it to pass unnoticed, did you, Father Lonigan?"

"As you observed earlier, milord, they are not of our faith. I hardly thought it was my place to denounce Lady Mary Margaret."

"Hmnn . . . You tolerate the Holy Well, however?"

"I am growing weary of this catechesis, Your Lordship . . . I have repeatedly denounced all the superstitions that are rampant in this place and were tolerated without complaint by my sainted predecessor. I have prevented some of the abuses of both the wakes and the patterns. If I could drain the water out of the well, I would do that too. Unfortunately it is not a well but a spring."

"Now, Father," he said, in a mollifying tone, "I am only counseling you to prudence."

"No, milord, you are accusing me of imprudence on the basis of falsehoods which you apparently believe. You can repeat all of them to the Cardinal if you wish. I cannot promise you that he will be pleased with you to hear them. Remove me if you dare, but I will not tolerate any further defamation."

I was the son of a Dublin lawyer, educated at Salamanca, adroit and articulate. He was the son of a poor farmer, educated, if you want to call it that, at Maynooth. He was no match for me. I knew I would feel guilty when he left.

"I notice you have brought a piano with you," he said more mildly. "I wonder that it survives in the dampness."

"I tune it often." .

"You have much time to play it?"

"For a half hour each day before tea."

"You surely do not have much of an audience at that hour."

Did he know about Eileen O'Flynn and her band?

"God and the angels may listen if they wish."

We chatted somewhat more amiably about the weather and politics. He believed that the English government would eventually grant us home rule. I argued that we would have to take it. He gave me his blessing at the door and wished me well. He did not shake hands. The sun had appeared. I wished him a safe and dry journey home.

He did not urge me to prudence.

"Was it a good meeting, Your Reverence?" Mrs. O'Flynn asked me.

"Despite your wonderful beef stew and apple crust, Mrs. O'Flynn, I don't think we'll see him again."

I walked over to the church to ask God on my knees for forgiveness. I had treated the poor old man contemptuously. He may have deserved it, but that was not for me to say. Mrs. O'Flynn told me this morning that it is noised about among the women of the townland that Lady Skeffington is with child. I nodded approval and observed that it was very good news indeed. It would not be appropriate to send my congratulations to the Big House. I would wait till His Lordship informed me.

When Mrs. O'Flynn had left my study, I could no longer contain my laughter. God or St. Colm or someone had a sense of humor. Nonetheless, I would denounce superstition at Mass the coming Sunday.

Outside the rain continued to fall. The massive rock was shrouded by low clouds. The stench of salt water and dead fish was, if anything, more pungent than usual.

— 8 —

I PUT aside Father Lonigan's journal. He was a bit of a wild man, a spiritual descendent of the warrior priests of the early middle ages. He'd die fighting. Yet he was sensitive and perceptive. He had made that horrible place in those horrible times come vividly alive. I was surprised when I looked out the window to see that after the morning rain our warm sunny Chicago spring was still alive.

A cab pulled up in front of our house. My wife and younger daughter emerged, the latter squirming in the former's arms. Nuala put Socra Marie on the ground as she paid the driver. Both were dressed in spring light blue, Nuala in a summer suit with a matching blue ribbon in her hair, the Tiny Terrorist in a dress and similar ribbon. Even Dolly wore blue. As soon as her feet hit the sidewalk, Socra Marie dashed down the street, doubtless in search of her playmate Katiesue down the block. Nuala snatched her up again.

Two beautiful women, I thought to myself. I'll spend the rest of my life taking care of them.

M<small>ORE LIKELY THE OTHER WAY AROUND</small>.

I walked down the stairs to assist in the task of dragging our little ball of energy into the house, though it was indeed a day for outside play.

"Da! Da! Da!" she shouted as I walked down the stairs, reaching out her arms to shift from her mother's responsibility to mine.

Nuala smiled with relief.

"Da! Socra Marie good girl!"

"I'm not surprised," I lied.

"Awesomely good," her mother told me, "weren't you, dear?"

"Awesome good, Da. Lady give cookies . . ."

"With raisins, I bet."

"Madame say Socra Marie pretty!"

"Naturally," I said, holding the door for Nuala Anne.

"Give candy!"

"She's found out that being a good little girl is a way to manipulate people," I said to her mother. "She'll be another Nelliecoyne in a few weeks."

"Och, Dermot Michael, wouldn't that be brilliant? I wouldn't count on it, though. Still wasn't she sweet today, on her very best behavior?"

"Socra Marie take nap now!" Our well-behaved Tiny Terrorist yawned. "Real tired."

She gave me her glasses, a sign that the waking world had lost all its interest.

"I'll put her down," I volunteered, "then we'll talk about what I learned today."

When the Mick was two, he hated the afternoon nap even though he was so tired that he was sobbing hysterically. Give the little devil her due: she was sound asleep by the time we got to the bedroom.

"I worry about that," Nuala said as I entered her study, the designated site for our serious conversations, designated by her of course. "Doesn't she sleep too much altogether?"

She had kicked off her shoes and relaxed in her favorite easy chair, to be occupied only when she had earned the right to relax, which wasn't very often. She had even opened the top button of her jacket, a certain sign that she was satisfied with her efforts.

"She earned her nap by virtue of the tremendous effort to be a good girl all day."

"She was that." Nuala permitted herself a yawn. "Madame absolutely adored her."

"And wasn't angry at you?"

"She cried she was so happy to see us, and meself feeling guilty that I hadn't talked to her in months . . . weren't you right again, Dermot Michael?"

We were back to the theme that I was the perfect husband. What was going on!

"What's her verdict?"

"Won't I have to go down there three days a week in addition to practicing at home?"

"Till when?"

"Till July, of course, Dermot love, if I'm going to sing on that mall place in Washington, that is if you don't mind?"

"You're singing at the Fourth of July concert? I haven't heard about that."

"You just did," she said. "And meself calling me agent to tell him that we'd decided that we could do it."

"And what are we going to sing for the whole nation?"

"I thought we might try those Aaron Copland arrangements of American songs. I know men do them every year for your Independence Day. Would it be a grand change for a soprano to sing about the dying cowboy on the streets of Laredo?"

She closed her eyes in complacent satisfaction.

"You've done them before."

"Not like I'll do them on July 4. And meself an American citizen now . . . You're not angry are you, Dermot Michael? Sure didn't I make up my mind coming home in Mr. Wood's cab?"

"I'm delighted!"

"I knew you would be and yourself not angry at all that I hadn't told you about the Washington invitation before."

"How would such a wonderful husband like me ever be angry?" I said, testing this new tone in our relationship.

"You're a living saint, Dermot Michael Coyne, to put up with all me moods and games and acts."

I probably was, but I never expected to hear it from her.

"Now," she continued, "if you're not too tired, would you bring me a tiny drop of the creature and tell me what you learned today about poor Damian's family."

When I came back with her drink, I wondered whether the open jacket to her suit was an invitation to love—or at least a promise of it later on.

However, she was sitting up straight in her chair, all business again. Apparently the new Nuala Anne was not abandoning her Sherlock Holmes persona. I was kind of happy about that. Nuala Holmes was fun.

She frowned and swilled the Bushmill's Green around in her Waterford tumbler and I made my report.

"They're strange people, aren't they now, Dermot love?" she said when I was finished. "Would you ever do me a favor and call your man at Minor, Grey and find out if that young woman will become a partner? I don't think she will and I want to be sure."

My contact did not ask why I wondered about the legal career of Maura O'Sullivan. His answer was quick and vehement.

"Hell, no, Dermot. It would have been a close call even if she were a fairly normal human being. There might be a place for her doing research for the firm. Her talents are not nearly as good as she thinks they are. If someone is really bright, the law doesn't mind them being abusive and arrogant. That's the style we look for in a litigator. She's just not bright enough to act like a hotshot trial lawyer. No one around here likes her."

"Tries to outmacho the machos?"

"Some women can get away with it. She can't."

"Ask him about her father," Nuala whispered.

"Has her old man been leaning on the senior partners?"

"Funny you should ask that. He does a lot of business with Conners and Cassidy, Notre Dame types. He's been hinting to our people that if she makes partner, he'll move his business to us."

"Not exactly ethical."

"If she were good enough, we wouldn't hold that against her. But like I say, Dermot, there are too many negatives."

"Poor thing," my wife said when I reported his reaction. "It'll break her heart and herself with enough on her mind as it is."

"So two of his kids are failed lawyers," I said.

"And the third one is working for his father too and not doing a good job, according to your friend from Marquette. I bet he flunked out of business school. I wonder if the pediatrician is any good . . . Maybe Damian is the only one of the children with any talent."

"The cream of the Irish, Jackie O'Sullivan called them. They have to be if they are to be like him."

"And the poor friggin' eejit, deep down, is afraid they're like their mother."

"About whom we hear nothing at all."

"You noticed that, did you now?" She grinned at me. "You noticed, didn't you, Dermot, that poor Damian is the only one in the family who couldn't have run over Mr. Keefe?"

"Because if he were so drunk as to be wiped out at the side of swimming pool, he would never have been able even to open the door of the BMW?"

"I know who was driving the car, but I don't know why Keefe was killed," Nuala informed. "I suspect that the various members of the family have different ideas about it. They're covering up for someone, but they don't talk about it and there's no consensus about whom."

"What makes you think that?"

"They're the kind of Irish family, Dermot Michael, who talk a lot—football, politics, golf, their own greatness, other people who aren't nearly so great, but they never talk about their own family life, their personal relationships, their fears. They don't have any problems, they don't have any fears, you understand, don't you now?"

"Woman, I do. It could have happened to my family."

"Only if your father were a friggin' gobshite, which he's not. Your friend Jackie O'Sullivan has turned them into a reflection of his own craziness. You don't ask questions, you don't talk, you take good care of everyone in the family because they're all Irish cream and they know that's true because their father has told them it's true."

"Where does Damian fit in?"

"I'm not one of your shrinks, Dermot, yet wouldn't one of them say that the rest of the family needs a scapegoat for their own terrors. If they worry about Damian and punish him, they don't have to worry about themselves."

"Shite hawks!"

"My word," she said wearily. "But there's a lot we still have to figure out, isn't there now? Would you be having a friend who was up at that club five years ago, if you take me meaning?"

"I don't hang around them North Shore aristocrats much, but there's a girl that I dated—twice—when I was at the Dome who lives up there. Her family were hereditary members. I didn't date her a third time because all she could talk about was how wonderful their club was."

"She's happily married, I hope, Dermot Michael Coyne?"

"As far as I know."

"What does she do?"

"I think she owns a boutique up there."

"She'd likely be a friend of the O'Sullivans?"

"Knows them anyway."

"Would she go out to lunch with you?"

"Sure she would! Don't women love to have lunch with D. M. Coyne?"

"What excuse would you use?"

"The truth."

"As good as any, isn't it now?"

"If you're right, Nuala Anne, they won't be able to tolerate any success for Damian."

" 'Tis true. Isn't that why I told the Caseys they should watch out for John Patrick O'Sullivan . . . Could they send poor Damian to jail?"

"For violating his probation? I suppose they might try; it would only be for the duration of the probation. This time Damian will have Cindy on his side. That'll make a difference."

"Will it ever! That sister of yours is a real shite-kicker, Dermot Michael."

"Takes one to know one."

My wife grinned happily. She and Cindy had bonded. Against me mostly, but that was back in the old days when I wasn't the practically perfect husband.

"Should we put her to work on a malpractice suit?" I asked.

"If I know that one, isn't she already working on it."

"It would tear that family apart to drag them into court when they couldn't tilt the playing field."

"We might be doing them a big favor, Dermot love . . . What's this woman's name?"

"What woman?"

"The friggin' shopkeeper with whom you'll be after eating lunch?"

"Lorene McMahon, now Lorene Carty, I think."

"She's perceptive?"

"She didn't use to be."

"See if you can find out something about Mrs. O'Sullivan . . . We don't even know her name."

Supper that night was a celebration of Damian's new career, about which he seemed to be very happy. The kids were all delighted. They demanded that Damian paint their pictures, so they could go down to the Gallery and see themselves hung.

"Me too, me too!" the youngest demanded.

What would the ultimate identity be like for this little one who, but for the grace of God and advanced technology, would not be with us?

It would not be a quiet identity.

Ethne and Damian chatted easily, nothing more in common between them than generation. Yet.

The dogs, aware that Damian was at the table, barked insistently. Nuala relaxed her rule, "just this once, girls," banning them from the meals. They were very good, for dogs. But they did beg shamelessly.

Nuala Anne sternly forbade our feeding them, but she broke her own rule.

After supper she went to her music room and I to my exercise machines. Then we shared the task of helping the older kids with their homework while Ethne put Socra Marie to bed. Ethne and Damian went out for a "cup of coffee."

Nuala put the older kids to bed, despite their protests, and joined me in my study, where I was rereading the Lonigan diaries. I handed them over to her.

She was wearing tennis shorts, a green Grand Beach tee shirt to get us in the mood for our first trip up there of the season (to plant flowers), and her favorite footwear—nothing at all, at all.

She put on her required reading glasses and "serious thinking" frown.

"Sure, he's a desperate man, isn't he, Dermot Michael?"

"He's all of that, woman."

"No murder yet."

"There'll be one, we know that."

"Won't there be more than one? And we'll have to figure them out, else Ned wouldn't have left it for us, would he?"

It was a given that Ned Fitzpatrick, long ago in paradise with his beloved Nora, had us in mind when he put this journal in the archives of Immaculate Conception parish on North Park. It was also a given that the good spirits of Ned and Nora were hovering around us, nudging us to get on with the task at hand. I had long since given up contending these points.

"Well we can't solve it till we know what it is."

"'Tis true . . . Now, love, I want to talk about women."

"One of my favorite subjects," I said, wondering what was in the wind.

"We're different than men," she began, averting her eyes.

"I think I've noticed that."

"Give over, Dermot. I'm being serious."

"All right."

"Our bodies are different, more complicated."

"Because they have to do so many more things than our bodies."

"Faith, don't you have the right of it, Dermot Michael, just like you always do?"

We were still in our "praise Dermot" mood.

BE CAREFUL, DERMOT, SHE'S UP TO SOMETHING.

When isn't she?

"Well, isn't sexual pleasure different for us?" she went on.

"Sometimes women are content with less than a full orgasm I'm told. Affection and closeness are important."

"'Tis true," she agreed solemnly. "And sometimes there is a lot more, isn't there?"

"If you say so," I said cautiously.

"Like the other night . . ."

This was getting awkward for both of us. Should be arousing but it wasn't.

"You seemed to enjoy it more than usual."

"Not the first time . . ." she said, her eyes fixed on the floor.

"No," I agreed. Then suspecting I was a little too clueless, I tried another comment.

"I can't quite remember such complete . . . abandonment."

"Och, Dermot Michael, I knew you'd understand."

STILL PRACTICALLY PERFECT.

"Abandon," she continued rapidly, "is the very word. Many of us know about it, but we don't talk about it much and there's no name for it. We're ashamed to talk about it because, well, isn't it so *animal*?"

"That's not true," I said. "You were an ecstatic human person, not an animal. Our dogs hardly notice when we mate them. I don't think any animal enjoys love that much."

"You enjoyed it too, did you now?" She considered me shrewdly. "Were you after being frightened?"

I thought about it.

"No, I loved every second of it . . . Is it kind of like a heightened orgasm or something?"

She shook her head, her long black hair briefly a halo around her tense face.

"You could call it that, but it's different, Dermot love. Maybe it's a little like God feels when he loves us—complete and total surrender to love, so much that it absorbs you completely, tears you apart, rips you out of yourself. It terrifies you and you don't want it to happen again, but of course you do."

"Men are cheated, aren't they?"

"They are, the poor dears . . . A woman first surrenders to her lover, then she realizes her body is pushing her further. She has a chance, if she wants it, to surrender to the storm of passion locked up in her own body. The man doesn't cause it. He's kind of a precondition . . . If he's gentle and sweet and loving and demanding like you are."

AHA, STILL THE PRACTICALLY PERFECT DERMOT MICHAEL COYNE.

"I'm glad I do some things right."

"It's not up to you, Dermot Michael, not at all, at all. Isn't it up to me when I find myself rushing towards the fiery waterfall to decide whether I let myself ride over it?"

"Oh . . ."

Silence.

Again she leaned forward and pondered the floor.

"My point is that it's not your fault if it doesn't happen."

She said "pint" of course.

"It's good to know that."

"My head has to be right and my body has to be right and even then sometimes I don't let it happen."

"Why not?" I asked, surprised.

"I'm afraid to let go. I don't trust meself or me life or me kids or me lover or me God."

"Oh," I said again.

"Sometimes, me body won't let me get away with that."

"Good for your body!"

"You did enjoy the other night, didn't you, Dermot Michael Coyne?"

"Woman, I did."

"I thought you did . . . Some women are proud of the fact that they never have orgasm."

"They're not," I said, an Irish way of expressing skepticism.

"They don't want to give their husband the satisfaction . . . and there are others who don't ever go over the waterfall because that gives their husband too much power. At least I think that's the reason. Aren't we afraid to talk about it, though some of us whisper to one another because we know the waterfall is there waiting for us."

"Do you feel guilty if you don't ride over it?" I asked. My Nuala Anne, you see, tends to feel guilty about almost everything.

She thought about it.

"A little bit, but not too much. After all, I do it often enough, though never like the other night."

"And why the other night?"

"Och, how would I know, Dermot? Maybe because I love you so much."

"That's a good reason, I guess . . . And afterwards?"

"Afterwards, Dermot Michael Coyne, didn't I fall in love with you all over again like I did that night at O'Neill's?"

She burst into tears and ran to my arms.

"Except then I was a silly virgin who had no clues about what it is like to possess a man of your own, how terrible, how wonderful, all-consuming. Just like God has us."

SHE SAYS SHE POSSESSES YOU. HASN'T SHE GOT IT ALL WRONG? BESIDES GOD KEEPS CHANGING AROUND.

If you're Irish, you can do anything you want with metaphors.

"And didn't I realize then what a terrible eejit I've been and meself not listening to you when you tell me that I shouldn't worry about the kids, especially about the little demon and about everything else too."

"So you decided you'd sing in Washington on July 4?"

She stopped sobbing.

"Sure, isn't that why I'm telling you all this terrible personal stuff?"

"Letting me into your most intimate emotions?"

SO SHE'LL POSSESS YOU EVEN MORE. HIGH-QUALITY SEDUCTION.

She nodded and produced the inevitable tissue to deal with the sniffles.

"And you feel good about telling me?"

"Do I ever!" She dabbed at her eyes. "You must not expect the waterfall trip every time, Dermot."

"Being a man and not having all the complexities you womenfolk have, I don't really need it, Nuala, though I'll enjoy it when it happens."

She cuddled in my arms.

We did make love that night. No fiery waterfalls, as far as I could tell. Still it was wonderful.

— 9 —

LORENE HAD been a babbling twit at the Dome. She still babbled but was no longer a twit. Rather she had matured into a svelte blond businesswoman whose North Shore boutique (begun with her father's money) had become a substantial success. She wore a pale lemon summer suit, molded to display her not inconsiderable breasts. She wanted to babble about my wife, understandably enough.

"What's she really like, Derm? I can't imagine you finding such a remarkable woman. Is she like on television—kind of ethereal and mystical?"

NEITHER CAN ANYONE ELSE.

"My wife is many different women, all of them adorable. The TV persona is very real."

"And those gorgeous kids? What are they like? Is that tiny preemie doing all right?"

"She has grown into a Tiny Terrorist at two years. She has some eye problems that they think they can fix when she's older. Otherwise fine."

We exchanged family pictures. Her husband, a theoretical physicist at Northwestern (with tenure, she said proudly) looked properly abstract and bemused. The two daughters were blondes like their mother.

We were eating lunch at an upscale café on Green Bay Road that concentrated on odd salads and soups. I had settled for split pea soup, Caesar salad, and carrot juice.

"Does she have any concerts coming up?"

"She's practicing the Copland American songs to sing on the D.C. mall on the Fourth. She'll make a big deal that now she's an American citizen though she can still vote in Irish elections."

"Where's she from?"

"Way out in Connemara where the next parish is on Long Island— or if you do the great circle route on the shores of Lake Michigan. She's an Irish speaker."

"Really! Do the kids speak it too? I think it's so wonderful for little children to grow up bilingual."

"Nelliecoyne, the redhead, is a full-fledged bilingual, switches back and forth like they're the same language. We spend a month or so over there every year, so the kids can keep up with the language. Then herself really becomes mystical and ethereal."

"So what's up, Derm? I don't mind being taken out to lunch by an old flame, but something's on your mind."

How to explain that my wife was the best or second-best mystery solver in Cook County, depending whether you rated the little bishop number 1 or number 2. Cindasue was an honorable 3rd.

"Nuala collects strays. I don't mean stray dogs. We have two wolfhounds that are authentic. I mean stray humans. Recently she collected young Damian Thomas O'Sullivan, who, it would seem, is a very talented young artist."

"He's such a sweet boy," Lorene babbled. "Not like the rest of those new rich vipers. We used to call him Damian the Leper because they treated him like a leper."

Lorene had never worried about putting too fine an edge on matters.

"She thinks he was framed on the manslaughter charge. I don't quite know how she arrives at those conclusions. However, she's usually correct. I have been deputed to find out more about that brood of vipers."

Lorene didn't catch the allusion to François Mauriac's title, not that I had expected her to.

"Fey, huh? I bet she's got you figured out, Derm!"

"From the first time she met me in O'Neill's pub in Dublin."

"They're terrible people, really they are. I no longer think the club is the greatest place in the world like I did when I was a little idiot down at the Dome. I also realize that what I'm about to say is snobbish. But they never should have let Jackie O'Sullivan in. He has a lot of money and a nice Irish smile and that's about all that's needed. My dad told me that if he hadn't offered to redo the locker rooms, he never would have made it. Me, I figure we should never let him out of the locker room."

"With his fancy scent."

"You noticed that, Derm? Nuala has done a lot with you!"

Arguably, as the little bishop would say.

"She would agree!"

"Actually, I'm not being altogether fair to him. There are a lot of others like him around the clubs these days—locker room cowboys with genial smiles that suggest an overflow of testosterone. They put Jackie up for president last year. It offended most of the other members, especially when Jackie brought in a famous architect to make recommendations for the 'improvements' he'd make if he were elected. He hinted that he'd pay for most of the improvements. Even if some of the old-timers liked the 'improvements'—'make it a golf course again,' Jackie said, which meant cut out some of the stuff for women and kids—they didn't like Jackie's gall. So he lost two to one. He didn't seem to notice. Still talks about the improvements as though he were president. He'll keep running until he's elected, my dad says."

"The wives won't like that."

"If Jackie had any sense, he'd support better locker rooms for women. He acts like they don't exist, except as objects to respond to his smile. He doesn't get it."

"Sounds like he doesn't get a lot of things."

"The Dome never really civilized him," she babbled on. "People like him the first time they meet him. Then they realize what a bore he is. His children all worship him and he figures that everyone else does too. Even poor Damian worships him, though Jackie shits on him all the time."

"Tell me about the kids."

"The boys—Sean and Patrick—couldn't quite make it as lawyers. Sean flunked out of law school, Patrick didn't make partner at Hodgis, Figgis which is not the best law firm on LaSalle Street by any means. Jackie has persuaded himself and them that they're geniuses. So they're working for him because he needs their talents more than the law does. They all believe it. Maureen is an associate at Minor, Grey mostly because her father leaned on the partners who belonged to the club. She's cute, maybe even beautiful when she gets around to smiling, but a real bitch. She believes more than the others Jackie's shit that they're the real Irish cream. The word in the women's locker room is that she's dead meat next month, though Jackie's doing his damnedest to buy her into a partnership."

"He's that dumb?"

"Not so much dumb, Derm, as unperceptive. He's smart enough, like my dad says, to have cut himself a nice little niche in the technology world, though his sons will probably run the company into the ground. He just is absolutely delusional about his family and determined to modify the world to fit his delusions. It's boring."

"The other daughter?"

"Kathleen?"

"The MD?"

"Yeah, well she is bright. Harvard Medical School without her father bribing anyone. Works with preemies, like your little one. Really good at it, they say. Jackie talks less about her than about the others. He was really upset when she went off to Harvard. He wanted her to go to Loyola, good Catholic school. Then a couple of years ago she marries this shrink from the Institute for Psychoanalysis. Jackie doesn't like him a bit, they say because he went to Boston College— that's the kind of guy Jackie is."

"They beat the Dome at football."

"They cheat," she howled with laughter, and refilled my glass of carrot juice.

I remember Belloc's marvelous lines:

> *. . . Catholic men that live upon wine*
> *Are deep in the water and frank, and fine*
> *Wherever I travel I find it so*
> Benedicamus dominio!

Me own wife doesn't feed us much beef (heresy for an Irish lass) but a vegan she's not.

"Anyway, she's always been a little bit different from the others. She buys Jackie's shit, but not completely. They just married a couple of years ago. She's older than we are, Derm, so Jackie should be happy she found a husband. But, if you're Jackie, how do you brag about his son-in-law the shrink. Tom McBride is a tough guy. He stands up to Jackie. There's going to be trouble there. Katie is expecting now and Jackie is already talking about some Holy Cross priest doing the Baptism. Tom wants a Jebby."

"Everyone in the club knows about this?"

"Everyone who's dumb enough to listen to Jackie . . . Tom is only one step above Damian on the family shit list. Jackie tells those who listen to him that Katie made a mistake marrying a guy from Boston . . . Would you believe it? And hints that maybe an annulment is in the works. Katie loves Tom as any idiot can see."

"And Mrs. O'Sullivan?" I asked gently.

"Madge? What about her?"

"She fits the scene?"

For dessert Lorene ordered us a glass of fruit juice, mango and strawberry. It wasn't bad. Not good exactly, but not terribly bad either. I would have to consume some chocolate-chocolate chip when

I returned to Southport Avenue. Or maybe some of the new coconut sherbet that Nuala had found at some ice-cream specialty store on Halsted Street.

"She's quiet, unobtrusive, almost invisible. People like her and feel sorry for her. She sort of disappears in the light of Jackie's radiance, if you forgive the metaphor. She just listens to him."

"I assume she's Irish."

"Not much class to begin with. She may adore Jackie or maybe she just puts up with him."

"Doesn't have a vote in family decisions?" I asked.

"No one has ever heard her disagree with him about anything, a vapid little mouse. Keeps to herself. Smokes a lot, drinks a little bit too much. It's like she's not there, know what I mean? She comes into my shop and buys something, enough sweetness to last a week."

None of my experience with Irishwomen had prepared me to understand such a phenomenon.

"My mom has a different take on her. Says she didn't want poor Damian, only ten and a half months after Maura, you know Irish twins. Had a miserable time carrying him and a very difficult delivery. Hated him ever since. Mom says she's mean and dominating. Maybe so, but she hides it pretty well."

"Damian is the only one who looks like her?"

"I'd never thought of it that way . . . Yeah, same blond hair, same sad face, same passive nature, same sweet disposition . . . Hey, do you think Jackie is dissatisfied with him because he looks like his mother?"

"Not an athletic star?" I said, ducking the question.

"The two other guys are overgrown apes, too clumsy to make it at football, but they are big and handsome. Jackie has elaborate explanations of why the coaches were against them . . . He cheats at golf too, though my dad says he doesn't realize he's cheating. He doesn't do it all the time, not with the guys he goes to Ireland with. He cheats, my dad says, when he thinks he can get away with it, know what I mean?"

"Sounds like he knows he's cheating."

There is nothing worse than the guy who subtracts a stroke from every hole or from every couple of holes. It angers the hell out of me, despite what you might hear about Dermot as a "live-and-let-live" kind of guy. So to get even I play my best golf and beat the guy anyway. It's not much fun.

"My dad says that Jackie goes through life figuring out what he can get away with and what he can't. It's second nature to him. He does it without thinking about it."

In this description, Jackie O'Sullivan sounded like a full-blown delusional sociopath, but one smart enough to launch a very successful electronics firm, which he might just run into the ground because of his delusions about his family.

"Kind of like he lies not because it is in his interest to lie, but because it is in his nature to lie."

I knew that Lorene would not recognize Pat Moynihan's description of Henry Kissinger.

"Yeah . . ."

"Tell me more about the sons."

"Grown-up kids, know what I mean? Sean flies the company plane, though they have a real pilot for it too. He wears an old flight jacket and some kind of captain's cap like he fought in World War II and sort of swaggers around as if he were a Marine pilot in an old film. Patrick has to tell you the latest inside gossip about the sex life of politicians, football players, and movie stars. They both know all about everything and will spend half the day telling you. I don't think they work much, too busy for it, know what I mean?"

Now, before she ran out of steam and before she could order me another healthy drink, I must ask the important questions.

"What was it like the night that Rod Keefe was run over?"

She rolled her eyes and grabbed a celery stalk to nibble on.

"A zoo . . . You know what the Calcutta is?"

"Sure . . . There's an auction of foursomes. If you buy a foursome and they win or do well, you make a lot of money from those who didn't buy into them. Sometimes people share foursomes. There's a lot of money involved, a lot of fear and loathing, and a lot of drinking."

"You got it! At the club it's a very big deal. Jackie always wins something, not top prize but something pretty big. Well that Labor Day, poor Damian plays the best game of golf in all his life. He comes in with an eighty-two, which shows he does know how to the play the game. He walks in off the eighteenth fairway with a happy smile on his face. His father shouts at him that he's an idiot like he always has been. His foursome, on which Jackie has not bet, is a cinch to win because of Damian's score and his huge handicap. That means that Jackie loses."

"People hear him?"

"There's not too many around. I'm waiting for the professor, who is in the same foursome and has played way over his game too. But it's all poor Damian's fault. So he wipes the smile off his face and starts to drink. I guess he doesn't stop till he's completely blotto. I don't see him, but a lot of people do. So they're willing to believe he ran over Rod Keefe."

"Then what happens?"

Lorene was warming to her story. No need to push her for details.

"He and his family are at the table right next to us. Jackie is drinking, not drunk—he's rarely drunk at the club—but he's drinking and he's really furious. Then Rod Keefe, who *is* drunk, comes up to the table. They rarely speak to each other at the club. Dad says that Keefe and Jackie have been fighting over the firm for years. Keefe shows up there just to collect his profits and complain that Patrick and Sean are ruining the company. This night they have a big argument about some patent. Then Rod taunts Jackie that he won't be able to cheat his way out of his big loss in the Calcutta. Damian is the only son that's worth anything and he just cost Jackie a couple hundred thousand dollars."

That's a lot of money, but it's in the range for some Calcuttas. That's why my whole family refuses to get involved.

"Then he goes on to shout that he ought to get rid of those two dolts and bring Damian into the firm. Jackie gets up to slug him and poor Rod just falls on the floor. Two of the waiters haul him out to the lobby and the fun goes on. Jackie just brushes it off as though it means nothing. Everyone knows what a drunk Rod is. My dad says in a loud whisper that people like that shouldn't be allowed in the club. He means Jackie too, but Jackie just says that he agrees completely."

"Does anyone leave the table after that?"

"Derm, you know what Labor Day is like at the clubs. Everyone has drunk a little too much—except my dad, who doesn't drink anything—and they're all running back and forth to the bathroom. Then that unspeakable little twit Maura comes in screaming. She's already blaming Damian."

"Why did Maura leave?"

"You can never tell why that little bitch does anything. She's all impulse, dumb impulse, thinks she's Angie Harmon in *Law & Order*. I guess she had a snit with her boyfriend, Jim Creaghan. Married the poor jerk since then. Supposed to be a good engineer. Domer. Chafes under her idiot brothers at the firm. If Jackie is worried about an annulment, that's the marriage he should look at."

"You think she ran over Rod Keefe?"

"Anyone in the family could have gone outside, got in that hideous German car and run over Rod a couple of times. I think we all knew that . . ."

"Or anyone in the club who had a set of keys?"

She sat up with a start.

"Anyone . . . me included. But the police seemed to settle on Damian pretty quickly, though as the professor says, he was too drunk even to start a car. Anyway, they didn't send him to jail."

"My information is that they tried."

"No one, not even Jackie O'Sullivan, would do that."

I didn't debate the point. Over her protests I paid the bill and promised that I would bring Nuala up to the boutique sometime soon. She pecked me on the cheek.

Purveyor to her royal highness, the Princess Nuala Anne.

I would never keep the promise. Since I wouldn't tell herself about it, I had no obligation to keep it. My wife did not need or want expensive designer clothes. She figured, quite correctly, that even on TV she looked brilliant altogether in simple clothes.

I had learned a lot from my old flame about the culture of the club and about the O'Sullivans. However, I had also learned that even an eyewitness could not guess who had gone out to the BMW. Moreover five years later, the people at the dinner that Labor Day probably did not want to remember.

Still it was interesting that Maura was blaming Damian from the beginning.

Well, I had done my part.

It would be no easy task for herself to figure out what happened.

As I drove home I realized that, though Lorene was an attractive enough woman, I had not a single lustful thought through the whole meal.

It must have been the celery.

Or maybe the carrot juice.

— 10 —

 WHILE MY husband was interviewing his old sweetheart, I took our youngest daughter to the pediatrician's office. Since I am being nice to Dermot these days, I did not give him a hard time about her. After all, I'd sent him on his assignment.

I've been giving the poor man a hard time since the first night in O'Neill's partly because I have Irish fishwife genes and partly because I'm frightened of the power of his love. It's time I stop and I know it.

La terrorista, as I call her, was on her best behavior for the pediatrician.

"Me do poopoo in the toilet," she announced at once and lifted her skirt. "Me wear big girl pants now."

"Wonderful!" the doctor said, as though she meant it. "Do you like your glasses?"

"Everything pretty!"

"And your brother and sister?"

"Take good care of me. Say me drive them nuts."

"Do you?"

She nodded solemnly.

After a few more questions and a few cursory probes, the young woman said to me, "She seems fine. I'm sure they'll be able to do laser surgery on her eyes eventually."

I explained my concern about her sleeping too much.

"Do you like to sleep, Socra Marie?"

"Nope. Ma say waste of time."

The doctor looked at me in surprise. I felt my face flame.

"I was talking to her da."

She chuckled, half-believing me.

"But you do sleep a lot, don't you, Socra Marie?"

"Me tired!"

"Why are you tired?"

The child sighed expressively, doubtless imitating her ma.

"Hard work to be two."

We all laughed.

"She's fine, Nuala Anne," the doctor said to me. "She built up a lot of energy just staying alive. Now she has to run it off."

"When will she have finished running it off?"

"Probably never."

I think I knew that already.

I was not reassured at all, at all. Yet as Dermot says, I like to worry about things, because I'm afraid that if I don't worry about them, they'll go wrong. He thinks that's silly, and he's right like he always is.

Our next stop was the neonatal unit. I like to visit them because they were so good to us when we were hanging around trying keep our little eight-hundred-gram preemie alive.

They made a big fuss over my daughter as they do about all those who come back and visit them. So she has to show off. She explained to Jane Foley, who had been the junior resident who gave us the choice of keeping her or not (as though there were any choice), about her mastery of poopoo and her big-girl panties.

Jane in whose eyes tears always appeared when she saw Socra Marie, picked her up and hugged her.

"You're really a big girl now!"

"Real big!" she said making a big circle over her head as children do.

My eyes were tearing too.

"Do you want to see the babies, Socra Marie?"

My daughter nodded solemnly. Jane caught my eye. Why not?

Socra Marie considered the unit solemnly.

"Babies tiny, Ma."

"Yes, dear. They came early. So they have to grow to be bigger before their ma and da can take them home."

"Me never tiny."

"Yes, you were, dear. But you're all grown-up now."

"All babies go home, Ma?"

Even at that age, children are somehow conscious of their mortality.

"Some can't grow up, so God takes them home to heaven, where they're bigger than we are."

That reassured her concern about justice for the tiny ones.

"We pray that God blesses all the babies," Jane whispered.

"God bless all babies," my daughter announced.

She had only the vaguest notion about who God was, though perhaps no more vague than anyone does. She did know, however, that God was good.

We paused where a mother at least half a decade younger than I was caressing her daughter gently, carefully, lovingly just as I had caressed Socra Marie.

"That was our crib," I whispered.

"Your daughter seems fine," the mother said hesitantly.

"Yours will be too," I said.

"She's doing fine," Jane Foley agreed.

"Who she?"

"Mary Jo," the mother said.

"Me Socra Marie."

"Do you want to touch her? She'd like that."

Socra Marie looked at me.

"Very gently."

So, as though she was touching an old and expensive piece of cloth, she put her finger on the child's forehead and quickly withdrew it.

"God bless Mary Jo. Me love you."

So now we were all in tears.

Dr. Foley asked me if I would sing a lullaby or two as I used to. So I began with the Connemara lullaby as I always did, then added a couple more. The tiny ones all stopped struggling and drank in the sound.

"Same magic." Jane Foley sighed.

I wished I could come every day and sing for them. I promised I would be back soon.

"God bless Mary Jo," Socra Marie said as we left.

I wanted to escape as quickly as possible, lest I break down altogether.

Jane and I hugged one another and my child and I slipped quietly into the corridor.

A tall, handsome woman with black hair, touched with gray, in a white doctor's coat and very pregnant was waiting for us.

"I'm Kate McBride," she said cautiously, brushing her short hair away from her forehead. "I'm the new director of the unit."

"Me Socra Marie." My daughter extended her arms to be lifted from the floor. "God bless all babies."

My little brat had made another convert.

"And God bless you too, Socra Marie . . . What a little sweetheart!"

"Manipulator!" I protested. "I'm Nuala Anne."

"Yes, I know. My maiden name is O'Sullivan."

"Oh . . ."

"I want to thank you for taking an interest in my brother Damian . . ."

Not exactly what I would have suspected.

"I hope you won't let my father frighten you away . . . He means well, I think, though sometimes I'm not so sure . . ."

"Not a chance," I said firmly.

"My husband and I have a little house in Michiana . . . Will you be going up there for Memorial Day?"

"Yes, we plan to."

"I wonder if I could come over and talk."

"Certainly," I said.

"Me be there too."

"Yes, I know, dear," she said, handing my precious daughter back to me. "You're very fortunate, Nuala Anne, very fortunate indeed."

"Wouldn't I be knowing that, though not often enough. And may God bless you and your child."

She sighed, not like I sigh but your native-born Yanks really can't do that.

"Thank you," she said. "It's a strange job when you're expecting. Janey tells me I'll get over it."

"God bless babies," my own ex-neonate said.

I wept most of the way back to Southport Avenue. For my miracle child and her father and her brother and sister and for the God who loved us all and had to put up with our weak faith. And for myself, poor clueless eejit that I was.

"Ma cry," my child observed.

"Sometimes Ma cry when she's happy."

"Me never do that."

The angels must have been watching me because I got back to Southport Avenue without any accidents.

"Mike the Cop call," Danuta informed me, her dust rag as always clutched in her hand, the same way Socra Marie clutched Dolly.

I put my child in her bed. She departed for the land of Nod, murmuring, "God bless all babies."

Then I called the Reilly Gallery.

"Nuala?" Annie Casey said to me. "That awful man was here today, just as Dermot said he would be."

"John Patrick O'Sullivan."

"Oozing phony South Side Irish charm. He warned us about his son. Said he would buy all the pictures we would hang, so long as we didn't hang them."

"How terrible!"

"Mike threw him out."

"Literally?"

"Not exactly . . . He had no idea who Mike was."

"He wouldn't."

"Mike is going to put a man on him."

"Good idea, though I don't think he's violent."

"Mike doesn't want to take any chances."

Dermot Michael came home at the same time as the kids returned from school and Socra Marie woke up. She had to tell us all about the tiny babies whom God blessed.

Then Dermot Michael and I shared stories. I didn't once ask him whether his old flame was beautiful. It was clear from his description that she was not his type.

"What's all this shite about Notre Dame? Do they think it's a Catholic Harvard?" I asked himself.

"For people like Jackie O'Sullivan from that era, better than Harvard because it is Catholic. You heard the joke about who the most obnoxious person in the country is? A Texan who served in the Marines and graduated from Notre Dame!"

"Oh," says meself, not understanding at all, at all.

"Like I say, it's a Catholic theme park, now more than it ever was, the Golden Dome, the Touchdown Jesus, the Grotto where youngsters marry, something for every kind of Catholic, Pre-Council, Post-Council, and the oldest football heritage in the country . . . Does that help?"

"Try again," says meself.

"Well, I flunked out, as you know, and my own fault. Still on Saturday afternoon I watch them play football on NBC and cheer loudly."

" 'Tis true."

"It's in the blood, Nuala Anne. Notre Dame is one of the great symbols of American Catholicism and of the struggle to become successful Americans and remain good Catholics. Till the 1920s their football teams were called 'the Catholics' only then did the name 'the Fighting Irish' emerge."

"And the football team now is mostly black."

It's also now a first-rate undergraduate college and on its way to becoming a great university . . . People like Jackie O'Sullivan pervert the symbolism to answer their own needs."

"Well," I said, changing the subject, because I still didn't understand, "I'd like some passionate loving tonight, if I find anyone who is interested."

"I might just be."

— 11 —

MEMORIAL DAY is a cheat.

I don't mean honoring the war dead, though I don't like the way we do that either. Somehow we make their deaths look like a confirmation of our loopy patriotism.

After a long, bitter, cruel Midwest winter, and the first two months of spring dominated by rain, cold, and nasty winds, we middle western Americans figure that we're entitled to a breath of summer, as we clear away the rubble of our perennials which have been wiped out by false spring. Memorial Day is, after all, by definition the beginning of summer, right?

Anyway, this particular weekend boded to be like all the others, low clouds, mist, and drizzle, par for the course. My wife and I do not agree about trips to the Lake. I argue that when the weekend is clearly wasted we should pack up and head for Chicago, even if it's Sunday morning. Being from Ireland, she expects the worst of the weather. Guess who carries the day.

"Give over, Dermot Michael. You Yanks are spoiled rotten by the good weather. Sure, isn't it unhealthy to have as much good weather as you? And bad for your character too?"

She maintains a similar philosophy about athletic matches, as she calls them. No matter how badly your team is losing, there's always a chance that they might work a miracle. So we don't leave the stadium or turn off the TV till it's over. On rare occasions, she's won that argument too, not that she had to be right occasionally to win it.

In statistical truth (I think) we're lucky to get one good day on the weekend. Maybe that's why we, without the dogs, drove to the Lake on Friday morning early, to get ahead of the idiots who would wait till noontime to start. We were using a rented Jeep Grand Cherokee (with a television set in the rear) to convey our massive supply of everything up to the Lake for our six-week stay before we headed to Ireland.

"Poor doggies stay home," our youngest lamented.

Both shaggy white heads peered out of the picture window on the first floor as we pulled away, a study in massive sorrow.

"The doggies will play with Day," I assured her. "They'll hardly miss us."

Nuala opened her mouth to contest my statement, then closed her mouth again. You don't contradict your practically perfect husband, even when he's read the same book you have, which says that dogs are always afraid that when you leave, you might never come back.

We sang American folk songs on the trip as my wife prepared for her show on the Mall in July. Nelliecoyne and the Mick have nice voices and blend in beautifully with their mother. The Tiny Terrorist sings loudly and forcefully and totally off-key.

"You're in good form, Nuala Anne," I said as for the third time we mourned the lost beauties of Shenandoah as we wandered across the wide Missouri.

"Sure, I'm not making any progress at all, at all, Dermot love, and meself about to make a friggin' eejit of meself on national television."

Which translated into Yankspeak meant that she was getting there.

"Dance, boatman," Socra Marie shouted. "Dance!"

So we did it once more. We were spared any more singing by the fact that, before we had crossed the "Oh HIGH Oh," she was sound asleep.

"She's all wound up," Nelliecoyne warned us.

"Tell me about it," I said.

"Mick and I were never that way, were we?"

"You went crazy the first weekend at the Lake," I said, "each of you in your own way."

"No way," they exclaimed.

"Yes way," I replied.

My wife giggled at my efforts.

When they were worn-out with their singing, Nelliecoyne observed that there was a TV screen in the rear of the Grand Cherokee.

"You can't play it unless you have tapes," I said.

"You DO have the tapes, Da!"

"Let me look around here . . . What do you know! I do have them! Shall we start with Barney?"

They cheered enthusiastically, even Nelliecoyne, who was a little old for Barney.

I passed the tapes back. Nuala Anne was, naturally, driving the car because, as she insisted, she was a better driver than I was. Being-nice-to-poor-Dermot did not include permitting him to drive the car— even though he never had an accident in all his life. Socra Marie woke for a few minutes of the purple dino, then went back to sleep.

We finally pulled up at the cottage and began to unload the Jeep. Nuala had put a strict limit on the number of toys that could be brought to the beach. Still the car was packed with kidjunk.

I lifted the comatose Socra Marie from her car seat and placed her in the driveway. I turned to remove a bag of food.

"There she goes," the Mick warned us.

I turned around to see her scuttle down the street at full tilt.

"Socra Marie Coyne, you come back here!"

Da was a goof to think that would work. So he chased after her. She had a two-house lead on him, but fast afoot that he is, he finally caught her.

"Me find Kaysue," she informed me as she struggled in my arms.

"Katiesue won't be here till tomorrow."

She continued to push me away.

"Me find Kaysue," she insisted.

"Kaysue still home," I said. "Come tomorrow."

I had slipped into baby talk again. The kid was corrupting me.

"Me find Kaysue!" she yelled, going into a solemn high tantrum. She fell to the ground and wouldn't move.

My wife and children stood mute.

"A time-out for you, young woman," I decreed, picking her up and carrying her back to the car.

"Aw, Ma," she pleaded.

"Da is the big boss, Socra Marie."

Her tantrum turned into inconsolable weeping.

"Me wanna go home."

Nuala took her from me and, when I had opened the door, carried her into the house.

"It's all right, Socra Marie," she said, "Katiesue will be here tomorrow."

"God bless Kaysue," she responded piously. "Me find her tomorrow."

I took a deep breath and pointed at a chair.

"Time-out!"

"Ah, Da," she said sadly, her face contrite.

I knelt before her time-out chair and took her tiny hand.

"If you hit a car you might have broken the car or the car might have broken you and that would have broken all our hearts."

"Me no run on street," she said, tears clouding her blue eyes. "Promise."

It was about as sincere as a two-year-old can be. However, I had to establish the policy that I could not be manipulated. Right?

"Good!" I said, choking back a remission of the penalty.

"We'll go out and look at the Lake after your time-out."

She brightened considerably.

"Me see Lake!"

I glanced around. My wife and older children were watching and listening to me with intense interest. Would I stand up to the little manipulator? The virtuous Nuala Anne, as the little bishop calls her, winked approval. Later she backed it up with a quick kiss, of which I had been receiving many lately.

"Weren't you the grand da altogether!"

As we were unpacking, a wind drove the clouds and the mist away and granted us for the beginning of summer a jewel of day—clear sky, calm lake, superabundant foliage, glittering flowers. However, it was necessary that we defer gratification. Nuala Anne insisted that we had to unpack our supplies, put everything neatly away, air out the house, plant the Memorial Day annuals, arrange for babysitters, and make sure all the appliances worked. The fact that this might be the only few good hours of the whole foolish weekend was irrelevant. She snapped orders at all of us though only Nelliecoyne and I were competent enough to obey.

Socra Marie pushed at the front door with grim determination.

"Socra Marie Coyne," her mother shouted. "Stop that now or you'll get another time-out."

The little face, bright with the excitement of her first real day at the Lake, curled up in a frown, which suggested that floods of tears were about to flow.

"Ah, Ma . . ."

"Moire Phinaughla Ain McGrail," I ordered her. "Cool it!"

When I speak her full name with an approximation of its correct Irish pronunciation, she knows she's in trouble.

She spun around, glared at me as though she were spoiling for a fight, and crumpled.

"Fair play to you, Dermot love." She leaned against my shoulder. "Come on kids, let's put on our swimsuits and head for the beach!"

As we were changing in the master bedroom, she leaned against me again, her bare breasts assaulting my chest.

"I'd become a screeching fishwife"—she sighed—"if it wasn't for you."

"I doubt it," I said gallantly, accepting her kiss.

I was making progress in taming this wild Irishwoman, not that I would really want a tame wife.

Fun and games in bed tonight.

MAYBE.

So, everyone anointed with sunblock and kids sealed in flotation jackets, we descended to the beach. Actually I had to make three trips to bring down all the kidjunk. We were each of us warned to stay away from the water, which was too cold for swimming.

Socra Marie must not have heard the order because her first move was the proverbial beeline for the water. Nelliecoyne caught up with her and grabbed the strap of her polka-dot swimsuit. They both slowed down at the water's edge because Socra Marie was not sure she wanted to try it after all.

I followed them.

"The water is real cold," Nelliecoyne warned.

Socra Marie delicately placed her tiny toes in an equally tiny wave.

The result of this venture was a sound that would mark the rest of the weekend, drowning out the roar of the offshore boats, the buzz of the wave runners, the whine of machine tools working their improvements on half the houses on the beach—the piercing screech of our onetime preemie announcing to the world that not only was she alive and well, but she was after having a grand time altogether. You would hear the screech when she was running on the sand, falling on her face or her butt, hugging other members of her family, cooperating clumsily, truth to tell, on the construction of sand castles, or shouting with delight on my promise that the doggies would come next time.

I looked around and pondered the situation.

When I was in college I would stroll down the beach and note with astonishment how many guys not much older than me were sitting under beach umbrellas with their wives watching a bunch of kids building castles, charging the waves, screaming with joy. The wife would be reading a magazine or a romance novel, the guy would be pondering papers he'd brought from work. Both would pretend that this was really living while in fact they were both prisoners to their offspring and bored out of their minds.

I resolved firmly that I would never be entrapped in that prison.

So here I was trapped.

There were some differences. Nuala Anne was startlingly beautiful in her white bikini. She was reading some Russian, Turgenev I thought. I was working on a poem about Memorial Day. Most American poets seemed to be addicted to melancholy Labor Day poems. I would show them up by writing a hopeful Memorial Day poem.

All right, I was not quite in the same trap as other men my age who were filtering down to the beach. No one had a wife who was quite the feast for the eyes as mine was. Yet I didn't think that watching kids on the beach was part of the contract when we were married.

Herself tossed aside the Russian.

"Wouldn't it be good for me to go soak my head in the water?"

"Woman, it would," I said because it was what I was supposed to say.

She dashed up the stairs to our cottage. Nuala never walks, she thunders. She never closes doors, she slams them.

She would have to exchange the bikini for a black tank suit, technically more modest, as though any garment that fit my wife's body could possibly be modest.

A few minutes later she thundered down the stairs, wrapped in a vast white terry-cloth robe. She threw the robe at me, pecked at my cheek, and dashed into the water, diving in the shallows to avoid the rocks. Then she swam out into the Lake with a powerful Australian crawl.

The whole scenario woke up everyone on the beach who might have been dozing. Every eye swiveled in our direction. The crazy Mc-Grail woman, the famous singer you know, was inaugurating summer. Yes, my dear, she has three little children.

Holding her robe (which I must have ready for her return) I wandered down to the edge of the beach. Like my younger daughter I tested the temperature of the waters. Just a little above freezing. The man who had said on the radio that it was fifty-six had not told the truth.

Me wife continued her assault on the melted glacier. I wished Cindasue Murphy was on the beach. She'd have a cell phone with which she could instantly summon the Coast Guard if . . .

Socra Marie was standing next to me.

"Ma swim," she observed.

"Ma crazy," I said, slipping into baby talk again.

"Me no swim."

"You're not crazy."

"Ma come back?" she asked cautiously.

"Sure Ma will come back," I said with more confidence than I felt.

To tell Nuala Anne that she couldn't swim because the water was too cold was to invite mocking laughter. Had she not swum with her own ma every day in Galway Bay, which was colder than Lake Michigan in May?

I doubted the daily part of the myth, but I had no doubt that winter would not have stopped the two of them from testing the Gulf Stream.

My two older children, used to the act, kept right on working at their sand castle.

Eventually, the swimmer turned around and attacked the Lake back towards the shore.

Dear God, how did I ever find one like this?

God did not see fit to answer. When she reached the sandbar, she stood up and hobbled over the stones—an Irish Venus without the half shell, her long black hair pasted to her arms and shoulders and the tight tank suit clinging to her body.

Again I wondered if the Deity could explain how I ever found her.

She hurled herself into the terry-cloth robe, which I had opened at just the right angle.

"Och, Dermot Michael, wasn't it grand altogether? And itself much warmer than Galway Bay?"

She leaned against me once again, either to share my warmth or share her cold.

"Ma crazy," Socra Marie said definitively.

"Am I now?" Nuala picked up *la terrorista* and swung her up in the air.

"Ma cold," the little girl chortled. "Me warm!"

Nuala kissed Socra Marie and handed her over to me.

"I have to get out of this swimsuit," she informed me and thundered up the stairs.

"Ma crazy," our daughter observed solemnly.

"I'll bring the kids up to the pool," I shouted.

I spent much of the rest of the day in our lap pool playing with the kids while my wife sat under an umbrella at poolside reading that Russian. She would glance up occasionally and blow a kiss at me.

Well, I had told her to cool it, hadn't I?

At first our youngest was reluctant to jump in the pool even if her da's arms were outstretched to catch her. Finally she decided to risk it. Generally the operation involved two screeches in rapid succession, the first when she jumped and the second when she landed in the water.

The older kids both swam like fish, having learned when they were infants. We had been afraid to risk it with our preemie. However, she flapped around the pool like her brother and sister, determined to catch up with them.

I knew the game. Youngest that I was, I always played catch-up with older siblings. Never did catch up. Not till I brought Nuala home. Then I lapped the field.

"Ma, why don't you come play with us in the pool?"

She frowned her displeasure, put aside her sunglasses, pulled off her sweatshirt and joined us. She was wearing, I noted, a different bikini, this one rose.

She pecked at my cheek as she climbed in and rested her breasts briefly against my chest. She was playing with me. Well, we'd see about that in bed tonight.

"Come on, little one"—she grabbed Socra Marie—"let's see if we can teach you to swim."

Socra Marie did not seem to have the slightest fear of the water, not as long as her ma was around. I found myself praying to God that Ma would be around for a long time to take care of all of us.

We opened the summer traditionally with a big multigenerational buffet at my parents' home. Nuala Anne had donned a lime minisundress, suspended from her shoulders by spaghetti straps. Traffic slowed as we strolled down Lakeview.

The village was alive with the joys of summer just beginning, especially since the weather was so benign. Neighbors asked the silly question of when you had come up and the more serious question of how the winter had been.

"It ended only last week," I would reply, truthfully enough.

Nuala would scoop up a grinning Socra Marie, also in lime (as was her big sister), and announce, "Wasn't there never a dull moment with this little one?"

Socra Marie would beam happily, convinced as are all small ones that the whole world loves them just like their ma and da.

The Mick was wearing a Grand Beach sweatshirt and black shorts, just enough to make him feel independent of the rest of our crowd.

My three lime-clad womenfolk introduced a moment of silence on my parents' big deck overlooking the Lake. Once more the gang was astonished that Dermot could have carried this off. Then the conversation and the laughter resumed and everyone admired our "baby" as they called her.

"She's not a baby," Nelliecoyne said fiercely. "She's a little girl, aren't you, Socra?"

"Me big girl," the child said, shaping the air with her hands. "Me TWO!"

She held up two fingers to confirm this truth.

"Me poop in toilet! Me wear big-girl pants!"

Nuala gave her to my mother, a keen-eyed nurse. She snuggled into "Gra's" protective arms.

"Me big girl."

"She's the picture of health, Nuala."

"Doesn't she tire real easily?" my wife said, still worried about the child's love of naps.

"Or maybe she's just lazy," I said, "like I am alleged to have been at that age."

They all laughed.

"Well," my dad said, "you certainly weren't a barrel of energy like this little dynamo."

I wasn't because I didn't have to be. That's why I didn't talk much till I was three.

Family mythologies never die. Poor little Derm, by far the biggest and tallest member of the clan, was your classic underachiever, a phenomenon that often happens to the runt of the litter. Admittedly, I had made a lot of money at the Merc, but I had been lucky. I had indeed written a couple of successful novels and won a prize for a collection of my poetry; but I didn't have a real job and thank heavens Nuala earned a good income with her songs. (They had no idea how good!) Still the myth was that I was a big, handsome, and lazy lout.

I knew how Day O'Sullivan felt, though I didn't mind the myth and had no doubts about family love. My wife, however, was furious every time someone said to her, usually in astonishment, that she "had certainly done a lot with Dermot."

"Isn't he the one who's done a lot with me?" she'd shoot back, her jaw tight and her eyes blazing.

The family learned to keep that idea to themselves.

They induced Nuala to sing for them, a routine at family parties, and one she didn't mind. So her voice, with the bells ringing over the bogs, soared through the still spring air and over the serene Lake as an approving sun seemed to delay its departure just to hear her and to spread rose-and-gold lights over the Lake in approval.

Heaven forgive me for it, but my desire for her became implacable as I watched and listened. She would not escape me tonight, not that I expected she'd try.

Her ready-made chorus, uninvited, joined in for the refrains, lamenting as she did the lost Shenandoah. Socra Marie looked appropriately sad and sang vigorously, way off-key again.

After the applause, my wife said nothing about her planned appearance on national TV in a month. It was bad luck to anticipate something till just before it happened.

"I might come down with a terrible sore throat and meself a friggin' eejit for bragging about what I was going to do."

Seven centuries of oppression have inured the Irish against counting unhatched chickens.

"Herself grows more beautiful every year," Cindy whispered into my ear.

"Sure, I haven't noticed it at all, at all," I replied.

"Then why did your mouth hang open when she was singing? . . . I have a suggestion on the Damian O'Sullivan case, by the way."

"Ah?"

"I go to the state's attorney with the evidence, including depositions from the public defender and the arresting police and ask him to agree to a motion for a new trial. Then we ask the judge to dismiss the case for lack of evidence."

"That's two big assumptions."

"This state's attorney believes in justice. One look at what happened and he'll realize that it was unjust. Besides it didn't happen on his watch. We'll make sure that we get Rick Mikolitis, the same judge who wouldn't send him to jail. He'll dismiss the case."

"Damian has only four and a half months more probation. Could the judge send him to jail?"

"Not if the state's attorney agrees that there was no evidence. Damian gets a felony conviction stricken from the record. And he can sue his lawyer if he wants, not that I would imagine he'd want."

"Old man O'Sullivan will fight it."

"He'll make a fool out of himself."

"He doesn't realize, Cindy, that the playing field can be tilted against him."

Nuala consigned Socra Marie to the babysitter's room, where a group of my teenage nieces were supervising their infant and toddler siblings and cousins.

"She's adorable, Aunt Nuala," one of them said.

"Sure, isn't she a tricky one now? You'll have to keep a close eye on her."

That caution was only for the record. The Tiny Terrorist would not be awake till morning.

As I was putting away my third swissburger, I found my father and asked him if he knew anything about a Dr. Tom McBride. My old fella had in his head a file-cardlike memory for every doctor in Chicago, especially if he were Irish and Catholic.

"Young psychiatrist from Boston? At Loyola. Teaches in the med school too. Little guy. Absolutely first-rate. Very creative and ingenious. Respected. Married to Katie O'Sullivan. Neonatology. Also first-rate. Daughter of Jackie O'Sullivan. Bad case of Notre Dame obsession. Not a nice man. I hear that Tom and Katie have rented a little place over in Michiana. I hear she's expecting."

See what I mean?

Dad himself had been a Domer, back in the days, as I tell him, when they had a football team.

We left the party early, pleading our exhausted children. I carried the sleeping youngest, while Nuala held the hands of the bleary-eyed older kids. I summarized the conversations with Cindy and my father.

"We'll have to see what Damian wants," I said.

"After all these years he probably doesn't much care one way or another . . . Poor kid, he still wants his family to love him."

"There's always a chance that the judge would want to send him to jail."

"Och, Dermot, is there any lawyer in Chicago who knows more about tilting the soccer pitch than Cindy?"

I agreed that there wasn't.

We put the unprotesting kids to bed.

As we walked to our room, Nuala began, "Dermot, it's been a long day and we're both exhausted . . ."

"It's going to be a bit longer," I said, flipping the spaghetti straps from her shoulders and letting the sundress fall to the floor.

"Dermot Michael Coyne!" she protested, picking up the sundress.

"And yourself teasing me all day long."

" 'Tis true." She sighed loudly as I closed the door. "Fair play to you!"

I flicked away her minimal underwear and drew her to the bed.

"You frighten me when you're this way," she murmured.

"Do I now? . . . 'Tis a good thing altogether for a man to have a naked woman on his bed."

"And yourself not having that often at all, at all."

"We're riding over the waterfall tonight, Nuala Anne McGrail."

" 'Tis a brilliant idea, Dermot Michael Coyne."

And so we did.

Beyond the waterfall we found a great silver lake of total peace and almost unbearable joy in which neither of us had ever swum before— endless ecstasy. This must, I thought, be the place where God is.

The next morning I tiptoed out of the house and drove to the Village Bake Shop in New Buffalo, where I picked up "Dermot's tray"— forty-eight raisin Danish made especially for the Coynes, which I would deliver before breakfast. This custom was naturally attributed to Nuala's good influence on me. It was my own idea, but I didn't dispute the allegation or pass it on to my wife.

I found my family at the table in the kitchen, the kids slurping up cereal, my groggy wife sipping at her tea.

"Wasn't it wonderful of you, Dermot Michael, to collect them rolls for us all?"

"Woman, it was . . . Didn't you sleep well last night?"

"Once I was asleep," she said, an impish smile flitting across her face, "didn't I sleep just fine?"

"Me finish!" shouted Socra Marie, ready to throw herself into another exciting day.

"Go into the parlor and play with your coloring books for a few minutes and I'll take you to the beach. Aunt Cindy will be down there and Annie Hurley will babysit you till we get back. Aunt Cindasue and Uncle Peter will be there and so will Katiesue."

"Hokay!"

New word.

"You're a desperate man, Dermot Michael Coyne," she said as she filled my teacup.

"Am I now?"

"You are." She looked at me over the rim of her teacup and sighed. "All I want to do today is float around in the pool and daydream."

"You will, however, play golf, swim in the Lake, frolic in the pool with the kids, attend Mass at the elder Murphys', and talk to Dr. O'Sullivan after Mass."

She sighed again.

"You friggin' Yanks and your Protestant ethic!"

She smiled, a complacent, self-satisfied smile.

"Where were we last night, Dermot?" she asked in a bemused voice.

"Close to the Lake beyond the Lake?"

"You mean God?" she asked.

"Isn't that what you mean when you engage in your Irish mysticism."

" 'Tis."

Pause.

"I love you so much, Dermot Michael Coyne."

She raised her teacup to me.

"Not as much as I love you, Nuala Anne McGrail."

We clicked teacups.

"Now let's play golf!" I demanded.

We were two very fortunate people.

The Grand Beach golf course (real name: Michigan Shores) is a nine-hole remnant of a twenty-seven hole layout that did not survive the Great Depression. It's short and not the most difficult course in the world. But it's right there within walking distance, though most of our neighbors rode over in their golf carts.

My wife firmly forbade such pampering.

"You Yanks," she informed me, "are obese because you're self-indulgent. We don't permit them things (dem dings) at Poolnarooma and you don't need one at this miniature golf course. You can get one if you want but I'll walk."

That settled that.

It was the second glorious day, a violation of the Memorial Day rules.

We were paired with two men in Notre Dame sweatshirts in their forties, serious golfers. They looked suspiciously at my wife in her white slacks and Galway sweatshirt. Gorgeous perhaps but an obvious duffer who would slow down the foursome.

"Ladies first," one of them said.

Without a word or a practice swing me wife teed up the ball and whacked it two hundred yards straight down the middle of the fairway.

"A little short," I observed.

"First drive of the year," she murmured.

My first day on a golf course after a long layoff is always my best because I don't give a hoot how badly I play. Then I begin to get serious and my score goes up.

Anyway I drove my tee shot some seventy-five yards beyond my wife's.

"Hooked it a little." She sighed.

I birdied the hole. She parred it.

"Should have had an eagle," I complained.

"You'll get better as the summer goes on."

She knew that wasn't true, but we were playing a game with our companions.

"My chip shots will never improve."

"Sure, 'tis all in the wrists, isn't it?"

I ended up with a thirty-two and herself with a thirty-six. Since I gave her two strokes handicap on the nine holes (which I thought was excessive for the sometime women's champion at Poolnarooma), I had won easily. Our companions congratulated us.

"You two could sweep the tournaments here this year."

"Wait till you see our daughter."

She complained bitterly as we hiked back to our cottage.

"If I were a gorilla, I could hit the friggin' ball that far too."

"Not a good loser, Nuala Anne."

"And yourself wearing me out last night."

"It was the other way around and yourself seducing me all day long yesterday."

"I did not!"

Then she laughed.

"Anyway, aren't you a pushover, Dermot Michael Coyne!"

"Every man is when a beautiful woman goes after him."

She giggled complacently.

"You ought to take golf more seriously, Derm love. Maybe you should when we're out at Rynville in August. Teach them Micks that a Yank can win their tournament."

"I might just do that, but only if I don't take it seriously. Golf isn't worth getting tied up in knots about."

"Your family is right about you. You're lazy."

"About some things."

She giggled at that line.

We had to rush to the beach in our golf clothes to make sure no disasters had happened. Socra Marie and Katiesue were busy trying to empty the Lake into a hole in the sand, a task they pursued with dedicated persistence. The two older ones, under Annie Hurley's direction, were building an elaborate sand castle.

"Two li'l she polecats a havin' themselves a ball," Cindasue informed us.

"Who won?" Pete Murphy, one of the Ryan Clan and an anthropology professor, rose to shake hands with us.

"The big lout shot a thirty-two," my wife complained. "I'll beat him at tennis this afternoon."

Our children barely noted our appearance.

We climbed back to the top of the dune. In our bedroom while we were changing into swimsuits, I caught my temporarily naked wife in my arms and kissed her soundly.

"My turn to do the remote seduction," I said.

"I'm a pushover too." She sighed. "I guess I have a weakness for gorillas."

"You'd better get dressed and do your swim in the Lake."

"Do I have to?"

"Woman, you do!"

"Then we'll play tennis."

"Tomorrow."

"You're getting old, Dermot Michael Coyne."

She carried the robe back down to the beach and tossed it to me at the bottom of the stairs. She charged the water as vigorously as she had yesterday.

"Ma's swimming," the Mick announced.

"Ma crazy!"

All three of them and Katiesue joined me at the water's edge.

"That 'un jest plum 'tack the Lake," Cindasue said. "Happen she ever get tired?"

"Not very often."

Cindasue, from a place in West Virginia called Stinkin' Creek, was a lieutenant commander in the Yewnited States Coast Guard. She could speak perfectly good radio standard English if she were a mind. But she had discovered that people like it when she talked "mountain" talk—"Just plain ole English 'fore them Puritan folks come through our hollers."

It was not exactly clear what she did in her office in the Dirksen Federal Building in Chicago. She insisted that she merely counted the boats on the Chicago River as they passed by. Everyone suspected that she was a gumshoe of some sort and really worked for the Secret Service, thinking work. As evidence of her identification she wore a white sweatshirt which said "United States Coast Guard" and carried the two and a half gold bars of her rank. As two outsiders, she and Nuala Anne had bonded instantly.

"This har shirt a getting' me some respect from them ratings a running around in that outboard."

She was a lovely little woman with a sweet smile and the flavorsome body of a sixteen-year-old. Young ratings cruising offshore, both of them women no more than twenty, would have a hard time believing she was an officer, even with the sweatshirt.

"Ma crazy," Socra Marie insisted.

"You're mother's a fine swimmer," Cindasue said in plain English.

"Ma fine swimmer! . . . Me love Ma."

"You better, chile."

"Me love Da too."

Then she informed us that she also loved Kaysue, Mickie, Nellie, and Aunt Cindasue.

I struggled for the words in my Memorial Day poem to describe the swarm of white boats on the Lake, either moving briskly in the wind or dragging skiers through the wakes. It was an explosion of summertime, when, contrary to Gerswhin, the livin' was anything but easy.

A ski boat pulled up alongside of my wife and someone tossed her a life belt and a skyline.

"That be your nefoo, Simon Coyne."

Aunt Nuala popped up out of the water and skied back towards shore, taking care not to cross the invisible line that would have brought the wrath of the Yewnited States Coast Guard ratings upon her.

"Ma ski," my youngest said dubiously.

"Ma is very good at it," I said.

"Me ski?"

"When you're a little older."

"I'm going to learn this year," Nelliecoyne said proudly.

"Me too."

"Me three," Mick promised.

I'd have to spend a fair amount of time over at Pine Lake trying to get Nelliecoyne out of the water. It would take a couple of more years. Prudent little punk that he was, just like his old man, the Mick wouldn't want to try.

Nuala dropped her ski offshore, tossed the belt to Simon, and swam towards the beach. A bikini-clad teenage lifeguard, whistle in her mouth, her body oiled in sunscreen ambled down the beach. She wore an open "New Buffalo" windbreaker and an "Oinks" baseball cap, Oinks being the local ice-cream supply station.

"Is that girl a good swimmer?" she asked skeptically.

"Ma fine swimmer."

"She's your mother?" The teen was impressed.

"Mine too."

"Mine too."

The kid lifted Socra Marie in her arms, an almost automatic reaction of a woman of any age to the Tiny Terrorist.

"Are you going to grow up to be a swimmer like your mother?"

"Me ski too!"

"You'll be real careful?"

"Shunuf!"

"And are you going to be careful too?" She handed my daughter to me and lifted up Katiesue.

"Shunuf."

If the kid noted that the two of them were talking mountain talk, she didn't let on. Nuala Anne waded ashore. I wrapped her in the robe.

"I didn't break any rules, did I?"

"Please exercise extreme caution on the Lake, ma'am. The water is still very cold."

"Not as cold as Galway Bay . . . But I will be careful."

"You have beautiful children, ma'am."

"The one in your arms goes with the Coast Guard woman. The others are mine. If they give you any trouble, let me know. My name is Nuala Anne."

"Yes, ma'am . . . And it would be better if you swam parallel to the shore."

"I will," she said. "Thank you for reminding me."

Poor child didn't know that she had a celebrity on her hands. Just as well. My wife had identified herself that way long before she had become a celebrity and didn't do it now as a gimmick.

" 'Tis me name, isn't it now?"

The next stop was the swimming pool, though we had to take time off so Nuala could call Damian to find out how the dogs were doing in her absence.

"Isn't he taking Ethne to see a film (pronounced "filum") tonight?"

"Shame on them both!"

"Give over, Dermot Michael, they're both sweet young people . . . Och you're having me on again, aren't you?"

After the pool we had to dress for the Mass the little bishop would say at the Murphy house. Poor dear man would have to drive out from the Cathedral, then drive back first thing in the morning. The idiots in charge ought to do something about the shortage of priests.

We all had to dress for Mass, myself in a sports shirt and slacks, the kids in "churchgoing" clothes, and my wife in a white skirt and her infamous "Galway Hooker" tee shirt, which she always wore for the little bishop.

He spun Socra Marie in the air much to her delight and hugged Nelliecoyne and the Mick. Then he performed a similar rite with Katiesue.

"Coast Guard and Galway racing boats," he observed. "A good way to begin summer."

All the summer enthusiasm began to weigh on me. It was an illusion. The weather would turn bad tomorrow. Summer would be fleeting. This Saturday might be the only good one. Life was fleeting too. We were struggling to keep alive an illusion we all knew was ephemeral.

O lente lente currite noctis equi, as the Roman poet had begged. Oh, slowly, slowy run you steeds of night.

My wife is the melancholy Irish person in our marriage, except when the black mood is upon me. Then I go down much more deeply into the swamp than she ever does.

Nor was I looking forward to the conversation with Katie McBride. There was so much pain in that family. Yet they doubtless had their own exuberant celebration of the coming of summer.

"The issue," said the little bishop in his homily, "is whether the tombstone or the flowers are more ultimate. It is perhaps odd that we Americans celebrate our day of the dead just when life flourishes and summer begins. Somehow we have our symbols confused. My parents called this festival Decoration Day because it is the day when we used to put flowers around the tombs. Now we put them everywhere and perhaps forget about the meaning of the festival and the tombs. We honor those who died in the country's wars—millions of young men whose lives were cut short before they had a chance to flourish. All war is foolish. Some may, however foolish, also be necessary. That is not for us to decide today. We must rather consider those long rows of white crosses—and Stars of David—and think of how much those young men might have contributed to the life of our country if they had been given a chance. We must also think of the parents, the wives, the sweethearts of those who are buried in the military cemeteries and how much their lives were blighted by early and sudden death.

"It might be said that they died for their country. It is more likely that they died because they were drafted and had no choice. They may also have died because political leaders or military leaders made tragic mistakes. We must not use this day of the dead to glorify war but rather to sorrow for those who died and for those who lost them.

"We must also ask God, with all due respect, why he permitted all these young lives to be cut short with such tragic results. We don't expect an answer but we must ask the question. Indeed he expects us to ask the question and not to lose sight of the tragedy in the military pageantry we will see on television.

"Yet we put flowers on the tombs and we surround our homes with flowers on this day. Hence the question: Which is more ultimate, the flower or the tomb? Death which the white cross represents or life which the flower represents? Do we just make the tomb pretty or do we defy it?

"I put it to you that as Catholics we defy the tomb. We do not pretend that there is no tragedy in all these deaths. We do not turn away from the stupidity, the futility, the ugliness of death, of any and every death and not merely that of a young man or a young woman in the prime of life. Because of our faith we seek to transcend it. Love is as strong as death the Song of Songs tells us. It is a kind of draw between the two. If, however, love cannot prevent death, so death cannot prevent love and thus in the end love wins. Consider the lilacs here on the Murphy lawn: they ought to have been wiped out long ago by the wind and the snow and the erosion of the dune. Yet they reappear every year at this time to remind us that there is beauty in the cosmos. If there is beauty then there is Beauty with a capital B. And if there is Beauty, death is not quite the end. There is yet more to be said. Beyond that today we cannot go and we need not go. All the beauty of this wonderful spring day and our celebration of the beginning of summer once again defies death and we join in that defiance. Life is too important ever to be anything but life."

— 12 —

"THAT GORGEOUS little redhead I saw at Mass," Katie McBride said. "She's the one in Damian's paintings, isn't she? The one with the two white hounds?"

"She is," Nuala agreed.

Before she could say something negative about our kids, a bad and thoroughly Irish habit, I interrupted, "She has her mother's beauty, her great-grandmother's red hair, and her dad's Irish smile."

We all laughed.

"I was astonished by the work in the Gallery on Oak Street. He is very gifted, isn't he?"

"Very," Nuala said solemnly, as she searched for the tone of the conversation.

We were sitting on the deck in front of our cottage, sipping port and Bailey's. The sun had set. The sky was dense with stars, the Lake content, the temperature comfortable if you had a sweater over your shoulders. Across the Lake the twinkling lights of Chicago defined the sky and swiftly moving lights marked the planes that O'Hare was firing off like firecrackers.

Tom McBride was indeed a little guy. However, his whimsical smile and his quick brown eyes suggested a gift of laughter and love. It must have required a lot of the latter to woo Kathleen O'Sullivan away from her father. He was silent through most of our conversation, but nodded approval for his wife's story as she told it.

"I'm so happy," she went on, "that you have helped Damian. I admit that as much as I wanted to believe that he had some artistic talent, I also wanted his exhibit at the Reilly Gallery to be . . . well, less than adequate. If he is really good—and he is—then my family has done him a great injustice. I went along with it, even when I had reasons to be suspicious, so I did him a great injustice.

"I thought I grew up in a wonderful family," she went on. "I have come to realize that it is in fact deeply dysfunctional. I am exploring this with a psychiatrist—not my husband—because I want to understand it and I want to avoid its influence on the family I will raise."

She touched her swelling belly.

"The first hint I had of the family culture," Tom McBride said quietly, "was the debate about our marriage being at the Notre Dame Grotto. It made no never mind to me. Katie thought it was a site for kids in their early twenties. I watched in dismay as they all brought pressure on her for us to marry in the Grotto as her parents and all the children had with the same doddering old priest presiding. It scared the hell out of me."

"Tom couldn't believe," Katie added, "that this was a serious attempt to exorcise his Boston College background. It became a celebration of our family unity . . ."

Her voice trailed off into the twilight.

"How can we help?" Nuala asked.

"I assume that you are attempting to reverse that terrible plea bargain that my father imposed on the case of the death of Rod Keefe. I was at the club that night of course. I knew that Damian was far too drunk even to open the door of the car. I told the police that and they agreed. He could not have driven it over poor Mr. Keefe. Yet later I somehow persuaded myself that he had."

"We're doing what we can," Nuala said softly. "You'd provide an affidavit about his condition if we needed it?"

Katie McBride hesitated.

"Of course I would . . . You've become the family he never had. It's astonishing to me that he has survived as long as he has."

"We're a resilient species," Tom McBride murmured.

"We were so happy as children," Katie went on. "Or thought we were. We adored our father, just like our mother did and still does. He was fun and funny and showered us with affection. We sang and we danced and we told stories and made up our little plays and went on vacations together and to Notre Dame games. Notre Dame was so much a part of our life. And our house at Lake Geneva. We could hardly wait to go up there in the summer. The family is there now and I feel a powerful tug towards them. I didn't tell them the truth. I said we wanted to be near The University of Chicago Hospital if the child came early."

She paused, understanding that she must break free and that it would be very hard to do so.

"We felt sorry for other kids who didn't have a wonderful father like ours or such a happy family life. I suppose we didn't get to know other kids as well as we might. We had all that we needed in the way of affection and relationships at home . . . The first hint I had that maybe there was something unhealthy was when my brothers were at Loyola Academy. They were big kids, kind of clumsy and not too interested in studying. They were not quite good enough to be on the starting team till they were seniors and even then they had a hard time staying in the game. They hovered on the edge of academic ineligibility. Dad blamed the Jesuits. He said they wanted them for Holy Cross. Somehow he got them through school, though he didn't seem able to persuade the coaches that they were as good as we all believed they were. I was at St. Mary's then. I wanted to go to Notre Dame, but Dad didn't approve of the admission of women students. He said it would ruin the school. It didn't make much difference to me . . ."

"Your mother went to St. Mary's?" I asked.

"Yes, she did. Dad said the women at Notre Dame would lose their virtue there. Mom just laughed because women at St. Mary's did too. Still, she supported him like she always did . . . As I say it didn't matter that much to me, but I had begun to suspect that just possibly we might be wrong about Sean and Pat. Maybe I thought we believed that some things were true because Dad wanted us to believe them. They didn't do all that well at Notre Dame either or make the football team. Looking back on it I think that was about the time when Dad's will-to-believe became an obsession. Or maybe I noticed it only then. Sean and Pat are good guys, they really are. If only Dad would have left them alone . . . When they didn't make it as lawyers he pretended to be delighted. He needed their special entrepreneurial talents in the firm . . . He even bought a company plane for them to play with."

We were all silent for a moment. The night air stirred lazily. The lights of a plane from O'Hare above us raced across the stars like twin meteors.

"You suspected that the story your family told itself might not be completely true?" I asked.

"Vaguely," she said. "I kind of knew it, but didn't want to know it."

"Why do you think your father was so driven to sustain the story?"

"Something in his own family experience, I suppose . . . The firm, the club, Lake Geneva, and above all Notre Dame—they were the stage for us all. Nothing else mattered. Looking back on it, I find it hard to believe that a man as smart as he is—and he is very smart—could have such a limited vision. I began to realize how limited it was when I went off to Harvard for my medical training and encountered a completely different world."

"And himself not wanting you to go to Harvard?" my wife asked.

"He couldn't understand it. Why would I want to attend such a pagan place? Wasn't Loyola good enough for me? They'd give me contraceptives. They'd make me perform abortions. They'd try to take away my faith. If I went to Loyola, I could live at home. He'd buy me a car of my own . . . Mom agreed with him as always."

"But you went off to Harvard just the same," Tom McBride said.

"Looking back on it, I'm astonished that I did. Then I discovered that Dad could . . . well, redefine a situation so it fit with what I now think of as the family myth. I was leading my class at the toughest medical school in the country and showing them that Irish Catholics were as good as anyone else. I wasn't quite on top of the class but there were plenty of Irish Catholics there to whom it would never have occurred that they had to show anyone anything."

"Mostly from Boston," her husband said. "Worst kind."

"Yet when I came home for my residency I fit right back into the myth. My brothers were both married to young women, graduates of St. Mary's. They seemed to fit in perfectly, though occasionally I think they were not happy that they could not spend some time on Christmas Day with their own families. Then the talk began that I'd better find a nice boy to settle down with before I was too old. I was only twenty-six and I resented the kidding. I would marry when I found the right man. I hadn't broken free of the myth yet, but I had begun to see it for what it was."

"And your sister?" I probed.

"Maura? Our family story is that Maura is an adorable little imp— pretty, tough, a lot like Dad. I always thought she was an obnoxious bitch who tried to be as tough as Dad but forgot about his persuasive charm. Now I feel sorry for her."

"And Damian?"

"Poor little guy," she said, the sound of tears in her voice. "For reasons that I could never understand he was defined as the family loser. He was so sweet. He loved to draw. He used to draw little birthday cards for the rest of us. We made fun of them and threw them away. Dad wanted him to grow up and act like a man. Heaven knows Damian tried . . ."

"And wasn't your father afraid that he might be gay?"

"That's pretty evident now, Nuala Anne. It didn't occur to me then. Like the rest of them I thought that Damian was a useless pest."

"Even your mother?"

"Especially my mother."

"It's remarkable that he survived," I said.

"Toughest one in the whole clan," Tom McBride observed. "He had to be. He wasn't gay either."

"I think Dad was so afraid that he might be gay that he did the sort of things to him that could make him gay . . . Though I know now that isn't possible . . . It's hard to change my mind about him." She reached for a tissue and wiped the tears away from her cheeks.

"Probably afraid of his own gay tendencies," my wife suggested.

That's what comes of her reading too many books.

"Looking back on it, Dad's world was coming apart. Notre Dame was a different place. The football team was losing. His sons were not the successes he had hoped they would be. He needed a scapegoat. Damian was not only a terrible disappointment, he was the cause of all the trouble."

"And, if we're to judge by the work at the Reilly Gallery," Tom McBride said, "he's the most gifted person in the family."

"Not the kind of gift your man can admire," my wife said, "not at all, at all."

"As the years went on," Katie continued her sad tale, "Dad began to rethink my situation. I had become kind of a dedicated virgin, almost a nun, who had given her life to the service of the tiny creatures I was keeping alive. He didn't seem to grasp that thirty didn't make you a spinster anymore. I had every intention of marrying when the right man appeared. If Tom had appeared when I was in medical school, I would have pursued him then. I began to worry that, like other of Dad's delusions, this might become a self-fulfilling prophecy . . . Then when I brought Tom around to meet the family, Dad barely spoke to him . . ."

"Boston College was just unacceptable." Tom laughed. "I wondered at first whether I should bother fighting the family myth. I decided that Katie was worth any fight I had to make. I wouldn't let her go."

"And he didn't," she said, "though it was dicey at times. I almost gave his ring back when he said that my family was dysfunctional . . . He was right, of course, though I still have a hard time putting the pieces together. Dr. Murphy is helping me to do it . . . I was surprised to see her at Mass today."

Mary Kathleen Ryan Murphy was the little bishop's sister and the grandmother and namesake of Katiesue.

"And your father was frantic by now?"

"He still doesn't talk to Tom and is spreading rumors about my getting an annulment, even though I'm almost eight months pregnant. I suspect a lot of people at the club and the parish believe them. It's hard not to believe Dad."

"Who do you think ran over Rod Keefe?" I asked suddenly.

"I don't know. I didn't do it and neither did poor Day. I'd like to think it was an accident. But the lights are bright enough in the parking lot. It would have been hard not to see him on the driveway."

Someone had told me the lights weren't bright.

"Can you exclude anyone else in the family? Your father? Your mother?"

She thought about it.

"I can't imagine Mom hurting a fly. Dad? It's not his style . . . There was trouble in the company then. Keefe was threatening to make some kind of trouble. I don't know what it was. I don't think my brothers were aware of the problem either. Jim Creaghan, Maura's fiancé then and a very bright young engineer, hinted to me that there was a patent problem of some sort and it was serious. It seemed to disappear after Keefe's death."

For the first time we had a motive.

"Och, your da's world is coming apart now, isn't it, Katie? Damian is on the verge of success. You didn't go to Lake Geneva . . ."

"And everyone outside of the family knows that no way is Maura going to make partner at Minor, Grey. She's able enough but she's too much of a bitch even for that profession."

So Jackie O'Sullivan was probably coming apart too. He might become dangerous. I'd speak to Mike Casey about that.

Our own lovemaking was very mild. Neither my wife nor I wanted to end up in that ecstatic lake again.

"Isn't it terrible, Dermot Michael?" she said as she snuggled in my arms.

"Marital sex, Nuala Anne?" I said.

"Well, not with you . . . I mean the mess that John Patrick O'Sullivan has made of his family. Think of how many lives he's ruined and how Damian and Katie will have to resist his myth, even long after he's dead."

"It's a mistake to believe that all the fantasies you had when you were at Notre Dame can come true."

"Or that you can force them to come true."

"What did we learn tonight?" I said, brushing my lips against hers.

"Didn't we learn about a possible motive, and that the mother is the high priestess of the Jackie O'Sullivan cult, and that this poor Jim Creaghan who married Maura might have figured things out?"

"So someone should see if Jim Creaghan wants to talk to us?"

"Ah, and now who would that someone be, Dermot Michael Coyne?"

The weather turned bad on Sunday morning as I had predicted it would. I played tennis with my wife, who mopped up the court with me. Then I settled in during the afternoon to read the latest transcripts from Father Richard Lonigan D.D.

— 13 —

February 2, Feast of St. Brigid, patroness of Ireland.

I have returned from my niece's wedding in Dublin. I had expected that I would enjoy the civilized conversation and warmth of Dublin. In fact I was bored. I had also expected that I would return to this terrible place with great reluctance. In fact I was almost eager to smell again the acrid stench of manure and peat, which permeates the West of Ireland, and only too willing to tolerate the oppressive reek of the sea. Nor did the great rock, hovering implacably at the end of the strand, oppress me quite as much as it had.

The sensation that I was happy to come home worried me. Had this wet, cold, miserable place become my home? Were these poor, illiterate, and superstitious peasants my family? Had I given up all hope that the Cardinal would relent and permit me to return to Maynooth, where I thought I belonged?

The answer to these three questions I must conclude is in the affirmative. I have become a native just as surely as missionary priests do in Africa. I must begin the practices which link me to the outside world. I must continue this diary and resume my half hour at the piano. I am not a Donegal native and never will be. I'm not a Dubliner anymore either. This is very dangerous.

The school goes very well indeed. Liam is a wonderful teacher and adored by the students, even the louts who were most likely to give him trouble. So good is he that some of the people—those who talk to the insufferable Branigan—complain to me about him. It's not good, they say, for a schoolmaster to be admired by his students. He is a bit of a Fenian, they say, he'll make trouble.

With the Ribbonmen around, I replied to Branigan (who, I suspect, has ties with them out of fear if nothing else), there's no reason to worry about a young schoolmaster.

Lord Skeffington is pleased too. I appreciate his approval of the choice I made.

"The parson," he says, "would never have found me a young man like that."

" 'Tis said he's a bit of a Fenian."

"No worse than you, Dick."

Milord is terribly worried about his wife. Her pregnancy seems to progress nicely. She is beautiful and blooming. He will take her to Dublin for her confinement at the Rotunda.

"I lost a child and its mother in India," he said to me once.

I hardly knew how to answer.

"She was a native of course. An exquisitely beautiful girl. I loved her deeply. I blame myself for her death."

"Fairly?"

"No. There was nothing I could have done . . . I had expected to stay on in India. When they died, I knew I had to come home. I told myself I would never love again. Then I met Mary Margaret, as different a woman as there could be, and I fell in love with her. I am a romantic, Dick, as you well know."

"You wife knows the story?"

"No. She could not understand. It wouldn't be fair to burden her with it."

Who was I to argue with him?

I must ask myself candidly whether I was also happy to see Mrs. O'Flynn again. Had I missed her dignified reserve, her native intelligence, her excellent cooking? Surely yes. And her womanly presence? Her classic face and her firm elegant body?

I would like to be able to deny that I found her attractive. Yet that would be to deny the obvious. Out of respect for her and my celibacy I must guard my feelings—and offer thanks to God that she lives in the house behind mine. I hope that she finds a husband worthy of her, one who does not mind if she continues to work at the parish house.

I now time my interlude at the keyboard to match the return from school of Eileen O'Flynn and her friends.

February 19, Feast of Colman of Lindisfarne, the last abbot of the monastery there before the English church took it over after the Synod of Whitby.

Legend has it that he then went to Inishboffin off the coast of Connemara, where his monks built the beehive huts.

Today I watched part of the process in the making of poteen. I denounce on every possible occasion the abuse of the drink. I am convinced that Father Mathew Theobald was correct in his total abstinence crusade. Yet I do not reject the tiny jar of the creature that Mrs. O'Flynn offers me on occasion when I come in from a ride in the bitter rain.

If the making of the poteen is part of the life of my people, I should at least know how it is done.

I am now convinced, after several hours of watching the work in the dark of night, that there is a serious craft to it, indeed one might almost say an art. There are perhaps a dozen farms in the parish where poor folk supplement their meager income from cattle and grain by the slow, careful, and loving creation of the "creature" as they call it. In the ongoing battle between them and the customs officials—usually Protestant if truth be told—the still masters usually win. The local constables are on their side and give them advance warning, for which they are rewarded with their own supply.

The care with the still masters' work and their loving concern for hiding their tools in part are precautions against the customs officers, but also part of the almost religious ritual with which they work.

Looking back on the night from the sober gray day I realize that I ran considerable risk. The customs officers would delight in arresting the local priest. The Cardinal would find his conviction of my imprudence confirmed.

Yet I was assured that there was no risk. The guards set out on the narrow road to the farm would raise the warning in plenty of time for the still master to cover the still and sweep the muddy earth over it.

And for the priest to ride away in the rain.

I have come to realize that there is much art in the way these people live. They are illiterate for the most part and superstitious. Yet they are not merely oppressed peasants. They carry with them a very old culture which has never needed literacy.

I can hardly credit that I wrote that last paragraph. Yet I believe it. They have invited me to their come-all-ye singing sessions around the fireplace because they discovered I could play the accordion as well as the piano. I have long despised the former instrument as unworthy and frivolous. Yet they marvel that a priest can play it and play it well. I do not remain long at these events. In my presence, they do not quite relax and they certainly do not drink as much as I'm sure they otherwise would. Still they unbend enough for me to see them as individuals. They put aside the masks of servility which they maintain for the "betters" and become interesting human beings.

Some of the men—though not the musicians and storytellers—are hard, unsmiling domestic despots who govern their wives and children with grim brutality. Yet other men are gentle and loving

and respectful to their wives. Some of the women are sour com-
plainers and the laughter of others is contagious and their affection for their husbands is obvious to all. In these respects they are
no different from men and women I might encounter in an infi-
nitely more formal setting in Dublin.

Sometimes as I ride home I find myself wondering which kind of
wife I would have chosen if I had walked down another path. Does
a young man know what kind of person lurks behind a pretty face?
I wonder if I would have chosen a woman with the mysterious reserve of Mrs. O'Flynn. What thoughts, what fears, what hopes,
what passions hide behind that reserve?

It is a question I should not ask, especially not on bitter nights
when the wind, all the way from Newfoundland, screams like the
terror of the damned.

Nor are they as passive politically as I had thought. They
know the stories of all the failed "risings" of the last century and
affirm that "someday poor old Ireland" will be free. They hate the
English and even more the Belfast Protestants who represent what
passes for government around here—the customs officers, the senior constables, the resident magistrates, the bailiffs. Indeed I am
surprised—though perhaps I should not be—at the virulence of
their hatred. No one mentions the deaths of the Famine, yet I
don't think they've forgotten them.

Violence lurks just beneath the surface. They do not talk of the
Ribbonmen but occasionally there is a sudden silence, as though a
Ribbonman might be listening at the door or even sitting among
us around the hearth.

When someone is cursing Tim Allen, Lord Skeffington's agent,
someone else will remark, "There are those who will take care of
him someday."

And another adds, "And the Widow Cudahy in the bargain."

Then the embarrassed silence, as though they realize they
should not be talking that way with the priest in the house.

"No one dare touch her," a woman will say. "Or the women of the
village will tear him apart."

I once asked Dr. Jarlath McGrath, a white-haired and white-bearded old man, who has served all his life here and seems to know all the secrets of the place, about the widow.

"Sure wouldn't your Mrs. O'Flynn been forced to the same thing, if you hadn't hired her and herself with a beautiful daughter too?"

"Were there no widowed men who might have courted Mrs. Cudahy?"

He sighed.

"She's not from here, don't you see?"

I didn't see.

They say little about Lord Skeffington in my presence because they know we are friends.

"He's not the worst of them."

"He's still a redcoat."

"Aye, but he's still not the worst redcoat in the world."

From the Irish such words border on praise.

About Lady Skeffington I hear only respect and affection.

"Sure, didn't she conceive after bathing in the Holy Well?"

"And herself a sweet young thing."

However, if the anger is as deep here as it seems to be, the Skeffington family should flee to Dublin or Belfast immediately should there be another "rising." I resolved I would tell Bob that when I found the occasion. Military man that he was, he probably understood it without my warning. Our hardscrabble outcrop into the ocean could become only slightly less dangerous than the Khyber Pass.

One particularly bad night when it seemed that the ocean wind would blow away the roof of my house, Dr. McGrath, the schoolmaster, and sergeant in charge of our RIC barracks (a surprisingly literate man) were sitting around my fireplace. Also present was an occasional visitor, Sean Toole, a recluse who lived back in the hills with his books and his butterfly collection. He was the local man of mystery, extremely well educated (especially in medieval Irish history) and brilliantly witty. He was about fifty, with broad shoulders, a lined, handsome face, and a thatch of iron gray hair. He did not come to church, denied in fact that he was or ever had been a Catholic—"Though with great respect for the Church's survival power." He had plenty of money and yet no apparent source of income. He was reported to be a veteran of the Fenian rising on the run, but it seemed most unlikely that the RIC would have permitted such a one to remain at liberty. He rarely spoke to anyone in the village or the townland and lived alone with a very old male servant. He spoke on occasion to the doctor, who must have told him about the occasional sessions in my parlor.

Present also was Dr. Boyd "Boysie" Lufton, a young English geologist who was exploring our rocky corner of the Isles (as he usually called the British Isles), "out of deference," he would say, "to the crowd of Fenians who surround me."

"By all rights," he said once, "this strange place ought not to exist. It is pure delight to a geologist like myself. Her Majesty's government is interested enough in it to pay me for poking around here when I am not engaged in the serious business of hunting and fishing with the schoolmaster."

Boysie was a wonderful comic contrast to us melancholy Celts. He even insisted that he supported home rule for England too, though it was not clear what he meant.

"Sounds like treason, young man," Dr. McGrath said with his booming laugh.

"Do I look like a traitor!"

We all laughed.

Yet for all his charm and comedy, Boysie seemed to me to be another man of mystery.

As usual we spoke of poetry and music and history and, rarely, politics. Sometimes Bob Skeffington would join us, but now he stayed home with his wife.

"I am surprised," I said tentatively, "about the undercurrent of rebellion I encounter in the parish."

"You should not be, Father," Sergeant Kyle said, sipping on the tiny glass of poteen I had provided. "There's them here that has long memories."

"The Ribbonmen?"

The sergeant waved his hand. "Ah, well, sure we all know that they're around conniving. They're up to no good."

The implication seemed to be that there were deeper emotions in the townland.

"If the English don't give us home rule," Liam Conroy added, "we're going to have to take it ourselves and drive them all out of our country."

"Then, dear one," Boysie said, "you must come to England and help us to win home rule from the British."

Liam's seditious words were spoken mildly. A verbal Fenian he might be, but I could hardly imagine his attacking Lord Skeffington's house with a pike.

Sean Toole spoke up.

"For most of Irish history, the Irish were more likely to be on the side of the invaders than on the side of Ireland. Thus at the Battle of Clontarf weren't there more of us fighting on the side of the Danes than with that poor senile fool Brian Boru?"

"Does that make it right?" Liam asked mildly.

Toole threw up his hands.

"I refrain from such judgments. My only point is that those who work with and for the occupying army on this island have a long historic pattern behind them. What would happen to the respectable Irish middle class if the protection of the English legal system was suddenly snatched away and they found themselves subject to the vagaries of the Brehon laws."

"Most likely," I observed, "we'd keep the English system without the English and call it by Irish names."

"That would be treason," Liam murmured softly.

"I wouldn't want to be that fella Tim Allen," the doctor said, puffing on his pipe. "There's them that would like to see him dead."

"I would have thought that Lord Skeffington had reined him in."

"He's not evicting people anymore," the doctor agreed. "Yet he harasses the tenants whenever he can. He's not only mean, but he's petty. He seems to enjoy it."

"And he harasses the Widow Cudahy," Liam added. "Which he also seems to enjoy."

"They wouldn't be so far from wrong who say that she enjoys it too," the doctor observed. "Not that she has all that much choice."

"There's talk of putting him down all right." The sergeant sighed. "But, sure, there's always talk around here."

"A good case can be made for the advantage of talk," Sean Toole said, "especially in a country so skilled at talk."

"Such as?" Liam asked.

"It's a lot easier and safer to talk about treason than actually to engage in it."

I could not banish the doctor's remark about the Widow Cudahy as I tossed and turned in my bed that night. I was not unaware that some women enjoy lovemaking with men. In Dublin that secret was carefully hidden. In Spain everyone took it for granted. Out here in this cold and barren place, it seemed to me, that some men and some women would seek warmth wherever they could find it. The strong affection that some women were not ashamed to display towards their husbands even when the parish priest was present was proof enough of that. Irishwomen may be modest, it has been said, but not cold.

I pondered a question about which I had no right to wonder: What had been the quality of Mrs. O'Flynn's relationship with her husband during their brief marriage?

Nor could I escape the dangerous question of whether she had yearnings about me like those I had about her. I told myself that I would never know the answer to that and finally, towards dawn, fell asleep.

Temptations are not sins, I argued to myself before Mass the next morning. The usual people were there—a half dozen elderly folks and Mrs. O'Flynn and Eileen. I was ashamed of my lascivious thoughts about her.

March 17, Feast of St. Patrick, patron of Ireland.

Father Jeremias Carey, the pastor of the next parish, finally came over to pay his respects to me the other day—giving up on any expectation that I would follow protocol and pay my respects to him first. He is a big, ponderous, bald man who moves slowly and speaks more slowly, as if weighing carefully every word. He arrived without advance notice at one-thirty, knowing that it was dinnertime.

"I'll put another plate on the table, Your Reverence," Mrs. O'Flynn said as she conducted him into my study.

"Lovely woman," Father Carey said when he had made himself comfortable in my largest chair.

"If you say so, Father."

"A lot of changes around here. Remodeled the house, painted the church, cleaned up the garden, hear you have a new schoolmaster and himself Catholic."

"All true, Father."

I offered him a splash of poteen.

"Poteen," he said as he sipped it.

"One of the major industries here as I'm sure it is in your parish."

"I have found it prudent to ignore it." He sighed heavily.

"And the Ribbonmen?"

"There are no Ribbonmen in my parish."

"You surprise me, but congratulations. They do cast something of a pall over the community."

He sighed heavily.

"They still talk a lot about the late Canon do they not?"

In fact, I had not heard his name in six months.

"I'm sure he is revered."

"The fellows wonder why you don't call."

"I've been very busy here."

"They say the lord's wife bathed in Colm's well."

"I wasn't there to observe it, but I am told that she did."

"And is now with child."

"Quite."

"Does she think it's a miracle?"

"They are very happy."

He would remember my answers and propagate them around the diocese.

"You get along with him? Some kind of colonel wallah from India?"

This catechism proceeded at a slow pace, almost like an absent-minded canon was questioning a backward and unprepared student. It was interrupted as he shoveled Mrs. O'Flynn's lamb stew into his big mouth and slowly and solemnly masticated it.

"Victoria Cross, I'm told."

"Unpopular with the people, I'm sure, like all of them."

"Not as much as his agent, whom he has restrained."

"Like it here?"

"Better than Maynooth."

"Pretty drab place, worse even than mine."

"Very lively people, however. Good people when you get to know them."

"Not very good Catholics."

"I wouldn't make that judgment.

"They say you sing with them."

I wondered who "they" were.

I refilled his claret glass as he cleared his plate of the second helping.

"And play the accordion. I find it helpful to observe them when they are relaxed."

"Not much to observe, I should think. All pretty much the same—ignorant, superstitious, sullen."

"That's not my experience."

"There should be another canon in our district."

Ah, that was the real reason for his visit.

"I don't think I'm a likely candidate. The Cardinal would hardly approve."

"Cardinals change their mind."

"I have not heard of such cases."

The catechism slowed to a halt. Heavily, he rose from the table, thanked me for my hospitality, did not bother to thank Mrs. O'Flynn, and lumbered towards the door. I gave him his hat, my groom brought up his buggy, and the poor old horse trudged down the muddy road. Another line of rain clouds was moving in over the ocean.

Mrs. O'Flynn was cleaning off the table.

"You'll have to make stew for yourself and Eileen when she comes home."

"I couldn't do that, Your Reverence."

"Yes, you can and you will. It's not your fault that that awful man came just at dinnertime."

"Did he come to check up on you?"

"He came to find out whether I might become a canon. When he learned that was most unlikely he left content that his chances were good."

"Are they?"

"No."

I walked over to the church to pray that God forgive me for my anger at that awful man. Poor fellow, he thought that if he became a canon he would at last achieve happiness.

Branigan was waiting for me to report that "some people" thought the schoolmaster "too handsome."

"Mothers of the girls in his class?"

"Come to think of it, those weren't the ones."

Old biddies, I thought with notable lack of charity.

March 22, Passion Week.

"They've murdered Tim Allen." Mrs. O'Flynn shook me. "He's dying over at the Widow Cudahy's house."

"Who? What?" I struggled to wake up.

I was sitting in my parlor in front of the embers in the fireplace. I had fallen asleep while pondering a tome of Suarez in which he defended tyrannicide.

Mrs. O'Flynn was wearing a robe and a long shawl over her night-dress. She was no less attractive for being awakened in the middle of the night.

"I'll go right over," I said.

"Be careful, Your Reverence. It's them terrible Ribbonmen. They may not recognize you in the storm."

"I must take that chance, Mrs. O'Flynn."

Brave talk!

I rushed out into the dark and was driven back to the doorway by the worst wind I had yet experienced. Sheets of rain drenched me instantly. The stench of the ocean seemed just across the road. Lightning crackled in giant gashes across the western sky. Thunder bellowed above my head. Fighting the wind, I stumbled into the darkened church, found the sacred oils, then groped through the rain for the stable.

My mare was not happy to be awakened and even less happy with the saddle and bridle. At first she simply refused to venture out into the mud and rain. I tried not to push her too hard, yet we had to get to the Widow Cudahy's house before it was too late. A man's immortal soul was at stake.

Especially if one did not believe in a God who was eager to for-give.

We were able to find our way only by the grace of an occasional thunderbolt. A couple of them struck trees along our path, terrify-ing my poor mare. I tried to soothe her, with little success. Still, gallant lady that she is, she kept on.

Finally, in the distance, I saw what might be a lighted window. It could be the Widow Cudahy's cottage, which was isolated at the far end of the townland. We plowed through the muck and deep puddles. A buggy was already tied to a post in front of the house. The doctor had come first.

I eased the mare under the eave of the thatched roof to protect her from the rain, tied her to the post, and burst into the house.

"Thank God you've come, Father," the doctor said. "He's fading fast."

Tim Allen, his chest covered with blood, was stretched out on the bed. He was breathing in deep gasps. The light of death was glowing in his eyes.

The Widow Cudahy, long braids on either side of her head, knelt at the bedside, her face wet with tears. She was wearing a long robe over perhaps nothing at all. She was indeed a striking woman.

"Father Lonigan, Tim," I said, kneeling on the other side of the bed. "I've come with the holy oils."

"You're a brave man, Father Dick," he said. "But I've always known that . . . I have a lot of sins to tell."

The wind wailed more loudly, like the cry of a thousand banshees.

I nodded to the other two and they withdrew to the corner of the neat little cottage. He confessed his sins and expressed deep sorrow by the light of a wavering candle. I gave him absolution and called the others back for the anointing. He answered the prayers in Latin.

Just as I was finishing the sacrament and Tim Allen was finishing his life, Lord Skeffington burst in. He took in the scene in a glance.

"Thank God you're here, Father."

He glanced at the doctor, who shook his head in the negative.

"I'm here, Tim," he said.

"Thanks be to God, Colonel," he said. "I knew you'd come if you could."

Bobby Skeffington ought to have been back in his spousal bed with his pregnant wife. However, a commanding officer comes to the deathbed of a dying soldier no matter what.

"Who shot you, Tim?"

"I don't know, sir. A rifle in the dark."

"We'll get them."

I doubted that.

"I don't think so, sir. Take care of Marie for me, please, sir."

Skeffington seemed to notice for the first time the anguished face of the Widow Cudahy.

"She'll receive your pension, Tim, as long as she lives."

"Thank you, sir." Tim Allen smiled, then died.

He had not lived a good life, but he had received the grace of a happy death. Who had prayed for him? Marie Cudahy. Who else?

God indeed had a sense of humor, and a gentle one at that.

Lightning struck very near us. I heard my mare squeal. I must get to her and try to calm her down. Then suddenly nature, as if pleased at the graceful departure of Tim Allen, became silent. Though a few drops of rain still bounced off the cottage, the wind died out and the lightning and thunder ceased, save for a few distant rolls.

"You will grant him Christian burial, Dick?"

"I have no choice in the matter, milord. No matter how he lived, he died a good Catholic."

"Fortunate man . . . The wake at his house at my estate or here . . . ?"

"I think here would be better, milord."

Marie Cudahy looked at me in surprise and smiled faintly.

I was violating all the approved rules of pastoral practice. Still, my instincts said it was the right decision. Besides, one did not want the Ribbonmen making trouble at the Big House with Lady Skeffington only a month away from delivery.

"I'll send some of my people over to help, Mrs. Cudahy."

Outside there was the noise of more horses. The RIC doubtless.

Sergeant Kyle entered the cottage.

"Sweet mother of God!" he exclaimed.

"Indeed, Sergeant," Milord Skeffington said softly. "I trust you'll find the men who did this."

"We will certainly do our best, milord."

Bob Skeffington and I rode back together to the village. The full moon, setting in the west, seemed to have reinvigorated my little mare. At least the poor thing could see where she was going.

"He said it was a rifle shot, didn't he?"

"He did," I replied

"Who in the village would have a rifle?"

"I doubt that the Ribbonmen would. They use clubs and old pikes and the occasional revolver."

"Do you know who the Ribbonmen are, Dick?"

"Not really. They're a small and shifting group, I expect. I could guess whether a given man might be a member but I might easily be wrong."

"I'm not asking you to violate any secrets."

"All I know is what my people tell me, one way or another. They're afraid of the Ribbonmen. So they do not speak to me about them."

He nodded.

"He may have been a bad man. I will be careful about my new agent. Still, I cannot let the murder of one of my people go un-punished."

"Or at least uninvestigated."

He was silent for a moment.

"Of course . . . How deep is the hatred against us here?"

"Fairly deep but mostly passive. I have found myself thinking, however, that should there be another rising, this region could be as dangerous as the Khyber Pass."

"I have considered the same thing. Perhaps I should return to England with my wife and child."

"I doubt that you are in danger at the present . . . How is your wife keeping?"

"She's fine. I'm taking her to Dublin next week for her confine-ment. I told her about my Indian family, by the way. Her reaction astonished me."

"Ah?"

"She wept for the poor Indian woman and for me and prayed for them. Not what I expected. Mary Margaret is much more sophisti-cated a woman than I would have thought."

Her reaction was what I would have expected. Rob confused so-phistication with compassion, the latter of which most women possess in an unlimited supply.

We arrived at the parish house at dawn. Mrs. O'Flynn was waiting for us.

"Your Reverence, milord," she said, nodding her head in respect, "you both look like you need a cup of tea."

Lord Skeffington, who was always respectful of women, leaned over from his white stallion and kissed her hand.

"I need to see my wife even more, Mary Catherine. However, thank you very much."

"There will be a wake this afternoon, Your Reverence?"

"There will. Up at Widow Cudahy's house."

"And a Christian burial?"

"He died a son of the Church."

I dismounted and gave the reins to my groom, who had appeared as he always does when I return, no matter the hour of the day or night. The mare neighed in delight. A toothless man of indeterminate old age, Phelan seemed to be able to read the minds of horses.

"She's a grand little girl isn't she, Your Reverence?"

"She's all of that," I said, patting the horse's head. She neighed again.

"And what will happen to herself?" Mrs. O'Flynn asked when I returned to the house.

"Mrs. Cudahy?"

Who else?

"Yes, Your Reverence."

"Lord Skeffington promised her Tim Allen's pension. He's a man of his word."

She sighed.

"He is indeed . . . Will Your Reverence take some breakfast?"

"Maybe later. I fear I must take some sleep first."

Naps, I firmly believe, are an indulgence. However, there are times when we have no choice but to indulge ourselves.

"Would you tell the sexton to begin the digging of a grave."

"Yes, Your Reverence. I have already told folk that there will be no Mass this morning. They understand."

"What do people say about the Widow Cudahy?"

"Women are very sympathetic."

They would be of course.

My sleep was deep and troubled, though when I awoke, groggy and confused, I could remember no dreams. I suspected that Mrs. O'Flynn and Mrs. Cudahy and Mary Margaret Skeffington were confused as one person in them.

— 14 —

"THERE ARE men waiting for you outside, Your Reverence," she told me when I finally stumbled into the parlor.

I went to the door. Three bearded and unkempt fellows, solemn and somber and hats in hand, stood in poses of grim determination.

"Lynch, Joyce, Regan," I said, remembering their names.

"You'll not be burying that heathen in consecrated ground," Joyce began.

"Which heathen, Mr. Joyce?"

"You know the one I mean."

"Why don't you tell me?"

I was in truth spoiling for a fight. I would not be intimidated by these ignoramuses.

"That bastard Tim Allen."

"He got what he deserved."

"That woman deserves a horsewhipping."

"And you stalwarts from the Ribbonmen are the brave Irish patriots who will do it . . . I warn you she's under Lord Skeffington's protection."

"We're not Ribbonmen . . . We speak for the whole townland."

"I rather doubt that."

"We won't let you bury him in consecrated ground."

"I'll make that determination without seeking your advice. I warn you not to interfere with the rites of the Church. I'll read you out from the altar if you do. And as for Mrs. Cudahy, you know as well as I do that the women of the parish, no matter what they might have said about her in the past, will protect her now."

"It ain't right," Lynch grumbled.

"I'll be the one to determine what the Chuch thinks is right in this community. Now, gentlemen, I bid you good afternoon."

I slammed the door in their faces.

Mrs. O'Flynn stood behind me in the parlor.

"Well, Mrs. O'Flynn?"

"They're blatherskites, Your Reverence."

"Ribbonmen?"

"They'd like to think they are."

Later in the afternoon as I rode up to the wake, under a serene blue sky and a bright sun, I stopped at the police barracks.

"Sergeant Kyle, there have been threats to interfere with the burial tomorrow morning."

"I'm not surprised, Your Reverence."

"Lynch, Joyce, and Regan."

"That doesn't surprise me either. The real Ribbonmen would not interfere with a rite of the Holy Church. They're all good Catholics. I'll keep an eye on them fellas."

"Do you think the Ribbonmen killed Tim Allen?"

"If they didn't, it was not for want of talking about it. Still, they'd not be wanting to battle Lord Skeffington. They're afraid of him, as well they might be."

"And they don't have rifles?"

"Not as I know, Father."

"They also threatened to horsewhip the Widow Cudahy."

"Their own women would horsewhip them if they tried, not to say the real Ribbonmen."

I did not ask who the real Ribbonmen were. When the inspector came down from Belfast I didn't want to know.

It was a small and quiet wake. A couple of Rob's men stood outside, hunting guns in the crook of their arms. Inside Lord Skeffington himself, grave in his red coat and medals, and a couple of servants stood at the wall. Several women sat near the Widow Cudahy, grim and graceful in her black dress and dry-eyed. They were, I noted, the influential women of the village, including my housekeeper and her daughter.

There were tiny jars of poteen on a sideboard, but no one was drinking. Yes, a different kind of wake. I led the Rosary in English out of deference to Milord Skeffington.

"Thank you for coming, Padre," he said, shaking my hand.

"You sound like we're in the Khyber Pass."

"I feel that way."

"So you ride over in your red coat to defy the Ribbonmen?"

He smiled thinly.

"You understand the British military mind all too well, Dick."

"And that's what a V.C. looks like." I nodded at his chest.

"It wasn't courage that won it for me, Padre. It was damned foolishness."

"Threats have been made to interfere with the burial. I doubt that anything will come of it. Sergeant Kyle will have some men there."

"And I'll send some of my men . . . We'll be on our way to Dublin tomorrow."

"With an escort to the train?"

"You think it's necessary?"

"I think it would be wise."

He nodded.

"A safe trip to you and herself and a happy return."

He shook my hand firmly and smiled.

"I'm sure that it will be very happy."

I offered my hand in sympathy to the Widow Cudahy and nodded to the womenfolk. Ordinarily they would be horrified that a priest had shaken hands with a scarlet woman. However, in their collective and implicit wisdom they now expected that I would. Or should.

It was a long way from the Cardinal in Dublin.

I winked at Eileen O'Flynn, who winked back.

Her mother had not asked my permission to come to the wake. She knew that I didn't expect her to. Even if I had, she would not have asked.

Branigan stopped me on the way back to my house. Naturally.

"They don't like burying him in sacred ground, Father."

"I expect *they* don't. Nonetheless, I make those decisions. *They* don't."

"There could be repercussions."

"I'll take that risk."

When Mrs. O'Flynn brought me my tea that evening, she said, "It was good of you to come to the wake, Father."

"I was happy to see the women of the townland committing themselves to the protection of Mrs. Cudahy."

"There's none of us who think the same thing couldn't happen to us."

"Especially if they are attractive."

She didn't reply. I hardly expected she would.

It was a most unusual exchange between us. Somehow I exulted in it.

There were no untoward events at the sparsely attended burial. I took it upon myself to make a few remarks, which I was sure would be carried to the farthest ends of the parish.

"There are none of us," I said, "who do not need forgiveness and none of us who are beyond it. Jesus came to tell us about God's forgiveness—not that we had to earn it but that it was there for the asking, for the taking. At every graveside we understand forgiveness. If it wasn't for that, none of us would ever join God and Jesus and Mary in heaven. So today we pray that we will find the forgiveness that God offers us and that Tim Allen will soon enjoy the fruits of that forgiveness."

When I left the burial site, my parishioners that were there turned their heads. Good enough for them. They knew what kind of a man I was. They ought not expect that I would back away from a confrontation.

The Cardinal would have said that my words smacked of Lutheranism. I would have replied that we had preached that doctrine long before Luther.

Sean Toole shook my hand afterwards.

"Nicely said, Father. Some in the clerisy would think you spoke heresy. You and I know that you did not."

"Thank you, sir . . . I'm surprised to see you here. Did you know the man?"

"No, Father, I did not. Save by reputation. I assume that handsome woman in black is his paramour."

"The Widow Cudahy."

"And what will happen to her?"

His eyes inspected her, delighting in every detail.

I had done the same thing, almost any man would. However, I had done it much more discreetly.

"Lord Skeffington has promised her Tim Allen's pension."

"Has he now? With any encumbrances?"

"I hardly think so. He is, as you know, well married to a lovely young wife."

"Who, I am told, is with child . . . Still the English have a long imperial history of discreet polygamy with captive peoples."

"Not for a couple of centuries here."

"Quite correct, Father, quite correct . . . Is it true that His Lordship appeared at the wake last night in his full regimentals, complete with his V.C.?"

"Indeed."

"One must give them due credit for the style in their follies . . . Doubtless you wonder why I join this pathetic little group of mourners?"

"Yes."

"This is a historic event. Despite all the provocation, the Irish rarely sanction traitors from within. Perhaps because they understand the temptation."

"Perhaps."

"It will be interesting to see how the occupying power behaves as well as the people in the townland."

"They will send down a horde of constables and an inspector from Belfast who act like they know everything and in fact will know nothing. They will blame the Ribbonmen . . ."

"Who don't own rifles."

"Precisely. They will try to persuade some of the local people to give false witness. Failing that, they will go back to Belfast."

"It would be different if the lord had been shot."

"There'd be redcoats everywhere."

"Yes, indeed. That, however, is most unlikely to happen."

"I would hope not.

It was a strange conversation. I would remember it later.

I had more immediate problems.

At both Masses on Sunday, the congregation was silent during the hymns before and after Mass, Irish-language religious hymns that I had resurrected from the past. They averted their eyes from me at sermon time as I denounced refusal to forgive.

I stood solemnly outside the church after the Masses, as I usually did. No one offered to greet me, except for some of my close friends.

"They are fools, Your Reverence," Mrs. O'Flynn said.

"More likely afraid of the Ribbonmen."

"Afraid of one another. They will get over it."

"I hate them all," the good Eileen insisted. "I hate them, I hate them, I hate them."

"You didn't understand my sermon, Eileen."

"Yes, Father. I'm sorry. Can I say that I dislike them?"

"That is certainly your privilege."

Two days later the police from Belfast arrived, led by the dour, lugubrious Inspector Crawford.

The day of his arrival he called on me.

"We meet again, Reverend Lonigan."

"So it would seem."

"It is obvious that the Ribbonmen are responsible for this horrible crime."

"Is it?"

"You of course know of the Ribbonmen in your parish."

"I have heard that such a group exists. I often think they are phantoms—like the faerie."

"We have here a very real murder, Reverend. Do you seriously propose that it was committed by the faerie?"

"I rather propose that everything is blamed on the Ribbonmen, like the older folk blame everything on the faerie. That is no proof that the Ribbonmen actually exist save as a fantasy, much less that they murdered Tim Allen."

"You had problems with Mr. Allen, did you not?"

"Despite past problems, I buried him in consecrated ground."

"Your people tell you everything, do they not, Reverend?"

"They only tell me what they want me to know."

"Surely they've hinted to you who the killers are."

"They have hinted no such thing, Inspector. I am not about to become an informer for the Royal Irish Constabulary."

"They must know, however, must they not?"

"In truth, I doubt it. You will question them, of course. However, I very much doubt that you hear anything but vague allusions. You may be able to bribe some of them to perjure themselves against their enemies, but I think not. That would be very dangerous behavior in this part of Ireland."

"You know men named Lynch and Joyce?"

"Those are common names in this part of Ireland, Inspector, as I'm sure you know."

He glanced at his notebook.

"Pat Jim Lynch and Jim Pat Joyce."

"I am familiar with them."

"To the best of your knowledge are they Ribbonmen?"

"I know nothing about that. If they are, the other Ribbonmen are fools."

He closed the notebook thoughtfully.

"I am told that you are a close friend of Lord Skeffington."

"I am not sure that I deserve that honor."

"This has been a terrible tragedy for him."

"His lordship is a former military commander, as I'm sure you know."

"We wonder if he is in jeopardy here."

I sighed.

"I think not, Inspector. He is well liked here as a generous lord. His wife is adored. Many other lords here on the outer edge of Ulster might be in danger. Yet I can guarantee nothing."

"If you knew of a plot which threatened him, would you intervene?"

"I certainly would."

"Even if you learned of it in the confessional?"

"You should know better than to ask that question, Inspector."

He shrugged, put on his absurd hat, and left the parish house. Doubtless he fancied himself a stern inquisitor, a man of the law who could easily trap the superstitious parish priest. It had been simple to cope with him. I wondered if the young lad who had been listening outside my deliberately open window would report the conversation accurately.

I review in my mind a list of men in the parish who might have guns that could have been used to kill Tim Allen. I don't have one, as I do not approve of hunting—or fishing for that matter. Dr. McGrath has a veritable arsenal. Finbar Smith, the storekeeper, has an old weapon from the Crimean War which probably does not work. His Lordship possesses a whole rack of weapons that he rarely uses. I assume that Sean Toole keeps guns in his aerie up in the hills. Obviously Sergeant Kyle has access to weapons. With the exception of the sergeant and Milord Skeffington, they all have the touch of the Fenian about them, though no particular reason to want to kill Tim Allen.

There doubtless were others in the village and the townland who owned or could find weapons if they wanted to badly enough, including perhaps some of the phantom Ribbonmen. However, the parish would know about them even if they didn't discuss the subject.

The man who killed Tim Allen either was very lucky with his shot or very close to him. Tim claimed not to know who the gunman was. It did not follow that he did not know.

Tim himself carried a gun with him when he made his rounds. I wondered if anyone had searched for that weapon.

The Widow Cudahy, despite her mourning, might have grown weary of her role as a virtual slave to his lusts. She might have shot him as he was leaving the house. She did not seem like that kind of woman.

I remembered the appraising eyes of Sean Toole as he considered her at the burial. Could he have wanted her badly enough to rid the world of Tim Allen? Mystery man that he was, Toole might have done anything. However, though Mrs. Cudahy was a striking woman, there were many attractive younger women he might have sought who would have been only too happy to find a husband, even one who lived something of a hermit's life back in the hills. Yet there is no accounting for the obsessions that might afflict the male of the species.

As I well know. I have more reason than most not to yield to such obsessions, yet I know what they are like and am never certain of my will to resist temptation. The risks, I perceived, not merely a body one wants to possess but a person one wants to be with.

My speculations are futile. I know no more than I told the inspector. I don't think that, outside of the confessional, I ever will.

May 1, Feast of St. Calla, who was first a monk, then a king, and later a monk. An interesting life.

Also the pagan feast of Beltaine. I presume they will stage a bonfire in the village tonight. There is good news of life to celebrate.

The postman rode up to our village from down below this afternoon with the telegram. The message was simple:

"Richard Colm Skeffington was born this morning at 3:30. Mother and son both well—and beautiful. Skeffington."

God continued to laugh.

June 9, The Feast of St. Colm, Patron of Ireland. The real feast and not the one they celebrate sacrilegiously here.

The gosson who had eavesdropped on my conversation with the inspector must have spread a good report. The next Sunday we sang the hymns and the people endeavored to be friendly after Mass. In response I was correct and reserved. I didn't like this shunning business and intended that they would know it.

Sean Toole appeared in my study this afternoon to engage me in a strange conversation.

"I find myself in something of an awkward position, Father Lonigan."

"I'm sure you'll find a way out of it, Sean."

"For twenty years I have not needed the company of women. My past experience has inured me to that need."

"Indeed."

"Now I find that once again, I do need the company of a woman, almost obsessively. As much as I hate to admit it, I must acknowledge that I can think of nothing else."

"You are not the first one to experience such feelings."

"I suppose not . . ."

"Any particular woman?"

"Mrs. Cudahy, of course . . . There is noble blood in her surely, a countess from long ago. I am considering whether I should assume the role of her protector."

"You surprise me, Sean."

In fact he did not.

"You need not fear, Father"—he turned away and moved his hands nervously—"that I will not be both honorable and respectful in such a role."

"You love her then?"

He sat upright.

"That is not a word I have used yet, but I accept that it is not inaccurate. Surely I want her body and soul."

"Ah."

"You will say that there is no fool like an old fool."

"No, I will not say that. No age is immune to the demands of love. Or its delights."

"I suppose not."

"Nor is there anything to be ashamed of if one is attracted to a beautiful woman."

"You agree that she is beautiful, Father? I find her so but I'm concerned that my passion deceives me."

"Surely not about her beauty."

He might have asked how a priest could make a judgment about womanly beauty.

"Naturally, we have not spoken directly about it. Yet I have the impression that she does not view the matter unfavorably."

His fingers moved nervously, poor man.

"You have been courting her?"

"In, ah, a manner of speaking."

"Well, I see no reason why you should not marry her."

"Marry her! That's not what I had in mind!"

"Surely there's not another union . . ."

"No, certainly not . . . I don't want to give up my privacy . . ."

"You must certainly realize, Sean Toole, that you have already lost much of it. You cannot feel the way you claim to about a woman without having already entrusted yourself to her."

"In theory, Father, I know that is true. Still . . ."

"Moreover, do you want to have to ride from one end of the parish to another in the kind of weather we have here?"

"I had not thought of that."

He rose from the chair to pace around my room.

"At the risk of shocking you, Father, your point is that from some points of view my life would be much simpler if she were in the same bed with me instead of at the other end of the townland."

"On a more philosophical level, Sean, intimacy requires some loss of privacy."

"And love demands intimacy, is that what you're saying?"

"At least the kind of love you're experiencing."

He sighed heavily.

"I am unable to debate the point effectively."

After he left I wondered when he had begun to desire the Widow Cudahy. While Tim Allen was still alive? A man in Toole's state of emotional involvement might stop at nothing, especially if he were a lonely romantic.

Should he take her under his protection, to use his own words, or marry her, would the parish begin to suspect that he had killed Tim Allen that he might have her?

There would perhaps be murmurs that Sergeant Kyle might hear. However, that man's ability to know only what he wanted to know—not unlike mine—would prevent him from taking action, especially since proof would be hard to come by.

The fact that Sean Toole had come to Tim Allen's funeral seemed to hint that he had already taken notice of Marie Cudahy and already wanted her. On the other hand, her grief, which was both unnecessary and unfeigned, suggested that she knew of no other possible "protector."

In any event, he must *marry* her. I would see to that.

June 20, Feast of St. Phelan.

Mrs. O'Flynn made a special dinner and a birthday cake for my faithful groom.

The Belfast constables have left us, disappearing without warning. The stubborn peasants of our townland would not yield up a suspect to them, no matter how strong the enticements may have been. Sergeant Kyle, I hear, has been charged with "continuing" the investigation. That means he will continue to listen.

June 29, Feast of St. Cocca, an abbess and a Cork woman.

According to the story she made a large rock, like the one that dominates this parish, move across the bay when St. Ciaran came to visit her abbey. Of an Irishwoman, anything is credible.

Speaking of miracles, today was the festival (I can think of no other word) in honor of the birth of Richard Colm Skeffington. Gentry from Donegal and Sligo—though not from Belfast—filled the Big House and the pavilion outside. God did not see fit to send rain. Doubtless he was still laughing.

Lord Skeffington had caused a second pavilion to be erected beyond the first tent. No signs said so, but it was for the local peasants. To give them due credit, they dressed in their best clothes and behaved respectfully. Lord and Lady Skeffington mixed easily with them and displayed their son—a serene and healthy gosson—with as much pride as they had displayed him to the gentry. It was among my own kind that I first saw my name-sake.

"We had the Baptism in Dublin, Dick," Milord whispered. "I didn't want to create any problems out here."

I could hardly have baptized this young Anglican, though in truth I would have liked to.

"We must have supper soon, Father," the radiant Mary Margaret said to me. "Just us three."

Would I have been as proud of a son of my own? That was not something about which I would have thought ever since the seminary days. Now I wondered. However, it was an irrelevant question.

The Feast of St. Etain of Cork, reputed to have been a beautiful woman, like all Irishwomen who bear the name.

It is an appropriate feast for the day here in the parish. Sean Toole and Marie Cudahy married one another yesterday. Again God protected us from the rain, though the stink of the ocean was stronger than ever.

It was a strange wedding and yet not so strange at all. There were only five of us in the church, the bride and groom, Dr. McGrath and Mrs. O'Flynn, and myself. Well, six if one counts Eileen O'Flynn, who had sneaked into the church, despite, I was confident, her mother's warnings that she was not to do so. The groom was shaven and brushed and handsome. The bride wore a light blue dress. Sean was both proud of his conquest and agitated. Marie seemed happy and relieved. I had wondered how she felt about the marriage. Was she merely exchanging one form of servitude for another less heinous? However, the occasional shy and loving glances with which she took in her husband were unmistakable.

The two of them were as much in love as any couple twenty years their junior.

Mrs. O'Flynn wore a fawn-colored gown. Next to the bride she seemed almost a twin, similar handsome faces, similar elegant grace, similar generous shapes, appropriately corseted for the occasion. Both of them distracted me.

"What do the women in the parish think of this marriage?" I asked Mrs. O'Flynn when she brought me my tea, still clad in the gown she had worn to the wedding.

"They are very happy for her. It is time that she have a good husband. They stayed away from the wedding out of respect for her privacy. She knows that."

"What do you think the chances are that it will be a successful union?"

"Oh, she'll take the rough edges off him and he won't even notice it."

So much for Mr. Sean Toole.

"You looked very handsome at the service, Mrs. O'Flynn."

I had not meant to say it. I had resolved not to say it, yet I had said it anyhow.

She was not flustered.

"Thank you very much, Father."

I had a second glass of poteen before I went to bed to protect me from a sleepless night in which I imagined the things that Mr. and Mrs. Toole would do to one another in their conjugal bed way up in the hills. And then I strongly resisted the overpowering images of my undressing Mrs. O'Flynn.

— 15 —

 WE LEFT early Tuesday morning to return to Chicago. The children, who had run themselves into exhaustion through the weekend, were sound asleep in the back of the Cherokee. Mick and Nellie had class and heaven forfend that we be late for school. I thought it was a sin against nature to have school after Memorial Day. My wife opined that rules were rules.

Our Tiny Terrorist had run wild on the beach, unable to resist the urge to explore it from one end to the other and greet all the people there present.

"Me Socra Marie!"

Naturally they supplied the adoration she expected as a matter of right.

Her mother and I gave up and took turns accompanying her on her excursions. Periodically she would wheel around to make sure that we were behind her. Once when she couldn't find us, she wailed, "Ma! Da! Faerie take me way."

So I scooped her up and carried her back to our section of the beach.

"Me lost," she told her mother. "Da find me before faerie."

"There aren't any faerie at Grand Beach, Socra Marie."

She seemed disappointed.

"Me *see* them."

Monday had been the kind of hot and humid day that we could not expect till July. I inflated the big Barney inner tube and we all played in the water. Nuala took her usual long swim, though this time she remained parallel to the shore.

The rains returned on Tuesday morning, thick curtains of rain. My wife navigated the roads on the way home with firm caution. I had a hard time staying awake.

"Well what did you think of Father Dick as a detective and himself a terrible lonely man altogether?"

"I don't think he has a clue."

"Fair play to you, Dermot Michael, and yourself having a clue yourself of course?"

"I'm not sure I trust that Lord Skeffington."

"Hmnn."

"Do you?"

"I have a pretty good idea. I'll write the name down when we're home."

I had played this game before. Nuala Anne always won.

"And I don't suppose you know who ran over Rod Keefe."

"That's evident, Dermot Michael, isn't it now?"

"One of the sons, maybe."

"Maybe not."

"You'll write that name down too."

"What will I get if I'm right on both?"

"What do you want?"

"One of them big Lincoln Navigator things."

"If you want a car like that, Nuala Anne, you can buy it."

"More fun to win it on a bet."

"Do you think Father Dick will make love with his housekeeper?"

"That'd be a terrible cliché, wouldn't it now?"

At that point the angels of Nod carried me away. I woke up when we pulled to a stop in front of our house. The hounds were at the window barking happily at our return. Damian opened the door to let them bound down the steps.

"Doggies!" Socra Marie shouted enthusiastically.

Nelliecoyne and the Mick, barely awake, embraced the snow-white monsters. Then the dogs rose up on their hind feet and insisted on kissing me and me wife. All of this was done very delicately. The hounds had learned long ago how to play with us. You did not, repeat did not, knock anyone to the ground in your passionate ecstasy.

I took the older kids over to school, despite their protests, and Nuala put the sleeping terrorist in bed.

When I returned Danuta was chasing the weekend's dust and looking suspiciously for wolfhound hair. Nuala and Damian were sitting at the kitchen table sipping from big mugs of tea.

"Damian heard some bad news, Dermot Michael."

"My sister, Maura—she's a lawyer at a big firm downtown—did not make partner. We all thought she was a cinch and she worked so hard. It's a big disappointment for the whole family."

He was talking like he was a member of the family, which he was not and had not been for a long time.

"Isn't that terrible, Dermot?" Nuala asked. "And herself with a new baby."

I wasn't sure how terrible it was. However, if Nuala thought that it was terrible, then it was terrible. For the moment.

" 'Tis."

"My father says they're discriminating against her because she's a mother and punishing her for not practicing birth control."

He would say something like that.

"He also blames some of the senior partners in our parish who don't like him. He say's he'll blackball anyone they nominate for the club."

That's really getting even.

This was the same sister who had fired the public defender who would have won an acquittal for Damian.

"Were you close to Maura, Day?" my wife asked gently.

"I'm not really close to anyone in my family"—he sighed—"not even my mother. Maura is only a year older than me. So I kind of knew her better than others."

"I see."

"Dad often said that I was an afterthought and not a good thought either."

What an incredibly cruel thing to say to a child.

"What's her husband like?"

"Jim Creaghan? Oh, he's a good guy. He always treats me like I'm a member of the family, which I'm not. He works for Dad, though I don't think Dad likes him very much. He graduated from Notre Dame too."

"Do you think he'd be willing to have a conversation with Dermot?"

"Sure. He doesn't buy the family enthusiasm. Dad is angry at him because he said that it was good Maura lost partner because she wants to spend time with their new baby."

Which is the opposite of what he might say under other circumstances. When he gets around to his doublethink, that's the line he'll be peddling himself.

"I'll give him a ring and ask him. Where?"

"Can he get away from work?"

"Sure. They don't let him do too much up there."

"Where do they live?"

"Over in Wrigleyville."

"A drink at five at the Billy Goat. Tomorrow maybe."

It would be the kind of place that might fascinate a Notre Dame engineer, who might think that a drink there was kind of transgressive.

Cindy called us that afternoon.

"I have all the material I need to ask for a new trial. The state's attorney tried to give me a hard time until he saw what I had. Who the hell did run over him he asks me? That's for you and the cops to find out. The point is this kid couldn't have done it. He agrees that he won't block a motion for a new trial. I think that if the motion is granted, he may drop charges for lack of evidence."

"Sounds great!" I said.

"Nuala," she asked my wife, who she knew was listening on another line, "do you know who really ran over Rod Keefe?"

"Not to say that I could prove it."

"OK. We don't need that. Damian has to authorize me to act for him. Can you work that out?"

"Won't it take a bit of doing now, and himself so ambivalent about his family? We'll persuade him. Still."

"Good. Let me know and I'll walk over to the Daley building and file with the judge who heard the original plea bargain."

"You'll talk him into it, Nuala love?"

"I will."

So that was that.

The next afternoon I was sitting under the Billy Goat with Jim Creaghan, who did indeed think it was kind of a legendary place.

"The first thing I gotta say," he remarked as he sipped on a Diet Coke, "is that I love my wife. I don't buy all the Notre Dame shit her family pushes. I mean I graduated from the Dome and it was all right. I got a pretty good education. Not MIT or even IIT but good enough for what I need to keep track of what's going on and what the good bets are for the future and what books I should read."

"Which you probably knew before you went to college and Cal-tech would not have added to."

He laughed. "Might have destroyed my instincts you mean? Maybe you're right. I want us to hire some consultants from those places. The old man won't hear of it. Notre Dame is good enough, he says."

"Figures."

"He's not a bad engineer, a lot better than his two sons, who don't know anything about engineering or anything else. Goofuses, if you ask me."

He was about five-foot-nine and wore thick horn-rimmed glasses. He did not, however, display the pocket saver full of colored pens. His brown hair was fine and his innocent smile and twinkling brown eyes suggested a man who didn't have a clue about guile.

"Hard to work for?"

"Not nasty or mean, just dumb . . . The old man bought a company plane for them to play with—single engine Cessna Caravan, ten-seater. They painted it navy blue and gold with the words 'Flying Irish' in big gold letters on the back."

"Kind of vulgar . . . Can they fly it?"

"Sean's been cleared for instrument flying. He's working on multiple-engine flight. He's not making much progress if you ask me. I try to avoid the plane whenever I can . . . They let me do the engineering, which is not bad for someone my age—a big and important company. But we're playing catch-up now. In the computer jungle we could lose out in a year."

"That's bad."

"Sure is. They certainly have strong family loyalties. Maura and I never have serious fights anymore except when we're with them. I've learned to put up with it. Otherwise, she's the best kind of wife that a man could hope for and a great mother. When she gets over the guilt about letting her father down, she'll be happy that she can spend more time with Todd. That's what she really wants to do . . . She'd come home from work often and sob because the work was so difficult. She had the reputation down there of being a bitch on wheels. She's not, Dermot. Nothing like that at all, except when she's trying to imitate the old man. Unlike him she can't be a son of a bitch and smile at the same time."

"Not a nice guy."

He hesitated.

"He can be awfully nice so long as you buy into his idiocies. Notre Dame is the fourth person of the Trinity, but he doesn't like the black football players or the black coach. He objects to women students, who he says just want to get laid, preferably by a black football player. When the Notre Dame women were playing for the NCAA last year he wouldn't let us watch the games when we were up at their house at Lake Geneva. They were just a bunch of lesbians, he told us. The money spent on them should be spent on the football team. That was the real Notre Dame."

John Patrick O'Sullivan was a throwback to his own era and a caricature of it at that. Yet he was a logical exaggeration of the way a lot of my own generation of Domers thought and acted. Jim Creaghan had it right. It was a good school, a fine liberal arts college, though hardly the best. It was also a Catholic theme park and hence a good place to ground your faith in something besides the wisdom and authority of the hierarchy. I had flunked out because they wanted me to study and I wanted to learn. Or so I tell myself. I wasn't angry at it. I just didn't fit. As I had told my uncomprehending bedmate, I still cheered for them on gray autumn afternoons. It's in the blood. I also cheer for the women's basketball and soccer teams and the men's baseball team and any other athletic outfit which seems to do well. Go Irish, beat Stanford!

Would I want Nelliecoyne to go there in eleven more years? Sure, if she wanted to. Unlike her father, she'd cream it.

"Highly selective commitment," I replied to Jim Creaghan.

"He doesn't like me much because he says I'm not committed enough. I met Maura, you see, after I went to work there. We clicked immediately, except when I was present at family gatherings. Then there were bad vibes. I still haven't figured it out. Somehow I was not reacting enthusiastically enough. It still happens. She wonders why I don't like her family. When I try to explain, she blows up. We don't talk about it anymore, so things work out pretty well. I'm not going to give her up. The old man is telling everyone that Kate and Tom McBride are thinking of an annulment. I see no signs of this, but his fantasies have a way of coming true. I'm going to fight them, damn. They're not going to take my wife away from me."

And this nice young man could probably beat a wet paper bag but not much else.

"What role does the mother play in all this?"

"Despite what you may have heard, Dermot, she's a real witch. She oozes sweetness but pushes the kids to go along with Dad. 'It'll break your father's heart if you don't come up to Lake Geneva. Kathleen is going to be there. You know how much your father wants to keep the family together.' Maura knows I hate those weekends. Yet she caved in and joined the general attack on Kathleen for being selfish. The Missus says that the sooner that marriage is annulled the better. Sean, Patrick, and their wives agree. So does Maura. The mother says, real sweet, 'Don't you agree, Jimmy?' and I say, 'I think it's up to them.' It's like I farted in the middle of dinner. They all clam up. Maura is furious at me. She cries all the way home. The baby is upset too. I tell you, Dermot, it's all sick, sick, sick."

"And Maura changes her mind the next day?"

"Effectively. She says she doesn't think they're planning on annulment. They seem very happy."

"And you?"

"I say I think they're very happy too and that's that. Someday I'm going to have to put an end to it."

"The sooner the better."

"Yeah, I guess you're right. I don't want to risk losing her. Yesterday he was blaming me for wanting the baby and that's why she didn't make partner. An odd position for a man who's a ferocious supporter of the right to life. Today the explanation is that she has decided to leave the firm because she wants to spend more time with the baby. They all believe it, even my poor wife who does indeed want to spend more time with little Todd—though a few days ago she was dying to become a partner. The people at the plant really don't pay much attention to Jackie's reports on family. They couldn't care less. The people at the club, jerks if you ask me, know how full of shit he is. Some of them actually voted to do Maura in, maybe because they dislike Jackie so much. However, what counts is that the family, especially the mother, thinks they've sold the new line. I suppose even Maura does. When we're up there again for some goofy reason she will be talking about how hard it was to give up the law but at this point in her life Todd comes first . . . I'm sorry I'm unloading all this shit on you, Dermot. It's good to have someone to talk to . . ."

"It's all right with me."

It really wasn't. I wanted to vomit.

"You know what I said about the people at the club seeing through his shit? That's not the whole truth. Some of them, the guys that go

to Ireland with him and the ones who vote for him for president of
the club every year buy it all."

We ordered a refill on our Diet Cokes.

"Do you want to talk to me about what happened that night that
Rod Keefe was killed?"

He pondered for a moment.

"First, my wife didn't do it. She swears to me she didn't do it and I
believe her. She knows who did it and won't talk about it. I'm pretty
sure it wasn't poor Damian. Kid would never hurt a soul, even dead
drunk. He was too drunk that night to walk to the car. It was natural
enough to blame him because they blame him for all their troubles.
They're raising hell about the pictures at that Oak Street gallery. I'll
be damned if I can figure out why."

"Maura knows who the driver was?"

"I think she does. I suspect that only she and the driver know. The
others all blame Damian. Like I say he's the perfect scapegoat. Anyway, they kept him out of jail."

I didn't add that it was no fault of the O'Sullivans, his wife included,
that Damian didn't end up in jail, roadkill for the jailhouse queens.

"What was the argument about between him and Rod Keefe?"

"It was about a patent we held, a very important patent. I did the
paperwork on renewing it and gave it to Sean. He always patronizes
me. Like don't bother me with this unimportant stuff. I have my airplane to play with. I insisted that the application had to go out over
his name. All he had to do was to sign it, put it in an envelope, and
send it off. He said he'd do it, like it was a personal favor to me.
I don't think he knew what a patent was. Well, the patent expired.
Rod Keefe had a bellyful of booze in him at the Calcutta dinner and
chewed Jackie out. He said that his kids were incompetent dummies.
He was so drunk that most of it didn't make sense to anyone else.
Jackie turned on me and blamed me. I told him I would show him a
copy of the paperwork the next day and all it needed had been Sean's
signature. He continued to say that I should have made sure. Maura
began to chew me out. I was a jerk. How dare I blame her brother.

I guess I lost it with her. Then Jackie went through one of his redefinitions of the situation. It was nothing to worry about. He'd take care of it. I should bring him the copy and he'd get the patent renewed. He told Maura to shut up. She didn't know what she was talking about. That's when she stormed out of the dining room and found Rod Keefe's body. I broke up with her the next day. We got back together later."

"Mr. O'Sullivan was able to renew the patent?"

"Sure."

"Did he bribe someone?"

"No other way he could have done it. Jackie always said that there was no such thing as an even playing field. It was either tilted against you or for you. Or he'd say that there were only two kinds of people, friends and enemies, and that sometimes it took money to make sure that the friends were really friends. He lived by that philosophy."

"He broke federal laws?"

"I never asked how he did it. I didn't want to know. Another time when we beat an EPA rap, he said that there was nothing he couldn't fix from a traffic ticket on up."

"What a dangerous way to live!"

"He loved it. Made him feel powerful."

Jackie O'Sullivan was scary. He could fix an expired patent at the same time that he was arranging to send his son to jail for a crime he didn't commit. Probably he had persuaded himself that Damian was guilty. If he defined something as real, then it was real. We were playing a dangerous game against a madman. I'd have to call Mike Casey and ask him for more protection.

Jim Creaghan thanked me for listening. He caught a cab on North Avenue and went home to Wrigleyville and his beautiful and half-crazy spouse. I walked up Clark Street and tried to make sense out of it all. We now had an excellent motive for the murder of Rod Keefe. He was threatening John Patrick O'Sullivan's reputation as a brilliant CEO. He had attacked the competence of O'Sullivan's two sons. Yet, if Keefe was a dangerous threat, why kill him that night immediately after they'd had a shouting match in the dining room of the club?

His whole world might have seemed to be coming apart. He might have lost it then and grabbed the opportunity of driving over Keefe's prostrate body in the parking lot. He had been able to tilt the playing field with the cops, who probably realized that Damian couldn't possibly have driven over anyone. Then his world spun around and turned right again. He could heave a sigh of relief. He would renew the patent and Damian would finally be out of his hair. When the judge had not sent Damian to jail, he could take the line that he had saved Damian from a jail sentence.

"Those other faggots would have eaten him alive."

Did he believe all the doublethink and lies?

Probably. More or less. It might not matter. Either way he was a very scary man.

Back on Southport Avenue, after supper and after we had worried about Socra Marie crossing the street again to join her sister and brother in school ("Me look both ways" she had said in defense as she was consigned to another time-out) and after we had put the kids to bed with stories, I rehearsed for Nuala my conversation with Jim Creaghan in her office. We sat side by side on the couch, testing one another's predisposition for lovemaking. There ought to have been no question about my attitude. I was always ready for action.

She had spent the afternoon with Madame and was still wearing her beige summer suit, which established that she was in her professional mode. One of them, there are several. This one was the exhausted professional.

"The poor lad." She sighed one of her best West of Ireland sighs. The one that suggests a possible attack of asthma.

"He claims he really loves his wife."

"She must be a good fock!"

"Nuala Anne!"

"Give over, Dermot Michael! If a young man has a wife who's crazy some of the time and he stands by her, she has to be really good in bed."

"You make young men sound like predatory monsters."

"Well, aren't they now . . . I'd like to get a look at her and see if she's really sexy."

"I'm not a predatory monster!"

" 'Course, you're not, Dermot Michael. But your wife isn't crazy."

"Just a little odd. She sees halos around people."

She giggled.

"And she's a very good fock too."

"Now that you mention it."

"Well, now I know that I'm right about who drove the car, just as I know that I'm right about who shot that poor Tim Allen."

"You've filled out the prediction and filed it in the usual place?"

"Haven't I now? And am I not always right about me predictions?"

" 'Tis true."

"I'm worried, Derm love."

"About us?"

"Sure we're not in any danger and Superintendent Casey taking care of us with them Reliable Security people of his . . . No, I'm worried about them. Something terrible altogether is about to happen to them."

"What?"

"I don't know yet. Their world is disintegrating, the only world they ever knew, and that mother keeping it alive for all these years . . . Maybe she's as crazy as he is . . ."

"A *folie a'deux*."

"And we're the ones who are taking it apart."

"How so?"

"Och, Dermot, we started out trying to save poor Damian. Now we're encouraging Katie McBride in her schism. You're after warning Jim Creaghan that if he wants to keep his sexy wife, he'll have to pull her out of collective neurosis. Now we know who killed Rod Keefe . . ."

"You know."

"I'm right like I always am. Still."

"We have to be ready to pick up whatever pieces might be left."

" 'Tis true."

She unbuttoned her blouse revealing white lace, net, and swelling nipples.

Looks like another good night for Dermot Coyne.

Don't take advantage of her!

Why not? She's seducing me.

"Woman, are you trying to seduce me?"

"Would I do that, Dermot Michael Coyne?"

"You've been known to."

She relaxed sensuously in my arms.

"It's been a hard day."

She pulled the blouse out from her skirt.

"Mine too"

"I'm tired."

She slipped the blouse and bra straps off her shoulders.

"Me too."

You eejit, you're crazy with desire.

"So, sure don't we have to relax together in the shower before we go to bed?"

Ah, a grand night for Dermot. Foreplay in the shower drives him round the bend altogether.

With eager and trembling fingers I peeled off the rest of her clothes and carried her, passive and docile in my arms, to the shower. She was already groaning.

It was one those nights when the game plan, the reasons for which escape me, was to be submissive and subservient to Dermot. I had a wonderful time. So, apparently, did she.

Yet as I was falling asleep, totally satisfied with myself, I wondered what terrible things might happen to the O'Sullivans and from which we would *have* to save them.

— 16 —

"THERE'S DIVILMENT afoot, Dermot Michael, and we haven't a moment to lose."

A paraphrase from Sherlock Holmes, conscious or not.

The seductress who had turned me into a screaming maniac the night before was sitting calmly at the breakfast table in her robe, drinking from a large cup of tea and writing on a yellow notepad.

I bent over and brushed her lips.

"What's happening?"

I had taken the two older kids across the street to St. Josaphat school and brought Socra Marie along so she could see what school was like. When the bell rang and the kids, good Catholic school pupils that they were, lined up in silent ranks and marched into the school, Socra Marie grabbed my hand.

"Me no go to school, Da!"

"Not for a couple of years."

"Me no go to school, Da!"

"Fair play to you, Socra Marie."

We marched back across the street to our home, being careful to look both ways. We had put the school monster back in its place for a while.

I sat down across the table from my disheveled wife.

She looked up at me, her eyes soft with affection.

"Och, Dermot love, weren't you brilliant last night?"

It had not been a night for the waterfalls and the lake, but a night of wild pleasure.

"I'm glad to hear it."

YOU KNEW YOU COULD GET AWAY WITH ALMOST ANYTHING, SO YOU DID IT.

You bet I did.

"Sure, don't you own me altogether?"

"Only when you want me to."

" 'Tis true." She sighed loudly. Another asthma attack.

I reached under her robe and seized a breast. She pressed my hand, so I squeezed harder.

"Dermot"—she sighed—"we have problems."

"Right," I said, removing my hand and settling down for serious business.

"Damian's probation officer phoned him yesterday and left a message on his line. He wants Damian in his office out at 26ᵗʰ and California at two this afternoon sharp. There's some grave problems about his probation."

"Jackie O'Sullivan tilting the playing field again."

"Och, your man never gives up, does he?"

"So?"

"I called Cindy this morning. She'll appear as Damian's attorney. She wants Mike Casey there too and one or both of us."

"And you have your appointment with Madame?"

"I'm afraid so."

"No problem. I'll go out there and try to look like Spenser."

She smiled faintly.

"Better that you look like Hawk."

"Wrong ethnic group."

I couldn't intimidate a ten-year-old kid with a soccer ball. Blond hair, fair skin, dimples—the big lout is a pushover. Before they found out that they were wrong, it was usually too late.

"Cindy says they can't do anything unless there's a lot of proof that he's really violated the probation."

"They could make him stop exhibiting his work for a couple of months. What good would that do?"

"It would show poor Damian that his father and mother were still calling the shots."

"Would they really risk sending him to jail for, what is it, five months?"

"Four and a half. Didn't your man yesterday tell you how vicious they can be when their collective neurosis is threatened? Poor Day is essential to it."

"So they tilt the playing field and we tilt it back?"

"The pitch, Dermot Michael."

"Right!"

So at one-forty-five I met our team in the corridor outside the probation offices in the bowels of the Cook County Courthouse at 26th and California, one of the most depressing parts of the world's most depressing building.

"We'll walk in," Cindy said, "in high dudgeon, I'll introduce you gentlemen—Derm, you are a gentleman for these purposes, none of your smart-ass comments."

"I'll do my best, big sister."

"I'll demand to know why my client is being harassed. I will threaten to get an injunction against the probation officer and warn him that in court he will have to reveal the names of those who have charged my client with violations. I'll add that his job, pretty worthless now, will be gone when I'm finished with him."

"Gosh, Mrs. Hurley," Damian, all slicked up in a business suit, said. "Should we do that?"

"Damian, you have to trust your attorney. Your attorneys since Superintendent Casey is also an attorney. And, Dermot, don't correct me by saying 'former superintendent.' And we reject all suggestions that we sit down."

"I wouldn't dream of that, Cindy."

"Good. At precisely two we go in there. If his assistant tries to stop us, we just bowl her over."

"Figuratively," I said.

My sister glared at me.

I was acting like the family smart-ass again.

"Now," Cindy said, glancing at her watch.

In we went.

The young black woman at a tiny desk in the small-and-cramped outer office rose to stop us.

"You can't go in there!"

"We can and are, young woman. My client is being harassed and I intend to put a stop to it."

The probation officer, a thin, worn young white man in his late twenties, with rimless glasses and thin lips, looked up in surprise.

"You can't come in here like that . . . Mr. O'Sullivan, this is completely unacceptable."

The guy seemed exhausted. M.A. in psych from Loyola or DePaul. Try probation work. Steady job. Maybe you could do some good. Go to night school and get a doctorate. It was already too much for him.

"My name is Cindy Hurley." She slapped her card down on his desk. "I'm appearing for Mr. O'Sullivan. This is Superintendent Michael Patrick Vincent Casey, whose gallery exhibits Mr. O'Sullivan's work. And this is Dermot Coyne, who arranged for the exhibition. We are here to demand that your inappropriate and questionable harassment of Mr. O'Sullivan cease at once. To exhibit his work in a prestigious gallery does not violate his probation. Your suggestion that it might comes dangerously close to malfeasance in office. If you persist, I will go into court this afternoon to seek a restraining order against you and John Patrick O'Sullivan."

A real mouthful.

My sister is a pretty, sweet woman with a bunch of good kids and a wonderful husband. I am always astonished at the harpy she can turn into when she dons her legal persona.

The probation officer stood up, since he grasped that none of us were about to sit down. He wore neither tie nor coat and his trousers were sustained by black suspenders. If he had been quicker on the draw, he would have denied that the exhibition at the Reilly Gallery was the subject of his intended warning to Damian and further denied any knowledge of John Patrick O'Sullivan. Instead, he tried to defend the warning. He picked up a sheet of paper with trembling fingers and read from it.

"I deem it inappropriate for a man serving sentence under probation to exhibit artistic work under the pretext that he is a rehabilitated criminal . . ."

Mike the Cop cut into the reading.

"What is your name, son?"

"Martin O'Grady . . ."

"Mr. O'Grady, I too am an attorney. I am appearing for my wife, Annie Casey, who owns the Reilly Gallery. I'm sure that a threat to probation on the grounds of an art exhibition would not stand up in court. Moreover, the suggestion that we are exploiting Mr. O'Sullivan's record is absurd and probably defamatory. I would remind you that you have spoken in the presence of witnesses. If we have to go into court to seek redress, we will, of course, question you about the complaints from Mr. John Patrick O'Sullivan."

Martin O'Grady surrendered.

"What do you want me to do?" he begged.

"We want you to sign the document indicating that Mr. Damian Sullivan has kept his probation since his last meeting with you," Cindy snapped. "And we want you to remember that we have witnesses to this meeting who will be only too happy to testify in court against you should Mr. Damian Sullivan have any more trouble from this office."

He slumped into his chair, searched on his desk for the paper, found it, signed it, and handed it towards Cindy.

"Damian, you'd better take that paper."

"Thank you," he said.

We left the office.

"You were great, Ms. Hurley," Damian said shyly.

"Thank you, Damian . . . Did you come over in your Benz, Dermot? . . . Give me a ride back downtown."

"And I'll take Damian back to the Gallery," Mike the Cop said.

"My dad won't like this."

"There are some playing fields, Day, that he can't tilt."

"I guess so."

"What a nice young man!" Cindy said as we drove towards the Loop. "Why would his family want to destroy him?"

"They needed a scapegoat."

"He's not free from them, is he?"

"I don't think he ever will be, Cindy. Not while that collective neurosis operates."

"Till his parents die, you mean?"

"That won't end it."

"Well you and your gorgeous wife have at least given him something to live for . . . Have you spoken to him about our petition for a new trial?"

"No, should I?"

"As soon as possible. I have all the ducks in a row. He'll have to designate me as his attorney. We should have no trouble. An assistant state's attorney will go in with me and will agree that the motion is appropriate. Then Judge Mikolitis will ask whether his office is prepared to prosecute a new trial. He'll indicate that it's unlikely. The judge will look at the papers and take the matter under advisement. He'll rule the following week. The state's attorney will tell him that his office does not intend to press charges and that they will reopen the investigation. The judge will dismiss the charges with prejudice, which means that they can't come back into court. That will be that."

"I'll have Nuala talk to him tomorrow."

"Will he want to do it?"

"No, but herself will talk him into it . . . Will the state's attorney really reopen the case?"

"He'll have to."

"So investigators will descend on John Patrick O'Sullivan to ask questions even before he knows what's hit him."

"Depends on whether the media picks up the story or not . . . What will happen then?"

"Something crazy, you can count on it."

"Who killed this Rod Keefe?"

"I don't know. Me wife says she does."

"Is she ever wrong, Dermot?"

"Occasionally, but never in a matter like this."

"Her instincts are not legal evidence, Dermot."

"Tell me about it."

I spotted Nuala walking from the L tracks towards our house and picked her up.

"The great singer is reduced to riding public transportation."

"How often have I told you that I like to ride the L and it being a nice spring day for walking in the fresh air."

"You didn't tell me to drive on."

"And hurt your feelings, Dermot Michael?" She said slyly, "Sure, I wouldn't do that would I now. Besides I'm tired and discouraged . . . How did it go out at the courthouse?"

"We won, naturally. My sister is a real bitch when she's hammering at a witness or a malefactor."

"Tell me the details."

So I did.

"Poor kid. He should get out of the job."

"Especially since he knows he's lost his integrity."

"John Patrick O'Sullivan corrupts everything he touches, doesn't he?"

" 'Tis true."

"I'll be glad when it's over."

"You still think it will all end tragically?"

"Unless we can stop it . . . and I don't know how we can do that."

We pulled up in front of our house.

"You're tired and discouraged, Nuala Anne?"

"Altogether . . . I'll never be ready for July 4."

"Woman, you will."

"That's what you say."

" 'Tis what I know."

"Och, Dermot, you've always been right before."

"So."

She giggled.

"What if you're wrong this time?"

"You need a long nap, Nuala Anne McGrail."

"Sleep, Dermot Michael Coyne. Just sleep."

"I take your point."

The next morning Damian was attempting a difficult task, with Ethne looking on in support. After he had taken the hounds for their morning run in the park, he was trying to take a picture of them and Socra Marie with a disposable drugstore camera. The "doggies" were tired from their run and wanted nothing more than to stretch out somewhere in the shade and sleep. Socra Marie was sky-high with excitement.

"Day take picture me and doggies!"

However, she could hardly stand in one place for a single moment.

"Day paint me!"

The idea was that the two hounds would lie peacefully on the floor and Socra Marie would stand above them as if she were the ruler of all creation—with her best manic expression.

The doggies didn't like it. They shifted and stretched and tried to walk away.

"Girls!" Nuala Anne ordered.

Socra Marie hugged Maeve, who was her favorite.

"Good doggy."

Damian fired and probably got a decent picture of Socra Marie and Maeve. But he wanted both dogs in the shot.

"Would you ever stand still for a moment, Socra Marie?" her mother asked with a touch of irritation in her voice.

Her little lip curled up. She was about to have a tantrum.

"Then we'll have a dish of ice cream!" I said.

"Me love ice cream! A big dish!"

She made the "big-girl" gesture and Damian shot again.

"Perfect!" Damian exulted.

"Nice doggies!"

The hounds rushed to the back door. I opened the door. They charged into the yard. After a brief exhibition of wrestling—which neither ever won—they sank into a spot of shade and promptly went to sleep.

Ethne served up the chocolate ice cream, a small dish for everyone. After our daughter had liberally smeared her little face with chocolate, Socra Marie announced, "Doggies sleep. Socra Marie sleep too."

Damian snapped a shot of grinning chocolate-covered face.

"Last shot," he said. "It might be a good segue into humans without dogs."

"I'll put her to bed," Ethne said, knowing that we wanted to talk to Damian privately.

"I'd better take this roll to the drugstore and get it developed. I'm painting up a storm these days."

"Would you ever give us a minute or two, Day," Nuala said casually.

"Sure . . . I hope nothing is wrong . . ."

"Not to say wrong, Damian. Dermot and I are convinced that you didn't run over Rod Keefe."

His face, alight with excitement over the photos, turned grim.

"Everyone says I did."

"There never was any real proof," I joined in. "Your sister Katie has signed an affidavit saying that it is her opinion as a doctor that you had too much alcohol in you even to be able to open the door of the car. The police up there have admitted that your blood alcohol level was so high that you could not have turned over the ignition key."

"I don't drink anymore."

"That might be good policy," I continued, "but that night you couldn't have possibly run over Rod Keefe."

He had a hard time absorbing that.

"But I was convicted!"

"Not quite, Damian," I said. "You accepted a plea bargain which we believe was a travesty of justice."

"Cindy Hurley wants to reopen the case," Nuala said. "The state's attorney agrees."

"Ms. Hurley thinks I didn't do it?"

"So did the public defender whom your father fired."

"Dad said she was just seeking publicity . . ."

"She's a smart lawyer, Damian," I argued. "Much better than the bungler who wanted to send you to jail."

"I didn't go to jail."

"Only because the judge had his doubts about the whole thing."

He shook his head sadly.

"I don't want to have to go through the whole thing again."

"My sister is convinced that you won't have to. When the judge grants the new trial, the state's attorney will say that his office does not wish to pursue the case because of lack of evidence. The judge will dismiss the case."

"If I didn't run over him, who did?"

"We don't know, Damian," I replied, shaving the truth because my spouse did know.

"That's not your problem, Damian."

"What is my problem?"

"To get that felony conviction off the record."

"Why bother? I'll be off probation in less than five months."

"Because you are not a killer and that should be as clear to everyone as it is to us."

"Dad will be furious."

"He's already beside himself with fury, Damian."

"You can't let him dominate your life," Nuala urged. "You must show him that the game he has played against you for all these years is over."

"That would certainly be nice, if I could do it . . . What will it take?"

"You appoint Cindy your lawyer and show up in court when she files her motion."

"When will that be, Dermot?"

"Friday morning."

"All right. I'll be there."

He went off, I thought, with a confident step.

"We'll get the bastards, Nuala Anne. We'll get them."

"I'm still worried, Dermot Michael."

"Why?"

"Bad things might happen to them. Probably will. They'll fall apart."

The next day they did.

— 17 —

 I PARKED the old Benz (old when I first courted Nuala Anne) in front of our house and climbed out. It was a hot day. Very hot. I was tired and ill-tempered after a session with my investment adviser who wanted me to make decisions, a conceit from which he has been unable to wean himself. I keep telling him that it was his job to make the decisions. He had done well so far; I trusted him. Still we had to go through the routine of his proposing alternative strategies, my asking which he would recommend, his making a tentative recommendation, and my accepting it enthusiastically.

As I turned away from the car, I saw two big guys, both more than a little overweight, bearing down on me. They were wearing jeans and blue-and-gold Notre Dame tee shirts. Their faces were twisted in anger.

They aren't really going to do this, are they? Nuala Anne would say it was a cliché. I sighed. They probably thought, as others had in the past, that I was a pretty boy pushover.

"You Coyne?" one of them growled, presumably Sean, the elder of these two comic Irish twins.

"Who wants to know?" I demanded, playing the story according to script.

"You're Coyne all right," said the other. "We're going to give you a good thrashing."

"As opposed to a bad thrashing . . . Well, thanks for the warning."

One of them moved cautiously around behind me, while the other stationed himself in front of me, just out of my immediate reach.

"We don't like you messing around with our family," said the one in front of me.

"Ah," I said. "What family is that?"

"The O'Sullivans, as you damn well know."

I remembered with zest the time in Dublin when three thugs from the North Side set upon me and I had thrown them through a plate-glass window. This ought to be easy by comparison.

"Aren't you a little old and little out of shape for this nonsense?"

I might be accused of egging them on.

The one behind me grabbed my arms and attempted to pin them.

The other aimed a punch at my face.

I fell forward to duck the punch. He missed and landed a good solid blow on his brother's jaw, knocking him to the ground.

"Pat, you fucking asshole, you hit me."

He grabbed at my feet. I kicked him away. The other one lunged at me. I grabbed him and threw him to the ground.

Some have argued that I enjoy violence. That doesn't fit the image of Dermot, the handsome and lazy lug. Moreover, it's not true. However, I do enjoy acting vigorously in my own self-defense.

Dazed, the two of them struggled to their feet and charged me.

I pushed them away with ease.

"Look guys, I'm Hawk. If you keep this silliness up, I'm going to have to hurt you."

"Freeze!" said a female voice. "Police officer!"

It was Anna Maria, the pretty little Latina sergeant, whom Mike the Cop often assigned to protect me. She was holding a very large gun in both hands.

Sean O'Sullivan made a very bad mistake. He swung his arm recklessly in her direction and knocked the gun out of her hands. It fired and one of the windows of my house shattered.

Now, I confess, I was very angry. I knocked him to the ground, fended off his brother, picked Sean up, and knocked him down again. Then I kicked the brother in his private parts and sent him to the ground too.

Then I heard the thunder of feet on our steps and a wild yell from Celtic antiquity—two very angry wolfhounds, accompanied by my wife with her weapon of choice, a canogi stick (cross between a hockey stick and a club). The dogs pounced on the two fallen men and affixed their jaws to the throats of the brothers O'Sullivan. On a single word from my wife, they would have torn out both their throats. We had a police officer as a witness.

"Everyone all right up there?"

"You shite hawks make a single move, the dogs will kill you. They're both police dogs."

Cindasue appeared on the run, in jean shorts and a tank top. She was carrying a service revolver that was almost as big as she was.

"Secret Service. If you polecats move, I'll kill you both."

Anna Maria had recovered her gun.

"I arrest you two on charges of assault and battery, resisting arrest, and causing a gun to be discharged."

I had been saved by two tiny women cops.

"I didn't realize you were a cop, Cindasue."

"Get this dog off me," Pat said, his voice in pure terror.

"We'll report you, for this," Sean said, trying to push Fiona off him.

"I'd advise you shite hawks not to move." Nuala closed in with her canogi stick. "These dogs are very nervous."

Both men began to sob.

"Don't kill us!"

"Our father will see that you are all punished!"

In the distance I heard the sound of squad cars.

The cavalry was coming.

"I think it's safe to call off the dogs, Nuala Anne."

"Girls," she said thickly, "let go."

Reluctantly the dogs pulled back and sat on their haunches, ready to go into action again at a minute's notice. I walked over to them and petted them both.

"Good girl, Maeve. Good girl, Fiona."

They relaxed, but not much. They sat on their haunches a few feet away from the O'Sullivans, breathing heavily. Anna Maria snapped cuffs on both men and read them their Miranda rights.

"You can't do this to us. We're important people."

I glanced up the steps. The next generation was about to get involved.

"Go back, kids. Everything is fine. Commander Murphy is here with her cannon and Sergeant Cruz with her nine millimeter, and your mother with her canogi stick. You heard me, Nelliecoyne, back into the house."

The kids ascended to the top of the steps, Nelliecoyne shepherding the other two. They paused at the top of the steps to watch. It was, after all, a good show.

Five squad cars pulled up.

"Cruz," said the first cop out of the car, "what the fuck is going on?"

"Keep a civil tongue in your head, Reynolds. There are civilians present. And what is going on is that I have arrested these perpetrators for assault and battery, resisting arrest, assaulting a police officer, and causing a gun to be discharged."

"No shit . . . sorry, ladies."

I held Maeve's collar. She didn't know police like her mother did.

Fiona for her part laid her paws on the cop's shoulder and kissed him.

"What the hell . . . hey good girl, good girl."

"She's a retired Irish police dog," I explained. "She loves cops."

A spit-and-polish African-American emerged from a car.

"I'm Lieutenant Craig Scot. Can anyone tell me what's going on . . . ma'am, I hope you're not going to hit anyone with that thing."

"It's not a thing. It's a canogi stick."

"I see . . . hey, dog, I'm one of the good guys, oh you want to be friendly, well, nice dog, nice dog."

"She's a retired Irish police dog, Lieutenant. She loves cops."

"Might I ask, sir, who you are?"

"I'm Dermot Michael Coyne, Officer. I live at this address. The young woman with the canogi stick is Nuala Anne, my wife. You know Sergeant Cruz, I presume. The other woman with the howitzer is our neighbor, Lieutenant Commander Cindasue McCloud of the Yewnited States Coast Guard and the Secret Service."

"Howdy, Loot, I don't mind if you say 'no shit.' "

"These two clowns are Sean and Patrick O'Sullivan. Their father doesn't like me much so he sent them to thrash me. Sergeant Cruz is a witness. The police dog who is trying to make friends with every cop in the detail is called Fiona and this one is her little daughter Maeve. I guess that covers it."

"I'll say it now, ma'am. No shit! Howard, put these two goons in the car and take them into Area Six."

"You can't arrest us."

"We already have. You want another resisting arrest charge?"

A detective car pulled up. Commander John Culhane of Area Six emerged.

"I heard the address, Nuala Anne, and I figured I'd better come over."

Fiona went mad. John Culhane was her favorite cop in all the world. Cindasue dashed back to their house down the street. Katiesue was standing in front of the house, trailing her "blankie" and crying for her mother.

Later in our parlor over splasheens of Irish whiskey we told the whole story to Commander Culhane. Ethne, who had just arrived, herded the children off to the playroom.

"Da fight bad guys," Socra Marie observed. "Ma come with club. Katiesue ma come with BIG gun."

"They sound like real loonies," John said in disbelief.

"I want to establish, John, that I was doing just fine by myself until these five females, three human and two canine, thought they had to intervene on my behalf."

"Shite hawks," my wife said, still tense and angry. "You could have got hurt. Someone up here could have got hurt."

"I think we should warn you, John, that they come from an unusual family. Their father firmly believes that there is not a playing field in the world that he can't tilt."

He grinned.

"Not the Chicago Police Department when they've assaulted a cop."

"They're spoiled babies," Nuala Anne snapped. "Throw the book at them, John."

"And watch the playing field."

After John left, the kids entered the parlor, along with the dogs. That's a big mob.

Socra Marie was continuing her running commentary on the event.

"Bad men try to hit Da. Doggies stop them. Good doggies."

Fiona and Maeve strutted around like soccer players who have just won a match. On a pitch.

Nuala Anne embraced the two of them.

"Aren't you two wonderful? Didn't you save me husband for me? Oh . . . good dogs . . . ."

"Good doggies," Socra Marie agreed. "Save Da."

Actually both of the thugs were flat on the ground before the arrival of the cavalry and me wife with her canogi stick. And Cindasue with her cannon. I had the good sense, however, not to question the revisionism.

I relaxed on my big easy chair—Nuala and the doggies already owned the couch. My adrenaline rush tapered off, my heart stopped pounding, I relaxed and every muscle in my body ached.

How come? No one laid a hand on me!

YOU FRIGGIN' EEJIT. IT WAS A BIG FIGHT.

The kids left with Ethne. The hounds remained ensconced on the couch. My wife and I continued to cool off. I noticed the shattered window. I'd have to call someone to fix it. Sometime. Someday.

Ethne's curly hair appeared at the door of the parlor.

"Isn't your man coming over to work on the garden? Sure won't you have to tell him about his gobshite brothers?"

We both groaned.

"I knew I was in no danger when I heard you and the dogs thundering down the stairs."

"Give over, Dermot Michael Coyne! We were the reserves! You'd already finished them gobshites and themselves pushovers anyway."

" 'Tis true."

"Now come over here and hold me in your arms while I cry."

That's always a compelling invitation. In her red halter and white shorts it was irresistible. The doggies made way for me, sensing I had prior rights.

My wife's heart was still pounding, her muscles tense. I found the smooth flesh of her belly and caressed it gently. She sighed.

"Don't you know all the tricks, Dermot Michael?"

"Only a few."

She moved my hands up to her breasts and squeezed them.

"Sure, aren't you thinking you won't have to make love to me tonight?"

"I suppose I can manage it, though you do wear me out."

"We could do a preview now."

My fingers found their way under the halter to the warm, moist skin of her breasts.

"Och, Dermot Michael, wouldn't that be brilliant? But there's people in the house and dogs and kids and we have to talk to Damian and isn't Danuta making supper?"

WE'RE RUNNING A FRIGGIN' HOTEL!

I'll still get her before supper. We have to celebrate the triumph of life over death once again.

A bell rang in the distance.

"Damian . . . Go sit in the chair, Dermot Michael Coyne, like a decent husband and not a hungry ravisher."

She rearranged her halter. The dogs didn't move.

Ethne came in with Damian.

"What's wrong?"

Ethne told him.

"Didn't your two gobshite brothers try to beat up on poor Dermot this afternoon and herself and the hounds going after them!"

That was a nice, terse summary. Except I was not exactly poor.

The dogs, faced with the alternative of embracing Damian or cuddling with my wife, chose the latter. She was, after all, the alpha person in our pack.

"Dermot," Damian said, his face twisted in anguish, "I'm so sorry. They're a pair of jerks. Dad must have shamed them into it. How badly are they hurt?"

No doubt in his mind who won.

We told him, Nuala incoherently because she was sexually aroused.

'Tis a good thing for a man to have an aroused wife and before supper at that.

I must not make her wait too long.

You always have just one thing on your mind.

Wouldn't you if you had a wife like her?

Idiot! I do.

'Tis true.

"My family is imploding," Damian sad sadly. "Maura's loss, my exhibition—it's all too much for them. Wait till they find out I'm getting a new trial. I feel sorry for them. None of this was supposed to happen."

"They're not likely to find out about the trial until it's over."

"That'll be worse," he said ruefully. "Someday I'll have to try to figure out what it all means. Maybe Dad is losing it as we get older. What could he have hoped to accomplish by turning those two spoiled babies loose on you?"

"Good question," Ethne agreed.

"Well, I better get to work in the garden. Let me know how it works out in court tomorrow, though I'm sure Mom will be on the phone weeping about it and blaming me . . . Coming, guys?"

The hounds bounded up from the couch and followed him out the door.

"Now that he's earning money on his own, we shouldn't make him work on the garden," I said as I took my wife by the hand and led her upstairs.

"He loves it and besides it gives him an excuse to see Ethne."

"You approve?"

"Och, you remember what it was like, Dermot love—the boys and girls together."

"I have no recollection of that phase of my life."

I locked the door of my office—a kidproof lock I always said— stripped her, exulted in her beauty, kissed her, spread her on the couch, and made very sweet and gentle love to her.

"Dermot"—she sighed afterwards—"I don't know what I'd do if anything happened to you."

"You'd be the brave Irishwoman that you are."

"Don't think this excuses you," she announced as I helped her on with her halter, "from fulfilling your marital obligation in bed tonight. I have me rights."

"I'll do my best."

Which I did.

Before then, at supper, Socra Marie continued her account of the great fight on Southport Avenue, a battle which was now approaching Cooley's Cattle Raid in its epic dimensions.

"Bad guys shoot gun. Break window. Ma and doggies go downstairs. Doggies bite bad guys. Katiesue ma come with BIG gun . . ." the service revolver was now as big as her outstretched arms. "Me holler at bad guys. Cops come and take away bad guys."

Out of breath, she sighed.

"Big fun."

Poor Damian laughed with the rest of us.

YOU DON'T REALLY THINK YOU CAN FUCK HER AGAIN.

Why not? You saw what she looks like when she's naked, didn't you?

THAT SEEMS KIND OF BRUTAL.

She wants it.

DON'T HURT HER, YOU EEJIT.

I never have.

AND STOP THE POUNDING IN YOUR HEAD!

Can't.

— 18 —

 CINDY AND I were in the back corner of the courtroom, trying not to be too obvious. A matronly black woman was the judge. On one side were two state's attorneys, a young man and a very young woman. On the other side were the Irish cream twins, shaggy and battered, in prison clothes. They looked like they felt that they had been violated, outraged. Next to them were their father, his face, knotted in an ugly grimace, and a beautiful young woman with a glorious body and a halo of black curly hair. I could report to my wife that she was both gorgeous and sexy if now exhausted and fragile.

I WOULD HAVE VOTED TO PROMOTE HER.

Yeah, sure you would.

My wife's last words to me before we left, I for the courthouse, she for Madame's final lesson had been, "I love you more every day we're together, Dermot Michael Coyne. I love you so much it breaks my heart. You deserve a better wife than me. But I have you and I'm not letting you go."

"I think I heard that message last night," I replied. "I don't think I'm trying to get away."

"All right, Mr. State's Attorney, what do you have for me today?"

Both young lawyers bounced to their feet.

"The State *versus* Sean O'Sullivan and Patrick O'Sullivan."

"Yeah? Irish huh? The charges?"

"Disorderly . . ."

"That you, guys? Stand up!"

John Patrick O'Sullivan stood up.

"Your Honor, there's been a terrible misunderstanding."

Maura tried to sit him down. Her sexiness I guess was natural, not learned. She was probably unaware of it.

"Yeah? Who you?"

"I'm the father of these . . ."

"You their lawyer?"

"No, but . . ."

"Sit down and shut up. Now, Mr. State's Attorney, the charges if you don't mind."

"Disorderly conduct, assault and battery, assault with intent to do serious bodily harm, resisting arrest, assault on a police officer, causing a dangerous weapon to be discharged into a house—all felonies, Your Honor."

"I know a felony when I see one, young man. You two guys were a real crime wave, weren't you? . . . How do you plead?"

"May it please the court?"

The lawyer wore a gorgeous white, tailored suit, a white shirt with a dark blue tie and matching handkerchief in his jacket pocket. His long white hair was perfectly groomed. His accent sounded not so much southern but Illinois rural.

"My name is Simon Weber. I have the honor to represent these young men who have suffered a truly harrowing experience. My clients, Your Honor, have been through a horrible experience and are at present too confused to enter a plea. In their name I plead not guilty on all counts."

"Hollywood send him over?" I asked.

"Simon is one of the best criminal defense lawyers in town. He knows that this case will end in a plea of some sort and it's his job to intimidate these young people into as good a plea as possible."

"Will it work?"

"Over my dead body. I'll have a word with Simon later. Let him know that this won't be a walk."

"Bail, Ms. State's Attorney."

"Your Honor, these are two dangerous men." Her voice was soft and singsong. "You'll note that they assaulted the victim without reason and caused a shot to be fired into the victim's house. It was only by luck or the grace of God, as you prefer, that his wife or one of his three children was not hit. We ask that the bail be set at a hundred thousand dollars for each of them."

"Uh-huh, Mr. Weber."

"Your Honor, these two young men have never been charged before. They are executives of a major Chicago-area corporation. They both attended Loyola Academy with honors and Notre Dame and played on the football teams at both schools. Patrick O'Sullivan was honorable mention all-American. The incident was the result of a grave misunderstanding . . ."

"Save it for the trial, Mr. Weber. Bail is set at a hundred thousand for each." She pounded her gavel as vigorous punctuation. "Next case."

"I wouldn't want to appear before her," I murmured to my sister.

"She's a cupcake. She just doesn't like the looks of those two thugs."

In the corridor, Simon Weber spotted my sister.

"Cindy Hurley, this is an unexpected pleasure. You look more lovely every time I see you. Your children are well, I trust."

"They're fine, Simon. Thank you . . . Now let's cut the crap. I'm appearing for the victim. He'll have a lot to say during the trial . . ."

"Mr. Dermot Coyne." He extended his hand to me. "Not the famous poet?"

"I don't know how famous, sir."

"I have been following your sequence on American festivals in *Poetry*. Excellent work, sir . . . I'm delighted to see you are not as seriously injured as my two clients."

"Like I say, Simon, cut the crap. My client is a gentle, poetic soul. He was acting only in self-defense, a point I will make in the civil trial after the criminal trial."

A quick rebound by my sister, who had no idea that I wrote poems that other people, even attorneys, read.

"My dear Cindy," the words oozed out of him like sunscreen, "surely you know that there won't be a criminal trial. The state's attorney and I will work out a satisfactory plea."

"If it is not satisfactory to us, we'll be in court the next day with civil charges."

"I see . . . What might a satisfactory plea look like to you?"

"One felony charge for what they tried to do to my client, big fine, probation, couple of hundred hours of community service."

"Jail?"

"No."

"Ah, Cindy my dear, you always were one to understand the quality of mercy, even if it be strained just a little. I'll see what I can do."

"You'd better."

"And, Mr. Coyne, it is an absolute delight to meet you. I trust we can look forward to a small book of festivals in the near future?"

"I'm working on the page proofs."

"What did that all mean?" I asked Cindy, when Simon Weber glided down the corridor, oozing his charm to everyone he met.

"It meant that I feel like an idiot for not realizing that you are a famous poet."

"Not as famous as my wife."

"Regardless. It also meant that the case is as good as settled as far as we're concerned. It's a tough penalty. The cops will be satisfied and we won't make martyrs of the two goofs. If they try to mess with you again, they'll go straight to jail. We'll also have the option to seek redress in a civil suit."

"Don't think you're going to get away with this, Coyne." John Patrick O'Sullivan grabbed the designer shirt my wife had bought for me (in her endless crusade to make me chic), spun me around, and shoved his face against mine. "I'm going to nail your ass to the wall before we're finished. And we'll get that bitch of a wife of yours too."

"Dad!" Maura Creaghan begged him, "Just don't say anything more, not a word. Please. And release Mr. Coyne. You're a step away from being indicted yourself."

John Patrick O'Sullivan released me, snorted derisively, and strode away, as though he had won the encounter.

"Half a step," my sister said. "We note the threat and the gesture and reserve the right to seek redress at a subsequent date."

Maura Creaghan was even more beautiful up close. She was also vulnerable and weary, not the bitch that Minor, Grey had rejected as a partner.

"Sorry, Cindy," she murmured.

"I also note that you hired a decent lawyer for these two thugs. Not exactly what you did for your youngest brother, which was an obstruction of justice by an officer of the court. No wonder you weren't promoted. In fact you should be disbarred. I might just notice you to the ethics board of the Bar Association."

Maura recoiled like someone had punched her in the stomach. Her eyes filled with tears and she turned away.

"You certainly kicked her in the teeth," I said to Cindy as we left the courthouse.

"She deserves it . . . Do you guys know who drove over that poor man five years ago?"

"Nuala does. She always does."

"What does she want this time if she's right?"

"A Lincoln Navigator."

She laughed.

"Does she need your permission?"

"Certainly not."

"Ask her where she's going to park it . . . Does Maura know who did it?"

"I don't see how she doesn't know."

"That's accessory after the fact to murder. She should be indicted as well as disbarred."

"Don't go after her until we clear this matter up."

"Why so concerned about the bitch?"

"She has a husband and a son and has a chance of surviving what their terrible father has done to all of them."

"OK, your call. Sometimes I think you're an even better priest than George . . . And, Dermot, I'm sorry I didn't realize that you're a famous poet. Would you ever send me a copy of that book when it appears?"

"I might even autograph it."

Back at the house, Nuala, in white shorts and a green sweatshirt with a mock *Book of Kells* script that said "Nuala Anne," was busy packing for the ultimate logistical move to Grand Beach as well as "preplanning" (her word) for the trip to Ireland. She stood in the middle of chaos with a clipboard and gave directions to Danuta and Ethne, who obeyed her instructions without question. I was impressed.

Ethne would come to the Lake with us and go back to Ireland, where she would see her family again. Danuta would have the whole summer off with pay and would return to Poland to visit her family. I'm sure that Nuala Anne had provided the ticket for her flight. Also "one of dem international phone dings for Ethne" so she can stay in touch with Damian during our Irish interlude.

"I take it that Madame says you need no more lessons from her in this go-around?"

"Madame is wrong. My voice is terrible. I'm going to cancel the concert on the mall and retire."

"You're not."

"I am so . . . Ethne, will you make sure that the kids' clothes are packed for the D.C. trip. We'll just have to rush in, pick them up, then rush to the airport."

She looked up and gave me a dirty look.

"Tell me about the day in court."

So I did, imitating all the actors. My wife relaxed and laughed. Then when I told her of Cindy's harsh words about Maura, she frowned.

"She won't really do that, will she?"

"Not unless we give permission."

"I never met the woman, but I think, from what her husband says, she might have a chance. We have to save some of them, don't we Dermot Michael?"

"We do."

"There's so many bad things that are happening to them."

"Is this the worst?"

"No, no, the worst is yet to come. I don't know what it is, but it will be terrible."

"Can we save all of them?"

"No, Dermot, we can try, but it's too late. There's so much evil. Now would you ever please help me with all this stuff?"

What else does a good husband do?

"You sure she wasn't a bitch? You're not saying that just because she's attractive?"

"All attractive women tend to be bitchy," I lied, "present company excepted of course. This one might have thought she had to be bitchy, but it was probably an act to prove how tough she was."

Nuala nodded.

"Not much hope. It's all dark."

I had never found a way to join my beloved in that part of herself where she was fey. I could sympathize but only as an outsider. However, it was usually not fun.

We were due to make the season's pilgrimage to Grand Beach on Friday. The continuing heat and humidity did nothing for my wife's bad humor. I knew that she'd get over it at the Lake. And several times each day she apologized to all of us for being a "terrible friggin' shanty Irish bitch."

"Your family's house in Ireland isn't a shanty," I would say.

"You never saw the one in which I was raised."

The plan was that we were to leave early on Friday morning. Nuala and Ethne and the kids and most of the luggage would go up first in the Grand Cherokee. I would follow in my old Benz with the rest of the luggage and the two hounds.

They like riding in the car and never asked whether we were there yet. But after the first hour or so, they got kind of restless.

We had to change the plans when Cindy called to tell me that the judge would deliver his response to our motion for a new trial on Friday morning. Damian had permission from his parole officer to spend Sunday at the Lake. He'd rent a car. He agreed to come home with me after the hearing—in the Richard J. Daley Center—and give the dogs a final run before we piled them into the Benz.

The hearing was set for ten. Judge Mikolitis emerged from his chambers at ten-thirty.

"Sorry to keep you waiting," he murmured as he ascended his bench. "Something came up on another case."

The only ones in the courtroom were the young state's attorney, the judge, Cindy, Damian, the judge's bailiff and court reporter, and meself.

"I really have no choice but to grant a motion for a new trial," he began. "Obviously the new evidence is substantial. So I grant the motion . . . Mr. State's Attorney, are you going to move for dismissal?"

"Yes, Your Honor. Patently there's no evidence against the defendant."

"Well, I'll grant that motion too. You have it in writing?"

"I do, Your Honor."

"I'll issue my decision formally before the day is over. Young man, you should enjoy a happy weekend."

"Yes, Your Honor, thank you, Your Honor."

"I hope you never drink that much again."

"Yes, Your Honor."

He leaned back in his big chair.

"I really have no choice. Clearly a mistake was made in the plea bargain. I was most uneasy with it. That's why I changed the agreement from five years in prison to five years' probation. I had the sense, Damian, that your family was not happy with that change."

"I was too confused to notice, Your Honor."

Even now he was confused, hardly able to believe that his family wanted to send him to jail.

"I can't escape the impression that you might have been the designated fall guy."

"I don't know, Your Honor."

"Mr. State's Attorney, I smell in these documents the scent of obstruction of justice, malpractice, conspiracy. I suggest your office failed to smell them five years ago."

"A different state's attorney, Your Honor."

"So I understand, so I understand."

He thought for a moment.

"I assume that this case will be formally reopened."

"Of course, Your Honor. After all these years, it won't be easy . . ."

"I am aware of that fact. Patently your predecessors were delighted with a plea that gave them more than they would have ever gained in a trial and did not look too closely at the matter."

"That's not for me to judge, Your Honor."

"Of course not."

"Very well. Congratulations on your new freedom, Mr. O'Sullivan. I regret that it was denied you unjustly for so long."

"Thank you, Your Honor," we all said in chorus.

"Next case."

"Are you guys going to go after the family?" Cindy asked the state's attorney as we left the courtroom.

He hesitated.

"I kind of doubt it, Cindy. Not unless we find some more clues. After all these years. You might want to file a civil suit against the lawyer for malpractice and implicate the family. That would be kind of dicey, it seems to me."

"I just want it to be over," Damian said. "Can't we just forget about it?"

"If that's what you want, Damian, I'm your lawyer. I'll do what you say."

He thought about it longer than I expected.

"What's it that Shakespeare says, 'leave them to heaven'?"

"My brother is the poet."

"They're going through a lot of trouble now. I don't want to make it worse for them just to get even."

Cindy nodded. "Good man, Damian . . . See you at the Lake this weekend, li'l bro?"

"God willing . . . Oh, will they notify the probation people?"

"I'll see to that this afternoon."

"Thanks very much, Ms. Hurley. I'll always be grateful."

"It's been fun, Damian."

An hour and a half later as the clock in my Benz touched two, I was at last on the way to Grand Beach, wrestling with the usual early-Friday traffic.

I had called our cottage from the house, while Damian was exhausting the dogs to report total success. Nuala had cheered, so did Ethne in the background.

Behind me in the car, the hounds, exhausted from their run and presumably with their eliminatory tracts properly drained, were sound asleep, too tired even to snore.

I let the events of the last couple of days flow through my memory. In four brushes with the law, we had reversed Damian's position and thrown his crazy family into disarray.

We knew a lot more than we did back on Memorial Day. We knew that Kathleen was in the process of breaking with her family. If they ever found out that her testimony had cleared Damian, they would be furious, but there was not much they could do. They'd already pulled all the strings on her and most of them didn't work anymore. We had learned that her brothers were immature, spoiled babies over whom their father had total control, maybe in part because of manipulation by their mother. We knew that Jackie O'Sullivan was out of control and his youngest, Maura, was close to collapse, trapped between her husband and new son and the family neurosis. She probably also knew that she had obstructed justice and acted as an accessory to murder. She had conspired with her father and perhaps others to make Damian the scapegoat. Damian knew this too and he was willing to forgive.

So could not the Holmes and Watson of Southport Avenue forget about it all? Our primary goal had been to salvage Damian. We'd done that, one of me wife's more spectacular successes. Why not leave it there?

I knew the answer to that question.

Still, I posed it that night out on the deck overlooking the silent Lake, protector of how many mysteries and witness to how many tragedies.

"Och, sure, Dermot Michael, don't you have the right of it as you always do? I know something terrible will happen. I don't know how to stop it. I'll have to wait to see what happens. Maybe we can do something while there's still time."

"Shall we put off the trip to the Holy Ground?"

"Och, Dermot, I wouldn't do that at all, at all. But isn't the trouble going to happen before then? Haven't they been crumbling for a long time? We've made it a little worse by helping out poor Damian, but sure it would happen anyhow. So don't worry about it."

I didn't even think of saying the same thing to her. It would have been a waste of time. Instead, I sipped at my Irish Cream.

Why, I wondered, would the creator of the universe, the ruler of all things, the one who ignited the Big Bang, bother to communicate his wishes to a simple, Irish-speaking peasant girl from the West of Ireland, a beautiful and remarkable woman and of course my wife, but not all that special among the billions of human women who had been born on our obscure little planet?

No explanation for it, at all, at all. Yet I didn't doubt the fact.

As my brother George the Priest has said, "The Lord has something for each of us to do. If we don't do it, no one else will."

And as his sometime boss the little bishop had observed, "One does not waste one's time trying to figure out the plans of the Lord God."

— 19 —

 I'M SO tired, spiritually, morally drained. I have worked very hard and tonight, distressed as I am, it all seems a waste of time to me.

It's been many years since I added to this diary. Young Richard Colm Skeffington is almost five. He has a little sister Mary Rose. They are both handsome, healthy children. Their parents are happy too. Motherhood agrees with Lady Skeffington. His Lordship is more relaxed than ever, having left behind the memories of the Khyber Pass and the woman he loved there.

I have been too busy working to keep a diary. I play my piano sometimes once a week, sometimes less often. Eileen O'Flynn does not come to listen anymore, though she promises she will whenever she comes home from the Mercy Sisters in Galway to whom I have sent her. She loves the school and does very well in her studies. I must begin to think whether she needs university training. There is always Queens in Galway, which is becoming an excellent school.

Obviously I pay for her schooling.

When she is home she is, as they say here, half courting with my shy schoolmaster, Liam Conroy.

My daughter and my son courting! Naturally I am pleased, though I fear they will leave for America and I will be childless again. Her mother will soon follow, I'm sure. And she should. She will be hard to give up too.

I wish I could say that she is no longer a source of temptation to me. But she is. However, I seem to be able to live with that. She is also a strong support and provides excellent advice though only when I seek it.

If only she were not so wise, not so strong, not so beautiful.

The new bishop, a contemporary of mine from school days, a class behind me in college, came the other night for Confirmation. I was not happy at the prospect. He never liked me and I never liked him. I was a Dubliner, a Castle Catholic, and he a wild man from Kerry. Not unintelligent, but far too vulgar for my tastes. I did not suspect that the Cardinal had sent him to put me in my place, but I did not doubt that such a prospect was all that far from his mind.

"Holy St. Brigid, Dickie, 'tis good to see you again and yourself looking as fit as ever!"

He still had flaming red hair and equally red cheeks. To my surprise he was still trim. Bishops tend to run to fat.

He embraced me enthusiastically in front of the church.

The parish had welcomed him with an Irish hymn and sang another as we processed into church.

"Glory be to God, you've resurrected them wonderful old hymns. I thought everyone had forgotten them."

"The people here have never forgotten them."

In the parish house I introduced him to Mrs. O'Flynn.

He rose out of his chair and shook hands with her.

"You're a grand woman, Mrs. O'Flynn, and yourself keeping me old friend in such good health. Brigid, Patrick, and Colmcille we're grateful to you for that. We don't have many like him these days, a scholar and a pastor all rolled up into one fine Irish gentleman."

"Your Lordship has kissed the stone," she said, "but 'tis true enough about His Reverence. He's a fine Irish gentleman."

"A good woman," Hugh said as she left the parlor. "You're lucky to have her. Thanks be to God."

At first I was profoundly skeptical about his enthusiasm. Then I realized that he meant it and I was embarrassed.

"They've been telling me wonderful things about you and I said I believe them all, because you did all things well at school. Faith, to tell the truth, Dickie, I didn't think you would be the kind of grand parish priest that you clearly are."

"I'm not so sure about that, Hugh."

"They tell me that there are no more faction fights at the patterns."

"So far."

"And the wakes have calmed down."

"They're still quite loud."

"And there's less of the drink taken."

"I'm not sure about that."

"And that the Holy Well is not visited as often."

"I'm sure that's not true. However, the belief that water is sacred and life-giving is part of the Catholic heritage too."

"Despite what your good friend the Cardinal thinks . . . And yourself with all this work still finding time to write articles for the Spanish theological journals."

"You read them!"

"Never thought I'd read theology, eh, Dickie! Well, I do. Father Conor here," he pointed at his silent but grinning young aide, "reads them all for me, then makes me read them as he thinks will do me good."

"I didn't know you were such good friends," Father Conor said, "when I gave him your first article."

"And the Lord named his first son after you."

"Richard Colm, I don't know whether he and Her Ladyship had me in mind."

"Colm?"

"I'm afraid she bathed in the Holy Well before she conceived."

"Holy Mother of God, and yourself there?"

"The women of the parish chased all the men away. Besides I don't go to the Holy Well as a matter of principle, though I'm convinced there's no great harm in it. I hear rumors that she bathed there again before conceiving their daughter."

"The Cardinal sent you here because he thought it would break you. Instead you flourish. That'll show the old man."

"It's a terrible place, Hugh. It is damp and cold, the winds roar in from New York. That ugly rock at the end of the strand cuts off the sun many days of the year. The stench of the sea never goes away."

"Ah, well, as a man from Dingle, don't I love that smell. Still, you have brought warmth to the place and light and I've never heard confirmands who know their catechism as well as yours do and can explain it intelligently."

"They surprised me altogether," Father Conor agreed.

"Lord Skeffington sends his regrets. He's at the House of Lords these days, preparing to make a speech on the Dual Monarchy idea of home rule—two kingdoms, each with its own government, united in the same crown like Austria and Hungary."

"Well, I suppose that would work. It's the way it used to be before that infernal Act of Union in 1801."

"With some changes. Catholics would control the Irish House of Commons anyway . . . But what we need is more important than shaking free of the Castle and Westminster. We need land. My people need to hold their own land and pass it on to their children with no fear of ever losing it. The village is happy today not just because the sun is out or because a friendly bishop has come to bless them. They're happy because the crops have been good and the cattle healthy for the last several years. Yet they need to know that in bad times their land is really theirs."

"Does Lord Skeffington evict many?"

"None, but it's not the same, is it?"

"So you'd support this Land League business?"

"I would certainly be so inclined. It also has a chance of winning now, which I'm afraid home rule does not."

"You might well be right . . . Down where I was raised in the Kingdom of Kerry everyone is a Fenian."

"The next thing," I said with a laugh, "will be home rule for Kerry."

"That will be the day!"

They left in high good humor with only a splasheen of the drink taken.

I think about it today as I write these words. I do not feel like a success. Mrs. O'Flynn is particularly attractive. I am tired. There's too much to do. I have little intellectual stimulation. I'm not sure what I believe anymore.

Hughie may not be a scholar, but he's no fool and, God knows, honest. I'm sure he would write a glowing report back to Dublin, not what the Cardinal wanted to hear. Whatever else might be said of Hugh, he is an honest man. Which is to say he always reports the truth as he sees it.

The truth here, however, is much more complicated than he realizes.

My evenings at home have diminished. Dr. McGrath is fading. Sergeant Kyle still comes often, but he is a listener rather than a talker. Lord Skeffington is busy in London much of the time and when he's home he spends his time with his glorious wife, which is perfectly understandable. Sean Toole rides down from the mountain, but only because Marie makes him come. And he leaves early, so eager is he to return to the marriage bed. Well, fair play to him.

They come to Mass every Sunday and make their Easter Duty. Though they are beyond the honeymoon stage and are a bit long in the tooth for such shallow romance, they seem quite satisfied with one another and obviously happy.

"I'll never be able to thank you enough for making me marry her, Father," he says to me.

"I didn't make you, Sean."

"Marriage is a good thing," he adds as his eyes appreciatively roam over her, just as they did on the day of Tim Allen's burial.

"With the right woman," I add.

"Aye . . . Still it is a good thing altogether to have the right woman in bed with you."

"So I am told, Sean. So I am told."

And I wonder about myself.

The weather is terrible today. Though it is the middle of summer, it is bitter cold, the rain and wind batter my house, and the stench of the sea mixes with the inevitable smell of manure and turf and invades my parlor like an effusion from hell. It makes me sick in my stomach. Not even an extra jar of poteen will heal me.

Probably it will make me sicker.

Yet Liam will come to talk with me tonight and I must be in fine fettle. It is rare enough that we have our old conversations, especially when Eileen O'Flynn is home from Galway, as she is now.

He has the most drastic ideas about the future of Ireland, though they have moderated through the years of our discussion. He wants not only home rule, but complete English withdrawal, confiscation of all English-owned land, suppression of the use of the English language, and of the Protestant religion.

"Like Isabella and Ferdinand after the fall of Granada who outlawed all Muslims and Jews."

"I know it isn't practical and it will never happen. I'm just arguing that it would be the ideal."

"A harsh and impractical ideal."

He'd laugh.

"You're right, Father. Naturally. I suppose I'll grow out of it."

We will roam all over the world of intellect. He is a Catholic and always will be, but he feels free to interpret Catholicism in his own fashion. In this respect, I think, he differs from the less educated men of the village only in that he is detailed and explicit.

"Aren't we as good Catholics, Father, as the bishops and them fellas in Rome? Probably better. I'm thinking that we're the Church as much as they are. Probably more."

Properly understood, he's correct. But without nuance and qualification, his position, I tell him, would lead to religious anarchy. In fact, it has not led to anarchy here in our parish.

"And what right do you celibates have to tell a man and a woman what they may do with one another in the marriage bed? What would you be after knowing about it? I don't mean you, Father Dick. You seem to know everything about everything. Some of these men are brutes. They wear out their wives with a new pregnancy every year and a new child to watch over. And the priests tell the woman you must continue to do it."

"I don't tell them that."

"I'm not talking about you, Father Dick." He smiles gently. "You shouldn't be so defensive."

In fact, I follow the instructions of the sainted Cure of Ars, Jean Vianney, and never trouble the consciences of the laity. I wonder if that indirect advice is responsible for the slight decline in Baptisms since I've been here. I can't believe that God intends a poor, worn-out peasant woman to have nine or ten children.

Our discussions are always polite and friendly. Liam has the mind of a radical, but the sweet disposition of a novice. I will miss him terribly when he and Eileen go off to America. Please God that will not happen for a couple of more years.

"I'd never do that to my wife, Father Dick, if I ever have one."

"I imagine that eventually some woman will take on the task of taming that hot temper of yours."

"I don't have a temper, Father, as you well know. Even if I did, I could never speak in anger to a woman."

He would, of course, but the anger too would be sweet and mild.

We never mention Eileen O'Flynn in our conversations. I do not want to embarrass him. He blushes easily enough as it is. If only there were a way in which he and Eileen could attend university as a married couple. That would be unthinkable in the British Isles today. Or anywhere else, alas.

June 24, Feast of St. Rumold of Malines, a missionary and
a monk who was assassinated by two men he had admonished.

Lord Skeffington has been shot. He was returning from his speech
in the House of Lords, which drew considerable attention in the
papers up here, so it had created a sensation in Dublin as well as in
London. He was riding up from the train station in Sligo and was
shot at the edge of our townland. Already the parish is swarming
with redcoats. I'm riding over to see him immediately.

THE MANOR HOUSE WAS surrounded by redcoats, almost a troop of
lancers. I rode straight up and was stopped by an officious and in-
solent young captain.

"You can't go to the house," he ordered me. "Please leave."

"I am a good friend of Lord Skeffington as well as a clergyman.
I demand the right to see him."

"Church of Ireland?" he asked.

"Catholic!"

"Then you certainly can't see him," he sneered.

"Will you please inform Lady Skeffington that Richard Lonigan
is here to see His Lordship."

"I will not."

"Then I will wait here till you change your mind, such as it is.
I also warn you that you will lose your commission because of your
rudeness and stupidity."

He glared at me, wondering whether I might have the power to
deliver on my threat.

"A certain amount of arrogance can be very useful, Father," the
Cardinal had said to me once in his peculiar lisping voice. "You
have more than enough of it."

"Rodgers," he said to the trooper next to him, "go ask Her Ladyship if it is possible that she wants to see a Roman priest."

In less than a minute, Mary Margaret was at the doorway despite the rain.

"Captain Blair, I remind you that this is my house and our friends are not to be stopped, much less insulted. Permit Father Dick to pass instantly."

"Yes, mum," he said, touching his funny helmet.

He pulled his horse away and even saluted me.

Mary Margaret embraced me as I entered the house.

"He's going to be all right, Dick. It is not a fatal wound. The doctors are with him now. I know he'll want to see you."

Robbie Skeffington was stretched out on a wide bed in heavy bandages. His face was strained, his eyes blurred by either pain or drugs.

Two doctors were fussing over him—the indestructible Jarlath McGrath and a man in the blue uniform of an Army medic.

"Dick!" he shouted at me. "Come on in! It's good of you to come. You did say that Donegal could be more dangerous than the Khyber, didn't you? The Pathan snipers could never get me. And some raw amateur who couldn't shoot straight managed to put a bullet in my shoulder after five tries."

He sighed and his voice trailed off.

"The doctors tell me I'm going to make it. So does Mary Margaret. So it must be true."

"He was shot in the back, Father," Dr. McGrath told me. The bullet entered beneath the shoulder and emerged cleanly in front. By the grace of God or good luck . . ."

"What is that you say, Dick? It's better to have both."

"I think I said I wasn't sure of the difference."

". . . The bullet shattered no bones and pierced no vital organs. Lord Skeffington has lost a fair amount of blood. Dr. Ross and I have cleansed the wounds and are both confident of his full recovery."

"Aye," said Dr. Ross with a deep Scottish burr. "His Lordship had a close one out there in the bog. Someone was looking after him."

"It was surely my wife's prayers. She storms heaven every time I go out the door."

"And will continue to do so . . . Father Dick, will you lead us all in the Lord's Prayer which we all share. Then I'll take you to see the children."

The Scotsman winked at me, as if to say, "I'm one of you . . ."

"I apologize for all the redcoats, Father. The brigadier is a fool. Always has been. Always will be. He thinks the Fenians are about to rise again. I'll get rid of them shortly."

Dick and little Mary Rose were under the care of their nanny, a local young woman who curtsied as I entered the room. The two children had been weeping.

"Your da is fine. He's going to be all right. There's two of them in there, one Irish like your da and one Scottish like your ma. So he'll certainly be all right in a couple of days."

"We're Irish, and English, and Scottish, Uncle Dick," my name-sake said. "The whole United Kingdom!"

"You left out Wales," said the nanny.

"Mum's part Welsh."

As I was leaving, Mary Margaret gave me an envelope and a note on her personal stationery.

"Notice to all army and police: Father Richard Lonigan is a personal friend of my husband and myself. No one is to interfere with his safe passage either to our home or to anywhere else. Mary Margaret, Lady Skeffington."

"Very strong," I said, smiling.

"I'm acting the role of the colonel's lady. Brigadier Pryce-Smyth is such a troublesome man. I think he expects Robby to salute and call him 'sir.' Instead, he calls him Enoch. Isn't that a terrible name?"

"And himself not holding the V.C."

"That piece of metal has been very useful. Do come back as often as you can, Father."

"I will."

The troopers saluted as I rode away.

"Pryce-Smyth," The brigadier snapped at me. "Two ys."

I nodded politely.

"I'm responsible for the protection of Lord Skeffington and the resolution of this problem of rebellion here in Donegal."

I looked out the window.

"I'm hard put to see any trace of rebellion, Mr. Pryce-Smyth."

I was not prepared to be impressed by his fancy red coat and his elaborate epaulets.

"His Lordship was shot by a sniper."

"One sniper does not a rebellion make, especially one who, thanks be to God, is a poor marksman."

"Nonetheless, we must take every precaution . . . You are, I believe not unacquainted with His Lordship."

"I consider him a close friend."

"Very well. You will then be willing to tell me who shot him."

"How would I know?"

We were both standing. I was not inclined to ask such an arrogant officer to sit down. Besides, I wanted to make sure the gosson lurking under my open window once again could hear every word.

"You Roman parsons know everything that happens in your congregation."

"We know only what they are ready to tell us, which often isn't very much."

He sniffed.

"Do you own a weapon, sir?"

I laughed.

"No."

"Not even a hunting gun?"

"I don't hunt or fish."

"We will search house to house for the weapon if we have to."

"That might be very unwise, Mr. Pryce-Smyth. It will offend the local people and make it even more unlikely that they will cooperate with your investigation. Moreover, whoever fired that rifle has doubtless hidden it."

"Do you know who fired it?"

"That is an offensive question, sir. If I knew, I would have reported it instantly. I would add that Lord and Lady Skeffington are very popular here. If any of my parishioners knew who did it, they would certainly have told me."

"Surely you know the members of the so-called Ribbonmen."

"I do not. You misunderstand the Ribbonmen if you think they are a formally organized group. They are more phantoms than anything else, a few leaders and a larger group of hangers-on who enjoy mysterious talk and vague threats. They are not very intelligent and they have only a few weapons such as old muskets and pikes and the odd unreliable revolver."

"You will tell me who the ringleaders are."

"I have not the slightest idea."

"Not even to protect your friend Lord Skeffington?"

"I repeat that I do not know who they are."

I wondered whether if I did I would tell him. Probably not. I might tell Robbie and let him make the decision.

The brigadier slapped his immense gauntlets together.

"Very well. I wish you had seen fit to be more cooperative. I might mention that we have every intention of solving this dastardly crime."

"And I might say that I don't believe you."

He flushed. How dare this wog medicine man insult an officer, indeed a general officer, in Her Majesty's Army.

"What do you mean, sir?"

"I mean that I'm sure you know that Lord Skeffington was returning from the House of Lords?"

"Of course."

"Where he had made a very strong statement?"

"Yes . . . What does that have to do with it?"

"You know what the speech was about?"

"Something about home rule."

"A dual monarchy actually. Do you really think that Catholics in this part of Ireland would be offended by such a statement?"

"I'm sure I don't know."

"Yes, you do, Brigadier Pryce-Smyth, with a double y. Those most likely to be offended are your Orangemen up in Belfast who have their own organizations like the Ribbonmen. When you be-gin to investigate the Orange Lodges, I'll take the efforts of British military justice seriously."

He snarled and strode out of my parlor and the house.

"Not a very nice man, Your Reverence. I did not like the way he looked at me. It was not respectful."

Women can tell when men are looking at them with desire. They like it or don't like it, I suspect, depending on who the man is and what the desire implies. Does she notice my glances? What does she think of them?

"Mrs. O'Flynn, you have encountered the kind of men who, when the British Empire finally collapses, will be responsible, the men who won the great victories at Yorktown, Balaklava, and Is-landhlwana."

"Yes, Your Reverence."

A tolerant woman's response to male bluster.

Robbie Skeffington, obviously much better, was appropriately horrified by my report of the interview with someone whom I imp-ishly referred to as his "superior officer."

"The man would not last five minutes in northwest India." He laughed. "I will order him not to search the homes of the townland for rifles. He will not question anyone from Belfast. Dublin Castle does not like to offend them. They're much more difficult than your people."

"Do you recall the names of the country folk who found you and called the doctor after they had brought you back here?"

"Of course I do, Dickie, though I have denied it to Pryce-Smyth. He'd reward their good deed by punishing them. They could have left me there to bleed to death, which they might have if they thought it was the Ribbonmen. I'll reward them appropri-ately when the lancers leave."

"The sooner we rid ourselves of that horrible man"—Mary Mar-garet Skeffington sighed—"the happier I will be."

I could only agree.

I was challenged by troopers several times on my return ride.

They saluted when they saw Lady Skeffington's pass. I could do without the salutes and, nice boys that they were, I could do without them.

THE REDCOATS ARE GONE AT LAST. Lord Skeffington is riding around again though still cautiously. He travels now with a couple of bodyguards, especially at night. I don't think there'll be another attempt, though I can't say why.

Why, I asked myself, did the same man who killed Tim Allen— and I rather thought it was—kill him with a single bullet, and then miss Lord Skeffington several times and then only wound him.

The most obvious answer and probably an accurate one was that Tim had been silhouetted against the door of Marie's cottage and the killer was only a few yards away in the darkness while His Lordship was riding rapidly at night.

A more intricate answer—and hence the one that, as an Irishman, I favor—is that he deliberately missed Robbie with the first shots and accidentally hit him with the last.

I assume I'll no more know the answer to those questions than I will know the answer to the question of whether Mrs. O'Flynn is aware of the power of my desire for her. In heaven, if I make it there.

— 20 —

I AM losing my son and daughter. Mrs. O'Flynn informed me that they want to marry soon and leave for America.

"She is not pregnant, Your Reverence. I think it will be good for them to go to America. They are both too intelligent and too ambitious to remain here as much as I will miss them."

I wanted to argue that they were too young, too innocent, too inexperienced to marry. We should try to persuade them to stay. I know that was the selfish man who hid always just below my priestly surface. It would also be an insult to Mrs. O'Flynn surging up from my own pathetic possessiveness.

"If you have given the match your blessing, Mrs. O'Flynn, I can only agree . . . Do they have tickets?"

"They have saved their money to buy a ticket in steerage."

I went over to my desk, removed a twenty-pound note, and put it on the table.

"This is my wedding present for them. It is for a first-class stateroom. They should have the privacy that such a cabin provides. Mind you, it is to be used for nothing else."

"Thank you, Your Reverence. You're very generous as always."

I wanted to weep. Soon I would lose her. The young people would be successful in the New World and they'd send her passage money. She would hesitate, but I would have to insist that she go. Away from this townland which was never her home, she would find a husband easily.

THEY'RE GONE—happy, expectant, anxious. My heart is broken now, but one recovers. The wedding was an exciting event for the parish. Our handsome popular schoolmaster exchanging vows with the most beautiful young woman in the townland, indeed in the whole of County Donegal. There was a tinge of sadness, however. We did not have the "American Wake" that has been common for years when someone leaves for the United States. The mother of the bride strictly forbade it. Liam, whose respect for his mother-in-law is at least as great as her daughter's, absolutely deferred to her in all things. He was, as is customary for grooms, far more nervous than she, both at the wedding and at the mild party afterwards, and as they boarded the buggy, which would take them to Sligo, and thence by train to Galway and Cork. Their ship would sail from Kinsale, where for so many before them the last glimpse of Ireland would be the diminishing church steeple.

He knew the risks. He had been assured by his friend in New York of a place to live temporarily and a good job at a bank that needed a young man fluent in both Irish and English. But it might all collapse. They might find themselves penniless in a tenement with no hope. Yet there was no turning back.

I preached on the bravery of marriage, the great risks every couple took, the love which would, with the grace of God, sustain them in danger and bind them together no matter what troubles they might undergo.

I put my heart into it, a very heavy heart. Eileen glowed, Liam fretted. I realized how much she looked like her mother and how beautiful Mary Catherine Reilly must have looked on her wedding day. We did not mention Seamus O'Flynn, her husband, a much older man who had died nonetheless too young. It was noteworthy that his family refused to attend the wedding. Seamus O'Flynn's bride was not to be forgiven for being an outsider to the very end.

However, the Skeffingtons did come to the wedding as was only proper since Liam was his schoolmaster.

The bride's mother wept, but no more than did the mother of any bride.

The parish priest did not weep, though he ached to do so. He contented himself with thinking of all the things that might go wrong. Then we gathered at the little cottage behind the parish house to say good-bye.

"We'll see you both again," Eileen promised with the serene optimism of the very young.

"The new schoolmaster will be better than I was," Liam promised me, with a touch of guilt in his voice.

"If he's half as good, he'll still be better than we deserve."

Eileen hugged me and kissed my cheek. Liam shook my hand once more.

A soft rain began as the buggy drove away.

The parish house will be quiet for the next couple of weeks until we get the first message from New York.

FINALLY, FOUR WEEKS after they sailed, Mrs. O'Flynn received a long letter from her daughter. It was a rough voyage. They were both seasick for much of the crossing, but recovered enough to enjoy the sights of the final days. They had little difficulty at Ellis Island. The first weeks they were overwhelmed with settling in their new apartment, tiny but very nice. Liam's job was better than they had expected. He would make as much money in a week as he did all year in Donegal. She was learning to play the piano. She thought she might be pregnant.

The first phase of their adventure was complete. And we would adjust to the infrequent letters written a couple of weeks before we received them.

The terrible storms continue. We have been most fortunate in the new schoolmaster. He is older than Liam and not as popular but the students respect him.

I resume my afternoon piano exercises. Astonishingly, some of the young people come to listen.

A TELEGRAM FROM NEW YORK. They have their first child, Mary Catherine. Mother and child fine.

A LETTER FROM EILEEN. They have a home of their own, a brownstone on Eighth Avenue near the park. Lovely. The bank is very pleased with Liam. They keep promoting him. Mary Catherine, called Cathy, is smiling all the time. They have a piano and a woman comes once a week to teach her.

Their own piano? Isn't that too much, too soon? Have they succumbed to American materialism? Little Cathy's grandmother also seems uneasy.

I am worried about Liam's rapid progress. Could it be some kind of confidence game?

Other young Irishmen, less intelligent and charming than my former schoolmaster, have done equally well.

Yet I worry. I will ask Lord Skeffington to look into the bank. I should have checked with him before.

BOB SKEFFINGTON ASSURES ME that his banker in Dublin tells him that the bank is first-rate. I tell Mrs. O'Flynn and she says that it is nice to know that. She is very lonely.

The Land League campaign is gaining momentum. Michael Davitt was in our neighborhood the other day. A powerful speaker.

Lord Skeffington was on the platform with him, much to Davitt's surprise.

Boysie Lufton stopped by to see. He's on one of his mysterious peregrinations through Ireland.

"So he went to America with his bride," Boysie said as he reclined at my fireplace with a jar of poteen. "He said they'd never do it. He reckoned as the school grew bigger they both would teach there."

"He was offered a very good position in a bank and is doing well."

"Old Liam would do well anywhere." He yawned. "He shouldn't have left. Still. Stay with the troops sort of thing. The mother-in-law still sees to you, I notice."

"Until they earn enough for her passage."

"Everyone says it's a shame to waste such a striking woman on a priest. I disagree. Priests are entitled to the best. Priests and lords. Brave deserve the fair, sort of thing . . . Your man left suddenly?"

"Not really. They decided to marry rather suddenly and that was the whole story."

He promised he'd visit the next time he came through.

A LETTER TO ME from Eileen.

They have bought a first-class ticket for her mother to join them in the States. In their new house they have room for a little apartment for her. She'll love the two children. Please beg her to come.

Mrs. O'Flynn comes to me with her letter and the ticket.

"I shouldn't go," she begins.

"Woman," I say, my heart pounding, "you should."

"I can't leave Donegal."

"You must."

"What will happen to this house?"

Nice touch. What is a figure of speech which equates a person with where he lives? A metonym!

"Someone else will keep it neat, though not as neat as you have. Someone else will cook the food, though it won't be as tasty as yours. Someone else will open the door, but without the grace and charm with which you do that task."

She flees the room in tears.

But she'll go.

AFTER SEVERAL DAYS OF TEARS, she agrees that she must visit her grandchildren. If she's not happy, she will return to Donegal. In the meantime she will find a new housekeeper for me. I agree, dishonestly, that, yes, she can always return.

SHE'S GONE. I escorted her by buggy and train to Cobh and boarded the ship, a new and elegant steamer, with her luggage. In her stateroom (I had added to her ticket) I gave her an envelope.

"Now listen to me, woman. There's money in here. I've been setting it aside through the years for your pension, so it's rightfully yours. I'm sure you'll be very happy with Eileen and Liam and the children. However, this is for you if something goes wrong. It will give you independence."

She shied away like it was a bomb.

"Woman, you will! Don't argue with me!"

I slipped it into her blouse.

"Thank you, Your Reverence." She bowed her head. "You're too kind altogether."

"Not kind enough perhaps."

The whistle blew, warning me that I should leave the ship.

"There's one more thing, Mary Catherine. You're a charming and beautiful woman. Men your age in New York will find you extremely attractive. You should not refuse to respond to that emotion, so long as you have encountered a fine Irish gentleman. Do you understand?"

"Yes, Father," she said simply. "I'm sure you're right."

"Do you think Sean Toole is a fine Irish gentleman?"

"After she polished the edges off," she said with a smile.

"You remember how he looks at her?"

"Yes."

"How would you describe it?"

"Half desire, half respect, half affection."

"When you find a man who looks at you that way, he might be the one."

"So long as," she said, blushing deeply, "he's a good Irish Catholic."

"Of course."

Another warning whistle.

I take her hand in mine and hold it tightly.

"Go with God, Mary Catherine."

"Thank you, Father. You've been very good to me."

A simple gesture. Simple words. A whole lifetime of emotion. Perhaps I should have kissed her, but I think not. That might have spoiled it.

She will always be the woman of my life.

We wave to each other as the ship slips away from the wharf and rises on the tide. Ironically, her last sight of Ireland will be the fading steeple of the Cathedral of St. Colm.

I AM NUMB, drained, empty of faith, of feeling, of hope. I will recover. Someday.

I am playing the piano again. Almost magically the kids reappear as if they were waiting for me.

The new woman is excellent. Not as good as Mary Catherine was, nor as beautiful, but still excellent.

I HAD SUPPER TONIGHT with the Skeffingtons. They were eager for the latest information about "the family in New York."

"Mrs. O'Flynn doesn't write. Eileen tells me that her mum is well and happy. She says she never realized how beautiful her mother was. Eileen is also making great progress at the piano. She asserts that soon she will be better than I am."

"Do you miss them, Dick?" Mary Margaret asks.

"Of course," I say easily. "Life, however, goes on. It's the way of it."

I'm not sure that I deceived them. Perhaps I did.

ANOTHER LETTER FROM EILEEN.

"*The most astonishing thing, Father Dick, has happened. Mom is in love. And the man, who has proposed marriage to her, loves her too. He is tall and good-looking, a rich doctor who lost his wife two years ago, perhaps a year or two older than Mom. When they look at each other there are stars in his eyes. She says to tell you that he's a fine Irish gentleman, which he certainly is. There have been suitors calling on her almost since she came to New York. No wonder. She is so beautiful. I guess I never noticed. My good husband says that every man in the townland noticed. I'm so happy for both of them.*"

I send a short note to Mary Catherine congratulating her on her engagement to the fine Irish gentleman whose name her daughter forgot to mention. She responds promptly with a short note thanking me for my blessing and telling me that her husband's name is Michael James Murphy and he's from Galway.

Married so soon? Well, why not? Why wait?

It's what I've wanted for her. So why am I sad?

She is too fine a woman to be wasted on a priest.

I AM TO LEAVE THIS PARISH and Donegal. The stiff and formal Latin letter from the Cardinal makes it clear that I have no choice. I do, however. I can simply refuse. In a struggle of wills between the two of us I think I can win. He's old and infirm now. And perhaps a little dotty, which would explain the letter.

I will ride over to see the Skeffingtons tonight. Perhaps they will give me good advice.

I'M BACK from the Big House. They were as implacable as the Cardinal.

"It's grand news, Dick," Milord says. "Your man in Dublin wants someone out there that guides the Church through the Land League Wars. Who better than you?"

"And you'll get away from the smell of the ocean," Mary Margaret adds with a laugh.

"I don't want to leave," I say stubbornly.

"You really don't have any choice," Dick says patiently.

"I can simply refuse."

"All your training and experience says you cannot and will not."

His point is well-taken.

"I like it here."

"I never thought I'd hear you say that," Mary Margaret says.

"Neither did I," I admit ruefully.

"You are not going to South Australia, old man. Besides, you need new challenges."

"I feel like I'm going to South Australia."

"Tuam is what, less than a half day's ride from here . . . Well if you're too busy to see us, we'll ride down to see you."

I write a crisp note to Mary Catherine that night, only the second I've sent.

"Dear Mary Catherine,

"I'm afraid that I must leave the parish and go elsewhere. I do not want to do so, but I have no choice. I will take many happy memories with me, however. I would not have expected that when I came.

"In any event, please tell your daughter and son-in-law that I have been named Archbishop of Tuam.

"I hope all of you will keep me in your prayers.

"Richard."

— 21 —

 "IS THAT all?" Nuala asked me. "Is that how it ends?"

"It is."

"A real Irish comedy," she said with a loud sigh. "A lovely grotesque ending."

"Grotesque?"

"Och, Dermot Michael, sure it is. Poor dear man has pretty much lost his faith as well as his family and his love. He faces a life of more failure ahead and isn't he made an archbishop? There's only four of them, you know. Dublin, Armagh, Cashel, and Tuam. Dick Lonigan was one of the most important men in Ireland for the rest of his life, especially during the Land League struggles. I'll bet we'll find a lot about him in the history books."

"Why did God send him our way?"

"He probably thought it was time that the book be published."

"Would Dickie Lonigan mind?"

"Give over, Dermot Michael. If he would, God wouldn't have sent this to us. You can look up the history of the time and write a wonderful book about it, now that *Festivals* is going to press. I don't want you to be bored while we're over in Connemara."

"Yes, ma'am."

"Wouldn't it be brilliant if we could find the letters?"

"Which letters?"

"The ones between him and Mary Catherine, what others?"

"How do you know they wrote?"

"Because he didn't keep the diary any longer. He could share his feelings with her now that she was safely married and he in Tuam."

"Love letters?"

"Not to say love letters. Weren't they letters between people who loved one another and not about love exactly?"

Was she guessing? Or did she know?

Don't ask.

I won't.

We were in a private jet flying from Midway. The two of us, the three kids and Ethne sound asleep, and two of Mike Casey's people as our bodyguards, Anna Maria and Amos, the latter a huge black man who did look like Hawk. The network had picked us up in a limo at Grand Beach and was flying us to National Airport, where another limo would pick us up and, with Secret Service protection (arranged by Katiesue's ma), take us directly to the backstage of the mall concert. Then they'd drive us to National (pardon me, Ronald Reagan Washington National) and put us on the plane that would bring us back to Midway and another limo to take us back to Grand Beach. All in the same day.

Red-carpet treatment for the celebrity and her entourage, which included her supernumerary husband. The reason said celebrity demanded it was not, as she had hinted, to get back to her family and friends for the rest of the weekend. The reason was to be close to the disaster that might hit the O'Sullivans almost any time.

"Well," I said, "we haven't solved the mystery."

"Sure we have. I thought I was right before. Now I know I am. I've brought the magic envelope with me. We'll open it when the other mystery is solved."

"Which will be before we leave for Ireland?"

"Haven't I said it would?"

Damian had arrived that morning to watch the dogs while we were away and chat merrily with Ethne.

Nuala Anne had finally approved the rental of a golf cart to drive the kids around the village. A never-to-be-forgotten sight was the picture of our three ruffians and the two dogs bumping along on the golf cart. The latter had their snoots in the air like they were the monarchs of all they surveyed, traveling on their own royal coach. They had ignored the barking of other dogs and permitted any kid that was interested to pet them. The event of the summer.

Damian had filled us in on the recent events in the family.

"They found out about my new trial and are all upset. My mother phoned me and begged me to plead guilty again. She says there's a shadow over the whole family now and Dad is very upset."

"And you said?"

He had shrugged and muttered softly, "I told them that I could not be tried again and now there was clear evidence that I didn't do it. She cried and said I was breaking Dad's heart. Then she hung up on me. Same old stuff, Dermot. It still gets to me, but I'm mostly immune now, thanks to you and Nuala."

"What's going to happen to your family?"

"I don't think they'll give up. It's too late in their lives for that. They'll keep trying and finally it will pull them all apart."

"What's between himself and Ethne?" I asked Nuala. "Are they courting?"

"Not to say courting. Not yet anyway. She thinks he's the nicest boy she's ever met."

"Oh my . . . You approve?"

"Well, Dermot Michael I don't exactly disapprove."

"To get back to Donegal, did Father Lonigan know who killed Tim Allen?"

"Probably. Though he missed it. He certainly knew who had shot his friend Bob Skeffington. So should you."

"I don't."

She sighed and kissed me.

"That, Dermot, is because you are such a good person, unlike me."

"Yeah, well."

Damian was acquiring a reputation at the Lake as a storyteller. A group of kids ten and under would sort of drift over to our house late in the day when he would begin to tell stories to our three. I had listened once to a story. It was about a very cruel and wicked king, a nice young prince who was mostly clueless, and a beautiful and very tough princess. Well, the young prince organized a revolt that overthrew the wicked king and freed his beautiful daughter though there was always some doubt whether the prince was bright enough to carry the day. However, the princess sent messages through a dove to the prince to tell him what to do.

Finally, when they had won, the prince cornered the wicked king in his throne room and pulled out his sword to kill him. The king pleaded for his life, the prince hesitated, and then what do you think the princess said to him?

"Chop off his head!"

"Stick the sword into him and throw him out the window!"

"Cut him up into little pieces and feed him to the birds!"

"Lock him up in the cell where he kept the princess and starve him to death?"

"What do you think, Nelliecoyne?"

Instant answer:

"The beautiful princess said, 'Forgive him. He's old and harmless now. Let him live long enough to see his grandchildren.'"

"That's what she said all right. Why did she say it?"

"Because we should always forgive people then they'll be sorry for what they did."

"That's right . . . How did you know?"

"Because that's the way stories should always end . . . And they all lived happily ever after."

"You mean you can't live happily ever after, unless you forgive?"

"No way!"

Damian was magic, so too was my daughter. I fled the scene lest my kids see the tears in my eyes.

The plane to D.C. was on time. We were whisked over to the mall. In a rough-and-ready dressing room, my wife arrayed herself in a shimmering, shape-fitting white dress with a blue sash and a red scarf over her bare shoulders. Then with our bodyguards and the network's bodyguards and a couple of Secret Service agents we walked the short distance to the wing of the main stage.

The MC introduced her as the world-famous Irish singer, she arranged herself on a chair next to a mike and fiddled with the strings on her small Irish harp, a necessary part of every concert.

"Sure, now I'm a citizen of this country, so I'm a Yank singer or that's what they'd call me back home. I can vote in both countries, though, which is kind of nice. So tonight I'll sing some very famous American songs."

So she walked through the streets of Laredo, and mourned for the loss of Shenandoah across the wide Missouri, and celebrated dancing on a boat on the O HIGH O!

She was better than ever. Even the dubious amplification system could not hide the sound of the bells ringing out over the bogs.

And she had almost sold it all out for a job at Arthur Andersen.

The applause exploded in the night air.

"Won't I be back later with my gang?" she said as she left the stage.

"Was I too terrible, Dermot Michael?" she demanded as she hugged me, leaning away to protect her makeup.

"Best ever," I said.

"Och, aren't you the sweetest husband in all the world."

"Ma sing good," Socra Marie said loudly. Backstage everyone laughed.

"You were wonderful," the director enthused.

"Directors always say that," she snorted in my ear.

She knew she had wowed them. However, it was bad luck, if you were Irish, to admit that you'd done well.

Before her other sequence three red, white, and blue chairs were arranged next to the harp. Then, to applause that was brilliant altogether, she led the mob out—Nelliecoyne in a white dress, the Mick in a blue jacket with white slacks, and the small one in a bright red dress. The last waved at the applauding audience.

It was a big risk to let her out on the stage. There was no telling what she would do.

Nuala introduced them. Each stood up in turn, Nelliecoyne and the Mick bowed politely as they had been told to do. Socra Marie waved both arms.

"The youngest not only looks like her mother. She acts like her mother."

Nuala has been criticized for exploiting her children, a charge she doesn't understand. "Sure, I sing for them and with them all the time, why shouldn't they think that their mother can't perform with them."

Then we chugged down the Erie Canal from Albany to Buffalo at the rate of fifteen miles a day. The kids pretended to pull the barge, Socra Marie in the opposite direction. Next we celebrated the fact that it was a simple gift to be able to turn and come round right.

"The Shakers lived a very difficult life, like nuns and priests. However, they were also very happy folks. There's another song written to the same tune that says the same thing."

The kids rose from their chairs and clapped their hands and sang the chorus, "Dance, dance wherever you may be/ I am the Lord of the Dance said he." The older kids sang on key and clapped their hands at the right time. Socra Marie was a little off on both but loved every second of it.

"Now they tell me I have to do two encores. So I thought both would be Irish, just to even things out a little for the other part of my heritage, one very short, the other a little longer. The first is the Connemara lullaby. Connemara is a barren and beautiful bit of Ireland so far out that the next parish is on Long Island. It's where I'm from and I think my youngest needs a lullaby just now."

She put the harp aside, stood up, raised the level of the mike, and picked up Socra Marie up from the chair from which she was about to slip.

"Sure, wasn't this one born terrible early altogether and aren't we happy to have her and doesn't she have tremendous energy these days?"

On the wings of the wind, o'er the dark, rolling deep
Angels are coming to watch o'er your sleep

Angels are coming to watch over you
So list to the wind coming over the sea

Hear the wind blow, hear the wind blow
Lean your head over, hear the wind blow.

She rocked Socra Marie back and forth gently.

The crowd applauded gently.

"Sure you won't wake her up at all, at all. Will you hold her, Nellie, while your ma sings her last song?"

Nelliecoyne very carefully enfolded her sister in her own strong little arms.

"This is a song about a young woman who sold fish in Dublin and isn't there a statue of her in College Green right outside of Trinity College where I went to school. She died very young, of TB I think. Yet as long as there is an Ireland or there are Irish we'll sing in her memory. I'm sure somewhere with God Mollie Malone is pleased that we Yanks are singing about her. Why don't all of youse join in the chorus. Incidentally, I once sang this song for a young man in O'Neill's pub which is also near Trinity. It was not a typical Irish love story because it has a happy ending."

A clip of the Mollie statue appeared on the monitor.

So she sang, for all of America and for me, the wondrous song about Sweet Mollie Malone. You could almost see Mollie's ghost wandering through the rainy streets of Dublin.

She scooped up the little one, waved to the crowd, and shepherded the kids off the stage.

"Was I too awful, Dermot Michael?"

"Terrible altogether."

She punched my shoulder. "You're a gobshite!"

The tumultuous applause continued.

She raised her eyebrow to the director, who waved her out.

Still holding the small one, she bowed again, waved, and said, "Sure I don't deserve all that, but thanks just the same."

Did she really think that she didn't deserve it? Well, not to say yes, but not to say no either.

She knew she had been damn good.

There were hugs and kisses and congratulations backstage.

"For your hour, Nuala, we'll have ratings higher than the other four put together."

Sure enough we did.

Ethne and Anna Maria took charge of the kids. Herself clung to me as she stumbled back to the dressing room.

"Did I make too many mistakes, Dermot Michael?"

"I'm faced with a dilemma, Nuala love. If I say you didn't make any mistakes, you won't pay any attention to me, and if I say you made tons of them, you'll hit me and call me a gobshite."

"Well"—she giggled—"it serves you right for marrying an Irishwoman."

"The audience loved you."

"Sure, they did that, didn't they?"

I helped her out of her gown and into her street clothes (jeans and a Marquette sweatshirt). We collected the kids and our entourage and headed back to the airport. As we took off the mall was glowing with fireworks.

Everyone slept on the way back, except me and me wife, who relaxed in my arms as much as the seat belts permitted.

"Do you think Father Lonigan should have made love to Mary Catherine O'Flynn?" she asked me.

"Wouldn't that have been a terrible cliché?"

"Well, as His Riverence would say, some men can't help being priests."

"His Riverence" is my brother, whom Nuala always treats as though he's only one step short of the Pope. On this matter even I was willing to concede he was right.

"You put a vigorous young man out there in a place like that without any other priests around to support him and of course he's going to be obsessed. Yet he made it and that's not a cliché."

" 'Tis true."

"My fellow poet Robert Browning once wrote, 'Why else does temptation come, save that we meet it, master it, and so be pedestaled in glory?' "

The Ring and the Book," she said sleepily. "Och, Dermot Michael, why didn't you remind me to call Damian and ask about the dogs?"

She pulled up one of the phones on the side of the cabin and punched in our number.

"Well now, Damian, are you having a loud, noisy party there? . . . Thank you very much. We had fun . . . How are the girls? Exhausted? Good enough for them. Anything from your family? Well, that's good. Don't wait up for us. It'll be late."

"The dogs are exhausted and sleeping. He's heard nothing from the family, which I don't know whether that's good or bad . . . What's the matter with them, Dermot Michael?"

"Some kind of collective neurosis. Probably their father's fault."

"No, Dermot Michael, 'tis the mother. A woman with any sense would have put a stop to that early on."

Probably she was right.

Then, her world taken care of, she sighed and went to sleep, leaving me awake to ponder the various crazy things we humans do to ourselves and our offspring.

Don't let us do the same thing, I prayed to the Deity as I too slipped into the land of Winken and Blinken and Nod.

— 22 —

MARY ELIZABETH McBride was born the following week, a little early, at St. Anthony's Hospital in Michigan City. However, she didn't seem to mind the rush. Indeed she looked out at her new environment, which I had been told she could not really see, with bright and interested eyes. She also refused to let go her grip on my finger.

Nuala and I had walked over to Michiana to praise the new human among us.

"Have you heard from your family?" Nuala asked tentatively.

"From Damian of course," Katie replied. "He's coming over here next Sunday morning to see Mary Elizabeth. Suddenly Damian is grown-up. And a strange call from Maura, who sounded terrible. Dad has found out about the new trial for Damian and is doing everything he can to reverse the decision. He's still trying to tilt the playing field, like he did when he got the FAA to reverse its decision against clearing Sean for instrument flying."

"There's really nothing he can do," Tom added. "Apparently he has some very expensive lawyers working on an appeal of the dismissal. Maura is trying to tell him to forget about it. But he never forgets about anything."

"And your mother?"

"Not a word . . . She's not interested in her new granddaughter."

"How sad."

"I don't understand it."

"Who's this lovely little girl named after?" Nuala asked innocently, lifting the baby into her arms and humming the Connemara lullaby.

"My family insisted that if it were a girl baby we had to name her Madeline after my mother," Katie replied. "Tom was agreeable though he preferred Mary Elizabeth, which is a traditional name in his family. I turned stubborn and said that Mary Elizabeth it would be."

"For generations back," Tom explained, "we alternated between Mary Catherine and Mary Elizabeth. Two of my ancestors who came over from Donegal to New York and then to Chicago. They worked for a priest up there before they emigrated. We have letters he wrote them after they came to America."

"Someday we'll have to sit down and read the letters," his wife said.

"What a sweet story!" my wife said, catching my eye triumphantly.

The dead, she believed with the ancient Irish, are always with us, watching us closely.

"You see why we're involved with all this shite, don't you now, Dermot Michael Coyne?" she said as we walked back to Grand Beach.

YOU SHOULD SPRINKLE THAT WOMAN WITH HOLY WATER.

"Woman, I won't argue with you."

"'Twould do you no good . . . There's no saving those gobshites," Nuala complained to me as we turned down Royal Avenue.

The following Sunday—that horrendous day—began with me oversleeping. The day before we had played tennis and water-skied and helped the kids build a sand castle. Then, after Mass, we took them to the movies because Nelliecoyne wanted to see *Powerpuff*

Girls. She loved it, her brother pronounced it boring, and her little sister went crazy. She stood up on her seat and shouted warnings to Blossoms, Bubbles, and Buttercup as the infamous MoJo Jojo attacked them. She cheered loudly for their triumphs and screamed in horror when they seemed on the edge of defeat.

People around us tittered.

"She really loves it," a woman said to us when we left the theater.

"Me Buttercup!"

The daylong effort plus some ingenious amusements with my bed partner must have knocked me out. When I woke up, there was no one in bed with me or in any of the other bedrooms. I rushed down to the kitchen to see the whole human household in robes and the canine contingent stretched out on the floor in sound sleep. The Mick's head lay on the table as though he was trying to sleep.

No one looked very happy, except Socra Marie. She was pounding the tray on her high chair and grinning happily.

"MoJo Jojo all gone, Da!"

"Good!"

"Bad." Me wife looked at me dyspeptically. "Your daughter kept us awake all night. You shouldn't take her to filums like that."

"And wasn't it my idea that we go?"

"It was, Da," Nelliecoyne agreed, selling me out.

It would be a long hot day.

Later it was catch-up nap time. The kids were napping in the house, Ethne in her room, the dogs at poolside, Nuala and I under the big umbrella on our deck. It was one of those times that one knows one should escape the greasy heat, go in the house, clean up, and get dressed, especially since a major weather front was coming through in a couple of hours. Sullen clouds already hung over the Lake. There was no kid noise on the beach. Everyone was going home to beat the storm.

I sighed contentedly—not a Nuala Anne sigh. Rarely do hers indicate contentment, except in bed.

I was content because we were to have two more weeks of uninterrupted bliss here before we left for Ireland. To tell the truth—what I had told no one—I didn't want to go to Ireland. I just wanted to vegetate in the warmth of a lazy Chicago summer.

"If 'tis vegetation you want," Nuala would have said, "sure, you shouldn't have married an Irishwoman."

"No," I would have replied, "I shouldn't have married the Irishwoman I did."

That would have been a silly argument, which I would have lost.

ADMIT IT. YOU'LL LIKE IT IN IRELAND WHEN YOU GET THERE.

I won't like leaving here.

The portable phone Nuala had brought out on the deck rang. Answer it, Nuala.

Fiona looked up reproachfully from the pool area as if to say, "Answer it, you eejit."

I sighed, this time in protest, and picked up the phone.

"Dermot Coyne."

"Kate McBride, Dermot. My family just left. They came for Mary Elizabeth's Baptism."

"That's nice."

"We hadn't scheduled a Baptism. They had Father King drive over from Notre Dame. He had baptized all of us and all the grandchildren. Apparently they decided that he would baptize Mary Elizabeth too. Mom kept saying, if the child dies without Baptism, she'll never go to heaven. It was surrealistic. They would not, could not believe that we had scheduled a Baptism at our parish in Chicago next week. They tried to force a Baptism, their kind of Baptism on us."

"You resisted."

"Certainly. There was a lot of sobbing and shouting, but we kept saying no. The little kids wailed too. I almost agreed but Tom told them to leave our house. Father King drove back to Notre Dame after telling me I was an ungrateful daughter. The others are returning to the Michigan City airport to fly back to Chicago."

"They flew over!"

"With the five kids!"

"I'll tell Nuala and get back to you."

I woke my bride and told her the story.

"This isn't a dream, is it Dermot?"

"No."

She bounced up off the lounge.

"We have to stop them. Look at that sky!"

It was growing more ominous by the minute.

She woke Ethne to leave her in charge. We threw on shorts and sport shirts and drove the Benz at top speed to the Municipal Airport, which was just around the corner on Highway 212. A light rain was already falling when we pulled up to the terminal building. Thought it was only a small general aviation airport with no control tower, Michigan City Municipal was usually busy on a Sunday afternoon. Now only one prop plane was on the ramp. A fuel truck was pumping gasoline into it. A couple of planes were firmly tied down off the ramp and the doors of the row of hangars were closed. Above us the sky seemed more menacing than when we'd left the house— low gray clouds rushing like scared squirrels under the brown overcast.

The redwood terminal building was a small, though comfortable, waiting room with a couple of model planes hanging from the ceiling, a small television set on the Weather Channel, and comfortable chairs. The O'Sullivans filled it with chaos. The four children were wailing, their nervous mothers trying to calm them, Sean and Pat were poring over a weather map, Madge O'Sullivan was weeping softly, John Patrick O'Sullivan was pacing back and forth shouting at someone on the other side of a counter.

"Is Palwaukee open?"

"Yes, sir, it is. For two more hours."

"And it's only a half hour from here to Palwaukee. What are we waiting for?"

"We don't advise it, Mr. O'Sullivan. The overcast is very thick."

"Fuck your advice. My son is cleared for instrument flying."

"No he's not, John Patrick O'Sullivan, and you know it," Nuala intruded. "You tilted the playing field so the FAA would reverse its denial of clearance."

O'Sullivan was startled to discover her presence.

"Mind your own fucking business, you fucking whore! Come on, Sean, let's get the hell out of here."

"You'll never make it," Nuala said softly. "You'll all die, even the kids!"

There was a moment of silence after Cassandra had spoken.

I sidled over to Jim Creaghan.

"She's fey," I whispered. "She sees things. Don't let your wife and child on that plane."

He nodded, I thought reluctantly.

His wife stood apart from him with the family, clutching their child. She seemed on the verge of hysteria.

Madge O'Sullivan, a pretty, plump woman with white hair and a sweet face walked over to Nuala.

"Can't you leave our family alone?" she begged. "Haven't you done enough harm?"

Nuala repeated her mantra.

"Don't get on that plane."

"For the last time, let's get the fuck out of here."

He strode out of the door into the rain. The rest of the family straggled out after him, Sean swaggering in his windbreaker and pilot's cap.

"A much more experienced pilot wouldn't try this," said the man behind the counter. "Most of our general aviation accidents are caused by people like him. At least he filed a flight plan."

The plane was indeed painted navy blue and gold with "Flying Irish" on both sides and on the rudder. It was a Cessna Caravan, a ten-passenger utility aircraft. Good, solid, one-engine plane.

The Creaghans were lagging behind the others, arguing fiercely.

At the door of the plane, Jim wrenched Todd out of his wife's arms and turned away. Hesitantly, she followed him. Her father's bulk appeared in the door. He shouted at her, though we couldn't hear what he said. Maura looked at her husband's back and her father's face, then slowly followed her husband.

"Thanks be to God! We saved *them* anyway."

They walked slowly back to the terminal. Jim returned the wailing babe to his wife's arms. They walked into the building.

The Cessna taxied out to the runway, turned around smartly, and took off. Almost immediately it disappeared into the dark brown overcast.

"They're nuts," I whispered to my wife.

She nodded solemnly.

"The children, Dermot, think of the children."

"You're Nuala Anne, aren't you?" Maura asked my wife.

"'Tis me name."

"Would you hold my little boy for a moment and sing that wonderful lullaby? I'm afraid we upset him."

So she did.

We then drove the Creaghans back to the McBride house in Michiana.

"Are they really going to die, Nuala Anne?" Maura asked after we dropped them off.

"Please God, no, but they're after taking a terrible chance."

"You don't have to be fey, Dermot Michael," she said to me, "to know that eejit can't fly that plane over Lake Michigan tonight."

Later we turned on the ten o'clock news on Channel 6 with foreboding.

The empty-headed blonde who was the weekend anchor and managed always to be upbeat no matter what brutal crimes she was reporting began with special joy.

"We have breaking news. A private jet airplane carrying thirteen people from Michigan City to the Palwaukee airport north of Chicago has disappeared from the radar screen over Lake Michigan. Residents on Lake Shore Drive at Fullerton reported a loud explosion at nine forty-five. We have a news team on the way to the site. Preliminary reports are that the plane was owned by the O'Sullivan Electronics Company in Northfield. We will have more on this breaking story later in the broadcast."

Nuala and I said nothing for several minutes as the anchors, the sports reporter, and the weatherwoman, played their game of happy little jokes.

"The children, Dermot," she said. "The poor children and their lives just beginning."

"You did all you could, Nuala. You saved the Creaghans."

"The mark of death was on all of them when they got into that plane."

"God will take care of them."

"He'll have to, won't he now?"

"Shall we go over there?"

"I don't think so, Dermot. Cassandra has never been popular."

"Our reporter Arleigh McGurk is at Fullerton and Lake Shore Drive. Arleigh, what is happening up there?"

Arleigh was a fresh-paced punk, just out of journalism school. Dressed in yellow oilskins, which created a nice effect, he was delighted with this triumph for a Sunday-night beat reporter.

"It would seem, Zenia, that there is a major tragedy in the making up here. Five children were on the plane, which took off from the Michigan City airport three hours ago for the half hour flight to Palwaukee airport north of Chicago. The plane was lost for several hours in the heavy overcast. However, it finally established contact with ground control at Palwaukee and was on distant approach. Then it disappeared off the radar screen and apparently crashed just offshore here. Chicago police boats are already searching for survivors. Police and Coast Guard helicopters are circling overhead. There is speculation here that the pilot became disoriented because he could not see the horizon."

The camera cut from McGurk's pretty face to the black Lake. Searchlights were probing in the darkness.

Back to McGurk and an African-American Chicago cop.

"We have here Sergeant Ron Stagg of the CPD maritime unit. Sergeant Stagg, is it true you've found wreckage?"

"Yes it is, uh, Arleigh. Also a body."

"A body!"

"Yes. Of a pretty little blond girl. We are conducting an intensive search for survivors. The weather is hampering our search as you can see."

"Thank you, Sergeant. Now back to you, Zenia."

Arleigh was ecstatic over his scoop. The cop looked like he might cry.

"Sergeant," Zenia bubbled, "do you have any comment at this early point in the investigation?"

"We're not investigators, ma'am. They'll come later. My only comment is that a man has no business flying a plane over the Lake with kids in it on a night like this."

At the end of the program, they switched back to the "site of the tragedy."

"With us now is a survivor of the family in the plane crash here off Fullerton Avenue, Mr. Dominique O'Sullivan."

"Damian."

"Mr. O'Sullivan, how did you survive the crash?"

"I wasn't on the plane. I was here in Chicago. I live right around the corner. I came down to see what happened."

Damian was emotionally exhausted but in firm control. I would have slugged Arleigh McJerk.

"Is it true there were thirteen people on the plane?"

He made it sound like an accusation.

"No, sir. I have just spoken with my sister Maura Creaghan. She and her husband and son are still in Michiana. They did not return on the plane."

"So there were only ten?"

"Yes, sir."

"Are you certain that was the number?"

"I am not certain of anything."

"So you have lost your whole family in this tragedy."

"No, my two sisters, Maura Creaghan and Kathleen McBride, are still alive."

"It still must be a heavy loss."

"Tell me about it."

"Thank you, Dominque. Zenia, we've just heard from Dominique

Sullivan, whose whole family including five children has apparently been wiped out in this tragic accident."

"Unbelievable," Nuala said. "They never learn, do they?"

Zenia was back on the screen.

"Dominique do you have any regrets about not dying with the rest of your family?"

"Well, as I said, my two sisters and their husbands and children are still alive. I'm sad about the loss, but glad I'm still alive."

"Cindy is driving tomorrow morning. Do you think we ought let Ethne go in with her?"

"Damian will need a lot of support, though he was brilliant altogether with them media eejits."

"Sure. I'll call Cindy."

"Does Ethne know yet, Derm?" my sister asked.

"She's sound asleep. We'll tell her when she wakes up."

"Is there a romance there?"

"Not yet. They're both grown-ups. They won't charge into anything. Herself isn't betting against it."

"Damian is older than you were when you chased after that gorgeous Irish witch of yours."

"It was the other way around. She came here, I didn't go there."

Nuala of course had listened in on another phone.

"I never chased after you! I just indicated my availability! And wasn't I the lucky one in finding you?"

It was still "be-nice-to-Dermot" time.

Kate McBride called us and begged us to come over. We did. Maura was on the phone talking to Damian.

"Oh, Nuala Anne is here with her husband."

"He wants to talk to you, Dermot."

"I still can't believe it, Dermot," he began. "All the little kids . . ."

"You've done well so far with the idiots, Day. Keep it up. My sister and Ethne will return to back you up."

"Good, I need backup. And, Dermot, Maura spent ten minutes begging for forgiveness. She can't believe that I said I did forgive her."

"She'll be all right, Day. She was almost on the plane."

"Nuala?"

"Who else?"

"May I speak to her?"

We stayed around with the bereaved. We Irish are good at that.

On the way home, herself said to me, "Sure aren't those two women devastated and themselves also relieved that it is all over."

We stayed up all night watching the news.

The eejits still saying that there were seventeen dead.

Until a tiny woman in white Coast Guard summer fatigues appeared with two and half bars sewed on her lapel.

"Have you found any other bodies, Commander?"

"Only another little girl, clutching her dolly."

"You'll have to find fifteen others, won't you?"

"Nossir. We'uns a finding only eight more bodies. John Patrick O'Sullivan, his wife Madeline, and their sons Sean and Patrick and their wives, and four children. Three members of the O'Sullivan family were not on the plane."

She allowed her rich mountain country speech to creep in.

"Down to Stinkin' Crek, West Virgina, where I come from, happen this kind of thing, folks'd be saying the man a polecat that takes them kind of risk."

"What mistakes did Sean O'Sullivan make?"

"A takin' off."

"Some pilots are saying that he was disoriented by the overcast."

"Happen that's up ta NTSB, National Transportation Safety Board. We uns jest find the bodies and clear the wreckage 'way."

During the night, the carrion media people came up with more information. They learned that Sean O'Sullivan had initially failed his test for an authorization to fly a plane on instruments, that the plane had been christened the "Flying Irish" and was painted navy blue and gold, that Sean and Patrick had been arrested for disorderly conduct and were out on bail, which they had violated when flying out of the jurisdiction, that neither son had in fact been all-American at Notre Dame, that Maura had just fallen short of a partnership at the renowned firm of Minor, Grey, that the Northfield electronics company had bought the plane for the CEO, and that its use for flying to a family Baptism in Michigan City might have violated the law.

Early on, I phoned Jim Creaghan.

"Tell your wives that they should answer no questions from the media. They should let Damian be their point man."

At nine o'clock there was a news conference on the shore. The sky was clear, the Lake a quiet aquamarine, a light breeze on the trees in the background.

Commandeer McCloud had a statement to make.

"Happen you notice that thar big craft out on the water . . . its the Coast Guard cutter *Mackinac*. It will try to locate the wreck precisely, to lift the fuselage of the aircraft out of the water and bring it over to Navy Pier. Our craft and those of the Chicago police are out there searching for possible survivors."

"Do you expect you will find any survivors, Commander?"

"Happen we do, we right proud and grateful."

The next hitter to step into the box was Damian.

"I want to say that my two sisters and their husbands and I are deeply sorrowed at the deaths of so many members of our family. We will miss them. We also look forward to meeting them again on some other and better day. The Irish believed in human survival long before St. Patrick came to Ireland and nothing since then has caused us to change our minds."

"Ordain him!" Nuala shouted in my ear.

"Damian, did you not know that your brother's clearance for instrument flying had been refused by the FAA, then approved."

"I did not know that. I hope it's not true."

"Have you really inherited the family firm?"

"A lawyer tells me that Dad left the controlling majority of the firm to his sons. I guess I'm the only one left. The lawyer says that there's no doubt about it."

"So you stand to benefit from this tragedy?"

Damian hesitated.

"I wouldn't say that."

"Won't you become the new CEO?"

"Hardly. I'm an artist. I have asked my brother-in-law Jim Creaghan to become temporary CEO until we can elect a new board."

"Have you made funeral plans yet?"

"No."

Cindy and Ethne stood behind him, glaring at the reporters.

"We are told that parents of the wives are both threatening suit against the company, would you comment on that?"

"They would certainly be within their rights if they did that."

"Did you know that your brothers were charged with felonies arising from a fight on Southport Avenue?"

"Yes, I knew that."

"And that your father was trying to find a plea bargain."

"I did not know that, but I'm not surprised."

"Thank you," sister Cindy said, ending the press conference.

"Will Mr. O'Sullivan be available for further questioning, Cindy?"

"I doubt it. There's time to answer questions and time to mourn."

"Good on her!" my wife said.

"She's a very smart lawyer and a fine woman," I said piously.

"She's not a famous poet . . . Did I tell you what the Christmas concert will be this year?"

"It will be called Festivals and will have a song for all the festivals that some poet wrote poems about."

"That," I admitted, "is a very good idea. Naturally you will want to buy the rights from this poet guy."

"Poor dear man."

— 23 —

 THE WAKE was a disaster area. The Lake Forest police had set up checkpoints for people coming and leaving, then a couple of Mike Casey's guys stood at the door, pushing back members of the media who argued that it was their right to shoot the wake scene inside. There was a lot of pushing and shoving.

We had driven up with the Caseys in Mike's car, so a reserved parking place awaited us. The media were not interested in us, so we passed through easily.

Before we left Grand Beach to drive to our house on Southport we had to explain to the kids that Damian's parents and brothers had been killed in a plane crash. Nelliecoyne had sobbed. The Mick had wept too.

"Why did God let them die, Da?"

"We all have to die sometime, Mick. God called them home early for reasons of his own."

"I hope God knows what he's doing."

• 309 •

"He usually does."

"God loves everyone," Socra Marie said piously, not understanding yet what death meant, not that any of us ever do.

After we had left them at my mom's, Nellie had run out to hug her mother again. She whispered something into Nuala's ear.

"What did herself say?"

"That the little girls are already in heaven."

"As a theory?"

"Och, Dermot Michael, do we Irish witches ever have theories. She said it as an established fact."

So that was that.

If the media vultures at the wake missed Nuala Anne completely, they hit a gold mine when the families of the two daughters got out of their limos. One mother, hopelessly obese, screamed at the camera.

"They killed our daughter and grandchildren. We're going to sue them for every cent they have."

The other said, "They took my daughter away from us, and now all they can give back is a closed coffin."

The families were both from small towns, one in Indiana, the other in Iowa. They were proud to have sent their daughters to St. Mary's and proud of their good marriages. They had no hint about the family circle into which their daughters had been drawn. Now they were finding out that it was a swamp of corruption and madness, the like of which they would never comprehend.

We walked into the funeral parlor. Both of us stopped in our tracks. We had never seen a wake with ten closed caskets, four of them small for the children. The mourners had placed a picture of each of the victims on the caskets. Such cute and vibrant little kids, such handsome adults.

What a horrible scene! Dear God, why?

I don't have to answer that.

Yes, but . . .

Were you around when I did the Big Bang thing?

I know that line you gave Job.

So why quiz me? Do you think I love these poor people any less?

No.

Good . . . And you and herself shouldn't feel guilty. Like me you did all that you could.

While we were waiting in the line of well-dressed people, the families of the wives barged up to assault Kate and Maura, both of whom merely bowed their heads and accepted the assault. One of the women slapped Maura. Mike's guys eased her out of the parlor. She screamed and punched and cursed all the way out.

Kate and Maura sat in chairs, their babes safe with babysitters in the undertaker's office.

Poor Damian had to greet everyone who came in, which he did with ease and charm. Ethne lurked behind him, ready to do battle if anyone threatened him.

"Thanks for coming, Dermot," he said to me. "This is terrible. Something like it would have had to happen. We're on our own now, whether we like it or not."

Our ride back to Southport was quiet.

"He's still doing great work," Annie told us. "He will become a very successful painter. That drawing of your little one and the dogs is wonderful."

In Nuala's office, we collapsed on our respective chairs. She pulled out the magic envelope and gave it to me.

"Where will you park that Navigator?" I asked her.

"I'll find a place."

I opened the enveloped and read the first note.

It's all pretty obvious, Dermot. In Ireland Liam is the man who killed Tim Allen. Perhaps Allen was hassling some of his girl students. All poor Father Dick could see was the nice intelligent young man. He did not realize that for all his gentleness Liam was a Fenian ideologue. It was a case of not looking at the most likely killer, because he didn't want to look. He didn't even consider the possibility that Liam had a gun—though he mentions he is a hunter. He considers all the other people who might have rifles and can't cope with the truth that none of them were the kind of hot-tempered young romantic who might actually have killed a traitor who, as he thought, was attacking an Irishwoman.

"The second time," she said to me as I put the sheet of paper down, "he must have known who shot Lord Skeffington. Why else the haste in getting them out of the country. The visit from Boyd Lufton, clearly an English spy, clinches it. I think Liam didn't mean to hit His Lordship, but did it quite by accident. He wanted him to stay out of Irish politics, which were none of his business. Of course he could have killed him accidentally. I suspect he confessed to Father Dick, who promptly arranged for the marriage to put Liam out of risk. You'll note he never mentions any suspicion of Liam, which is really strange when you consider how smart Father Dick was. He knew all right, probably before the second shooting. But he didn't want to know."

"Why didn't I see it?"

"Because you're such a good man that you don't suspect other good people when sometimes you should."

I opened the second note.

*Madge is the woman in the case. Dux femina facti. You notice how long it was before we learned anything about her. So because we hear nothing we assume that she's a pushover and couldn't hurt anyone. She's too sweet to run over a drunken man. However, I've begun to ask myself what kind of a woman it is who will buy into the collective neurosis around her husband. Either she's a total simp or she is the neurosis. She engineered it, orchestrated it, and enforces it. I don't know why unless she needed to control her husband and found that this was the way to go. So my vote goes for her. Besides, I **know** she's what Cindasue calls the bad un.*

"I think," she said aloud, "that everything since then confirms my hunch. A grandmother who won't come to see her new granddaughter in the hospital and doesn't even call . . . Dermot that's a bad woman."

"And she does finally come to force an unwanted Baptism!"

"It took a long time for us to figure out what she's really like. By then we're like Father Dick, not able to see what she is . . . Her aura was the ugliest I've ever seen."

"But that doesn't prove she ran over Rod Keefe."

"We know that the sons were too weak to kill anyone but themselves and their families. The father's style isn't murder but tilting the playing field. Once he figured out a way to do that he calmed down and so too probably did the sons. We can safely exclude Katie. That left either the mother or Maura. My inclination was to think a woman who would persecute a kid all his life because she didn't want another child and because the pregnancy was difficult would do anything to preserve the ideal family she had created for herself. She probably left the dinner to get something out of the car or to go home early, that we'll never know . . ."

"It still could have been Maura. She wasn't always as pathetic as she is now."

"No, it couldn't. She knew the kind of trouble that an apparent murder would stir up for the family would be worse than a public fight over a patent. Besides, she knew her father would tilt the field once again, like he always had."

"Maybe."

"I'd guess that Madge saw him lying in the driveway on the parking lot. She was so angry at him for the attack on her sons that she ran him down and then, frightened by what she had done, she backed up over him again. Then she tried to get away and went over him a second time. Then she ran back to the parking lot, leaving her keys in the ignition. She wasn't very bright to begin with and she'd probably had a bit too much of the drink taken like the rest of them. Maura spotted her mother's key ring, took it away and later slipped it into her mother's purse. She knew all along. However, she was willing to sacrifice her brother to save her mother, especially because she didn't know that her father had persuaded his corporate lawyer to see that Damian went to jail. For all these years she has been carrying around guilt for both events. She and Day have made peace, but she'll have a lot to work through."

"That's all speculation, Nuala Anne, though I admit that it's good."

"No it's not speculation. Didn't herself confess it all to me at the wake? She wondered if she should make it all public."

"And you told her?"

"That her first obligation was to Damian. For her to go public would be another terrible blow to him. I said she should tell it to a priest, then forget about it. She could atone by loving her husband and her son and her brother and start a whole new family culture. That can be done, you know, Dermot Michael."

" 'Tis true."

"And we have to be their parents, don't we now?"

"Do we?"

"Aren't they orphans? Don't they need a mother and father? Aren't we that already?"

"Fair play to you, Nuala Anne!"

"God will just have to take care of the others. We did all that we could. Doesn't he love them as much as he loves us?"

" 'Tis true."

I was in no mood for theology. Or anything else. With possibly one exception.

"Can we go up to Grand Beach now? Sure, it isn't too late? I miss the kids!"

"No. We need a good night's sleep to get that wake out of our system."

"You're right, Dermot Michael, as always. Sure, I want to see the little one now that she has an identity."

"Has she now?"

"Didn't you hear what she said to that nice cabin attendant? 'I go Ireland.' She's an 'I' now. She's developing her own nice little ego."

"Nice it will be, little, I'm not so sure."

We laughed, then were silent for a moment, pondering perhaps all our responsibilities new and old.

"I can hardly wait till we get to Ireland." Nuala sighed. "It will cleanse our souls of all this bullshite about Irish cream."

"Irish rain will clean out anything," I agreed.

We both sighed and were silent for some time.

" 'Tis true that they made love in the fields after wakes in the old days," she said, as if in deep thought. "Didn't me ma tell me that her granny said that she knew people that did it."

"They never did," I insisted, though I knew that they had.

"Och, they did, Dermot. Weren't they saying 'fock you, death!' "

"Sounds to me like very muddy and messy behavior . . . and pagan at that."

" 'Tis a very Christian symbol—life and love are stronger than death."

"Too bad we don't have any pratie fields here."

"We do have an empty house . . ."

" 'Tis true." I sighed as though it would mean hard work that I didn't want to do.

"No kids, no dogs, no Danuta or Ethne."

" 'Tis true."

We both sighed again.

I rose from my chair, dragged her to her feet, and we folded into each other's arms.

Then at some length and with great vigor and not a little creativity we celebrated our belief that life and love were stronger than death.

— Author's Note —

My story is based on an incident described in *The Outer Edge of Ulster* by an Irish schoolmaster from Donegal, Hugh Dorian (edited in a new edition from Lilliput Press by Breandán Mac Suibhne and David Dickson in 1990). A new parish priest pried loose a local school from Protestant control, which had been tolerated by his predecessor. My imagination began to wonder if a story might be built around that incident. However, the story is not a fictionalized version of the event. It is a story stirred up by my reading about the event. None of the characters in this story are based on real people or real places. St. Colm's well looks like the one in Glen Colmcille, but the town is not Glen Colmcille. Because it is a work of imagination I have not given my imaginary townland or its imaginary geography a name.

However, Hugh Dorian (who died in abject poverty in 1914, God be good to him) was not only a masterful observer, he was also a first-rate amateur sociologist, though he might have denied the charge. His book is the most vivid portrait of life in rural Ireland of the time between the

Famine and the Land League Wars that I have ever read. It is the culture and the social structure of that era that I have tried to re-create in my story.

His chapter on the making of poteen is especially delightful. I direct any reader of this story who wants to make his own poteen to the book. The custom of making it has by no means disappeared from Irish life.

The Irish Church's conflict with wakes, holy wells, and "patterns" in the last century is documented. Now some Irish clerics argue that the struggle against them was a mistake and are attempting to revive them without the abuses that crept in during earlier years.

The Irish have the lowest rate of per capita alcohol consumption in Europe.

AMG
Grand Beach
June 2002

— Family Tree —